# Horse Woman's Child

*A Novel About Clashing Cultures
on the American Frontier*

by
Roger Stoner

Wanata Publishing
Peterson, Iowa

Published by: WANATA Publishing
Peterson, Iowa

ISBN 13: 978-0692366486
ISBN 10: 0692366482

Library of Congress Control Number: 2015930528
Copyright © 2011 Roger Stoner

This is a work of fiction. Characters, names and events, as well as places, organizations and dialogue are products of the author's imagination, or are used fictitiously. In the case of those characters that are historical, dialogue and circumstances are used fictitiously.

Second Printing January 2015

For
Jane, Wade, & Wendy

## Acknowledgement:

I could not have completed a work of this size without advice, criticism, suggestions and praise from people who read it throughout the various stages of writing and re-writing until I finally got.it right. I want to thank the following people for their candor and kind words: Shirley Clark, Matthew and Melinda Stoner, Mike Hansen, Carolyn Roberts, Devon Rud, Sharon Maaland, Wade Stoner, Jean Tennant, and Elsie Mae Brown. I hope the final result meets your expectations.

*Roger Stoner*

# Author's Note

It is written historical fact that while the men of the Lewis & Clark expedition traveled up the Missouri River, they had relations with the women of the various Indian tribes they encountered. From the recorded descriptions of Inkpaduta, I feel that he was of mixed blood and of an age that could have placed his birth near the time of the famous expedition. But there is no documented evidence that this is true. This is one liberty with written history that I took. Most all of the rest of Inkpaduta's encounters with the white settlers, described in this book are accepted facts. Also most all of the characters in the story were real people and for the most part, performed the actions herein described. From these actions and from descriptions of the people in various reference materials, I tried to give each character a personality consistent with his or her role in history.

Because there is little written about the *Wahpekute* people before encountering and interacting with the white race, I've used my imagination to fabricate a plausible story of their "pre-white" existence. In many cases the Native American men's names are recorded in written accounts, but there were few women's names documented. Many histories merely stated that this man had a wife or that man had a daughter. I took the liberty of giving the female characters names that I hope are appropriate and not offensive. I tried to portray the customs and lifestyles of the *Dakotah* people as that of a proud, primitive culture, in direct conflict with the more modern culture of the Caucasian population of that time. It is not my intention to condemn or condone the actions of either faction in this story. It is only my desire, to relate an accurate account of the clash of cultures reflected by the life of Inkpaduta: outcast, renegade, and chief, in the most complete and factual manner possible.

Roger E. Stoner
Peterson, Iowa
2011

Also by Roger Stoner

*Life with my Wife: the Memoir of an Imperfect Man*

(nonfiction)

# A Dakotah Calendar

January . . . *The Moon of Frost in the Tipi* . . . The cold of winter penetrates even through the thick buffalo hide walls of our home, forming frost on the inside, which melts from the heat of our fire and drips on us. It is wet. It is cold. We are hungry.

February . . . *The Moon of Dark Red Calves* . . . The buffalo calves have grown their winter coats and appear very dark against the white snow. Thrive young bulls and cows, for as you survive, so do we.

March . . . *The Moon of the Snowblind* . . . The sun of spring rises bright and glares off the endless plains of white snow. The days get longer and the hunters grow restless. But beware of the bright sun and the white snow, for a blind man cannot survive.

April . . . *The Moon of the Red Grass Appearing* . . . The snow melts and the dead grass of winter peeks through to greet the sun. The promise of new life pokes its green shoots up and the sweetness of life beckons.

May . . . *The Moon when the Ponies Shed* . . . The shaggy winter coats fall from the horses. The hunters brush them and paint their medicine signs on them. The buffalo will soon drop their calves. It is a time of confidence. It is a time of hope.

June . . . *The Moon of Making Fat* . . . The buffalo graze and grow fat. We take our first meat, young bulls and barren cows. We cook the fat and store it in bladder bags to be used when we make pemmican.

July . . . *The Moon of Red Cherries* . . . The berries are ripe. We eat them. We dry them and grind them. They help to make our pemmican sweet. The hunters pray for the buffalo to come. Our meat drying racks are full!

August . . . *The Moon when the Cherries Turn Black* . . . The summer sun is hot. The overripe berries fall to the ground. It is dry. The prairie burns.

September . . . *The Moon when the Calves Grow Hair* . . . All of the golden baby fur has fallen from the spring buffalo calves. Their coats are long. They dance with the coolness of the dawn.

October . . . *The Moon of the Changing Seasons* . . . The migrating birds flock together. They gather and they go. The nights are filled with their whistling wings. There is frost in the mornings and the grass turns brown.

November . . . *The Moon of the Falling Leaves* . . . The leaves have turned brown and are falling to the ground. They are dead. The cold time comes. We make our winter robes ready.

December . . . *The Moon of the Popping Trees* . . . The cold time is here. The white trees freeze and split from the cold. They whine and cry out in the wind. The children are hungry and cry in silence.

## Names & Phrases

Sioux - from the French - Nadowwessioux - which was derived from the Ojibwa - Nadowessiwak - meaning snake or enemy.
Dakotah - friend or ally. (A name they called themselves.)
Minnesota - minne (water) sota (clear)
Minnewakan - minne (water) wakan (spirit) - Spirit Lake
Minnetanka - minne (water) tanka (big) – (The big water) – West Lake Okoboji
Okobooshi - A Place of Rest – East Lake Okoboji
Inyaniake - Little Sioux River
Wagachun - rattling tree (Cottonwood)
Wasichu - white men
Pahuska - long hair (A name used for George Armstrong Custer)
Shyela - Cheyenne
Blue Clouds - Arapahos
The Greasy Grass River – The Dakotah name for The Little Bighorn River

Tribal Divisions

Teton Dakotah: (Western Division of the Sioux Nation - Lakotah)
Hunkpapa (Cutthroats)
Sihasapa (Blackfeet - not the same as Blackfeet Tribe of Montana and Alberta)
Minneconjou (Those-Who-Plant-By-The-Water)
Itazipcho (Sans Arc - No Bows)
Sichangu (Brules - Burnt Thighs)
Oohenonpa (Two Kettles)
Ogalala (Those-Who-Stand-In-The-Middle)

Yankton-Assiniboin: (Northern Division of the Sioux Nation - Nakotah)
Yanktonnai
Yankton
Assiniboin

Santee Dakotah: (Eastern Division of the Sioux Nation - Dakotah)
Mdewakonton (People of the Mystic Lake)
Wahpekute (People Who Shoot Among the Trees)
Wahpeton (People of the Leaves)
Sissiton (People of the Swamps)

# TABLE OF CONTENTS

# Horse Woman's Child

## Child

*A Novel About Clashing Cultures
on the American Frontier*

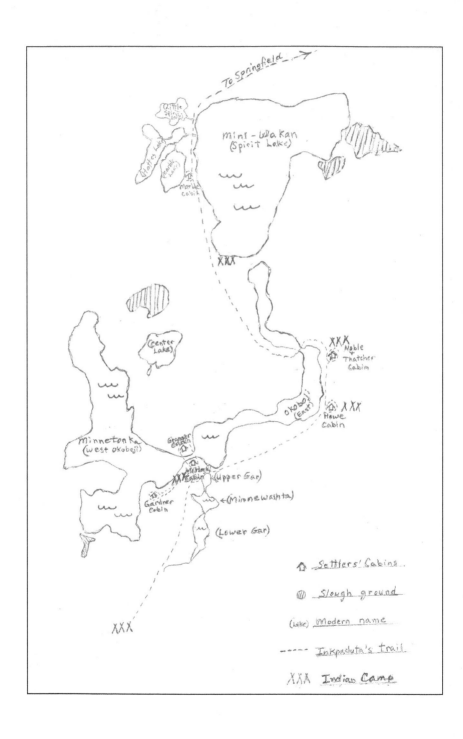

# PROLOGUE

The old man lay propped back under a short-limbed tree. His head and shoulders were bent against a wolf skin pillow that was stuffed tight with horsehair. A cool Canadian breeze filtered through the early morning air. Even with the thin, faded, trade blanket covering his bony body, goose bumps prickled the flesh of his upper arms as they lay outside the blanket, crossed over his sunken chest. His gray-white hair stuck out from beneath his blue army cap and hung stiffly down over his shrunken ears. The short-billed hat sat slightly askew, shading only half of his wrinkled, pockmarked face. His eyes, once sharp with the bright black of coal, glowed milky now and saw only dark, dancing shadows.

Yes, his sight was gone. It had left him slowly, over the years. Some blamed it on the white man's disease that had caused him a high fever and horrible, itchy, pus filled sores and left his face pocked with scars. But the disease had come and gone many, many years ago, when he was a young man. He was an old man now. A very, very old man . . .

# PART ONE

# Chapter 1
## *The Woman (1804)*

The young girl rolled over slowly, her eyes searching the darkness around her. Red coals glowing in the small fire pit in the center of the tipi circle threw just enough light for her eyes to make out the dark forms of her sleeping family. Close beside her lay her mother and father, sharing the same robes. On the other side of them, lay her father's old wife, Woman Who Watches the Babies. She was old, as old as her father and she no longer cared to share the robes with a man. She could see the four separate, uneven mounds of her brothers. The older two were sons of her father and Watches the Babies. The two younger were sons of her mother and father. They lay sprawled on their beds of dark robes across the fire from the girl. The dim light of the dying embers threw their shadows against the gray walls of the tipi.

As the girl listened in the darkness, familiar nighttime sounds reached her ears. She could hear old mother faintly snoring and a small smile played across her lips upon hearing one of the boys break wind, causing a muffled, sleepy mumble of protest from one of her younger brothers. As she gazed at them across the fire pit, their movements ceased and one by one, she could sense that they had fallen back asleep. She heard her parents' robes rustling and could tell even in the darkness, that her father had rolled over and positioned himself on top of her mother. In her mind's eye, she could see the rhythmic movement of their carnal dance and followed its progress by the sounds they made. A sudden quickening of their breathing, punctuated by her mother's soft moans and her father's quiet, but urgent climactic grunts of passion brought an end to rustling motion in the bed of robes beside her. Soon, their slow, even, breathing told her they were asleep. In the stillness of the night, with the sounds of her family's quiet slumber, she drifted off into a contented sleep herself.

Hours later, she awoke feeling a familiar pressure in her stomach, and she knew it was time for her to rise and take care of her morning business. Quietly she folded back her sleeping robe and stood. As she straightened up, she began a long, luxurious stretch, feeling the muscles in the calves of her legs strain against the stiffness a long night of sleeping. A long, reluctant yawn pulled her mouth open and ended with her jaws snapping shut with a loud click in the morning quiet. One of her brothers mumbled and rolled over. Cautiously, she moved through the darkness, careful not to further waken any of her sleeping family. After stepping around the sprawled forms of her brothers, she found the door and slipped silently through the opening.

She went out into the gray light of the pre-dawn and sniffed the fresh air of morning, drawing it deep into her lungs and blowing it out again. Inhaling the cool, damp air chased the last vestige of sleepiness from her mind. Taking a familiar path to the edge of the village, she stepped a few feet into the tall grass. Squatting, she sprayed her bladder empty, feeling instant relief and then stood and pulled her sleeping robe tightly around her shoulders. She stepped back on the path and trotted up the slope leading to the top of the rise above their village. At the highest point of the rise, where she could have the best view, she sat on her haunches and waited for the sun to rise.

Before the blazing ball's golden eye peeked over the horizon, its own zenith announced the coming of the new day! It rose slowly, its rays sprinkling the waving prairie grass with iridescent shoots of pink, crimson and orange. The slight breeze that lived with the darkness quieted and the morning star shone its brilliance for the night's last few seconds, before disappearing completely.

Morning Girl faced the rising sun, her eyes drinking in the aurora of its colors until she was forced to look away by its brilliance. As its light slowly spread toward her across the darkened earth, she searched for any unnatural movement disturbing the waving grasses of the endless prairie. Suddenly, as if in a hurry to frighten the darkness away, the sun jumped up from the horizon and brought new life to the sleeping land. She sniffed the breeze that had begun to pick up again. Her ears listened, trying to hear the world awakening. She prayed to the Creator of the People that the day would be a good one.

She could hear the dogs in the village below as they awoke and began to greet the sun with a chorus of yips and whines, and could identify the cries of a litter of pups that belonged to her father. They were yipping for their breakfast. She knew that their shaggy yellow mother would soon return from her night of scavenging the edges of the village in a constant search for scraps of tossed away food. The sudden silence of the pups told Morning Girl that the yellow dog had dropped to the ground behind the tipi and accommodated the hungry puppies with two rows of swollen teats, dripping with warm milk.

When the sun had completely cleared the horizon, she turned to face it, closing her eyes against its bright light and raising her arms as she sang her morning prayer song.

*"Oh Father Sun - Greet the morning with your smile - Warm us when we are cold - Shine on us when we are lost - Help us find our way"*

She finished singing and turned away from the sun's light. Once again, her eyes surveyed the area around her. Her shadow led toward the village, down the hill from where she stood. The village was positioned where the slope flattened and ran somewhat level before continuing its gentle descent to the river bottom. The village site had been chosen because it lay high enough up the slope to be safe from unexpected floods, yet it was close enough to the river for it to be a handy water source. Beyond the town, on the river's edge, cottonwood trees grew tall and stately to heights of sixty or seventy feet. They alone broke the flow of the prairie, which was an endless, rolling ocean covered with a thick carpet of tall grasses and early spring flowers.

Her eyes scanned the vastness before her habitually, watching for any sign of life or unnatural movement in the waving grasses. Once again, her nose tested the scents blown upon the breezes, and her ears listened closely to the sounds of the world awakening. Since birth, it had been her way to awaken before the dawn. As soon as she had reached the age of independent thought, she had yearned to see the sun rise each morning and prayed to the power of the *Dakotah* God.

\* \* \*

Wamdisapa rolled over and groaned. The restlessness of his soul had awakened him and he knew that sleep would probably elude him for the rest of the night. With an angry jerk, he threw his sleeping robe from him and stood up. No fire burned in the center of the tipi and in the total darkness, he tried to see the sleeping forms of his family. His wife, Rain Dance Woman, and their two-year-old son lay nearest him, but on a separate mattress of furs. Across the tipi, slept Old Grandmother, Rain Dance Woman's mother. Not far from the old woman lay New Grass Woman, his wife's sister. He thought momentarily about slipping into New Grass Woman's bed, where he knew he would be welcome. Rain Dance Woman had encouraged him to take her sister for a second wife. Her husband had died last year from wounds he had received during a battle with mortal enemies of the *Wahpekute*, the Sauk and Fox and she needed a new husband. He had shared her robes occasionally but found her to be lazy and unexciting and he had no desire to call her one of his wives.

By the door lay Old Silver Owl, his wife's father. Old Silver Owl was very old and worthless in Wamdisapa's mind. The old man could hardly climb to his feet and walk unassisted anymore. His mind wandered. He seemed confused most of the time and talked more and more about how good things were when he was young and how bad things were now. He could feed himself but had trouble making water, often standing and moaning with pain at the edge of the village for long periods of time before finding relief for his swollen bladder. In truth, the old man had to be cared for in all ways, which took up much of Rain Dance Woman's time. Old Silver Owl talked often about having outlived his days. Soon, Wamdisapa planned, he would build the old man a shelter and move him and all of his possessions into it. Then, when the village moved, as was the way of their people, Old Silver Owl would be left behind to spend his last days alone.

Skirting his sleeping family, Wamdisapa ducked low through the tipi door and went out into the night air. Hearing the gurgling of the river, he moved to a nearby tree on its bank and leaned against it watching the water flow in the starlight as he contemplated the problems of his life. He wasn't a young man. He had lived for more than twenty-five winters. He had traveled far and fought well and had gained some prominence in his tribe. He looked to no other man to lead him and went where he pleased, when he pleased, and most of the people followed him. With this realization, there came added responsibilities. He was considered the leader of the band and though he was highly respected by his peers and their families, he was also blamed when things didn't go right. If the scouts couldn't find the buffalo; if the rivers dried up and there was no water to drink, if it rained too much and the river flooded their village, if the winter was too cold or the summer too hot, some of the people would find a way to blame him!

Adding to his stress of leadership, since the birth of his son, an uncommon restlessness had nagged him. He knew the short-term reason stemmed from the long cold winter of inactivity. In the fall, he had led his people to a small copse of thickly branched evergreens near the shores of a blue water lake for a winter village site. The trees growing across the low hills on the north side of the lake were a natural shelter from the winds of winter. The people were content to wile away the cold months on the shores of the blue lake, spear fishing for the huge pike that lurked beneath the ice and hunting for the elk that yarded up in the trees when the wind blew blizzards of snow from across the empty plains. It had been a long cold winter, and Wamdisapa was growing anxious to be on the move long before the cold winds of winter subsided, but his restlessness was due to more than just the long season of inactivity.

Finally, during the *Moon of the Red Grass Appearing* the snow disappeared, except for small patches that found shelter from the warming spring sun at the base of tall bluffs or deep in the evergreen woods. On a clear morning, with the coming of a warm southerly breeze, he told Rain Dance Woman to pack. When word that Wamdisapa was leaving spread, the rest of the camp struck their tipis. And by mid-morning, he was leading the band south and west. They continued their spring migration stopping for only a few days at a time. Each time they stopped the restless feeling continued to plague him as it was this night.

\* \* \*

She lingered, basking in the sun's light, knowing that she would never see the sun rise from this spot again. Their headman had stated the evening before that he would be moving again with today's light. As was the custom of her people, the rest of the village could pack up their belongings and follow him or stay where they were and choose to follow a different headman. But Wamdisapa was one of the most respected men in their tribe, and she knew that her father would continue to go where Wamdisapa led. Wamdisapa had decided it was time to move down river and to the west in search of a great herd of buffalo. If they could have but one successful buffalo hunt, meat could be dried for the next winter, hides tanned for warm tipi skins and sinew stretched for bow strings and horns carved into spoons, and bladders and stomachs cleaned and stitched as liners in water bags. The livers and intestines would be eaten on the spot, and there would be lots of salty warm blood to put the strength that the long cold winter had taken from the People, back into their bodies. It would be a time of great celebration!

Her daydreams of a successful hunt brought saliva to her mouth. She swallowed and stood up, realizing that people were beginning to move about in the village. From far off, down the hill, she could hear her mother calling her name. She turned and could see the woman standing with hands cupped around her mouth, looking up in her direction. The girl laughed, imagining the look of mild disgust on her mother's face. She raised her hand and waved, acknowledging that she had heard the summons. Morning Girl giggled again, knowing that her mother was scolding her for being late in doing her morning chores. Her mother turned and stooped low to enter their tipi, where old Watches the Babies was probably already starting to pack all of their worldly goods in bags made from buffalo, deer and elk skins. They would be loaded on travois and pulled by their dogs, as they traveled toward the hunting grounds.

She knew she should hurry down and help, but she couldn't bring herself to leave the rise just yet. After all, she had been named for her habit of rising early and running out to greet the sun at its rise each day. Spurning her father's warnings about the dangers that dawn often brought to the unprotected and the unwary, she visited the sunrise each day to pray to the creator of the People and talk with her ancestors.

She heard her mother call again and knew that she had to hurry or chance making the woman really angry with her. Quickly, she dropped to her knees and began attacking the thick buffalo grass carpet. She pulled handfuls of the grass until a small portion of the tough, deeply rooted stems came loose, leaving a small brown wound in the green blanket. Removing a small leather pouch from a leather thong around her neck, she carefully opened its mouth, protecting it from the wind and pinched a small portion of the soil between her thumb and forefinger and deposited it in the pouch. Tying the top securely, she hung it back around her neck. Then, ceremoniously, she grasped a heavy blade of the buffalo grass between her thumb and finger and slid it across the fleshy part of the thumb on her other hand, making a shallow grass cut. She shook the droplet of blood that appeared into the wounded earth and covered the spot with the grass she had pulled.

She believed that the spirits of her ancestors lived in the soil, and she always took a small part of them with her when they moved. In times of danger or sickness, she clutched the pouch containing the dust of her ancestors and prayed for their spirits to rise out of the pouch and scare away the danger or cure the illness. She prayed again now.

"Bright Morning Girl!"

She jumped at the closeness of her mother's voice. The woman had made the long trek up the hill.

"You must come down now. Your father is impatient to be moving. The old mother and I need your help," her mother said in a quiet, but firm voice, adding, "Bright Morning Girl, you know it is important to your father that we follow close behind Wamdisapa. If we're not packed before the rest of the people, someone else will sneak in ahead of us."

Grinning at her mother's use of her full name, Morning Girl jumped to her feet and raced over to the woman. She locked arms with her, and they turned and started down the hill to the village. "Father is just afraid that the great Wamdisapa will see some of the other young women in the village and forget about his Bright Young Daughter," Morning Girl teased.

"Bright Morning," her mother scolded. "You shouldn't talk that way. You are much too young for a man like Wamdisapa. Besides, he already has a good, young wife and probably isn't looking for another."

"Ah Mother, you know his young son is still sucking and his 'good young wife' sleeps without him," Morning girl said. "That's why he prowls the village at night. He's lonely."

"Hush that gossip!" her mother hissed. "Wamdisapa is the head-man. He has many things to worry about."

"His fat sister-in-law for one," Morning Girl giggled.

"Hush that gossip!" her mother hissed again. "Besides, you are too young to become a second wife to a man Wamdisapa's age. Your father knows that. He knows that it will be two or maybe three years before you are ready to marry. He knows that I will not allow you to leave the tipi at night in answer to the flute songs. He knows that I will soon have to begin strapping your legs together at night to keep the Unwanteds from sneaking in and defiling you. He knows . . ."

"He knows that Wamdisapa has horses," Bright Morning Girl interrupted her mother and added, "and he knows that he will trade one for a good, young, second wife to share his robes at night."

Her mother frowned, but didn't answer. They were near the tipi and it wouldn't do to have her father hear this talk. He was a stern man, who made the decisions for his family and wouldn't like it if he were to hear them discussing, what both of them knew was on his mind. They entered the tipi and Morning Girl began carrying the filled packs back out. Her mother gathered and folded their sleeping robes and carried them out. It was almost time to strike the tipi and fold it and pack it. It was just the beginning of what would be a long, hard day, filled with sweat and toil for the women of this *Wahpekute Santee Dakotah* village.

# Chapter 2
## *The Man (1804)*

Though the rifle was of Pennsylvania stock, it was called a Kentucky Long Rifle. Its long, slender barrel had been forged and bored by a skilled blacksmith who specialized in fine firing weapons. Special care was taken to spiral a rifling groove down its hollow inside to give a fired ball spin and make it fly true. The intricate trigger assembly was of the finest steel. It had been filed and honed to a perfect fit and would release with the slightest of finger pressure. The sights had been fused to the barrel and adjusted, tested, and readjusted, until the rifle would shoot with pinpoint accuracy.

This metallurgic tribute to the ingenuity of man was fitted into a stock of the finest cherry wood. The reddish brown stock had been lovingly shaped with gentle strokes of a drawknife and carved to a comfortable feel with a narrow grip and a curved butt plate that was covered with padded leather sheath. The forearm was checkered by using a small wooden mallet and tiny chisels, giving it a coarse gripping surface. The ramrod was of the hardest oak wood, carved straight and sanded smooth for easy passage down the .32 caliber bore. The rod was stained black from the powder residue left in the barrel after each firing. Its slender length slid into brackets beneath the barrel and was easily accessed when it was time to ram the ball to the bottom of the barrel. Many hours of hard labor had been put into the creation of this rifle. Its beauty and functional accuracy were proof of its creator's love for a job well done.

"Ain't she a beauty, Will?" the red-headed young man asked as he held the weapon up for inspection. "We brought 'er out, all the way from Virginny. Pap bought it off the Dutchers up north, west o' York when he was surveyin' up there."

"Aye," answered a big, rawboned man, dressed in a military uniform with a tricorn hat that didn't cover the rusty red curls of his own hair. He reached out and took the rifle and smiled as he sighted down the barrel. "It's almost too pretty to shoot, Hugh."

"It shoots straight enough, and I keep it greased up to keep the rust off. It'd be a fine rifle to take west Will," the young man said, hinting that he knew the reason Will Clark had come visiting his father. In all of his eighteen years, Hugh McNeal had never admitted to eavesdropping on the conversations his father held with visitors in his small office at the back of his smithy. A decade earlier, the McNeals had landed their flatboat, loaded with forge and anvil and hammers and awl, on the rocky landing on the south shore of the Ohio River. Since that time, Hugh's father, Amis, had made a fine living shoeing animals, mending harness, and fabricating and sharpening tools for the northern Kentucky farmers and plantation owners near Louisville. Hugh had worked in his father's smithy since that landing and had become skilled in the craft. But a young man's restlessness had come over him in the last year. He was tired of spending long hot days sharpening the scythes, and long handled hoes used by plantation slaves. He was bored with bending harness rings and forging bridle bits. He wanted adventure!

"Come on Will, ya gotta take me with ya!" Hugh blurted. "I heard ya talking ta Pap about yer secret trip through them Frenchy lands."

"I came to recruit your father," a bemused Clark answered. He remembered his own yearnings as a young boy, to follow his famous brother, George into battle against the Red Coats and Indians during the revolution.

"Hell, he can't go!" Hugh exclaimed. "He's got too many mouths ta feed already and damned if he ain't got Ma in the family way agin. There ain't no way she's gonna let him run off explorin' when she's got six youngins, one still on the tit, and a seventh kickin' the inside of her ribs, ta keep from squealin' with the hungries."

"Aye," the thirty-three year old Clark admitted. "Your father told me as much." He chuckled, remembering Amis as he ticked off the reasons he couldn't accept his offer to join the Corps of Discovery. Each reason was the name of a strawberry-headed child that could be heard squealing with delight as they romped in the yards surrounding the McNeal house and smithy. But Hugh, the oldest, hadn't been included in the list. Will Clark looked at the young man standing before him, up and down. He saw a strapping youth, broad at the shoulder, with long, sinewy, freckle covered arms. It was obvious the young man could take care of himself. He stood almost as tall as Clark himself and had large, strong hands, the hands of a blacksmith. And a blacksmith is whom he came to recruit.

"I heard ya talkin' ta Pap," Hugh stated boldly. "I know what yer plannin', Will. And I just gotta go along, I just gotta," he begged. Then upon failing to get a response from Clark, he added, "I can smith fer

14

ya, near as good as Pa. I can hammer shoes. I can mend harness, sharpen tools, make knives, axes and hatchets and put a edge on 'em that you can split hairs with! Hell and damnation Will! You said you were even takin' one o' yer niggers. It'll bugger me the rest o' my life if some old slave gets to travel the western land like a free man while I have to stay here, chained to my Pap's anvil."

Clark's brow narrowed as he looked into young Hugh McNeal's eyes. He saw a determination in them that he liked and thought again about his promise to Captain Lewis to bring a blacksmith to the rendezvous in St. Louis. Hugh McNeal was young. But he had been trained by the best. Amis McNeal had a way with a hammer and steel and could grind an edge on a knife that a man *could* shave with.

"There'll be no forge on the river. Just the heat from a fire and one small anvil. You'll have hammers and a small peddle grinder. Capt'n Lewis is expecting an accomplished smithy, one who can keep knives, bayonets, axes, and hatchets sharp and in good repair. You'll have to make rope, carve paddles and do some general carpentry on the boat. And you'll be expected to pull your own weight when it comes to a day's travel. The smithy work will be done at night. While the rest of the crew is resting or playing dice, you'll be working. This is not a lark, Lad. This is not an adventure. This is . . ." He stopped talking as he saw the broad, toothy smile play across Hugh's face. William Clark smiled back and shaking his head, he walked around the young man and back into the smithy. It might take some fast talking, but he was going to convince Amis that if he couldn't go himself, he should let his eldest, red-headed son go in his place.

*       *       *

Thomas Jefferson, President of the United States, had secretly commissioned the expedition. It was his greatest desire to explore the vast wilderness west of the Mississippi River that the young nation had purchased from the financially strapped Napoleon. He wanted not only to find a water route to the Pacific Ocean, but also to beat the British in exploring the coastal land on the western ocean, thereby giving the United States claim to it. He needed a reliable man to lead the expedition and had chosen Captain Meriwether Lewis for the job. He was a close, trusted friend, who had served him as a loyal secretary.

Lewis immediately picked his friend and former commander in the army, William Clark, as his adjutant, and the two men set out to recruit hardy individuals to form what they called the Corps of Discovery. The Corps that rendezvoused in St. Louis early in the spring was made up of seventeen regular soldiers, eleven enlistees,

Clark's large dog and his Negro slave, York. The soldiers had been picked for their military backgrounds and good service records. The enlistees were picked for specialties they had. John Shields was head blacksmith. Young Hugh McNeal was his assistant. The half-breed, Drouillard, was Chief Interpreter with two French-Omaha assistants, Pierre Cruzatte and Francois Labiche. Patrick Gass was a carpenter, and Moses Reed and La Liberte were hunters. The rest were rivermen, whose knowledge of currents, snags and sandbars would prove to be invaluable in getting the Corps up the big Missouri River.

The three vessels that launched from the St. Louis docks on a cool, bright spring morning, May 14, 1804, were unspectacular craft. They slipped away from the wharf slowly and pushed up river without being noticed by the loungers and other scoundrels who inhabited the riverfront. The largest, a keelboat, was approaching sixty feet long and was twelve feet wide. It was built with a broad flat bottom, ideal for carrying heavy cargo in deep or shallow waters. Two small swivel cannons were mounted, one foreword, the other aft, on the deck. Thick planking provided a wide walkway on either side of a lean-to cabin that sheltered the steps leading down into the cargo hold. Teams of men poling against the current propelled it.

All of the supplies for the trip were stored there, deep in the bowels of the boat. The list was a long one including barreled salt pork, bags of corn meal, and dried peas. There was also a small supply of jerked beef to be used when the pork ran out or became too rancid to eat. Kegs of rum were the last item of food supplies. Each man would be issued a small draft with his evening meal for as long as it lasted.

The middle of the boat's cargo space was reserved for powder, shot, cannon balls and the smithy tools; anvil, sledge, small hammers, five splitting wedges, iron rod, bars of lead, harness leather, bit rings, kegs of square nails, axes, hatchets, knives and scythes. There were also five extra rifles and a fowling piece lashed to a rack along the low wall. Grain for the small herd of horses they drove along the bank was bagged in burlap and piled against the opposite wall.

In the aft, presents for the Indians were stored. These gifts were intended to be used as bribes to gain good favor with the natives. There were hardwood boxes containing multi-colored glass beads imported from France, Italy and England, stacked from the floor to the deck. They were imperfectly shaped beads; some were round, some oblong, and others almost square. But all had holes through the middle and river traders knew that the brightly colored beads were a favorite among the up-river tribes. Small hand mirrors were stored in crates filled with shredded wood to protect the fragile mirrors from rough handling. Army officer uniforms and lead medals, cast with the likeness of President Jefferson were gifts for chiefs and important men. Bolts of bright cloth were gifts intended to catch the eye of the Indian women. There was sugar cane from Barbados for the children. Cheaply made, and low quality steel hatchets, knives and sharpening stones were more gifts that could be used for bartering. The last item earmarked for the Indians were several casks of watered down trade whiskey. It was a vile liquid that few of the whites would consider drinking. If served undiluted with river water, it was believed that it would burn a hole in a man's stomach and cause internal bleeding. But if diluted correctly, and served in copious amounts to the lead men of a village, whiskey was known to be invaluable when trading with the Indians.

The other two boats in the fleet were called "piraguas" by the Spanish or "pirogues" by the French. Made from the trunks of huge trees, they were larger versions of dugout canoes. They had two sailing masts and a built-in rudder. Compared to the cumbersome keelboat, they were smaller, lighter and a more maneuverable, faster craft that could be paddled, poled or pushed by the wind. All of the men's personal gear including rifle, powder and shot, skinning knives and belt hatchets, were stored in the pirogues.

As the days passed, the men learned to work together. The keelboat's pace was almost sluggish yet headway was made each day. But they were long, arduous days, filled with toil. They rowed when possible, then pushed on the poles. When the currents were too strong for the oars or poles, a crew of men had to jump into the black, rushing water to pull like common dray horses on ropes fastened to the bow of the boat, dragging it ever onward, up the river.

Hugh McNeal had fit in with the corps of men well. Even though he was the youngest and was sometimes teased about being inexperienced, John Shields was quick to realize that he was a skilled smithy. As the days passed into weeks, Hugh's job of repairing broken hatchet handles and sharpening dulled knives and axes at night at his peddle stone, became a place where the crew gathered to visit. His skill at putting an edge on the curved scythes they used to cut lengths of river grass to feed the horse herd at night didn't go unnoticed. Even Captain Lewis clapped him on the shoulder and told him his job was "well done."

But sharpening tools till well after dark each night didn't get him out of pulling on the ropes in the morning. Hugh was a big man, nearly as big as Clark's slave. Therefore, he found himself pushing on the poles, rowing the oars or straining on the ropes to pull the keelboat up the river. When close enough to shore, they could pull from dry ground. But more times than not, sandbars, snags or shallows near the shore forced the men back into the cold rushing river. The greasy bottom made them slip and slide as they fought against the current. The mud pulled at their feet and sucked their moccasins off to be lost forever. Rocks and sunken tree limbs gouged their bare feet and the cold water made their joints ache. There were also hidden undercurrents, snags and deep holes that were treacherous to even the best of swimmers.

Hugh found that his turn at herding the horses wasn't easy either. It seemed that every one of God's creatures and plants was a potential enemy to the horse herders. Under every rock or low growing shrub, there lurked a snake or spider or rodent that didn't like being disturbed by the stumbling white men. Swarms of bees covered the spring flowers and rose up in anger when the horses tromped through their nectar fields stinging animal and man alike.

Gooseberry bushes, prickly pear, and bramble patches tore at the drovers' legs and ankles. Plum thickets with long spike-like thorns dotted the river bank, grabbing anyone walking too near, scratching or gouging a wound deep enough to bleed. Green flies were quick to pester any such wounds, causing infection and slow healing. Mosquitoes and gnats rose in dark clouds from stagnant pools of water. Their small bites caused swelling and itching, and their sheer numbers made it hard to even breathe. Fields of cane grew in thick stands along the river. The cane was too tall to walk over and too thick to push through. Long detours, sometimes reaching miles out into the prairie, had to be made to circle around the cane fields.

After weeks of travel, the conversation around Hugh's grinder each night turned from their agonies to their apprehension about the Indians. It was understood that meeting up with the red men was an unavoidable certainty. In fact, according to Captain Lewis, it was their desire to meet as many indigenous people as possible. It was in their best interests to make them friends and allies of the United States. But how this large group of white men, intruding upon their lands, would be accepted by the aboriginal inhabitants was a question that weighed heavily on each man's mind.

Nevertheless, the Captains sent the hunters, Reed and La Liberte farther and farther afield each day, hoping to make contact with the red men. They knew that there had been earlier traders to pass up the river, and they were anxious to ply their trading abilities with the friendly down river tribes, who had experienced white man wares, before having to deal with more hostile people farther up the river.

# Chapter 3
## *The Husband*

**W**amdisapa groaned as he rolled over. It was the middle of the night, and the restlessness in his soul had awakened him again. It seemed that nothing could quiet his yearnings. It didn't matter how long he traveled, or how fatigued he was at the end of each day, the hunger in his loins would not allow him to sleep the night through.

With a frustrated jerk, he threw his sleeping robe from him and ducked low through the tipi door, breathing the fresh night air deeply into his lungs. He moved to a tree on the bank of the small river they had been following. He had led his people in a southwest direction from the lake where they had wintered. They had been traveling for many days, taking their time and watching for buffalo sign. *The Moon of Red Grass Appearing* had ended, and *The Moon When the Ponies Shed* had come. The temperature, while warm during the day, remained cool at night. A slight breeze touched his face, and he felt goose flesh grow on his arms and legs. He looked up and studied the night sky, trying to guess how long it would be until dawn arrived.

Thinking of the sunrise brought to his mind the girl called Bright Morning. He was aware of her early morning habit of visiting her ancestors on the rise above their camps. He had watched her from afar many times. He knew precisely how far from her father's tipi she would walk before she stopped to relieve her night filled bladder. He could predict which path she would follow and the exact spot where she would squat on her haunches to watch the coming of the sun. Many times he had crept in close and listened to her songs.

He knew that she was only about thirteen winters old. But she appeared to carry a wisdom beyond her years. He could see it in her jet black eyes that shone with the intensity of a burning ember. She had a long, slightly hooked nose, with high cheekbones and a small mouth. Her sparkling white teeth were seen frequently, as she had a happy disposition and laughed often. Her hair was as dark as her eyes and was always brushed to a shining brilliance or braided with her scalp painted a bright vermilion. She was tall for a girl her age, and though she was slender, her body was that of a young woman, not a child. Thinking about the young girl's simple beauty brought a smile to his weary face.

His wife, Rain Dance Woman, was a good wife. She too, was young and pretty. And she also seemed wise. But when he compared Bright Morning with Rain Dance Woman, there was a difference. Bright Morning was truly like the slender shoots of new grass poking through the late snow of spring. Her slender young body was fresh and full of promise. She had never lain with a man. She had never carried a child and had never felt the responsibilities of motherhood.

Wamdisapa sighed. Thinking of the young girl while standing naked in the night breeze had aroused him. This was his never-ending problem. His son, Pinched Cheeks, named for the small dimples on each side of his mouth, was two summers old. *Dakotah* mothers let their children nurse for as many years as the child wanted, sometimes to the age of five or even six years. It was a good custom for there were always many mothers with milk at their breast and any child, when hungry during a day's march or a day's play, could go to any mother for a suckle lunch. But the custom also prohibited frequent sex between the parents of small children. It was feared that if a nursing mother became pregnant, her milk supply would dry up to feed her child within, thus depriving her already living child. The child mortality rate was high due to the harsh life on the plains and the health and well being of their living children was foremost in the minds of most of the *Wahpekute* people.

Consequently, young fathers in the village were in an almost constant state of sexual deprivation. There were a few accepted remedies for this problem. Many men took a second, and sometimes even a third, wife. Another remedy was to make war and take a female captive as a slave to help with the women's work during the day and to share the warrior's bed at night. But this remedy wasn't always acceptable in the family unit. This was Wamdisapa's problem.

In the two years since his son had been born, Rain Dance Woman and he had shared the same robes only a few times. During the first year of the child's life, not at all. During the second year, occasionally. But the infrequent sex had only made the problem worse. Joining with his wife once every few months had only served to rekindle his yearning and add to the guilt his conscience felt each time they took a chance.

His misery and frustration grew until finally, almost a year ago, he had slipped off and captured a young Fox girl and presented her to Rain Dance Woman to keep as a slave. All had went well at first, as the Fox girl had been quite willing to couple with him at night and share in his wife's work during the day in exchange for her life. With each passing night, the girl became more satisfying for Wamdisapa. But as the days passed into the second week, Rain Dance Woman became less and less satisfied with the slave girl's work and more and more jealous of the time the girl spent with her husband.

As time passed, the slave girl grew more and more comfortable with her relationship with Wamdisapa, and he began to react toward her as something more than just a slave to be used. Rain Dance Woman's jealousy grew deeper and one day when Wamdisapa left on an early morning hunt she decided to act.

When he returned late in the afternoon, he found the slave girl's prone body tethered by the neck to a stake outside of his tipi. Both of her hands and her feet had been smashed with a large rock hammer. The tethers around her neck were of green rawhide that had been soaked in the creek and wrapped around the girl's neck and tied to the stake. She had suffered in the warming sun as the wet green leather shrunk tighter and tighter as it dried. Her swollen tongue was clamped between her teeth and had turned black with dried blood. The slave girl was dead.

Wamdisapa was furious! In a terrible rage, he turned from the dead girl's body and bellowed his wife's name. Rain Dance Woman appeared at the tipi door, naked and crying out apologies. She dropped to her stomach and, oblivious to the sharp grass stubble, belly-crawled to her man, scraping her breasts and stomach across the ground. When she reached him, she came slowly to her knees, still crying, still apologizing, and begging him to forgive her. She untied his clout and pulled the garment from him. Slowly stroking him with her hands, she stood to face him. Shards of dried grass clung to her where her full breasts had dripped milk, which ran down her body, joining with blood oozing from hundreds of small grass cuts. She raised one of his hands and placed it upon her breast. Her crying eyes beseeched him to forgive her.

Wamdisapa grabbed her roughly by the hair on the back of her head. He cuffed her across the mouth with an open hand and then spun her toward the tipi entrance. He pushed her to the door and shoved her down through it. As she hit the tipi floor, she fled ahead of him, frightened and whimpering. Her parents snatched Pinched Cheeks from his small bed of robes and slipped quickly out of the tipi as Wamdisapa came in. He snatched up a kindling switch and whipped her across the back and buttocks as she cowered, whimpering, away from him while protecting her breasts with her arms. After several red welts rose on her backside, he threw the switch in the fire pit and pushed her onto her back. He dropped his clout and kneed between her legs, thrusting himself deeply into her with a savage passion born more of anger than of love.

When he was finished, he stood and glared down at her for a moment. As she pulled a robe over her face to hide her eyes, he turned and stalked out of the tipi. His anger had drained from him and had been replaced by a strange sadness. The slave girl, whose body someone had taken away, had filled a void in his life that had become more than just sexual gratification. He realized that Rain Dance Woman, having sensed that truth, had followed her instinctive jealousy to protect her position in the family unit. Somehow, that knowledge only saddened him more.

For her part, Rain Dance Woman had not regretted killing the Fox girl. She understood, though, that her husband would not wait much longer for her to become sexually active again. She also understood that his anger would be swift and terrible, if she were ever to deprive him of a cherished possession again.

So, a few weeks later, Rain Dance Woman offered her sister, New Grass Woman, to him. Wamdisapa understood what she was up to. Rain Dance Woman knew that her sister had no chance of surpassing her as favorite wife. She hoped that he would make New Grass Woman pregnant and make her his second wife. After her child was born, New Grass Woman would have milk and therefore could feed both the baby and act as a wet nurse for Pinched Cheeks, which would allow Rain Dance Woman to once again share her robes with their husband, as a principle wife should.

Wamdisapa only used New Grass Woman occasionally over the many months that had passed since. But, she was as lazy under the bedding robes as she proved to be at working at the many jobs Wahpekute women performed each day. And lately, her unexciting sexual performances had left Wamdisapa even more frustrated than satisfied . . .

A wolf howling on the prairie brought Wamdisapa's mind back to the present. He couldn't help but compare the girl, Bright Morning, with the slave girl. They were both very young and very beautiful. The thought of taking Bright Morning Girl as a second wife was even more exciting than having the slave girl as a sexual substitute. The fact that she was so young would mean that she would have many years to give him more sons.

He watched until the eastern horizon showed the first signs of slipping from darkness to light. His experienced feet tread silently through the prairie grass and found their way up the gentle slope leading to a rise in the ground a short distance from the village camp.

He sat still, watching the landscape before him grow lighter and lighter with each passing minute. Wamdisapa heard her prayer song before he saw her. She sat on her knees facing east, singing as she chopped at the ground with a dull stone knife. He could hear her grunting with effort as she tore at the tough buffalo grass. Stalking slowing forward, he stopped when he was only an arm's reach away from her busy form.

"Mother Earth holds her children tightly," he said softly.

Startled, she spun to face him, the stone knife raised defensively!

"It can be dangerous for one so young and pretty to be so far from the village in the early morning," Wamdisapa said with an easy smile as he looked boldly at her young, naked breasts rising and falling with her frightened breathing.

"Yes, it's true," she answered, her voice trembling a little.

"Are your ancestors from the grass?" he asked indicating the chopped blades lying askew by her knees.

"The soil," she answered simply.

From the leather sheath at his waist, he drew his war club. It was a stout staff, with a stone head, sharpened on one side, blunt on the other, attached to it by sun-shrunken wraps of rawhide. With a few strokes, he chopped the tough grass away and scarred the ground deep enough to remove the grass roots. She reached forward and pinched a few grains, depositing them in her pouch. Then she stood and faced him, not knowing what to say or do next. She felt nervous and was short of breath. Her voice trembled even more, and she was conscious that her hands shook, even as they hung at her sides.

"The sun rising is like *Manito* coming back to life after being dead all night. The night frightens me."

"You have no need to fear the night," Wamdisapa said gently. "You have a father and four brothers in your tipi." His eyes drank in the young girl's beauty as the light from the rising sun revealed the contours of her body. Her long dark hair had already been brushed. There were no sleep tangles and no tiny bits of grass or bark in it. In the slowly coming light, her skin looked smooth and clear of any imperfections. Her eyes were alive with youthfulness. Her small breasts looked firm and lovely to him, the dark nipples puckered tight, standing against the dawn's coolness. He could feel his heart pounding, wondering how a man of his experience could be so affected by one so young? Clearing his throat nervously, he said,

"You have more to fear here at sunrise than you do from the darkness at night." With an effort, he tore his eyes from her and glanced across the prairie. "It is now, with the light of a new day, that the Sac and Fox or the Pawnee will come." He reached out a finger and traced a line from her forehead, down her nose and added, "And they would be very pleased to find one so young and pretty to steal away from us."

Even in her youth, she could see the longing in his eyes and sense the desire in the touch of his finger. Confusion entered her soul. This was the mighty Wamdisapa: headman, great hunter, killer of enemies and owner of horses. He was the most respected leader of the Wahpekute people. Gentleness and polite conversation with children were not his common practices. Still, she could see his eyes as they passed across her and was keenly aware when they stopped on her bare breasts. She blushed a bit, realizing that she was still dressed as a child, with only a short clout in warm weather, even though her body had taken the shape of a young woman.

"Sunrise would be a good time to die," she stated bravely, not knowing what else to say.

He smiled, saying nothing. They both turned to watch the sun burn itself over the horizon. Feeling a breeze touch their shoulders, they both sniffed the scents it carried, but there was no danger on the wind. Wamdisapa knew that this wasn't the usual way of his people. Normally, when a man wanted a woman for his wife, he spent many weeks courting her.

First, making eye contact with her whenever the people gathered at social functions, like when successful hunters distributed food to all in the village, who were not so successful, or when they danced before a hunt, or going into battle. Then a suitor, taking a warm horsehair blanket or buffalo robe, would sit outside the girl's father's tipi at night and play soft tunes on his eagle wing flute and chant songs encouraging the girl to come out. If the girl's parents were agreeable to a possible union, they would allow the girl to go out and sit beneath his robe with the man. In this way, matches were made. He had followed this tradition with Rain Dance Woman. But this girl would be a second wife. He didn't have time to spend weeks courting her, nor the sexual inclination to wait that long.

Not looking at her, he said, "Your father has two wives. One is old, and one is young."

"Yes," she agreed.

"Which is your mother?" he asked.

"The younger, Catches Birds Woman," she answered.

"Your father has a big family," he stated, adding, "and many mouths to feed."

She merely nodded in agreement.

Wamdisapa took the girl by the shoulders and turned her to face him. He felt an unexplainable need to tell her what he was thinking.

Any final decision would be made by her father, Blue Nose, no matter how the girl felt. He planned to make his offer to the old man no matter what her reaction was now. But Wamdisapa knew that the girl's father was more apt to agree to the union if the girl wished it too.

"I wish to feed one of these mouths for him," he said, looking down into her eyes.

Bright Morning's heart leapt in her chest, and she could hear it racing as it pounded in her ears. A thousand thoughts flashed through her young mind in the flutter of a butterfly's wing. If she were to marry a younger warrior, who didn't already have one wife, she would bring her husband into her father's tipi to help provide for him in his old age. This custom of their people gave girl children great worth. It made her very valuable to her father.

"My father's four sons will one day find wives and leave his tipi and he will have no one to help him hunt in his old age," she said, knowing the practicality of her marrying as a second wife was not good for her father in the long run.

Wamdisapa smiled. He could hear the underlying excitement by the quivering in the young girl's voice and see her chest rising and falling with her rapid breathing. But he could also see that she was, for the most part, undaunted by this sudden change in her young life. The fact that she would craftily try to bring the highest price for her father proved his belief that she was wise beyond her years. Old Blue Nose was known as a good bargainer, and the Wahpekute enjoyed dealing almost as much as gambling.

"I have many warm robes, sharp knives, spears, arrows, well balanced war clubs, gut bags of pemmican, dried deer, elk, and buffalo, a white wolf skin, the hide of a red deer, bear claws and a black dog with seven suckling pups," he stated proudly, indicating that he was wealthy enough to pay a good price for her dowry.

Bright Morning Girl knew he was a rich man. But it was none of the items he had mentioned that proved his true wealth. She knew Wamdisapa possessed the one commodity that represented wealth throughout the *Dakotah* peoples. He had horses.

"My father would like all of those things," she said. "But," she added coyly, "I'm not so sure my mother will be interested in trading away her best helper for more possessions for her to carry on her back."

Wamdisapa couldn't help himself; he laughed. The girl was as sharp as newly chipped flint. For one of such few years to understand the true political intricacies of governing in the family unit was remarkable. He knew that he would pay what ever the price would be

25

to get this young woman. She was no longer a "near child" in his mind. He thought of her now only as a young woman, and her bold confidence and self assured manner lent credence to his belief.

"Will your father be in the village when the dogs seek the coolness of the morning side of the tipis?" he asked, referring to the time in the mid-afternoon, when the village dogs could be found snoozing in the shade provided by the tipis.

"He will be in the village," she answered.

He smiled and dropped his eyes once more from her face to her naked breasts, and then spun on his heel, walking down the hill. His mind was on preparing for the bartering session facing him in the afternoon. He needed to sweat and bathe and paint his face and torso. But first, he would go hunting. A movement caught his eye as he neared his tipi and he spotted New Grass Woman scurrying back into it. She had been spying on him, and he smiled to himself, knowing the disappointment she would be experiencing before the afternoon sun settled behind the western prairie.

# Chapter 4
## *Explorers*

The Corps of Discovery's apprehension about meeting hostile Indians during the early weeks had proven to be unfounded. The bands of Otos and Omahas they encountered were helpful and friendly. Each village welcomed them with open arms. The men, women and children poured forth from their lodges and ran to the riverbank in small rivulets of humanity. Laughing and calling out in their native tongue, they greeted the whites by waving and smiling. The young men didn't hesitate to jump in the river and swim out to meet the boats as the vessels swung towards the shore. Dodging the oars of the pirogues, they clung to the sides until the water was shallow enough for them to find their footing, when they pushed the large canoes and beached their prows on the rocky shore.

They clambered aboard, shaking the white men's hands and patting them on the back. So friendly was the greeting at the first such meeting, that the Corp's apprehension melted away, and the white men immediately relaxed their vigilance. The next morning, several of the men's personal items stored in the pirogues were missing, stolen by the friendly young men. It was a lesson learned well and early in their expedition. Stealing from visitors, who were not careful enough to stow their gear in a safe place, was not considered a sin among the river tribes. After the first of such thievery, the pirogues were used to transport the men and gifts for the Indians from the keelboat to the shore, but were moored at night to the anchored keelboat, well off shore and put under guard.

These Indian villages had experienced the bounty of white traders before. The people lived close to the big river for much of the year and ranged up and down it, taking fish in nets made from twisted tree bark and horse hair. They set deadfall traps along the paths of deer, elk and buffalo. In the spring, the ducks and geese, in flocks so large that they darkened the sky at mid-day, migrated along this stretch of river, before wheeling due north to head for the wetlands of the upper mid-west and Canada. Great numbers of the fowl could be taken with bow and arrows, spears or skillfully thrown nets. Life along the big river was good. They were a thriving, happy people, who were eager to trade with the influx of white traders that had worked the lower reaches of the big river for the last few years.

After the rituals associated with greeting visitors, the chiefs were always anxious to council with the whites. The Otos and Omahas had many furs and the white traders they had met in the past were always very generous with gifts, hoping to gain favor with the lead men and secure exclusive trading rights with the tribe. They were not disappointed when Captain Lewis and Will Clark told them through the interpreter, Drouillard, that they had come as emissaries from their Great White Father, who resided in the place of the sun rise.

They passed along his wish for friendliness and peace with his red children and asked them to stop waging war upon one another as well. As a special show of the power that the Great White Father had, they fired the air gun mounted on the prow of the pirogue and the small cannon mounted on the keelboat. They handed out scarlet red uniforms to the principal chiefs and gave them medallions with the likeness of the Great White Father's face on one side. There were many other gifts, small mirrors, steel knives and axes, handed out to the lesser chiefs and warriors and brightly colored beads and sugar cane were given to the women and children.

When the council was over, the friendly atmosphere almost always called for a celebration. Huge cook fires were built, and venison haunch, buffalo hump and the delicacy of the camp, spitted pup, were placed over low burning coals. Cakes of ground corn and dried squash flavored with berries and small bits of meat were baked on the hot rocks near the fires and served with the meal.

The white Captain ordered a small cask of the watered down trade whisky brought ashore and was generous in serving the main men of the village. After the meal, the cook fires were built high against the growing night sky, and the Indians and explorers danced around the flickering flames and sang at the top of their lungs against the silence of the plains, until the stars grew bright and the day's exhaustion overcame them.

It was always near the end of the dancing that the female starved men of the expedition found opportunity knocking. Clark's slave, York was always the sensation at each village they visited. His dark skin and curly hair were a great curiosity to the Indians. Men, women and children crowded around the big black man, pushing and shoving, trying to get close enough to touch him. It was a bewildering situation for the slave. He was used to staying in the background and being quiet and unobtrusive. To be in the limelight made him nervous at first. He stood in the center of the crowd, quivering with fear and the desire to break free of all the throng of outstretched hands. It was only after Drouillard explained to him that the Indians thought of him as being "kin to the buffalo," because of his curly black hair and dark skin that he began to relax and enjoy the attention. And it wasn't long before he was taking advantage of the situation. He trimmed his beard to a shaggy point, resembling the long tuft of hair that hangs from a bull buffalo's chin. He stomped his foot, flared his nostrils and grunted from deep within his chest in a near perfect mime of a randy bull. This act always pleased the people and encouraged them to be even bolder in their attempts to touch him.

York's popularity soon became a problem. La Liberte discovered that some of the Indian men were bringing their wives and daughters to York's bed at night, hoping that the women would become pregnant from the "buffalo man." When he reported this finding to the rest of the men, who had been on the river for several weeks without the favors of women kind, it made the whole crew unhappy. A small mutiny was at hand until Clark convinced Captain Lewis to open the store of gifts and allow the men to trade them for the favors of the Indian women. Many of the red men were willing to trade some of their wives' time for a new steel knife or hatchet.

The liaisons between the men of the Corp of Discovery and the Indian women became quite commonplace and gave each man a reason to pull harder on the ropes, push harder on the poles and work the oar strokes with more force. The faster they moved up river, the sooner they would come to another village. But as the days and weeks passed, the villages became fewer and fewer. Each day was filled with toil that caused the men's muscles to ache and their hands to bleed.

The sameness of their labor would have caused boredom to set in, if it hadn't been for the element of danger that leaving the relatively safe lands of the Oto and Omaha presented. The Corp was entering the lands of the people the French called *Nadouwessioux*—a name given them by their ancient enemies, the Ojibwa. It meant "snake, or enemy." The Americans had shortened the name to just "Sioux." But everything they had heard about these people who fought with the Omaha, if they traveled too far up the river, was bad. They were a large, powerful nation that had had little interaction with the white race. Their war-like habits with their neighbors had borne them a combative reputation for jealously protecting their territory.

One of the old Oto chiefs had tried to warn them away from entering the lands of the *"Dakotah,"* as he called the Sioux. So much was his fear for his new white friends that he cried large tears when his warning failed to persuade Captain Lewis to turn the expedition around and go back from where they had come. Each man in the Corps of Discovery knew that how the Sioux would greet the white men on the river was a question that would not be answered until they met face to face.

The days dragged on, but Captain Lewis, nor his adjutant Clark, would allow the men's boredom or fear to interfere with their performance. The leaders led by example and worked as hard as anyone. Their spirits were indomitable, as they were almost always cheerful even under the hottest of suns, coldest of rains, and pulling against the strongest of currents. At night in camp, when everyone was ready to fall in their blankets for a well deserved rest, both Captains, (for Captain Lewis had named Clark his equal even though the official commission had not come through before the expedition slipped away from the St. Louis docks) wrote in their journals, caught strange insects, and sketched drawings of wildlife and flowers they had seen during their day's labor.

Specimens were packed away to be sent back to President Jefferson, and they encouraged all of the men to keep journals, too. They lectured them about the fact that they were making history, and someday, the greatness of their adventure would astound the entire world. Lewis and Clark, it seemed to most of their men, never wavered in their beliefs, never tired, never hurt and never quit. It made the men wonder at their ability to remain well when everyone else was sick and their ability to keep going when everyone else wanted to stop. With any lesser men leading the expedition, it would have failed by now, for already there was quiet talk of desertion when the Captains were out of earshot.

The hard labor of fighting their way up the river had added even more muscles to Hugh McNeal's lanky frame. The large young man had a bushy red beard now, and his bright blue eyes twinkled in the fire light at night as he worked his small bellows and hammered bent rope stakes straight again on his portable anvil.

The burning summer sun had penetrated the thin coat of golden hair that covered his chest and arms, causing his fair skin to freckle and burn, adding to all of the other discomforts of traveling up the wild river. But, he was as tall and broad as Captain Clark, larger than the rest of the men, except for York. And because of his great size and strength, he often found himself as leadsman on the rope crew, trudging up the river, through ankle deep muck and waist deep water, towing the floundering pirogues and keel boat, when ever the current was too fast for poling or paddling.

It had been a long, hard three months since they had left St. Louis and only Hugh's great loyalty to Will Clark kept him from having second thoughts about signing up with the Corps. His days were filled with toil that he had never dreamed of. Even though he had worked hard everyday of his life, his hands were callused from rowing and poling, and his shoulders and arms burned from pulling on the ropes. His joints ached from the cold water and the pressure of the merciless current. But the weaker men were in far worse shape.

It was late in the day, and the banks of the river were coming closer together, indicating the chance of a stronger current. Captain Lewis ordered Hugh's crew over the side to pull on the ropes. Hugh tried to ignore the cold as it crept up his legs, numbing them. Freezing mud tugged at his moccasins as he swung to the right bank, searching for shallower water. The chest deep water swirled against his body as he and his crew looped the rope over their shoulders and leaned into the rope. The current's constant pressure pushed at them, threatening to wash them off their feet.

Hugh had to concentrate on putting one foot ahead of the other, making his struggle against the river a personal battle. Everything else had to be forgotten. It was his strength, his brawn, and his brute stubbornness against the cold, the mud, the snags and the overpowering surge of the current. It was Hugh McNeal against the Mighty Missouri River! The current was a relentless, unwavering force, but Hugh and the men on his crew strained on their rope struggling in the deep mud, stumbling ahead, slowly gaining on the river one stubborn step at a time.

The afternoon wore on with only short rests between seemingly endless hours of pulling on the long rope. During one of these endless hours, with his mind all but blank from pains in his body and exhaustion, Hugh heard a hail from the north bank. Raising his head to see who had called out to them, he saw one of the hunters, standing on the low bank, excitedly waving and pointing to the trees behind him.

Hugh turned to lead the boat to that shore. When his feet hit solid ground, he clambered up the bank to help tie the rope to a tree. The rope crews from the pirogues did the same and soon, the current swept all three boats over to the bank, where they came to ground on a small sandbar.

Hugh's whole body shook with cold as he wiped the sweat from his forehead. It didn't seem possible to be so cold, and yet still be sweating. He sat with his head in his hands, experiencing a period of dizziness, not uncommon among the tired men after a long time on the ropes. All around him, the men who had been pulling on the ropes sat or lay in various poses of utter exhaustion. Behind them, two of the hunters were talking excitedly to the Captains. Drouillard had seen an Indian up river. He had been stalking slowly along the tree line, which followed the river when he saw the lone man coming.

Drouillard thought the Indian looked to be a runner or messenger of some type. The man appeared to be in a hurry as he trotted across the prairie from the southeast and had entered the trees about a quarter of a mile from where Drouillard hid. Drouillard then backtracked down the river until he found the other hunter, John Newman, who was gutting out a buffalo cow he had shot. The two men finished dressing out the buffalo while they waited for the party on the river to catch up. When the boats rounded the bend, it was Drouillard who had signaled them to put ashore.

Captain Lewis was excited by the sighting. They had been in the land of the Sioux for days, and he had been expecting to run into these people at any time. His voice shaking with excitement, expressed more confidence than apprehension about a hoped for meeting with the Sioux in the next few days. Captain Clark ordered the tired men to set up camp. They would stop early today and celebrate the sighting of the Indian as well as the good luck of having fresh meat to sup upon. York built a big cook fire and soon large chunks of buffalo cow were spitted and hung over the flames.

Something in the captains' manners roused the men's spirits. They would stay camped here on this bend of the river long enough to make a try at finding the Sioux. Everyone was in motion again. Space was cleared to set the tents and a great pile of firewood was gathered. The men unloaded the boats and staked them securely to the shore. Pickets were set around the small herd of horses that had survived the trip thus far. While the men set up camp both Leaders followed Drouillard and Newman up river to the place Drouillard had spotted the Indian. By the time the Captains returned, the men had gathered around the fire, savoring the aroma of the fat cow, sizzling over the flames.

The Captains couldn't hide the disappointment on their faces. They had trekked several miles beyond the point Drouillard had last seen the man, but no further sign of the man could be found. Both the Otos and Omahas had assured them that if they stayed on the river they would soon find the Sioux. Captain Lewis privately suspected that the runner was a messenger sent by the Omahas to their red cousins, to inform them of the coming of the expedition, which might mean they would be met with friendliness or an ambush. To protect against any devilment the Sioux might attempt, he doubled the guard for the night and his thoughts turned to two of the men who were absent from the camp.

La Liberte had left their camp on the morning before. He had left word that his mission was to scout ahead and try to find the Sioux. La Liberte claimed to know their tongue and hoped to make contact with the Sioux and explain the expedition's peaceful intentions, but his mission was self-imposed, for neither of the Captains had given him orders or granted him permission to leave the main body of the expedition.

Moses Reed was the other man absent from camp. He had asked for and gained permission to leave with the morning sun to return to the campsite of the night before, to retrieve his knife. He claimed to have stuck the knife into the trunk of a tree while finishing his morning meal and had forgotten it when called to load the boats. Neither man had yet returned, and Captain Lewis feared that both could have fallen at the hands of the Sioux. Every man in the company slept with one eye open that night.

The next morning, Captain Clark awoke with the suggestion that both men had possibly deserted. His reason for the accusation was simple. La Liberte had been a good hunter and boatman, but had never before been overly anxious to meet with the Otos and Omahas without someone there to watch his back. So why would he now desire to meet with people reputed to be hostile, all by himself? Plenty of time had passed for Moses Reed to find his lost knife and return, because a man traveling on dry land could travel much faster than men dragging boats up the winding river against the current. By short cutting all of the twists and turns in the meandering river, a man on foot or certainly on horseback would easily be able to catch up with the struggling boats in a matter of a few hours.

Will Clark wanted each man to know that he would not be forgotten. If the two men were lost, they should be found. But if it was found they had deserted, they would be hunted down and punished. He requested permission from Captain Lewis to take an armed guard of men back to the last Oto village. He was sure that he would find both men there, snuggling deep in the robes with a fat squaw. Lewis refused, stating that he would give the two men the benefit of the doubt. His orders were for the men to make any repairs on their personal gear that was needed while they waited for La Liberte and Moses Reed to arrive in camp, and he sent scouts out to look for sign that might have been missed the day before. By noon, Reed and La Liberte had still not returned and Clark again urged Lewis to take action to find them. Lewis bowed to Clark's request and wrote orders for a troop of men to return to the last Oto village and search for news of the two men. If they were found, they were to be brought back to face company punishment. If they resisted, they were to be shot dead on the spot. These orders were read in full view and hearing of the entire corps of men, so that every man would know the severity of the accused crime of desertion. With the orders tucked away in his medicine bag, Pat Gass led his mounted troop of men off to the southeast along the river.

The Captains agreed that it was time to start pushing the boats up the river again and gave the orders to load the boats and get ready to move. Sergeant Charles Floyd had taken sick a few nights before and was experiencing a lot of abdominal pains. He was a brave man, who didn't complain, but his pain was obvious in his face. When Captain Lewis asked him if he felt up to traveling, he merely nodded his head and moved slowly to his place in the keelboat. With one backward glance after the troop of riders, Lewis ordered the main party of the expedition to continue up river again.

# Chapter 5
*The Dowry*

**B**lue Nose glared across the matted buffalo robe spread before the entrance to his tipi by Wamdisapa. He had just taken a good tongue lashing from Bright Morning Girl's mother. The girl, after returning from her morning ritual a few hours before, had drawn her mother outside of the tipi, where a whispered conversation had taken place. The conversation had ended with this, his second wife, the young one he still enjoyed sharing his bed with, crying and moaning with anger. The exasperating thing was that while she seemed to be angry with him, he knew nothing about what ever it was that had made her mad.

"She is too young!" Catches Birds Woman had spat at him when she came back into the tipi after whispering with Bright Morning Girl outside.

"Too young?" was all that Blue Nose could get out before she interrupted him.

"And he is too old!" she snarled, her face twisting into a grimace as she tried to choke back a sob.

"Too old?" He labored to keep up, but was confused by his wife's ranting.

"You will not allow it! You will stand up to him! You will refuse him!"

He thought she was done and started to ask her just what she was talking about, but she cut him off once again, her anger and fear pitching her normally gentle voice to a high whine. "I don't care how much you like him, you will not let him do this! You will not let him take our young daughter! She is still a child, not nearly old enough to be taken as an adult man's second wife!"

Blue Nose pondered his wife's words now, as he sat cross-legged on the robe just outside their tipi door, facing Wamdisapa. His baleful eyes showed none of the respect, everyone knew that he held for their leader. Now he understood what had prompted his wife's dire warning that if he allowed this to happen, his "bed would soon be cold and lonely," just before the woman had fled the tipi and ran out to hide in the tall grass of the prairie. All threats aside, Blue Nose knew Catches Birds Woman was right. Bright Morning Girl was much too young to be a wife to the Lead Man of their village. He thought there must have been some mistake. Wamdisapa already had a young, pretty wife and a plump sister-in-law to share his bed with. There was no reason for this great man to want his young daughter, too.

The reality of the situation came down hard on Blue Nose when he noticed that the people were gathering, standing in small, whispering groups, peeking between the tipis, to watch. He saw the growing pile of gifts Wamdisapa had laid on the robe between them and heard the sounds of appreciation the watching people made at each addition. He knew this was a serious situation. After seeing two finely tanned buffalo sleeping robes, a white wolf skin, and two gut bags stuffed with jerked deer meat placed on top of the pile, Blue Nose was sure that Wamdisapa wouldn't take his rejection of the fine gifts well.

"Blue Nose," Wamdisapa said, "I offer these gifts in exchange for your daughter, Bright Morning. She has grown into a fine young woman."

"But my daughter is just a girl," Blue Nose answered, remembering his wife's concerns. "She was born in the summer, thirteen summers ago and is still just a child. I can not accept these gifts." There was a sharp intake of breath from the assembled crowd. How could an old man like Blue Nose refuse these fine gifts and refuse a man like Wamdisapa?

"Then she is a child who has grown far beyond her young years," Wamdisapa answered. "Her breasts are formed, and her hips are wide. Her womanly shape has caught my attention, as I'm sure it has for many of the men in this village. I've heard the flute players calling to her each night." Wamdisapa pulled a newly made war club from a pack at his side. The club's head, a smooth round stone with a groove chipped around its girth was held to a dark wood handle by colorfully beaded leather strips. He added the club to the pile of gifts. "I offer these gifts in exchange for your daughter."

Blue Nose sat and thought deeply about the value of his young, strong daughter, who normally would be counted upon to bring a young man into his family to help provide for him in his old age. The pile of gifts was considerable, but certainly not enough in comparison to facing the wrath of Bright Morning's mother.

"My young daughter's mother says you are too old for her daughter. My daughter's mother says she has kept her child safe from the flute players and has tied her legs together each night to protect her from those who would steal her childhood. She is strong and healthy and, as her mother says, unused by a man. I can not accept these gifts." This rejection caused a loud murmur from the watchers.

Wamdisapa sat staring at the old man. Blue Nose was arguing the value of this daughter well. These bargaining sessions were sometimes known to last for hours, but he was in no mood to spend all day. Before he could sweeten his offer, Blue Nose went on.

"My sons will all marry and leave my tipi. The girl is my only hope to add to my family. She is very valuable to me."

Wamdisapa stood and motioned with his hand in a "come here" gesture. His first wife, Rain Dance Woman walked from between the tipis, leading a pinto mare by a war halter rope snugged around its bottom jaw. She led the horse up to Wamdisapa, handed him the rope, turned and left, not looking back. A freshly killed buck sagged across the horse's back, tied with a rope looped around its hind quarters then passed under the horse's stomach and looped around the deer's front quarters.

Wamdisapa loosened the rope and dropped the deer next to the pile of gifts. Then, he spoke. "Old one, I was born in the winter, many winters ago. But I'm not so old that I can't provide for my family." He pointed at the buck on the ground at their feet. "What other hunter in this village would be better for you to have as part of your family? I can provide for your daughter as my wife in my tipi, and you and your sons and wives in your tipi." He stood with his chest puffed up with pride and tapped at his heart as he spoke. "I am a great leader of the People. I know my people. I believe your daughter's mother has protected her from the night rovers and flute players. I know your daughter is a beautiful and strong, young woman. I understand your reluctance to lose her. I know how valuable she is to you."

He stopped talking and stood quietly for a moment looking intently into Blue Nose's eyes. Slowly he raised his arm, extending the lead rope from the war bridle in his hand toward the old warrior. All motion in the village halted. Everyone, the men reclining in the shade of their tipis, the women squatting by the cook fires and even the children at play, stopped what they were doing along with those who had gathered to watch, as if frozen in place without a sound. Even the camp dogs stopped chasing their tails, snapping, sniffing and quarreling over scraps and sat silently watching the scene. The only sounds that could be heard were the crackling of the fires and buzz of insects for several heartbeats after Wamdisapa raised the lead rope to Blue Nose.

"I know your daughter is dear to you." Wamdisapa's voice, though calm and quiet, carried throughout the camp. "I know that a man's last daughter is valuable to him. That is why I offer these many gifts and . . . this horse with spots, which will serve you in both peace and war, in exchange for her."

Old Blue Nose stared at Wamdisapa's hand holding the lead rope. He had always wanted a horse, but had lacked the courage to go steal one. He had never even dreamt that his daughter's bridal price would include a horse. Suddenly, even Catches Birds Woman's threats faded from his mind. In another year or so, his daughter would be courted by the flute players anyway. And soon after, one of those young men would be offering much fewer gifts than what laid before him now for her. And he would have to take them. No! Catches Birds Woman would have to understand!

Slowly, as if he expected Wamdisapa to pull the rope away and proclaim this all a joke, Blue Nose reached out and grasped the beautiful spotted horse's lead and looked directly into Wamdisapa's eyes and said quietly, "I will send my daughter to your tipi tomorrow morning. Her mother will need this night to prepare her."

"Hoka-hey. It is done."

\*       \*       \*

New Grass Woman was very angry. She was angry because Wamdisapa's new young wife had arrived, carrying a small bag of possessions, at their tipi that morning. She felt humiliated. After all of these months of living with him in the same tipi, honoring his wishes and helping Rain Dance Woman with all of her chores, sewing his buckskins and caring for Pinched Cheeks, he had ignored her evident right, earned by sharing his sleeping robes even more often than Rain Dance Woman had. It was insulting for him to disregard all she had done for him and bring home a new young wife.

By taking this young girl for his second wife, he had dashed any hopes she had held of becoming one of Wamdisapa's wives. Oh, she could still live in his tipi and would probably even be called upon to share his bed on occasion, especially if the girl soon became pregnant. However, New Grass Woman knew she would never be considered equal to Rain Dance Woman or even to this young girl he called Bright Morning. Wamdisapa had left early, before the girl had arrived. He'd left instructions for Rain Dance Woman and New Grass Woman to treat her well and make her feel welcome until he returned.

The morning had passed with Rain Dance Woman and Bright Morning Girl sitting beside the tipi breaking down a tanned deerskin. Rain Dance Woman explained the process of using animal brains along with salt and the sun's drying powers to tan hides. Bright Morning girl already knew the process, but was too polite to say so.

New Grass Woman was disappointed in the way her sister seemed to accept this stranger into their home. She felt betrayed, which only added to the anger in her soul and refused to join in visiting with the girl. Muttering low curses in her throat, New Grass Woman uttered warnings to the girl as she stomped about doing her chores. Her face was contorted into an angry frown that grew uglier with each passing minute.

Late in the afternoon, Rain Dance Woman and Bright Morning Girl finished softening the deerskin and put away their tools. Rain Dance Woman started to prepare their evening meal by chopping strips of dried deer meat and dropping the meat into a clay pot of water, sitting on a bed of hot coals beside the fire pit.

She felt disappointment that her husband had decided to pick a new, young girl, instead of making her sister, New Grass Woman, his second wife. But she knew from the amount of dowry her husband had paid, that he wanted this girl badly, so she kept her disappointment in check. She did like this girl, though. Their conversation throughout the afternoon had established that Bright Morning Girl was unusually intelligent and friendly. She tried to council New Grass Woman to keep her distance from the girl and just wait and see what time would bring, but she could see that her advice was not being heeded.

With uncontrollable anger in her heart, New Grass Woman glared at the girl, sitting silently beside the tipi, curled there, like a defenseless little mouse. She was gathering firewood to feed the fire, and the sight of the girl sitting in the shade of the tipi, while she and Rain Dance Woman worked, pushed her into madness. She circled the fire pit and stopped before Bright Morning and shook a stick of firewood in the girl's face.

"Sit there shit worm that hangs from the dog's ass!" She fumed and swung the stick back and forth before Bright Morning Girl's face. "Sit in the shade and watch the real women of this lodge work!" she snarled. "He'll have you working soon enough! After he has ridden you like a stud horse rides a mare, he'll put you to work too. Then, you won't be so pretty!"

Bright Morning could sense the madness in New Grass Woman's voice and shifted from her seat to her haunches. She was ready to spring to her feet and run. She quickly glanced around the tipi area, looking for something she could use for a weapon to defend herself with, but New Grass Woman turned and walked away, still muttering to herself. When the big woman had entered the trees that lined the stream they were camped by, Bright Morning Girl relaxed a little and sat back down by the tipi.

She let her mind drift and a small, proud smile played across her lips at the memory of the price she had brought for her father. Buffalo and deer robes, beads, pemmican and jerked meat, a white wolf skin, a war club, the list seemed to go on and on, but it was the horse that she felt most proud about. Few men in the village had horses and acquiring one, no matter how, raised a man's stature amongst the People. Her father would be looked upon with greater respect by the rest of the People. Her brothers would walk a little taller amongst their friends. Even her mother would know a certain notoriety over the fact that her husband now owned a horse because the *Wahpekute* People had few horses, unlike their *Dakotah* cousins who lived out on the flat plains along the big muddy river. Only men rich enough to buy horses from their cousins or brave enough to steal them from the *Pawnee* had horses. Unless of course, she thought proudly, a man had a daughter so beautiful that her wedding price included a fine horse!

The afternoon sun moved to where it shined its warmth on her face. Bright Morning Girl felt sleepy. She laid back and, closing her eyes, locked her fingers behind her head. It had been a good day so far. She had enjoyed helping Rain Dance Woman with softening the deer hide and appreciated the way the older woman had visited with her.

She looked through half closed eyes and watched Rain Dance Woman place meat in the clay pot beside the fire and add heated stones to the pot. She poured blood from a bladder bag into the pot to flavor the broth and stooped to enter the tipi. The hot stones made the water hot and cooked the meat. She could smell the cooking meat and wondered when Rain Dance Woman would come back out of the tipi to remove the stones as they cooled and add more hot ones? The warmth from the sun and the good smell of the cooking pot coaxed her to close her eyes and relax.

Suddenly, her reverie was broken by a loud screeching shriek coming from the trees. She awakened instantly and slid up on her haunches again. New Grass Woman had abandoned her search for fire kindling and now carried a great club length branch high over her head as she ran screaming back to Wamdisapa's tipi. She ran directly at Bright Morning Girl with murder in her eyes and swung the club with all of her strength, but the young girl was far too quick for clumsy New Grass Woman. She easily dodged the wild blow and danced around the fire pit stopping near the pile of small cooking stones that were waiting to be heated in the fire pit.

"I'll break this club across your face Shit Worm!" New Grass Woman screamed and ran around the fire pit in pursuit of Bright Morning Girl. "Then we'll see if he still thinks you are so beautiful!"

The agile young girl easily eluded the older, heavy woman and raced around the tipi ahead of her. Hearing her sister's screams and curses, Rain Dance Woman came running from inside the tipi. She grabbed New Grass Woman from behind and held on tightly, struggling to keep her hold on the big, anger crazed woman. She knew how dear to Wamdisapa this young girl must be for him to pay such a high price for her. She also knew the price she would pay if the girl was injured. Frantically, she tried to calm her sister. And finally, after much talking and warning and threatening, Rain Dance Woman succeeded.

"All right, all right, I'll quit," New Grass Woman shouted to get Rain Dance Woman off of her back. Her great chest heaved with her efforts to slow her own breathing and her trembling hands started to steady. "But next time, Shit Worm, I won't let you know I'm coming, and I'll bust up your pretty face yet," she added.

A horse whinnied behind her, and she turned and saw Wamdisapa sitting astride his hunting pony. A fat doe was on the ground behind him. A rope was tied around its neck. He had dragged it to the village from where he had killed it. For an instant, she hoped that he had just ridden up. But one look in his eyes told her he had seen and heard too much. Rain Dance Woman immediately fell to the ground, groveling into the wicked grass stubble. She was afraid of the expression she had seen on Wamdisapa's face. She cried out apologies and begged for forgiveness. Her face was buried in the dust of the village thoroughfare. She was afraid to look up. She had felt his wrath once before and had barely survived the beating he had administered.

Wamdisapa's eyes were half closed, and his lips were pulled back in a snarl of anger. He looked from his wife's writhing form to New Grass Woman. The big woman's chest was heaving up and down again as she sobbed breaths of air into her fear-constricted lungs. Her fear was so great that her pendulous breasts quivered with each breath she drew in and shook violently when she exhaled. All of her anger was gone, melted by the heat of her terror.

Wamdisapa dug his heals into the pony's flanks and the startled beast leaped forward in surprise. In two jumps, it crashed, chest first into New Grass Woman. The blow knocked her to the ground and sent her rolling into the fire pit. Screaming, she jumped up from the fire, brushing at the coals that had burned into her forearms and stuck there! The clay pot full of cooking meat and broth beside the fire was knocked over and broken in her mad scramble to escape from the burning brands. Wamdisapa dropped from the pony's back and picked up the club New Grass Woman had dropped when the horse crashed into her. He swung the club in a low arch, causing New Grass Woman to instinctively duck. But the blow was aimed at the backside of her knees, knocking her back to the ground where she sat, dazed and shaken. He then began methodically beating her about the head and shoulders with the club.

The force of the blows rolled her onto her stomach, and she covered her battered head with both arms. The angry man then began moving from her shoulders on down, raining blows on her back, buttocks and the back of her legs. Struggling, she gained her hands and knees and tried to climb to her feet, but the relentless club kept falling. Her clothes were ripped and torn and came loose, leaving her nearly naked. Still he hit her with the firewood club, each blow smacking into her fat body, leaving an immediate welt. Blood, from a dozen different wounds, splattered each time the club landed, and it became slippery in his hands.

When Wamdisapa stopped to wipe the club's handle dry, the battered woman tried again to gain her feet, but after getting her hands and feet under her, she lacked the strength to straighten up. Her torn body tried to escape, walking on all fours like a bear. A fearful, desperate keening filled the air as she struggled to get away. Wamdisapa followed kicking her until she fell and could rise no more.

With New Grass Woman a mere bloody heap, he turned his attention to his first wife. Rain Dance Woman witnessed what had happened to her sister and saw him coming. She cringed to the ground, trying to become part of the earth. He towered over the small woman raising the bloodied club to deliver a blow, but before he swung, he felt an insistent tugging at his shoulder. Spinning, he saw Bright Morning Girl with tears running down her face.

"No, don't do this thing!" she cried. "She saved me! She stopped the Crazy One!" and she began crying like the small child she really was.

Wamdisapa's anger melted, and he took her gently in his arms hugging her tightly and patting her reassuringly on the back. With a trembling voice, she told him how it was New Grass Woman who had went crazy and attacked her and that Rain Dance Woman had come to her rescue. Rain Dance Woman still lay whimpering on the ground in front of the tipi.

Wamdisapa went to her and helped her gently to her feet. With great tenderness, he pulled the stubble sticking to her breasts and stomach. He told Bright Morning Girl to bring water and to take her into the tipi, and clean the older woman's body. When they entered the tipi, two old people, a man and a woman sat, huddled together on the far side of the lodge. The old woman held a whimpering child. Bright Morning Girl wet her hands and carefully washed Rain Dance Woman's face and torso, then laid her back on some robes and covered her. She was trembling from both fear and the coolness of the water. Bright Morning took the child, a young boy, from the old woman and rocked him, singing a soft song;

> *Oh young warrior, do not cry!*
> *Father Sun has come to warm you!*
> *Mother Earth will hold you safe!*
> *Brother Wind wants to play!*
> *Sister Rain sings you this song!*

At first, the child struggled against the sound of a stranger's voice, but soon the soft sounds calmed him and he lay back watching the singer's face intently. After four times through the song, the boy was yawning and Bright Morning took him to Rain Dance Woman's bed and placed him under the robes with her. Loud smacking and suckling noises began immediately. She could hear the soft sounds of Rain Dance Woman humming quietly to the child as he nursed.

Bright Morning Girl looked around the tipi's interior and felt a moment's trepidation. This was totally different than her parent's lodge. It seemed dark, and she looked up through the smoke hole noticing that the sun was gone. With no fire in the center pit, there was no light source.

She slipped out of the tipi and scooped up some hot coals from the outside fire, bringing them in. There was a small pile of tinder by the pit, and she placed it on the hot coals, blowing on them gently until they glowed red. Soon small wisps of smoke rose from the small sticks and flames flared. Patiently, she added larger and larger sticks until the flames grew in strength. She made another trip outside and gathered more sticks to feed the fire. Finally, with the fire burning brightly, she looked around the tipi and immediately missed her brothers. It was so quiet. She was used to hearing them argue and joke and wrestle. Here, the only sounds came from the suckling baby. There was slight rustling and she turned to see the old couple looking at her. The old man stared up at her and smiled. The old woman just stared. Neither said a word.

Nervously, Bright Morning Girl left the tipi once again. When she emerged this time, it was full dark. She looked over to where New Grass Woman had collapsed, but she was gone. The deer that Wamdisapa had brought home from his day's hunt was gone also. But the tongue, liver, heart and a steaming pile of intestines lay on the fresh deerskin. She assumed Wamdisapa had taken the rest of the meat to share with others in the village and her father. She took the small stone knife from her belt pouch, cut foot long length of the gut and quickly cleaned them by pulling them between her thumb and forefinger to discharge their contents. She took them into the tipi and skewered them on cooking sticks propped over the fire.

Soon the sizzling fat began to drop into the fire, causing brief flare-ups of light and the wonderful aroma of cooking meat engulfed the tipi interior. The old couple was glad to accept the food when she took it to them. This time, even the old woman smiled at her. Rain Dance Woman and the boy were both sleeping. Bright Morning Girl stood for a moment watching the flames grow and fall in the small tipi fire place and wondered if maybe she should go back to her father's tipi.

The reality of her situation was far different from her romantic musings of even just one day before. A large angry woman had threatened to kill her and then chased her with a club. The violence Wamdisapa used in punishing New Grass Woman frightened her. But it was Rain Dance Woman's abject fear of their husband's anger that scared her even more. Suddenly, she yearned for the known qualities of her father's tipi, wrapped safely in her mother's arms, the spoiled and often pampered "only daughter."

When she stepped out into the night, she knew it was too late to flee to her parents' tipi. Wamdisapa was back and she shuddered to think of how angry he would be if she were to run back to her parents. He sat by the fire, slicing the deer liver in thin strips and eating them raw. He had slivered the tongue and had small pieces broiling over the coal end of the fire. He motioned for her to come and sit beside him and offered her a slice of liver, which she took and swallowed without chewing. The warm, bloody meat awakened her own hunger. She hadn't eaten since leaving her father's tipi that morning and the fresh liver tasted good. She ate more as he sliced it and passed it to her. When the tongue was browned, he pulled the skewers away from the fire and held them out to her. She took one, blew on the hot meat to cool it and chewed it off of the stick. It was good, too.

"I told your father that you were a child grown beyond your years," Wamdisapa said quietly as she ate the browned tongue. "You've proven me right today. I'm sorry New Grass Woman tried to hurt you. She won't ever again. She's banished from this fire. Tomorrow, I'll have her sister remove her things from our tipi and set them on the edge of camp. She can pick them up there."

"You mean," Bright Morning Girl hesitated, but then finished her question, "she isn't dead?"

"No, she's not dead." Wamdisapa laughed a short laugh. "I didn't kill her. I just punished her badly, so she will never try to hurt you again." He reached over and took her chin between his thumb and fingers. "I can hardly blame her for being jealous of you," he added smiling.

"Rain Dance Woman and your son are sleeping," Bright Morning Girl informed him. "I fed the old people," she added and pointed at the gut pile on the skin. "Do you want some?" she asked.

Laughing, he took a short section and stripped it between his fingers and placed one end, uncooked in his mouth. He held out the other end to her, and she took it between her teeth and both began swallowing without chewing working toward the middle. When their lips touched, Wamdisapa cut the intestine between them, and they each swallowed it down. It was enough to eat.

They sat quietly, watching the fire. Wamdisapa smoked a short pipe loaded with a mixture of shredded plum and mulberry bark. Bright Morning Girl sat nervously, her eyes never leaving the flames. She knew that a big moment in her life would come yet that night, and she only hoped she was grown enough for it. She was less frightened of him now. Knowing that he hadn't killed New Grass Woman seemed to help. Now, he was being gentle and seemed almost kind as they ate at the fire. She was apprehensive about this night. She had never been with a man and hoped he wouldn't be disappointed.

With a grunt, in the middle of her thoughts, Wamdisapa stood and walked around behind her. He reached down, his large hands reaching under her arms and cupping her small, firm breasts as he lifted her to her feet. She dropped her head back against his chest and a low moan, filled with a passion she knew nothing about escaped her lips. She could feel his hard penis pressing against her back and shuddered wondering what she should do. Wamdisapa took her hand and led her into the tipi. The fire that she built earlier had died down and only the glow from the embers provided light. As he lowered her to his bed of robes, his hand slipped into her clout and pulled it down over her slim, girlish hips and she lay, naked and frightened before him.

Oblivious to the other people in the tipi, he dropped his clout and lay beside her. His hand stroked her lower belly, and he murmured reassuringly in her ear. She felt instant arousal when his lips caressed her suddenly very hard nipples and gasped when she felt his finger searching her pubic area. An involuntary grunt came from low in her throat when his finger found her vaginal opening and pushed deeply, but slowly, stretching her child size to accommodate his adult organ. She began to respond to the movement of his finger and found herself pushing with her pelvis and moaning in passion, reacting to his gentle touch. She sensed a change in him as he moved over her and spread her legs with his knees. He leaned forward and she felt his hard penis probing for her opening. His entrance was slow and deliberate and his first strokes were shallow, but each one pushing deeper and deeper until finally, it reached her membrane and then one, swift, hard thrust brought a soft cry from her lips. As her arms clutched him tightly around his back, he continued the hard thrusts faster and faster, until he moaned a low, lust fulfilled moan of relief, and she felt a powerful heat pouring through her loins, and his body collapsed dropping his full weight upon her.

Moments later, he rolled off of her and onto his back.

"You are now to be known as Bright Morning Woman," he whispered.

# Chapter 6
## *Crime & Punishment*

**S**ergeant Nathaniel Pryor rode at the head of the column of six riders in his party. They had ridden slow, searching the land thoroughly all the way back to their camp from two nights earlier. Pryor was hoping that La Liberte had accompanied Moses to search for his lost knife. It was possible that after retrieving the knife, while trying to follow the twisting, turning river back to the Corps, the men had become lost. But Pryor and his troop could find no sign of either man. The Sergeant felt certain now, that Reed and La Liberte had deserted. He decided to stop searching and led his party to the south, riding hard. There was a friendly village of Otos not too far down the river from where they were. He felt certain that if La Liberte or Reed had come this way, he would find them in that village.

They arrived in the Oto village late in the evening, and it took only a cursory search of the camp to find Moses Reed hiding in one of the dark lodges. On the last night the Corps had stayed in the Oto village, Reed had used sign language and by speaking a little French, struck a deal with one of the minor Oto chiefs. He started the deal by trading his knife for favors with the chief's wife and promised even more presents if the chief would agree to hide him and provide him with food for his long journey back down the river, when he returned. Thinking that the Captains would not want to take time to look for one man, Reed waited until the expedition had traveled several days up the winding river before deserting. But he had misjudged Lewis's and Clark's devotion to both their mission and to their men and was surprised that the Captains had sent a party after him. Now, the two cloth shirts with pockets full of blue beads that Moses had given the Chief upon his return, were not enough for the chief to risk trouble with the heavily armed troop of white men who had shown up looking for Reed, and Moses surrendered with no resistance.

Sergeant Pryor was disappointed that La Liberte wasn't found in the village, too. Pryor thought the men had acted together, but Reed adamantly claimed to know nothing of the whereabouts of his fellow hunter, La Liberte. The troop searched the entirety of the Oto camp and questioned all of the men in the village. But it was all to no avail, La Liberte had vanished.

Pryor's men also reported that they could not find the horse Reed had stolen from the Corps. When questioned about the horse, the Otos merely shrugged their shoulders and shook their heads and Pryor knew that the horse was probably staked miles out on the plains. It was well after dark, and he knew there was not much of a chance to find it even if it were daylight. Knowing that an extended absence from the Corps would cause his Captains deep concern, Pryor decided to give up the search for La Liberte and the horse. After putting a heavy guard on their horses, the troop stayed the night in the Oto village and left before sunrise the next morning to return to the boats. Reed would walk the entire distance.

On the return trip, they traveled as fast as the walking Reed could keep up. The man's hands were tied together and a length of twisted horsehair rope tethered him to the tail of the last horse in line, pulling him along at the pace the horse's rider chose. If he didn't keep pace with the horse, each step the horse took, jerked his arms straight away from his torso, tugging his slow moving body along. By mid-morning of the first day, his stride was clumsy with fatigue.

It took three days for them to catch up with the horse herders. Captain Clark was walking with the herd when Sergeant Pryor and his troop caught up with them. Clark sent a man to the river's edge to hail the boats when they came into sight and called an immediate halt. The herders picketed the horses and set up guard posts for the camp. Pryor and his men dismounted and led Reed to a nearby tree and tied him to it. He stood by the tree, leaning his forehead against its rough bark. Shame creased his face. His legs trembled with fatigue and pain. His shoulders and arms ached. Prickly pear and cockleburs were stuck to his clothes. His hat was gone, and the sun had been unkind to the skin of his face and neck. His face was burnt fire-red and large patches of dead skin were already peeling from his cheeks and forehead. Moses Reed was in a miserable condition. Clark ordered Pryor to loosen the rope, so the man could turn around and sit down. Moses sat, head down, staring at the ground. He ignored the men who came to look at him. Only a few tried to speak to him. He didn't respond to them.

An hour later, the boats came into view and they were hailed to shore. Though it was not yet noon, Lewis ordered the boat unloaded and a night camp set up. Sergeant Floyd, who had awakened that morning retching his night's meal and having severe pains in his lower stomach, was carried ashore and placed on a soft bed of robes under a tree shaded from the merciless hot sun. The Captains' tent was set up, and the rest of the camp set up around it. Wasting no time, a small, hand-hewn writing desk was set upon a short section of log, set on end in front of the Captains' tent. Captain Lewis seated himself behind the desk, and Clark stood at his side. When all was ready, the men were assembled and on Clark's order, Moses Reed was brought forward. He stood with guards on either side in front of Captain Lewis. When summoned, Sergeant Pryor stepped up to recite his report on the finding and arrest of Moses Reed.

"We searched the ground hard all the way back to the night camp Moses said he lost his knife at," Pryor said, clearing his throat, before he continued. "I knew they had to be on this side o' the river, and I figured they wouldn't a drifted to fer from its banks. I's hopin' they was lost, and we'd find 'em wanderin' around in circles. But we couldn't find no signs of either Moses or La Liberte. So, I decided to ride on down to the Oto village and see what we could see."

At this point, Pryor cleared his throat again and eyeballed the water bucket sitting by the Captains' tent. He wasn't used to speaking formally and found his mouth dry.

"Continue," Lewis ordered.

"We found Moses hunkered down with that toothless chief's fat wife. She was inclined to put up a squabble, but neither Moses or the Chief wanted any trouble with us. Them Injens musta run off with his horse, 'cause there weren't hoof ner hair of it to be found in their camp. So we tied ol' Moses foot ta hand, and then took a night's sleep our own selves. We didn't find no sign of La Liberte. My best guess is he got kilt by the Injens or et by a bear! And that's about all I got to say unless you got questions you want ta ask."

But the Captains asked no questions and Lewis ordered, "Captain Clark, read the charges entered this day, 19 August, 1804 against one Moses Reed, a member of this Corps of Discovery."

Clark stood before Moses Reed and listed the charges against him in a loud, clear voice, so that all the assembled men could hear. A slight breeze began to blow, rustling the cottonwood leaves.

"Moses Reed, you are charged with the following: Number One: The accused did leave this company under false pretenses with the explicit intention to desert and not return. Thereby failing the oath he took upon his enlistment with this company of men.

"Number two: The accused did steal certain articles of public properties listed as: one public horse, one public rifle, one public shot pouch and public shot, one public powder horn and public powder. The rifle, powder and shot were retrieved, the horse was not." Clark lifted his eyes from the written sheet he had prepared, to look at Reed. But Reed's eyes never left the ground. "The accused actions not only endangered the lives of the men sent after him, but also put into jeopardy the health and happiness of the entire Corps of men by causing the splitting of our force in known hostile land. Indeed, the success of the entire expedition was put into question by such an action as desertion."

"Have you any answers to these charges, Mr. Reed?" Captain Lewis asked.

At these words, Moses Reed looked up from the ground, and he stared blankly into the faces of the rest of the men. Then he merely shook his head and looked back down at his feet.

"Have you anything at all to say in your own defense?" Lewis then asked.

Reed raised his head once again, his eyes blinked several times quickly as small, dirty, rivulets of tears rolled down his dusty cheeks. His voice shook when he spoke for the first time since being captured.

"I cain't argue my guilt," he said first, pawing at the tears on his face with his tied up hands. "All I can say is that I'm lonely fer my family and afeared of the comin' unknown." His eyes darted about at the men. "I unnerstand that everyone here has those same feelin's, so I know I done wrong. And fer that I am sorry." He turned and looked at the Captains and in a voice cracking with emotion he continued, "But from here on out, I'll do ya right. I beg ya Captains to be as favorable to me as yer oaths will let ya be."

With those few words to defend himself, Moses Reed dropped his chin to his chest and stood staring once again, at the ground.

"We will recess to deliberate these facts and decide on a sentence," Lewis stated. He stood and turned to Sergeant Ordway. "Keep the prisoner on his tether, but let him wash himself clean. See that everyone, including the prisoner, has some hardtack and jerky. Be ready to re-assemble the men shortly." With that, he and Clark retired to their tent to discuss their options.

Inside the tent, York had spread their bedrolls, and the two leaders sat close together, with their faces only inches apart. They kept their voices low, so that the men just outside the tent couldn't hear.

"What do we do, Will?" Lewis whispered, but answered his own question, "Every military tenant dictates that deserters be tried, found guilty and shot!"

"I believe that is only specific in cases when an enemy is present, like a coward running from a battle," Clark said. "We've actually not seen an enemy."

"But we are in hostile lands! Who knows when the *Nadowwessioux* might take umbrage with us for trespassing on their lands and attack us in force! You called it from the very beginning. I thought Reed and La Liberte were probably just lost, but you . . . you read the men so well, and you knew in your heart that they had deserted. You told me you were afraid they might have run away to go home on the first night they didn't return."

They sat for a few minutes and listened to the rustling of the men as they moved around the camp. All the voices outside the tent were low, subdued by the grave nature of the current situation. Twice before, men had been disciplined. One of the French boatmen had been whipped for stealing rum from the keelboat, and Peter Wiser had been caught napping while on guard. He had received thirty lashes and had his rations cut for two weeks. But this was the first serious incident that, unless handled correctly, could put the success of the entire mission in jeopardy. The Captains would have to deal with it without the luxury of a long deliberation, and both knew that their actions now could have lasting effects on the rest of their men.

"Aye, Captain, I can read the men," Clark started to whisper, but stopped upon hearing a soft cough outside the tent door.

"What is it Ordway?" Lewis snorted, disgruntled with the interruption.

"Got some tac and beef fer ya," came the voice from outside the tent.

"Set it in then," Lewis ordered and rose to accept the food from the Sergeant. Ordway turned and left the tent.

Munching on the stringy meat and dried biscuit, Clark continued. "Aye, I can read the men. And I don't think shootin' this skunk would set well with them." He swallowed the beef. "I'm purty sure there's plenty of them mad at Reed for runnin' out, but I don't think you'll find many of them who want to shoot him. One of the Frenchies might be willin', but that won't set with them either. Naw, if ya gonna shoot 'im, it'd have to be a bona fide firing squad that done it." Clark thought for a few seconds and Lewis was content to let his friend finish forming his thoughts. "Captain, you know that if you stand Reed agin a tree and order five or six of them men to load up take aim, and fire, they'll do it. . . . but it won't set right with 'em."

"What then, Will?" Lewis asked. "We can't have the men even thinking about deserting. You know that. We've a long trip ahead, filled with unknown dangers and hardships. We have to be able to count on every man to do his part. Moses Reed has to be the last man who even thinks of deserting."

51

When he left the tent after dropping off the Captains' food, Ordway hurried over to a group of men who were watching York digging the night's fire pit. Nate Pryor, George Shannon, Hugh Wheat, John Shirley and John Potts sat in a semi-circle, some leaning against trees, others reclining on their sides as they watched the large black man dig with a small spade. Hugh McNeal dropped two large rocks he had lugged from the river to bank around the fire pit, and joined the group just as John Ordway walked up.

"I think they're gonna shoot 'im!" he whispered. "They're discussin' it anyway."

"That's make two dead men for today," Wheat stated matter-of-factly, nodding his head toward the blanketed Charles Floyd who laid under a nearby tree. "His guts are full o' pison. Ol' Floyd's a gonner fer sure."

"Quiet with that talk!" Sergeant Nate Pryor hissed. "Sergeant Floyd'll be okay by morning. Captain Clark bled him this morning and gave him a dose of salts. That'll fix him right up. He'll be back riding your ass by this time tomorrow, Wheat."

"Maybe, maybe not," Wheat mumbled and sauntered over to stand where he could see the prisoner. Reed had been tied to the same tree with Privates William Bratton and John Collins standing guard over him.

"You might wants ta put a edge on this hyar spade, Mista Hugh." York's deep baritone voice rumbled. "Dis groun' is mighty rocky ta be diggin' in."

"Do you really think they'll shoot him?" Hugh McNeal asked, ignoring York's request. At only eighteen years of age, Hugh had seen two dead men, one who had gotten drunk, fell in the river and drowned before anyone could pull him out. The other was a sick man who had just died. Nobody knew why. Neither of those men's deaths had really bothered Hugh. And seeing their bodies had had little effect on him. But, he was sure that he didn't want to see someone get shot.

Without warning, the Captains emerged from the tent and called for Ordway. The Sergeant who had Day Duty called out to assemble the men, and everyone hurried to form ranks before the Captains' tent. There was a quiet expectancy in the air.

"Mr. Reed," Captain Lewis addressed the prisoner, "the severity of the charges against you should warrant immediate death by firing squad!" There was a quiet gasp from the men upon actually hearing the words and Moses Reed began to tremble uncontrollably. "However," Lewis continued, "in reviewing your past service to this Company, you've been a good and capable member . . . willing to share your part of the load, and up until this incident . . . dependable."

Upon hearing these words, Reed gained a little hope. He brought his trembling limbs under control, and he tried to stand straighter.

"Therefore," Lewis went on, "Captain Clark has prevailed upon me that a lesser punishment should be commanded." At this, he turned to face the assembled men and added, "But hear me now." His cold blue eyes raked the men, and his voice was as hard as the steel in his sword's blade. "Should anyone else deem it wise to desert in the future, no matter what the circumstances may be, the leniency shown here today will be forgotten and immediate death by firing squad shall be theirs!" He spun on his heel and motioned for Clark to read the sentence.

"Moses Reed, in so much as you have been found to be guilty of desertion and theft of public property, you are hereby commanded to run a gauntlet, made up of our entire company of men four times. It will be the duty of each man in the company to gather and exhaust a supply of nine switches on your bare backside! Sergeant Charles Floyd is the only member exempt from this duty." Clark stopped and watched the eyes of the men as his next words sunk in. "And from this point until it is time for you to leave this company, you shall not be considered a member of this company. You shall be with us . . . but not a part of us."

Clark's last words rang loudly in the small clearing. Moses Reed was all but banished! His rations would be cut. No rum for Reed from here on out. He would be chosen to do all of the extra duty, but not trusted to stand guard. Maybe even worse, he would be left out of most conversations. His opinion would no longer be considered, by anybody. He would sit at the edge of darkness around the night's fire and not be asked to join in the banter. Most of the men were glad that death wasn't his penalty. Even so, they would be glad to lay into Reed's back without mercy for he had stolen something from each and every one of them. Desertion had not been a stranger to any of their minds at one time or another during the rigorous months of fighting their way up the river. It had been something they could play with in their minds, something to think about to help pass the time and dull their aches and pains. But now, with Lewis's harsh warning of death to the next deserter, few men could ever even think about it again, not even to just past the time.

Before Moses was ready, Sergeant Pryor took his arm and led him to the edge of the clearing. All of the men were lined up in two lines with a narrow passageway leading between them. Some of the men were whipping the air with the long switches they had gathered from the underbrush. Reed trembled again as Pryor used his knife to cut the filthy torn clothing from his body. His hands were still tied, and they would stay that way.

Naked, embarrassed and ashamed, tears began to drain down Reed's face. A sudden fear spread throughout his body, and for a moment, he was afraid he might lose control of his bladder. He wretched with the dry heaves, but mercifully, a shove from Pat Gass started him in motion down the avenue of pain before him.

He started slowly, but the switches flashed vigorously and the stinging blows soon pushed him to run as fast as he could. But his gait was clumsy, as his hands, being tied in front of him, wouldn't allow the pumping action of his arms to lend him both balance and speed.

When he exited the end of his first passage through the gauntlet, Moses was slightly elated. He'd made it through the first gauntlet all right. He felt the pain, but it served to energize him. He was angry! Tearing off the bonds tying his hands together, he walked back to the beginning and without waiting, began running through a second time.

With his hands free, he ran much faster, but this time, the blows came from heavier switches, that didn't just sting, but bruised deeply beneath his skin. He fell to the ground when he came to the end of his second run through the gauntlet and lay panting for air. But he bravely climbed to his feet without assistance, his lungs aching as he sucked for air, drawing in great draughts of it and wheezing the tortured used air back out as he walked back to the front.

Again without pause, he started through for the third time. A sudden heavy blow, high on his neck, knocked him down. He thought to lay there and catch his breath, but the whipping switches wouldn't let him. He rose and staggered on. When he reached the end again, he fell and lay gasping in pain and misery.

John Colter and John Newman lifted him to his feet and dragged him back to the front of the gauntlet again. By this time, his nose was broken and a blow above the eyebrow had opened a gash that bled into his right eye, making it hard for him to see. He lurched forward, blindly seeking the end. Halfway through, he staggered and fell. He lacked the strength to climb to his feet, but the slashing switches didn't stop and he finished his fourth and final trip through the gauntlet crawling on his hands and knees. When he passed Colter and Newman, he collapsed into unconsciousness.

Hugh McNeal and York dragged Reed's inert body back through the camp, where they laid him under the same tree as Sergeant Floyd. Captain Clark arrived soon and applied salves and poultices to some of the cuts and bruises that covered his face and head. But Reed's back, buttocks and legs were one large red welt with blood oozing from hundreds of wounds. Large black and blue areas were already forming. Clark shook his head and wondered if he had done Reed a favor by talking the Captain out of the firing squad? He hoped Reed's wounds would heal and not cripple him. But this beating had been more severe than either he or Lewis had anticipated.

He moved from Reed to Sergeant Floyd and was surprised to see the man's eyes open. Sergeant Floyd's morning had been filled with the passing of diarrheal spatter and vomiting a gray fluid spotted with dark masses, that Clark had thought were clots of blood. Finally, Floyd had fallen into a coma and had been sleeping for most of the day.

"Are you awake Charles?" Clark asked.

"Aye, Captain," Sergeant Floyd answered in a barely audible whisper. "I'm thinking I'd like to send a letter home. Would you write it for me?"

"Sure, I will," Clark answered, "I'll just go get paper and a quill." But before the big Captain could leave, he heard a soft gasp of air leaving the Sergeant's lungs, and saw that though Floyd's eyes were open, the light was gone from them.

They dug his grave deep, wrapped Floyd in his own blankets and covered him with river rocks, hoping to keep the wolves away from his remains. His death had been quiet, but his sickness had been horrible to watch. With the punishment of Moses Reed and the death of Sergeant Floyd coming on the same day, a certain uneasiness came over the entire Corps. The pickets stood to their posts and the rest cleaned up the camp and rolled into their blankets with one thought on all of their minds: Who would be the next to die?

# Chapter 7
*Sisters*

**R**ain Dance Woman carefully laid her small son back in his robes and watched him intently for a few minutes to make sure he was going to stay sleeping. Movement in Wamdisapa's robes had stopped and the sounds of love making by her husband and his new bride had ceased. She could hear Bright Morning Woman's soft, steady breathing and mild snoring from Wamdisapa, indicating that both were asleep. She rose and silently gathered all of New Grass Woman's belongings. Cautiously, she ducked through the tipi door and waited to see if either of them had awakened to the soft sounds of her exit.

When she heard no protests, she moved quietly. Searching through the village, she circled the lodges along the fringe hoping to find some sign of New Grass Woman. The village gossips had probably already circulated the story about the fight and New Grass Woman's banishment from Wamdisapa's tipi. She hoped, but doubted if anyone had offered her sister a place in their tipi yet. The People, though normally very kind to those in need would probably want to wait to see just how angry Wamdisapa was before offering his estranged sister-in-law shelter.

Not seeing anything of her sister in the village proper, Rain Dance Woman drifted toward the bank of the small river. It was a small slow moving stream with low banks, overgrown with gooseberry bushes, grapevines and tall grass. Wamdisapa had been leading the People along this river, following it to where it converged with the big western river, where they hoped to meet up with other *Dakotah* people.

Rain Dance Woman moved slowly and quietly through the briars and grasses peering carefully into each small stand of river willows. Moving closer to the river's edge, she heard a low moan and soft keening, and soon found New Grass Woman huddled by the huge trunk of a tall cottonwood tree. As Rain Dance Woman approached, New Grass Woman rose painfully to her feet and started to flee, but upon hearing Rain Dance Woman call her softly, she collapsed back to the ground. She tried to pull her torn clothing back into place but had little success and was shivering with cold.

"I've brought your things," Rain Dance Woman whispered walking softly up to her sister's prone figure, and laid the bundle of her clothing and her digging tools on the ground beside New Grass Woman's bed. "I brought some jerky too."

"Why didn't you help me?" New Grass Woman hissed as she grabbed the bag of meat and bit off a piece chewing it furiously.

"I tried to warn you to stop," Rain Dance Woman said. "But you wouldn't listen."

New Grass Woman didn't respond. She sat with her left side gingerly leaning against the cottonwood trunk, angrily chewing the sun-dried meat, her angry eyes glaring up at her sister.

"Come, let me tend to your wounds," Rain Dance Woman said softly and reached out her hand. With a grunt, New Grass Woman took her hand and pulled herself up. She allowed Rain Dance Woman to lead her down to the edge of the water. She sat on a rock as her sister gently washed her welted back with the cool river water. Rain Dance Woman waded into the shallows and dug up handfuls of smooth, cool mud and gently spread it across her sister's injured back.

"This mud will help cool the fires," she said, "and help keep the flies from laying their eggs in the deep wounds."

New Grass Woman slumped forward on the rock, allowing Rain Dance Woman to pack mud on the torn flesh where Wamdisapa's club had cut deep. She was still angry and felt betrayed by her sister for not helping her during the beating and wanted to disown Rain Dance Woman. But she knew that if the wounds festered and grew with infection or maggot infestation, that a fever would follow and she could die.

"You must keep the flies from your wounds," Rain Dance Woman stated. "I will meet you each night and clean them and coat them until you are healed. I will bring food whenever I can sneak some away from our fire, but I must be careful that my husband doesn't find out. So stay away from our tipi and stay away from the girl." She added a stern warning, "Next time, he'll kill you."

New Grass Woman turned her head away, refusing to look at Rain Dance Woman. She stood and shuffled up the sloping bank, stopping at the cottonwood trunk. Stiffly, she bent to retrieve the bundles of possessions that Rain Dance Woman had brought her and then without saying a word or looking back at her sister, she slowly trudged off into the darkness.

In the weeks that followed, New Grass Woman lived as a beggar. She slept wherever she could find shelter and sometimes, on cool nights huddled with the camp dogs. At first, she met Rain Dance Woman each night and allowed her to administer to her wounds and took what food her sister brought for her. But never did she speak a word of gratitude.

On days she found edible food thrown away before the camp dogs did, or when someone with plenty of food was kind enough to give her some, she didn't seek the nightly rendezvous' with her sister. As her wounds healed and she became stronger, she darted around the village proper gathering food and discarded clothing, always watching for Wamdisapa, fearing that if he saw her, he would undoubtedly kill her. She also spied on his tipi, whenever he was out of camp, watching Bright Morning Woman and Rain Dance Woman settle into a friendly domestic relationship. A growing hatred of Wamdisapa, his new wife, and even her own sister grew within New Grass Woman's breast and she swore on her own soul to get revenge in this life, or the next.

Time had passed quickly since Bright Morning Woman moved into their tipi. After the inauspicious beginning to her life with Wamdisapa and Rain Dance Woman, things improved dramatically. Rain Dance Woman knew that while any kindness that she showed toward her exiled sister, would raise Wamdisapa's ire, any kindness she showed to his new young wife, would be looked upon with favor by her husband.

It became easy for her to feel little pity for New Grass Woman's plight. Her sister hadn't uttered a friendly word or shown any appreciation toward her, even though the ministrations Rain Dance Woman performed on her wounds in those first few weeks probably saved her life. As the wounds did heal, she noticed an even darker tone in New Grass Woman's attitude and soon after, recognized the hatred she saw in her eyes. With no fanfare, she severed the relationship with her sister and slipped out at night to meet her no more.

She began treating her husband's new young wife as a friend and helped the girl in the difficult transition from childhood to adulthood with gentle advice. Rain Dance Woman showed Bright Morning Woman the duties she expected the girl to perform, being part of the family unit. She was surprised and pleased to find that Bright Morning Woman was a fast learner and an eager worker. The girl showed no tendencies of being a spoiled child, expecting special treatment, because she was young and pretty and their husband's favorite. She rose early each morning to go out and greet the sun and always had a fire going with strips of dog or deer or fish broiling over hot coals for Wamdisapa's breakfast. Rain Dance Woman found she had time to stay in her bed and let little Pinched Cheeks suckle without being interrupted by the necessity of making food for Wamdisapa each morning. This was a luxury she had never experienced when New Grass Woman lived with them.

As the days turned into weeks, Bright Morning Woman seemed to fit into the family well. She was kind to Rain Dance Woman's mother, Teal Duck Woman, helping the old lady soften skins for moccasins by scraping them thin using a buffalo's jaw bone. She rubbed the old crone's bone needle on a rough stone to sharpen it and never failed to remark on the beauty of the old woman's beadwork. She treated Rain Dance Woman's father, Gray Bird That Swoops Low with the respect that an old grandfather deserved. During the few weeks she had lived with them, she had lifted the burden of caring for the old man off of Rain Dance Woman's shoulders. Bright Morning Woman helped old Gray Bird That Swoops Low rise each morning and took him for a walk to relieve himself and loosened his age-stiffened legs before the day's journey. When necessary, she hand-fed him his meals, searched for lice and ticks while brushing his long gray hair and took the old man to the river for a bath, whenever possible. All were things New Grass Woman had refused to do for her own parents. Rain Dance Woman was pleased to notice that Wamdisapa had even stopped grumbling about it being almost time for the old man and old woman to stay behind to live out their lives by themselves when the village moved.

The unforeseen benefit was that Rain Dance Woman suddenly found herself with time on her hands to play with her child and time to tend to her husband, which made him happy too. Her personal relationship with Wamdisapa was better than it had been since before she had killed his slave girl. He was sleeping through the night again. He woke each morning cheerful instead of frustrated and was friendly toward her instead of accusingly angry at her. And with the absence of the tension between them over New Grass Woman's place in their home, their relationship was once again that of a normal husband and wife. She knew that Bright Morning Woman's presence was, in no small part, the reason for the turn around in her happiness and she began calling the girl "Little Sister" in private. The name pleased them both.

"Little Sister you are tired," Rain Dance Woman said as they spread the sleeping robes inside the tipi after having hung them outside to air out for the day. "Let me help my old gray haired father to his bed." The robes were always laid in a circle around the fire pit, close to the flames in winter and out along the walls in summer. The walls were usually rolled up on hot nights to let the cool breezes drift across the sleepers.

"It's been a long day," Bright Morning Woman answered and added, "As was yesterday and the day before." The People had been traveling for several days, stopping only today to set up the village, a sign that they might camp in the same spot for two nights in a row. Their travels had brought them close to the big western river, where they rendezvoused each year with the *Yanktons, Tetons, Oglala* and *Minneconjou,* the tribes of the western *Dakotah* people as well as many of their cousins from the Eastern Fires of the *Dakotah* nation, the *Wahpeton, Sisseton* and *Mdewakonton*. The *Wahpekute* men of their village were very excited about the rendezvous, as there would be story telling, trading and gambling. And the women looked forward to seeing sisters and brothers and other relatives who had married outside of their tribes.

"Will we stay here long? Or will we be leaving for the rendezvous tomorrow?" Bright Morning Woman asked.

"Wamdisapa will make that decision when he returns from his scout," Rain Dance Woman said. "He left this morning to see if he can find the place of the rendezvous. If it is not far, we will probably stay here one more day. If it is far, we will probably leave early in the morning," she explained, adding with a twinkle in her eye, "I know that you are so very tired Little Sister, so if you want, you can go to your bed now and rest up for when our husband returns."

"But our husband is tired too, Older Sister," Bright Morning Woman said, smiling. Putting her hand on the older woman's shoulder, she added, "Maybe tonight, you should tend to the needs of our husband. I'm sure he would be glad for the rest your more experienced touch would bring him."

"Yes, it is true. Our husband would not be so tired if it weren't for your young, inexperienced touch each night." Rain Dance Woman liked this girl very much. For one so young to joke about her sexual prowess with an older woman showed how comfortable she had become in her new life as the wife of the village leader. "The poor man gets little sleep since you have started sharing his robes," she added. And laughing said, "But I know that it is probably necessary for a young girl like you to keep practicing over and over again each night so that you can one day be as skilled and experienced as I. I only hope that all of this practicing doesn't wear him out and make him as limp as a gelded travois horse."

Grinning with a self-conscious smile, Bright Morning Woman shook her head vigorously up and down. "This is true," she cried in a fake lament. "For our husband's own good, tonight, I will move my sleeping robe outside. I will hide in the tall grass and when our husband calls for me, I will not answer. Then when he returns bulging with passion from thinking of me, but frustrated because he can't find me, you can take him to your bed robes, my beloved Older Sister and then you can try to keep him from tiring himself out!" she answered and they both laughed at the vision of the randy Wamdisapa walking about the village roaring in frustration for his new young wife.

They settled back to the work of unpacking, feeling certain that Wamdisapa would find the western tribe's lodges and tomorrow the camp wouldn't be moving. But after a few moments of silence Bright Morning Woman solemnly asked, "When will our husband return to your robes for his night time pleasures?"

Rain Dance Woman smiled at the deep look of concern on the young girl's face. She stooped to pick up her young son answering, "Only when this one no longer shows interest in the titty."

"Oh, but that could be a long time!" Bright Morning Woman said remembering that her young brother had nursed from her mother for over five years. She had been too young to notice that her father hadn't shared the bed robes with her mother for that period of time. After a moment of thought, she added, "I had never known the pleasure of a man and woman before Wamdisapa brought me to live in this tipi. I had heard that it was pleasure and now I know that it is. How, my sister, how can you go so long without this pleasure?"

"It is sometimes hard," Rain Dance Woman answered with a small smile. "But there have been times, only a few times, when I was told in my dreams that I would not become pregnant, that Wamdisapa has come to my bed robes. These times are moments of great pleasure for both of us."

"If I were you Older Sister," Bright Morning Woman said with a devilish grin, "I would start having these dreams much more often!" Both women laughed merrily at this joke. Rain Dance Woman decided that this young girl was more of a sister to her than New Grass Woman had ever been.

When their laughter died down, they heard a shout from outside the tipi and knew that Wamdisapa had returned from his scout. Rushing out to meet him, they immediately knew something was wrong. His eyes were shining with excitement. He demanded his medicine paints be brought to him and paced back and forth until Rain Dance Woman, who ran inside the tipi, retrieved them for him. He began singing as he prepared to paint his body. The excitement in his voice proved to the women that something very important had happened.

*This swift warrior saw them on the river!*
*They come floating on the water!*
*This brave warrior saw them on the land!*
*They camp where the rivers meet!*

The women huddled quietly by the tipi wall, listening to his song and watching him paint his body. Carefully, he colored his right side black, signifying war and death, and the left half of his body, he painted white indicating friendship and life.

*Are they friends of the People?*
*Are they enemies of the People?*
*Are they men?*
*Are they Gods?*

Using the sacred color red, he painted the sun on his left buttock. On the right, he painted the moon in yellow. On his left breast, he traced the shape of a tipi with stick children playing in black. On his right breast, using white paint, he painted stick warriors with bows and arrows and lances and war clubs. The conflicting stories depicted on his body showed the women the confusion he felt in his soul.

"What is it, my husband?" Rain Dance Woman asked in a timid voice.

Wamdisapa glared at her with a stony face, his eyes peeled wide open, almost as if in a trance. Then he stood tall and pointed south toward the big river. Both women stretched high on their tip-toes, straining to see what he was pointing at, but neither could see anything beyond the underbrush and trees in their camp area and the ocean of tall, waving grassland that reached out beyond it.

"There are men with white skin camped on the big river." His voice was just above a whisper and the fear they saw in his eyes alarmed the women, for they had never thought it possible that the mighty Wamdisapa could be frightened. "They come up the big river, some paddling big dugouts, others walking in the water. These men are followed by a large canoe with a wooden lodge on it," he added.

Wamdisapa stopped talking and looked back to the south again. A small shiver shook his body. His wives drew together, frightened by their husband's intensity.

"The *wasichu* drive horses on the land and these white skinned men chop a path for them through the fields of river cane with long knives that glisten in the sun." Wamdisapa continued, his voice hushed, "I've watched them all day and have seen many things. Once, I was close enough that I could have struck a man whose hair was the color of winter grass, with my war club." He turned to face his wives and his voice cracked with emotion. "They all carry sticks that shoot fire. I watched one kill a buffalo cow with his firestick. He pointed the stick at the cow. Lightening flew from its end and thunder clapped loudly! The cow ran off down the hill and I laughed thinking these firesticks were just for making noise to scare animals out of their way. But then, the cow fell over on its side and died."

Wamdisapa took each of his wives by their outside shoulders and squeezed them even closer together as he looked at them, his eyes darting back and forth between their faces. "I must go and visit these *Wasichu* with the magic weapons. I must have one!"

## Chapter 8
### *First Contact*

Hugh McNeal was dreaming about his brothers. The tribe of little tow and red-headed urchins, with feathers stuck under leather bands tied around their heads and smears of charcoal soot spread on their freckled little faces, were sneaking up on his mother and sisters, who were at work in the cabin sewing clothes for the boys, and in the summer kitchen cooking food for the whole family. With blood curdling screams, the boys brandishing toy bows and arrows and stick clubs, jumped though the cookhouse door and into the main cabin room surprising the women at their toils, like a bunch of "wild Indians" as his mother would call them. But in his dream, the boys changed from his small siblings into grown men with dark skins and real weapons and the screams were screams of terror from his sisters and mother!

He felt someone touch his shoulder and he rolled quickly to his back, his eyes flying open as both of his large hands grabbed the figure crouching over him by the throat!

"C'mon Hugh, wake up," he heard the voice of Pat Gass croak as he started to squeeze the man's throat.

"Sorry," he said as he released the short, stocky man and added, "I guess I was dreamin'."

"Well it's yer watch," Gass said, in a raspy whisper, silently vowing to always wake the big blacksmith's apprentice by shaking his foot rather than his shoulder in the future.

Hugh rolled to his feet and looked around the camp letting his eyes adjust to the darkness that surrounded them. Trees blocked the light from the stars. The thick stand of trees including oak, maple and cottonwood was a rarity along the river and the Captains had called an early stop the day before, to take advantage of the supply of firewood the stand of timber provided. Most of the crew was put to chopping dried windfalls into manageable lengths to take with them for future fires. Hugh was kept busy sharpening axes and wedges the men used to split the larger logs into burnable kindling and helping stack the harvested firewood on the keelboat. Reuben Field had shot a buffalo cow that afternoon and they feasted around the luxury of a large fire that night. Drouillard warned the Captains that the light from the fire could be seen from miles away, and interpreter Drouillard's assistant, Pierre Cruzatte a man of French and Omaha Indian blood with only one eye, announced around the night's fire that he had the feeling they were being watched.

McNeal yawned, stretched and then dug inside his pants to scratch at the itchy red bumps that had formed beneath his scrotum and then spread to his inner thighs. Captain Clark had diagnosed them to be a heat rash caused by the salt in his sweat and told him to try to keep the infected area as dry as possible. Hugh chuckled at these instructions. It seemed that if he wasn't in the water pulling the keelboat, he was on the bank pulling, or on the boat poling. Each activity provided its own agony, contributing to the rash by either causing him to sweat profusely or his legs to chafe together as he struggled at the ropes.

He picked up the rifle, powder horn and shot pouch that each man carried while on night guard and moved off into the darkness, away from the low glow from the fire pit. He moved quietly through the sleeping camp to his post at the edge of the trees and looked out over the ocean of grass on the prairie. Here, he could see the stars rising from the horizon in a flickering mass of brightness that shed an eerie light on the landscape stretching out before him. The countless twinkling lights in the huge endless sky only added to the vastness of the rolling, wavering prairie. Hugh leaned back against the rough bark of an oak tree. Mindful of Captain Clark's warning to "keep sharp" in case Cruzatte was right and they had visitors watching the camp, he vowed to not get too comfortable. But the three hours it would take for dawn to arrive, would make this a very long night.

He could see little, as the pale light from the stars lent only shimmering shadows to the grasslands in front of him. Hugh knew that watching was only part of being on guard. He listened for sounds that might be unnatural. During the last three months of traveling in the wilderness, he had become so accustomed to the monotonous singing of crickets and the constant croaking of frogs from the river, that he tuned their sounds out. He could also ignore the foot stomping of the horses, which were tied inside the tree line for safety, and the swirling splash of the river current and the quiet slapping noise it made on the side of the keelboat. An owl hooting drew his attention. He had always heard that Indians mimicked the night birds. But then he saw a flying shadow of one of the birds light in the tree above his head and relaxed.

He watched, his eyes roving back and forth over the emptiness, reaching out to each shadow, making sure it was just a grass shadow. He listened, his ears tuning out the normal night noises, but focusing on the slightest scurry in the grass, the smallest unidentifiable cry from out on the prairie and the muttering of a sleep talker back in the bed rolls by the fire. He was alert to find anything that was out of place, anything at all that wasn't as it should be. He knew that the life of every man in the company might depend on his diligence on guard duty.

But after each sound and each shadow was identified as normal and not harmful, guard duty was boring. To pass the time, he began thinking about the recent days' happenings. Sergeant Floyd's death had proven how helpless they were against sickness and disease. He prayed that the rash between his legs was not the beginning of some awful disease that would leave him puking yellow bile and shitting green mash for days before he died and was buried on the riverbank. The desertion, capture and punishment of Moses Reed had had a lasting affect on Hugh also. One of his favorite pastimes while toiling on the ropes had been to remember his life back home at his father's smithy thinking about what each member of his family was doing right at that very minute. He had loved to visualize his father pumping the bellows to get the coals red-hot and then hammering horseshoes on the anvil, the muscles of his right arm bulging with the effort. And his mother, still full with child, steeping corn in lye water to make hominy and his little brothers romping in the mow and his little sisters grubbing in the garden. But all of these thoughts lent him a melancholy that made him a bit homesick.

He had not enjoyed flaying Reed's back with the switches as he was ordered to do, but he hadn't shrunk from it either. By stating that the reason he had deserted was because of his lonesomeness for his family, Reed had awakened a certain feeling of guilt in Hugh when he daydreamed of home and since Reed's return, his only dreams of home were unhappy night time dreams like the one he'd had this night, while sleeping.

And then there was La Liberte. He was still missing. Was he walking back east at his own leisure? Or, was he lying dead somewhere on the prairie? Was he killed by the *Nadowwessioux*? Was he gored by a bull buffalo? Or mauled by one of the great bears or big cats they'd seen sign of along the riverbanks?

The night breeze picked up and a puff of wind caused the tall grass to rustle, standing and then falling back, throwing a shadowy shape, not unlike a man's shape, in the dim light, breaking his reverie. But when the wind died back down, he dropped back to searching over his life so far, reaching back to his childhood. He remembered his fear of the dark. From out of the dark came all kinds of dangers. And as a child, moonlit shadows had held their own special terrors. He had been afraid of swimming in the swirling waters of the Ohio River, when other children his age dove and swam like young otters on a lark. He had withstood their taunting, sticking to his own convictions, waiting until he was older to swim when he was sure that he swam because he wanted to, not because his friends made fun of him for being afraid. As a boy, he had been totally afraid of Indians because he'd heard, over and over again the stories of attacks and atrocities committed by the Shawnee, who supported the British during the Revolution.

He had to chuckle. After all of his fears as a child, here he was standing alone in the dark, with shadows forming and reforming, moving and swaying. He had plunged fearlessly into the muddy swirling waters of the Missouri River almost every day for the last three months. And he had been dealing with real Indians for weeks and had found nothing to fear from them. He shook his head, smiling at himself. Leaning deeper into the tree trunk, he lowered his rifle and rested its butt on the ground. He stood this way, watching and listening for the next two hours.

The stars dimmed in the sky and receded completely as the horizon began to lighten. It was dawn. Hugh leaned away from the oak tree, straightened and stretched. He drew in a deep breath through his nose and had it only partially blown out, when an unconscious fear crept into his soul. His sleepy eyes were suddenly wide-awake. The hair on the back of his neck stood on end, sending a tingling sensation down his spine. A heavy weight settled in his gut and a pressure on his chest made it hard for him to suck air into his lungs. A sudden silence hung over him. No owls hooted. The crickets and frogs were unusually quiet and even the horses had stopped snorting and stomping. He noticed too that the usual cacophony of birdsongs, greeting the sunrise was oddly absent. Something was wrong. The animals knew it.

Frantically, he searched the shadows in the grass as the day's light slowly crossed the plain towards him. His eyes and ears strained to their limits, trying to detect what it was that had unsettled him so. Finally, he realized it was not something he saw or heard. It was something he smelled! It was a greasy odor, smelling of rancid animal fat and soot that tickled his nostrils. It wasn't polecat or coon or any varmint that he had ever smelled before. It was something that shouldn't have been there. His eyes ached from staring into each shadow that materialized, dissecting each small dark area, trying to see what lay hidden within it. His ears pulled his head from side to side, straining to hear any noise that shouldn't have been made. In his fear, he could feel his pulse pounding in his veins and hear it hammering in his head.

In desperation, he began sniffing the air, like a coonhound that had lost the scent, trying to smell the fleeting odor again and pinpoint its origin. All the while, his brain screamed at him to call out a warning and awaken the camp. But his mouth had gone dry and his throat felt constricted. His tongue was thick with fear and refused to cooperate. Every hair on his body stiffened with anticipation as a sixth sense pulled his head around to look behind himself . . . into the camp! As his body turned, a hideous black and white face loomed at him from out of the still dark shadows under the trees.

He sensed, rather than saw a blow coming and ducked, trying to avoid it, but was too late and pain charged to his brain as a coup stick caught him on the side of the head, driving him to the ground. Stunned by the blow, Hugh lay on his back trying to shake the fogginess from his brain. Vaguely, he felt his rifle being tugged at and instinctively closed his fingers in a tight grip around the weapon's barrel and butt stock and held on. All the while, his semi-conscious brain was sending the message to his non-functioning lips to form words of warning and shout out. But a low, growling sound was all that he could manage.

Suddenly, a mighty jerk pulled the rifle from his grip! The realization of the loss of his weapon sprang through Hugh's foggy consciousness and his mind cleared instantly. He jumped unsteadily to his feet and was surprised to see the figure of a man, his body painted half white and half black, just standing before him looking down at Hugh's rifle.

The man held it awkwardly with the barrel near his body and the butt sticking out, toward Hugh. He was not as tall as Hugh, but was taller and leaner than the Omahas and Otos the Corps had encountered so far on their journey. He was well muscled and his uncropped hair hung about his shoulders and blew up in small wisps in the morning breeze. He was completely naked and the half-white and half-black paint reached to every extremity of his body. It was the paint, Hugh now realized, that was giving off the odor he had smelled just before the man had attacked.

Oddly, Hugh felt no fear and calmly reached out and snatched his rifle back. The Indian didn't give up his grip and a short tug-of-war over the weapon ensued. Hugh, being the bigger, heavier and stronger, soon wrenched the gun from the Indian's hands and the man stepped back with a disgusted grunt. Sounds of the struggle finally reached the ears of another of the night guards and John Colter moved from his post at the south end of the camp.

"What's goin' on Hugh?" he called.

At the sound of Colter's voice, the Indian turned toward the prairie and started to run. Instinctively, Hugh threw his rifle to his shoulder. He took aim at his assailant, who was running with amazing quickness out into the prairie. It was almost full light now and he could see the man quite well. The man carried a long, sturdy stick in his hand and at his side flopped the short, sturdy handle of a war club. Hugh realized immediately that if the man had meant him real harm, he would have used the war club and probably killed him. In that last instant, Hugh raised his sites from the middle of the running man's back to aim just above his head and squeezed off a round.

Wamdisapa ran hard for the security of the tall grass, but before he had gone far, he heard a whining whistle as a projectile flew past his left ear and then he felt bowel-loosening fear as the explosion of lightening blasted behind him! He expected to feel the blast of its power. But nothing more happened. He stopped, looking up into the sky in confusion. He had seen one of the white men shoot fire at a buffalo cow the day before. And he had watched as the cow staggered in a stumbling run for the river and saw it drop to its side dead. Confusion filled his soul and he chanted a quiet song of thanks to his God:

*Oh great One who lives in the sky*
*Oh great One who lives in the earth*
*Oh great One who lives in the wind*
*Oh great One who lives in the rain*
*Hear me say thank you ...thank you*

The explosion of the rifle shot brought the sleeping men in the camp to life! Without dressing, they jumped from their beds and ran to their stacked weapons, checked the loads and took up defensive positions in a half-moon shaped perimeter protecting the horses and boats.

When the smoke from his shot cleared, Hugh was surprised to see the Indian standing still, not fifty yards distant. The man stood with his head tipped back, looking up in wonder, singing in a deep, sonorous voice. The men from the camp left their defensive positions and moved to stand in a line by Hugh. Several of them cocked their rifles and took aim.

"Hold your fire," Captain Lewis ordered in a clear, but quiet voice. "We don't want to scare him away." He walked slowly out to stand in front of the men. Over his shoulder, he called for Drouillard to join him and then asked in a whisper, "What in tarnation happened, Hugh?"

"That Injun snuck through our pickets Cap'n. He was in our camp!" Hugh answered with a short, nervous laugh. "I knew sumthin' was wrong, but couldn't see ner hear nothin'. Next thing, he come from behind me, inside the camp and swung that stick at me. I ducked right into it and it knocked me right down, it did!" He reached a cautious hand up to feel his aching jaw. Already, a bruise, reaching from his chin to his ear was beginning to swell.

"Coup stick, Hugh," stated Drouillard. "He proved he was more brave fer smackin' ya with that stick than he would a' if he'd slit yer throat from ear ta ear."

"What breed do ya read him to be?" Clark asked as he moved out from the men to join Lewis and Drouillard.

"Dunno fer sure," Drouillard answered. "Somethin' I never seen before. Might be *Nadowwessioux!*"

Lewis sent a man to the boats to bring back a bundle of gifts. If this man was indeed a member of the powerful *Nadowwessioux* nation it was important that they make contact before the man bolted back out onto the prairie. Though the man didn't seem to be adversely affected by being shot at, Lewis wanted to make sure the man left under friendly conditions. From what he had heard of these people from the lower tribes, he knew that if they were unfriendly, it could spell doom for the Corps of Discovery.

With the gifts held high out in front of them, Drouillard and William Clark walked slowing across the prairie toward the man. The Indian stood his ground, warily watching the approaching whites. When only twenty steps separated them, Clark read the apprehension in the man's face and stopped. Drouillard spread a buffalo robe and laid an assortment of gifts on it: a blue officer's uniform, a metal cooking pot, a steel knife, a small square of red cloth, a bag of colored beads and a small mirror. The men sat down on the edge of the robe and Clark took out a long stemmed pipe and a twist of tobacco. He held it out toward the man and beckoned for him to come and smoke.

Cautiously, like a deer moving upwind, taking one step at a time, checking each wind current, not exactly frightened, but very wary and ready to bolt at the slightest sign of danger, Wamdisapa moved up to the opposite side of the robe and sat down.

Clark presented the pipe to the four sacred directions and to the mother earth and to the sky above. Using flint and steel, he placed a glowing piece of char cloth in the pipe's bowl, and sucking hard on the stem, ignited the tobacco. Soon, a deep, rich smoke rolled into his mouth and spewed into the air with each puff and he reached out, offering the pipe to the Indian.

Wamdisapa took the pipe and puffed several times, inhaling the smoke deeply, enjoying the mild burning sensation in his lungs. This smoke was much better than the smoke produced from the *Wahpekute* blend of moss, plum tree bark, and dried grass. He sucked on the stem of the pipe several more times, inhaling each puff until the bowl was almost burnt out. After handing the pipe to Drouillard, his eyes rested longingly on the tobacco twist sticking from Clark's pocket.

Noticing the Indian's gaze, Clark pulled the twist from his coat and dropped it on the robe with the other presents. This gesture made the Indian smile. Using a mixture of Oto, Omaha and sign language, Drouillard interpreted as Clark began a prepared speech. He brought greetings from the Great White Father, who lived where the sun rose, and wished all of his children health and happiness.

He presented the man with this fine buffalo robe and all of the gifts that lay on it and asked if he could meet with all of his people, promising even more fine gifts at that time. Finishing his speech, Clark leaned back and waited for the Indian to respond.

To Clark's chagrin, the black and white Indian merely gathered up the corners of the robe and stood up. Flinging the bundle of gifts over his shoulder with one hand, he pointed his coup stick up river and jabbered something Drouillard didn't understand. But then dipping the end of the stick, he made a sign in the air that Drouillard thought meant *where the sun sets.*

With that, the black and white Indian spun on his heel and disappeared before their eyes into the endless ocean of tall prairie grass.

# Chapter 9
## *Dangerous Gathering*

The summer rendezvous of the *Dakotah* people was a loosely planned gathering where several tribes of people, speaking the same or nearly the same dialect got together to trade, gossip with family members who had married into different tribes, and gamble. People representing the *Yanktons* and *Assiniboins* from the northern fires, the *Tetons, Hunkpapas, Minneconjous and Ogalalas* from the western fires, and the *Mdewakonton, Wahpekute, Wahpetons,* and *Sissitons* from the Eastern Fires traveled the long trail to the most centralized location on the Missouri River for the occasion. The event happened most years, but not always the same people attended. The rendezvous village this year was not as large as some years. The people from the Eastern Fires were only sparsely present. Wamdisapa's village was the only group of *Wahpekute* people there and a few *Mdewakanton* villages from the far north lake country were the only eastern fire tribes to make the long trek. But there were enough of the western tribes to spread the gathering of tipis for two miles up the river's western bank. Tipis were set up in a helter-skelter array in small circles of family groups, wherever the lay of the land along the river was flat enough so that no one would have to sleep with their head above or below their feet. Wamdisapa's people set their tipis near a village of *Ogalalas,* as Wamdisapa's good friend, Sun At Night, was an *Ogalala* who had married a *Wahpekute* woman and moved into her father's tipi many years before. Sun At Night hoped to hear word of his family.

Hundreds of cook fires smoldered in front of the tipis, filling the air with a smoky haze, which smothered the lungs and stung the eyes of the young boys playing in the small fields between the lodges. Since the arrival of Wamdisapa's people, the entire encampment was abuzz with excitement. On each man's lips were words of speculation about the *wasichus* and every woman and child waited anxiously for the arrival of the large, white skinned men that Wamdisapa had excitedly spoken of two days before, when he led his band into the big camp. He told a tale of meeting with a party of large, white skinned men, traveling up the river in big canoes. These men had powerful medicine. They had sticks that shot fire! They pulled a huge canoe that stood as high as a lodge pole above the water, was as wide as two lodge poles laid end to end and as long as three lodge poles laid end to end, against the mighty river's current. This big canoe was filled with the most amazing gifts!

Wamdisapa danced at the *Ogalala* fire that first night and told how brave he was to sneak into the *wasichu* camp and count coup on one of their guards. The guard, he bragged, was a huge demon, with a ring of fire-colored hair surrounding his face. Wamdisapa only intended to touch the guard gently with his coup stick and sneak away, but the demon had turned and caught him in the act. He had had to swing his stout stick hard and hit the guard a blow to the head that would have killed most men. Wamdisapa had taken the opportunity to steal the guard's fire shooting stick, but the demon arose from the dead and fought with him over the weapon! When the other guards came running, Wamdisapa had turned to flee! But before he had run far, the demon shot at him with the fire stick and a bolt of lightening passed so close to his head that he felt its heat and his ears were still ringing from the thunderous clap it made! He was sure that while he was struggling with the demon for the weapon, he had gained some of the firestick's medicine, because he had seen with his own eyes that buffalo died when shot with the fire from the stick. Yet he was still alive!

The second night, Wamdisapa related his story to a larger group of people, who passed his story along, until everyone in the town had heard of the white demons coming up the river. Many men scoffed at such a tale and believed that Wamdisapa was making it all up, just to gain the attention of the western tribe leaders. A man from his own village was the biggest disbeliever. Tasagi was a widowed man of about Wamdisapa's age. His wife had ventured out on a frozen lake after an early freeze during *The Moon of the Falling Leaves* a year ago and fell through the ice. The woman drowned before anyone could reach her. Tasagi, having been alone for most of a year had decided to take pity on New Grass Woman, and he invited her into his lodge as his wife. By becoming Tasagi's wife, she had regained her place among the People. She still hated Wamdisapa and his new wife and even though Tasagi was once Wamdisapa's friend and loyal follower, she had turned her new husband against him.

Tasagi walked about the town, stating his disbelief of Wamdisapa's story about the *wasichus* on the big river, to the general populace at each gathering of tipis and did all he could to discredit him.

Tasagi's assertion that he had seen no signs of any white demons on the river and that Wamdisapa was a known liar in their village angered Wamdisapa. From this time on, there would be bad blood between the two men. To prove that he was telling the truth, Wamdisapa donned the fine cloth officer's uniform given to him by the *wasichu*. Carrying the shining metal pot, with the bag of colorful beads and the square of blood red cloth stuffed in it, and the steel knife hanging at his hip, he walked around the separate towns, sticking the hand mirror before the faces of everyone he encountered. These fine gifts were enough proof for most of the people and a barely controlled excitement swept through the entire camp.

The *Dakotah* were a diverse and powerful nation, controlling a large tract of land stretching from the upper reaches of the Mississippi River in the east to the foothills of the Rocky Mountains in the west and from southern Canada in the north to the northern plains of Kansas in the south. Most were nomadic hunters, whose travels were dictated by the movements of their food sources which ranged from the vast herds of migrating buffalo, low country elk and mule deer in the west, and whitetail deer and black bear in the east when times were good, to crickets, spiders and snails when no other game was available, and everything in-between including all the birds in the sky and all the fish in the lakes and rivers. Their neighbors, including Omahas, Otos, Pawnee, Mandan, Sauk, Fox and Ioway feared them and tried to avoid battle with them for they were a numerous race whose members were healthy and strong. The strength of their nation would eventually work against them. They protected their territory so fiercely that their reputation frightened many would-be intruders away. Consequently, their neighboring tribes were united in their dislike of the *Nadowwessioux* and more receptive to the benefits of encroaching white culture.

Added to this self-imposed isolation, from the quickly advancing world, was the fact that the *Dakotah* people lacked a governing body with leaders who were delegated the powers necessary to guide their nation, their tribes, or even their villages. There were societal rules to follow, but each tribe, village and man was an independent entity. No man could govern another man. Each individual went his own way and chose to follow whom he wished until he became disenchanted with that leader and then, he chose another man to follow.

The next day, to Tasagi and New Grass Woman's chagrin, scouts returned to the town, with news of a strange looking party of light skinned men herding horses a few miles down river on the other side.

And to add to their displeasure, it was said that the leader of the men had hair the color of fire! Further proof of Wamdisapa's story! When more scouts, sent out to watch the river, came back excitedly telling of two large canoes and an even larger vessel making its way up river, Wamdisapa became a very important man.

Excitement rippled through the town and many of the principal leaders came to talk with Wamdisapa and congratulate him for telling a brave and true story. They listened again to the telling of the story and were even more impressed with his bravery. His stature among his peers rose and most held only contempt for the man Tasagi. It was said that the man's new wife had put him up to trying to change the true words. It was a sad thing when a man could be controlled by his woman. Many men went to Tasagi and offered to beat his wife for him.

Darkness fell on the town with the people looking forward to the morning, with mixed emotions. Some of the people were afraid of the *wasichus'* strong medicine and pulled up their tipi stakes and moved back out onto the prairie. Others, in their fear, became angry and wanted to attack the white skins and kill them all. But the incredible gifts that Wamdisapa displayed again and again, whenever anyone asked to see them, kept most of the people interested in meeting the strangers themselves.

In the morning, when the vessels of the Corps of Discovery rounded the bend and came into sight of the *Dakotah* encampment, eight hundred red men, women and children lined the bank. Most were screaming, creating a tremendous din that was not a friendly sound and many were gesturing at the white men with their bows with arrows nocked and their war clubs waving high! There was pushing and shoving in the crowd. All of the young men wanted to be close in case there was a fight. The girls and young women stood back from the bank, in small groups, whispering to one another and pointing at first one white man and then another. Small children clung to their mothers with fear clearly in their eyes.

The young men were filled with bravado. They waved their weapons and shouted brave, insulting words at the white skinned men, and some even shot stone tipped arrows in the water around the boats. But they all scurried up the bank and away from the river's edge when the boats turned toward them. When still sixty feet from shore, the big keelboat dropped anchor and swung down stream until the chain tightened and held. The pirogues hurriedly tied up to the keelboat and suddenly, it became deathly quiet as every Indian on the bank stopped shouting and watched to see what the men in the boats would do next.

The sudden silence was commanding. Captain Clark, who had left the horse herders on the eastern bank to join the men in the boats, looked at Captain Lewis and exhaled the air out of his lungs before taking a deep breath to try to calm his nerves as he looked at the Indians standing on the western bank. Lewis examined the amassed sea of hostile faces and for the first time realized the paucity of their small corps of men, when compared to the job they were charged with doing. This was the largest village they had visited by far. He was filled with questions about these people. He wondered if this was a common sized village? And if so, how many villages there were? Why were they so hostile? Where was the man they had met two days before? What had he told them? And then, Lewis saw the man, standing resplendent in his officer's uniform, in the middle of the crowd.

He quickly ordered a landing party, consisting of Clark, Drouillard, McNeal, and the towering York into a pirogue and told the paddlers to aim for the very center of the crowd. He then told the rest of the men to carefully and quietly ready their rifles, in case there was trouble.

Clark and his landing party stood in the prow of the pirogue, ready to step out and make the first meeting with these, the most primitive and hostile Indians the Corps had yet encountered. It was their job to break down the wall of fear and mistrust and set the stage for Captain Lewis to deliver his standard speech about peace and friendship.

As the pirogue neared the bank, the silence was broken. Some of the women were overcome with fear and squealed as they grabbed their children and scrambled back away from the river. The frightened children began wailing.

The men, standing their ground against these unknown intruders shouted their defiance of the fear they too, felt rising in their breasts. Soon, an all-encompassing din rang in the ears of the approaching white men. Clark, along with Drouillard and York, had been the first to encounter the Indians in their villages before on this trip. But this was Hugh McNeal's first time at being first in. It was obvious that these Indians had never seen white men before and the tension in both groups grew with each paddle stroke closer they got to the bank. Hugh knew that all it would take would be one wrong move, one misinterpreted action or gesture, and a rain of stone tipped arrows would fall upon them. He felt the hair on the back of his neck stand on end and tried hard to make his knees stop shaking.

When the prow of the pirogue scraped bottom, Clark stepped boldly into the shallow water and advanced, totally unarmed and seemingly without fear, up the bank. With only a second's hesitation, Drouillard, Hugh and York followed him. Clark sought the uniformed warrior and saw him standing with four other men. They wore the gaudiest paint. Some had bones through the lobes of their ears and noses and they had the most feathers in their hair. Instinctively, Clark had found the most powerful men at this gathering of tribes.

Hates His Horses of the *Yankton*, Wamdisapa of the *Wahpekute*, Runs In Circles of the *Teton*, Pushes Hard of the *Ogalala*, and Shell Fish Eater of the *Mdewakonton* had gathered to face this danger together. Wamdisapa recognized the red haired Captain as the man who had given him his gifts and also recognized the younger red haired man he had struggled with at their camp. He bravely stepped forward and held up a hand in greeting.

Clark signaled York for his pipe. Silence overcame the crowd once again as they watched in awe as the big black man wadded tobacco in a char cloth and packed it in the bowl. There was a quick intake of breath when he struck his steel to flint showering the pipe bowl with sparks while Clark sucked on the stem, drawing air through, coaxing the char cloth to glow and start a slow burning of the tobacco. Once it was lit, Clark drew the smoke deeply into his lungs and offered the pipe to the four directions, the earth, and the sky, while slowly exhaling the smoke with much ceremony. He then handed the pipe to Wamdisapa, who also puffed deeply and blew the smoke out slowly, using his free hand to draw the fragrant smoke back into his face and through his hair.

He passed the smoking pipe to each of the other leadmen standing with him and after they had finished their ritual, it was handed to Drouillard who finished the pipe circle, knocked the ash out on his heel, and gave the pipe back to York.

Clark began to speak in his strong, sure voice and Drouillard interpreted, using a mixture of sign language and Oto. "We bring greetings to the mighty *Nadowwessioux* People from the Great White Father who lives in the Morning Sun's home. The Great White Father sends his love for his *Nadowwessioux* children." After Drouillard's interpretation, speaking in Oto, there was a loud, angry sounding murmuring from the crowd.

Runs In Circles stepped forward. He had fought the Oto and Omahas for many years and knew their tongue. "If the Great White Father loves us so much, why does he insult us by calling us by the name our enemies call us?"

"Cap'm Clark," Drouillard whispered in a nervous voice. "They don' like being called Sioux."

Unruffled, Clark smiled and then laughed, throwing the gathering off their guard. "The Great White Father likes to play jokes on his children," Drouillard, trying to laugh as convincingly as Clark, interpreted.

Runs In Circles stood for a moment, switching the words from Oto to his own language and dialect, and then he smiled. Pointing at Wamdisapa, he said "*Dakotah*." And then pointing at Hates His Horses, "*Nakotah*," and ended pointing to himself, stating "*Lakotah*. We are friends. We are allies."

"Call 'em *Dakotah*!" Drouillard whispered urgently. "That's what they like."

"The Great White Father's emissary, Captain Meriwether Lewis is in the keelboat. He has sent me to ask permission to smoke the pipe with the leaders of the Great *Dakotah* Peoples," Clark stated, adding, "He wants to explain our peaceful purpose and wants to assure the *Dakotah* of our friendship. He brings many gifts," he said, gesturing toward Wamdisapa in his officer's uniform, "from the Great White Father." He turned to Hugh and York and pointed toward the pirogue.

The two men waded back out to the pirogue and gathered their arms full of Indian gifts and brought them back to Clark. The Captain solemnly presented Runs In Circles, Hates His Horses, Pushes Hard and Shell Fish Eater identical gifts to the gifts he had presented Wamdisapa with and shook each man's hand, a practice totally unfamiliar to the *Dakotah* men. But upon seeing the gifts being handed out, all fear left the rest of the people. The young warriors were the first to push forward for a closer look. When the women and younger girls saw the young men receiving gifts of steel knives and mirrors, they were quick to lose their timidity. Chattering and pointing, they crowded to the river's edge and soon the air was full of their voices as they quibbled over the bright cloth and colorful beads they were presented.

The sudden addition of several hundred women and children clamoring for their share of the gifts caused a press of bodies that slowly forced Clark and his small crew of men to the water's edge. When the pirogue was emptied of gifts, Clark signaled and the second pirogue, laden with more presents for the Indians, pushed off from the keelboat and beached itself a few yards up river from where Hugh and York stood ankle deep in the water. With all of their fear gone, the people immediately flocked to it and began snapping up the gifts handed out from the second pirogue by Colter, Collins and Pat Gass leaving Hugh and York room to walk back onto dry land.

Clark and Drouillard continued talking with the headmen, promising even more gifts and asking for a council fire that evening, where the Great White Father's emissary Captain Meriwether Lewis could address all of their people.

Hugh started to relax and looked around at all of the people. He had never seen this large of a gathering of people, white or Indian in his entire life. The commotion was astounding and with their fear gone, they became curious and a large crowd soon gathered around York. Pressing close, they tried to touch his black skin and rub his tightly curled hair.

At each person's touch York flexed his highly muscled chest, making it jump and ripple. Suddenly, he stomped a foot and snorted, then grunted low in his chest, mimicking a bull buffalo. Many of the women were startled, squealed and jumped back. But their inquisitiveness brought them back. Some were even bold enough to tug his belt loose and peek down his pants to see how much of a bull he was. Low murmurs of admiration followed.

Hugh grinned. It looked like these women would be just as anxious to have buffalo babies as the Indian women down river had been. Old York would be busy tonight! Hugh turned his focus on Captain Clark and Drouillard and the men they were talking to. He noticed that the man who was fully dressed in the officer's uniform, the man he had encountered three nights before, was looking at him. The man's coal black eyes seemed to be looking right through him, never wavering, never blinking.

It made Hugh nervous and he was glad when Captain Clark turned away from the group and headed for the pirogue again. There would be a council fire that evening and he wanted to brief Captain Lewis about what he had learned from these proud, brave and very suspicious people and to advise him to be careful about what he would say and how he would say it.

# Chapter 10
## *Conception*

**W**amdisapa took Bright Morning Woman aside. "There will be a council fire tonight. All of the people are invited to listen to the Great White Father's message. It is said that these *wasichu* want only to pass up the river in peace." It was a warm evening and he was sweating, causing dark spots under the arms of the officer's uniform he still wore.

"I will attend this council. You will not." Rain Dance Woman came out of the tipi and he motioned for her to join them, but kept talking to Bright Morning Woman. "I want you to find the giant white man that I hit with my coup stick. You will recognize him by the red hair he has on his face and on his head. It is lighter red, more the color of fire, than the hair on the white man called Clark. Also, his face is bruised from when I hit him."

Bright Morning Woman glanced nervously at Rain Dance Woman, then said, "Many of the People say these white skins are demons. I'm frightened by them."

"Some of the holy men call them demons because they do not understand the power of the firesticks and they saw the black white man strike fire in the pipe by striking an arrowhead stone against his knife blade. They believe these men possess magic and are afraid they might cast spells on the People and bring us bad luck," Wamdisapa explained. "But I have scouted these men. They live like men, not demons. I have touched their hands. They feel like men, not demons. And I have shared their pipe and tasted their smoke. I know they are not demons. But they are men with very strong medicine as can be seen by the wonderful gifts they gave us. I felt the medicine of their firestick when I held it in my hands. But I know it is not magic. It is strong medicine that I must get and you can help me do this. When you find this man with the bruised face, don't be frightened. I want you to bring him back here to the tipi and pleasure him."

"I heard that many women are offering the white man with black skin hunting shirts and moccasins to bed with him hoping they will have a buffalo baby," Rain Dance Woman offered.

Wamdisapa shook his head. "Forget the buffalo man. Many of the women are fucking the other white men in exchange for more gifts. And that is what I want you to do," he said, making it clear to her. "But I don't want beads, or cloth, a hatchet or another steel knife, pot or mirror. I have all of these things. What I want is the man's firestick. I felt its medicine when I tried to steal it and I must have it! You can get it for me if you pleasure him right."

"This you must do for me," he continued. "Get him to mount you like a stallion breeds a mare, from behind." He patted her gently on the rump. "This will tire his legs; he will have to lay back and rest them and may even fall asleep. Watch him and when he lays back and closes his eyes, you grab his firestick and run away from the tipi, out onto the prairie with it. Hide there until the *wasichu* leave in the morning." He tipped her head back so that he could look directly into her eyes. "Do this as I have said and he will understand that he should have to pay more than just a trinket for such great pleasure and he will not search long for you. What ever happens, do not fail to get his firestick!"

He turned the girl and gave her a gentle push toward the river and then turned on his heel and hurried for the council fire. He could see the people gathering around a large fire a quarter of a mile down river from his tipi. He didn't want to be late.

\* \* \*

The girl came to him as he sat on a long log on the beach by the north pirogue. Hugh and John Colter were to be on watch over the pirogues while the council was in session. Except for the few men left on the keel boat to keep any nighttime swimmers from boarding, the rest of the men were at the council fire or scattered, looking for willing women to couple with. Hugh could see that the girl who was approaching him was no more than a child in years, but something about the way she carried herself, proud, self assured, told him she was not just a little girl. Without speaking a word, Bright Morning Woman walked up to him and reached out a cool hand to caress his swollen cheek.

"Only a mighty warrior could stand such a terrible blow to his face," she said softly. With a gentle fingertip, she traced the long welt that reached from his chin to his ear and then spread across his face to blacken his eye. "Come with me mighty warrior, I will sooth your pain."

She reached down and took his hand and struggling against his weight, pulled him to his feet. Standing, the top of the girl's head barely reached as high as Hugh's armpits. She started off along the river path, but when he didn't follow, she came back and took his big hand in both of her tiny ones.

"Come with me, big white man. I will make you happy." Though he couldn't understand her language, her soft words and gentle actions struck a chord with Hugh. He had felt a growing void in his heart for the simple grace of a woman's compassion ever since he'd left his mother in Kentucky. He had missed the kind and tender attention only a woman can give, more than he thought was possible. She took off again tugging at his arm.

"John," Hugh said. "What do I do? She wants me to go with her."

John Colter laughed. "Go with her boy!"

"But I'm on guard duty."

"I'll watch yer end fer a while. I doubt it will take you long," John Colter snickered.

"But, John . . ."

"Don't worry, boy, I already got me some and I need ta rest up b'for I git after some more."

"But she's so young."

"Yew ain't so old yer own self boy. Don' worry bout it. These Ingens start 'em off young," Colter said. "Give her yer knife or yer shirt or sumthin and it'll be all right."

Bright Morning Woman boldly led him away from the river trail, through the narrow strip of trees lining the bank and up a short path through the tall buffalo grass. She stopped in front of a tipi that stood on the edge of a small town of tipis that spread out with no apparent pattern.

He felt a little nervous, being this far from the river and the rest of his party. But the girl stood in the door of the tipi and reached up to tug on his beard beckoning him to come in. He stooped low and crawled in. It was very dark inside and at first he couldn't see anything. But the girl was there beside him, tugging gently on his beard, leading him to a bed of piled robes.

Giggling, and jabbering at him in her native tongue, she coaxed him out of his buckskins and shed her clothing as well. His eyes grew used to the dim light. The sight of her small firm breasts as she stood, straddling him aroused him instantly. She bent over to hug his bearded face into her chest and giggled at the feel of his beard tickling her nipples. He reached his arms out to help her as she slid down his torso. When she felt his erection poking her, she turned and kneeled down, facing away from him.

For a moment, Hugh was confused, but then rolled from his back to his knees between her legs. She reached up and expertly guided his hard penis thrusting herself back at him. Surprised to find that her young body would hardly accommodate the bigness of the young giant, she cried out and her muscles locked onto him. A low moan of passionate pleasure she had never felt before, escaped her lips. His forward thrusting pelvis lifted her off the bed and she squeezed her muscles tighter almost afraid the motion would lose the pleasure she felt. She felt his large hands grasp her narrow waist and slowly begin pushing her forward as he leaned back and then pulling her back against his forward thrusts. Finding a rhythm, they began moving faster and faster, grunting with their efforts.

Bright Morning Woman's head was spinning. For an instant she visualized a mare, being bred by a young strong stud horse. She felt wild, unbridled power in his thrusting loins and tried to match his strength meeting each of his forward thrusts by slamming back harder and harder against him. A continuous low moan of pleasure worked its way from the pit of her being until finally, with his arms locked around her, holding her against his pelvis, all of his muscles straining to push forward and all of hers shoving back, she reared back squealing like a mare in heat as a tortured groan of satisfied lust roared from deep in his throat. He lifted her with one last explosive thrust of passion that drove her forward into the bed of buffalo robes and collapsed in a heap on top of her.

If this man is not a demon, he must be a god, she thought. If this was not magic, it was very powerful medicine. Wamdisapa had told her to take him like a horse, and she had felt him become a horse! She had never felt such passion when coupling with Wamdisapa and she was convinced that no mere human could have performed so powerfully. She felt his great weight pinning her down making it hard for her to breathe and squirmed against it.

Hugh felt the girl trying to move and carefully disentangled his legs from between hers and rolled over on his back, breathing heavily. Bright Morning Woman knew she should grab his firestick and run out the door, but before she could catch her breath, his big arm had encircled her and he hugged her against the side of his body. She was suddenly frightened by what he might do if she were to try to run away. They lay there several minutes, Hugh not sleeping, but resting deeply. It felt good to hold the girl by his side. She was so pretty and young.

"You had better grab his firestick and run!" Rain Dance Woman whispered to Bright Morning Woman.

Upon hearing these words in the native tongue, Hugh realized that they were not alone in the tipi. His eyes hadn't been accustomed to the dim light when they first entered and he'd been blinded by his passion until now. He sat up and saw an old couple sitting across the tipi from the bed he sat on. They sat, grinning toothless grins and nodding their heads at him. Just to their left sat a young woman holding a child of two or three years suckling at her breast. She smiled at him, but then spoke urgently to the girl once again.

"Get his firestick and run! Wamdisapa will be very angry if you don't."

Hugh wondered idly, what she was saying, but then glanced up through the smoke hole at the top of the tipi, noticing that it was full dark outside. How long he had lain recuperating in the tipi, he didn't know. He did know however, that he couldn't be absent from his guard post too much longer. If either of the Captains found out he had left his post, even with Colter's permission, there would be hell to pay.

Quickly, he started to pull his pants on. At his movement, he saw the girl jump to her feet and step around him. He saw the naked young woman stoop at the waist and pick up his rifle with the cherry wood stock. Grunting with effort, he sprang to his feet and dove after her, just as she neared the tipi door. His hand caught her ankle and she cried out in alarm.

He pulled the girl back into the tipi and gently took the rifle from her small hands.

"I must have your firestick for my husband!" she shouted at him.

Hugh smiled and pointed to his leather hunting shirt and his belt knife and hatchet lying by the bed.

She shook her head and shouted at him once again. He knew she wanted his rifle, but losing a firearm to the Sioux was one thing he knew the Captains wouldn't like. He shook his head back and forth, noticing that his bullet pouch and powder horn lay back in the tipi where he had originally laid his rifle. He started back in to retrieve them, but the other woman had lain her child down and stood between him and the pouch and powder horn. She too began screaming at him.

With all of the noise they were making, he was sure many of their people would soon be coming to find out what was going on. Hugh decided to abandon the powder horn and bullets, but by god, they weren't getting his rifle. He left the tipi and started down the path to the river, but Bright Morning Woman followed him and still shouting, grabbed the rifle in both hands and tried to jerk it from his grasp. With a furtive glance at the darkness surrounding him, Hugh pulled the rifle from the girl's hands and gently, but firmly, shoved her to the ground. He turned quickly and jogged away. He could hear her shouting after him, but couldn't tell if her voice was angry or desperate. A sudden shiver of fear traced his spine and he wondered what the next few hours would bring?

\* \* \*

Wamdisapa returned from the council fire in a bad mood. Hates His Horses and Runs In Circles, had both received one more present than he, from the white leader called Lewis. It was only a small, round medallion, with the likeness of the Great White Father pressed into it, but since only two were given, it was a great honor to receive one. After the *wasichu* left, the two men puffed up their chests like prairie grouse in the spring and pranced around showing the medallion to all who would look at it. Wamdisapa was jealous, but he knew that the firestick would regain his important standing with the people because he would have the only one, as the weapons were one gift the whites would not give.

When he arrived back at his tipi, he was elated to find the bullet pouch and powder horn by the bed. But his mood changed quickly when Rain Dance Woman told him in a shaking, frightened voice what had happened. He stomped angrily around the tipi, kicking through the bed robes and through provisions that had been carefully stored away.

"Bright Morning Woman did all that you asked," Rain Dance Woman said. "She took him as a mare takes a stud, but he was very strong and held her after he was finished. He wouldn't let her up until he was rested. And when she grabbed the firestick and ran, he caught her, pushed her to the ground and took it back."

Wamdisapa hit her, knocking her to the ground, then turned on Bright Morning Woman, who stood cowering with fear. Pulling the new metal knife he carried at his belt, he grabbed the young girl by the back of her neck and held the knife over the bridge of her nose. Rain Dance Woman screamed in fear for her adopted little sister! She was sure Wamdisapa was going to punish her for adultery by cutting off the end of her nose. But suddenly, he laughed and spinning the girl away, he pushed her down on the bed where she lay cowering from him, pulling the robes over her still naked body. He reached down and jerked them away from her. Dropping his clout, he rolled her over onto her knees and entering her from behind, he used her until he was satisfied. After, she lay by his side, quiet and still afraid of him, but not impressed with his performance as a stud horse. He rolled over and took her face in his hand, squeezing her cheeks a little too hard.

"Tomorrow," he growled, "you will get my firestick for me."

* * *

Bright Morning Woman crouched in a small hollow on the riverbank, near where the *wasichu* boats were tied. Several bushes concealed her from both the men readying their boats and the people watching them from the high bank behind her. The white skins had spent the early morning hours demonstrating the power of their firesticks and small cannons on the prow of each pirogue. The noise, smoke and devastation of the targets they fired at did impress the People. Now, at mid-morning, as she watched from her hiding spot, the party of white skinned men was ready to leave.

"There is something going on with these people," Clark said to Lewis as they walked away from shaking hands with the lead men one last time. "It doesn't feel right. There is a tension among them. I almost feel like they might turn on us as we are leaving."

"We'll keep our eyes open and try to avoid anything that might cause trouble," Lewis answered. "All we have to do is make it to the canoes and then paddle out to the keelboat. The river is slow enough and shallow enough here so that we can pole it up river and not risk putting any men in the water."

They finished their conversation as they neared the river's edge and Clark stepped into the first pirogue and his paddlers shoved off. Lewis waited as the rest of the men manned the second pirogue and then stepped in and pushed it away from the bank.

Bright Morning Woman's heart leaped in her chest! She knew that now was the time to act. She was frightened of the whiteskins, but she was more frightened of Wamdisapa's wrath if she failed him again. Screaming a wild shout, she burst from her hiding place, running through a group of men and women who had gathered at the water's edge to watch the white men depart. Her feet threw a fine spray as she splashed through the ankle deep shallows.

"Inkpaduta!" she shouted. "Inkpaduta! Your firestick! I must have your firestick!" She was screaming in an anguished voice, crying tears as she waded after them through knee-deep water.

Captain Lewis glared at the girl. He knew that this must have been the trouble that Clark had felt coming.

"What is she shouting, Drouillard?" he asked the interpreter, who hadn't left his side during the entire visit with the Sioux.

"Sumthin' about red end or, red stick, mebbe red hair," the interpreter answered, adding, "I dunno, but this here looks like real trouble ta me Cap'm."

Upon hearing this, Hugh McNeal, sitting directly behind Drouillard stopped paddling and turned around. Guilt had ridden him hard all night. He had never experienced a sexual encounter like he had with this girl. All of the other Indian women he had been with had just been quickies behind the bushes. There had been no passion, just a release of tension. Bedding the girl had been the most special time of his life. And then he had just run off and left her crying. He felt responsible for what ever it was that had her so upset this morning.

The girl was only a few steps from catching up with the canoe, when Hugh saw a warrior, carrying only a knife, run from the shore and his long leaping strides caught up with the young girl in the waist deep water and grabbed her, throwing his arm around her throat. A wild glare shone from the man's eyes as he stared directly into Hugh's face. He held the girl roughly by her long hair and shouted at the white men."

"You took my wife without my permission!" Wamdisapa shouted at them. The crowd of people on shore was growing rapidly. Upon hearing Wamdisapa's accusation, many people joined in with angry shouts at the whites.

"Let's get these canoes out to the keelboat," Lewis commanded in a calm, but urgent voice. They were not out of bow and arrow range.

"What's he gonna do?" Hugh shouted when Wamdisapa yanked Bright Morning's head back and placed his knife on the bridge of her nose.

Horror filled Drouillard's voice as he answered Hugh, "It's their custom to cut off the nose of a wife who cheats on her husband!"

"No!" Hugh bellered at the top of his deep voice and jumped out of the pirogue.

"McNeal, Halt!" Lewis ordered. "Don't interfere."

But it was an order Hugh ignored. He stumbled through the water toward the struggling man and woman. His shame was riding hard on his shoulders. He couldn't bear to see this beautiful young woman mutilated because of something he felt he may have been to blame for. Hugh's shout had stopped Wamdisapa's knife, but he glared with anger at the huge white man sloshing through the water toward him. He threw Bright Morning Woman aside and stood ready with his knife. But Hugh slowed when he saw the man release the girl. Ignoring more shouts from Captain Lewis, he slowly advanced toward the warrior until only two feet separated them.

"I'm sorry for what I dun," he said softly to the man. "Don't hurt her. It wasn't her fault," he added and then reached out his rifle with the cherry wood stock and handed it to the Indian. Then, turning, he waded back out to the pirogue, his eyes avoiding Lewis's glare.

Wamdisapa stood in the waist deep water, watching as the *wasichu* pulled their man back into the canoe. Smiling then, he turned with his precious firestick and waded back to shore. Seemingly forgotten, Bright Morning Woman stood in the water and watched the canoe in which her red haired, white stallion sat looking back at her, until it disappeared around the up-river bend. She slowly turned and waded back to the rocky landing and sat on the grassy bank, holding her head in her hands.

# Chapter 11
## *The Child (1805)*

In the week after the departure of the *wasichu* the *Dakotah* people's summer rendezvous slowly dissolved as the various groups packed their belongings, and said their farewells. They had all enjoyed their short time together, trading and gambling and visiting. The big topic in the village that last week was how the *Wahpekute*, Wamdisapa, had tricked the red-haired white man into giving him his firestick!

Tasagi's wife told all who would listen that Wamdisapa had really intended to cut his wife's nose off for coupling with the red-haired white man, adding that it was only luck that the *wasichu* had given him the firestick. She stated boldly that Bright Morning Woman was an adulterer and should have her nose cut off! Wamdisapa, she said, was a weakling and a poor leader for not doing it. Tasagi, she said, was the clever man. He had instructed her to give the black-skinned white man a full set of buckskins to have sex with her. The medicine of the black-skinned white man was strong. It was said that he could call the buffalo and that no one who shared his medicine would go hungry. Tasagi was a wise leader, whom the People should follow.

Wamdisapa told everyone that chasing his wife into the river and threatening to cut her nose off had merely been the final part of his plan. He had instructed his second wife to seek out the red-haired white man and lure him to their tipi. She was supposed to seduce him and, acting like a mare in heat, then tire his legs by breeding with him horse style. His first wife and her parents had witnessed that the two had rutted like a stallion and mare.

A laughing Rain Dance Woman told the people that she had whispered, urgently telling Bright Morning Woman to steal his firestick and run, when they were done. But the young girl had collapsed from her exertions and the red-hair had fallen on top of her!

"She couldn't get up!" she giggled at the memory of Bright Morning struggling under the weight of the huge white man. "And the red-hair's medicine was too strong. He stopped her from stealing the firestick, and made her lay with him, letting her absorb much of his powerful medicine."

"My young wife," Wamdisapa bragged, "has much power of her own. She has the power to make men desire her. She didn't have to trade buckskins to get his attention! Her medicine was so strong that the red-hair would do anything to keep harm from coming to her. I knew," Wamdisapa added, "that seeing the pretty young horse-girl about to be mutilated would break the red-hair's heart, and I knew that he would give her the firestick she had asked for."

It was a good trick and most of the people believed that Wamdisapa had planned the whole thing. His stature among the people grew with each telling of the story. The question on all of their lips now was if Wamdisapa would be able to find the magic of the firestick and acquire the power to use it?

Wamdisapa had paid close attention, when the whites demonstrated their great medicine by shooting their firesticks. He knew now that it was not lightening, but a small lead ball that was shot out of the barrel. He also understood that it was not magic that caused the "gun," as the whites called the firestick, to fire. He learned the intricacies of loading the "gun" by watching closely when the whites held an impromptu shooting match to show off the big medicine of their weapons.

When the rest of the crowd drew back in awe, covering their ears with their hands at the sound of the explosions and were running to look at the holes in the cloth targets the men had hung, Wamdisapa watched closely as the white men reloaded, and he committed their routine to memory.

First, the dark powder was carefully poured down the barrel from the powder horns they all carried. Then a small round lead ball was hammered into the hole in end of the barrel with the butt of the hand and then rammed to the bottom of the barrel using the slender oak rod that was attached under the barrel. More of the dark powder was then poured into a small pan located back by the bottom of the barrel. It was a simple thing then to pull back on the lever that held a small piece of arrowhead stone, "flint," and then pull the trigger assembly which released the flint to fall forward, striking the metal edge of the pan, showering the powder with sparks. The powder in the pan flared and smoked and then the powder in the barrel behind the ball, ignited and exploded, sending the ball out the end of the barrel! In a way, it *was* magic!

Wamdisapa had learned the secret to the firestick's magic, but it was not a lesson that came easy. The first time he fired it, shortly after reaching shore after grabbing it from the outstretched hands of the red-haired giant, had almost ended in catastrophe. Mimicking the white men, he placed the gun to his shoulder, but took a careless aim, not really sighting down the barrel and pulled the trigger.

The resulting explosion sent the lead ball whistling between the heads of Hates His Horses and Runs In Circles who stood only yards away. They shouted in fear and ducked to the ground. The noise and smoke excited everyone and they all laughed at the two powerful men cowering on the ground. Both men angrily jumped to their feet and, not fully recognizing what result would have happened if the ball had hit one of them in the head, demanded to shoot the weapon too. But Wamdisapa was adamant that no one else touch his weapon. It was his strong medicine and anyone else even touching it might take some of its power away.

He carried the firestick back to his tipi and told Rain Dance Woman to hide the firearm under his bed of buffalo robes and to watch it so that no one could steal it. As the week wore on, more and more of the People began packing their belongings and bidding friends and family farewell. One week to the day after the white men left to go up river, Wamdisapa told his women to pack their belongings and get ready to leave the next morning. When word spread that Wamdisapa's women were preparing to move, the entire *Santee* contingent, both *Wahpekute* and *Mdewakanton* villages struck their tipis to follow. He was definitely a man with strong medicine and no one wanted to be left behind.

Even Tasagi, whose new wife often told him that he should be the leader rather than Wamdisapa, decided that he would follow along with the rest of the People.

Early the next morning, the convoy of horse and dog drawn travois traveled in a northwesterly direction. Wamdisapa told the men that they would hunt buffalo for a few days. It was now late in the *Moon when the Cherries Turn Black* and they would need to take in a supply of meat for the coming winter that would soon come roaring over the plains.

They spent the *Moon when the Calves Grow Hair* hunting for buffalo, having only varied success. The herds were scattered and hard to find. Wamdisapa tried several times to use his firestick gun but missed the animal entirely more often than not. Most of those he hit were not hit in a vital spot and they ran off. Occasionally, they could track one down and find the carcass before the wolves got it. At these times, Wamdisapa was very proud.

By the third week, he had used up all of the lead balls for his firestick gun and they reverted back to the old methods of creeping close to the buffalo herds and using bow and arrow or lance to kill the mighty creatures. This was more successful and soon the women were busy drying strips of buffalo meat, grinding it and mixing it with rendered fat, salt, dried plums and berries to make pemmican.

As the season passed, the forty or so families following Wamdisapa were glad to see that their wandering path was taking a more northeasterly route each day. Wamdisapa had announced that they would winter in a place back east in their *Santee* land. They had spent the cold time in the land of lakes and marshes for decades before. *Mini-wakan* (Lake of the Spirits) and *Okobooshi* (A Place of Rushes) had clear water, teeming with fish.

There were small groves of hardwood trees that provided the opportunity for nuts and clumps of conifer forests that would break the cold north wind. They would be able to catch fish through the ice and hunt for small game in the woods around the lakes. It would be good. Wamdisapa had chosen wisely once again and they were anxious to go there and set up their tipis and prepare for the cold times ahead before the first snows fell.

The first snows found them tucked safely away in their tipis near a grove of trees that graced a peninsula reaching out into the south side of the lake they called *Okobooshi*. The winter season came upon them fast with cold temperatures descending upon the land early in the *Moon of the Falling Leaves*.

One early morning, Bright Morning Woman rolled from her bed and ran out of the tipi, without even wrapping herself in a warm robe. She made it out the door and a few steps down the snow packed trail leading toward the edge of the village where most people went to relieve themselves, before she vomited her night's supper. Noticing the cold snow on her bare feet, she wiped her mouth on the back of her hand and headed back for the warmth of the tipi. Twice more that morning, she had to run out to throw up and by the third trip, only a bitter bile came up burning her throat and the inside of her mouth. Throwing up her supper each morning became a daily habit and after the third day, she began to worry that she was sick, even though she seemed to feel fine for the rest of the day. Finally, she mentioned her sickness to Rain Dance Woman.

"I think our pemmican might be rancid," she said one afternoon.

"Why is that Little Sister?" Rain Dance Woman asked.

"Each morning, I throw it up before I can even make it out far enough to pee."

"Did you throw up this morning?" the older woman asked.

"Yes."

"We ate fresh rabbit last night."

"Then it must have been from the pemmican the night before."

"No one else got sick."

"But each morning I throw up," the girl said again.

"You are pregnant, Little One," Rain Dance Woman said with a knowing smile. "Wamdisapa will be proud."

\*     \*     \*

Even though the cold weather came early and the lake froze over fast, more snow didn't fall until the middle of the *Moon of the Popping Trees.* But then, the extreme cold drove the lake ice deep. Its thickness made it hard to chop the holes they needed to keep open for a drinking water source and to fish through. The holes had to be chopped open each day. The fishermen had poor luck and because the snow was not deep, the deer and elk didn't herd up making it hard to hunt them. By the *Moon of Frost in the Tipi* the village knew hunger and they passed the rest of the winter rationing their meager food supplies.

The men went out hunting and fishing every day and even with their limited success, the People survived. Luckily, spring came early during the *Moon of the Snowblind* bringing relief from the cold temperatures. The sun shining off of the snow fields caused many of the men to return from hunting with headaches and their best hunter, Bear Runner, had to sit in the darkness of his tipi for three days before he could see again. With the warming heat from the sun, the snow began to recede and the lake ice began to rot. Early one evening, the hunters were successful in chasing a small herd of buffalo out onto the thinning lake ice about a mile from the village. The small diameter of the animals' hooves along with their great weight and the poor condition of the ice caused several of the animals to fall through into the freezing cold water before they had advanced far from shore. Panic spread through the herd as the animals that fell through thrashed and bellowed in terror. Some of the frightened animals on thicker ice turned and ran into the gaping hole, joining their drowning compatriots; others broke for the shore where they were met with a hail of arrows.

Three cows were slain on shore. Five buffalo, including two bulls, swam in the lake, trying to climb out, but each time the ice broke off, making the hole larger and larger. One of the bulls found stronger ice and driving his front hooves in, pulled his front quarters back on top of the ice where he laid half in and half out, heaving for air, before slowly sliding back into the dark water. In a half hour's time, the five exhausted buffalo in the lake drowned. Seven escaped the arrows on shore and fled to the south and three pitiful yearling calves still stood, trembling with fear, far out on the lake, where the ice was still thick.

Brave men who could swim quickly scampered out across the thin ice and dove into the freezing water. They tied horsehair ropes around the drowned buffalo's heads to keep them from sinking to the bottom of the lake. Wamdisapa and Blue Nose brought their horses to pull the dead animals back to shore.

Fires were built and the women came from the village to butcher the eight creatures. This buffalo kill was a lucky thing. The meat from the animals was divided equally between the forty families and would provide food for the People a few weeks, at least until the warmer weather returned. Another lucky thing was that two women in the village were with child. Wamdisapa's second wife, Bright Morning Woman's stomach was starting to grow noticeably larger and Tasagi's wife, New Grass Woman was even bigger with child. Everyone was anxious to see if New Grass Woman's child would be a buffalo-man baby as she bragged daily about the black skinned white man being the father.

New Grass Woman was quick to claim that it was the child, developing in her womb that had brought the buffalo so near their camp at this odd time of year. If this was true, it was good news for the village and would add much to the claim that Tasagi was a wise man who would make a good leader. New Grass Woman's constant complaining about Wamdisapa's leadership was starting to turn some people's heads. It was good that two of the important men in the village's women were pregnant, but the bad blood between Wamdisapa and Tasagi grew only worse over the hungry months and was not improved by this quirk of fate.

\*   \*   \*

Wamdisapa grew restless early in the *Moon of the Red Grass Appearing.* The morning was cool and hoarfrost covered the dead grass that was beginning to thaw and stand up with the disappearing snow. He stood beside a tree and urinated, enjoying the relief of an emptying bladder. The faint, far off honking of geese filtered down from above the early morning clouds. Wamdisapa listened to the gabbing geese until they flew beyond his range of hearing. The fresh sounds of the northbound geese lifted his spirits. It was a sound he waited for each year to know that spring was truly on its way. The snow, except for pockets where the winter's winds had deposited deep drifts behind the groves of trees, was gone.

He had the itch to move and the deteriorating climate between he and Tasagi was not improving with the coming of the warmer weather. Tasagi's wife was openly haranguing to the village women about Tasagi having stronger medicine than Wamdisapa. She was quick to point out that Wamdisapa's pregnant wife was in poor condition compared to the vitality of her own pregnant health. Bright Morning Woman was especially thin from the malnutrition brought on by the hungry months. Her arms and legs were emaciated. Her hands looked large and her elbows and knees were bony and protruded. Her smallish breasts, which should have been firm and full in preparation to lactate, were sagging, not even beginning to show signs of making milk. Her stomach was huge. It was hard and tight, stretching every bit of skin from her young frame.

New Grass Woman's explanation for Bright Morning Woman's poor health was centered on Wamdisapa's failing medicine. He had been a great and powerful man when he tricked the white man out of his firestick. What happened to his strong medicine? If the firestick's medicine was so strong, why did they experience the cold time hunger like they had every year before Wamdisapa acquired the magic of the firestick? The truth, she told them, was that the firestick was bad magic that had fooled Wamdisapa, who was not a smart man, into believing it would be a good helper to the People. Actually it was not a good helper. Its presence scared the game away and contributed to their hunger all winter. It was only the powerful medicine of the buffalo baby she carried that had brought them food when they most needed it.

With her voice filled with disdain, New Grass Woman told them once again how her husband, Tasagi, was the wiser man of the two. He knew enough to have her bed the black skinned white man and gain them the medicine of the buffalo man instead of fooling the whites into giving him a worthless firestick. Wamdisapa was the one who was fooled!

Rain Dance Woman heard all of the hateful statements about Bright Morning Woman and Wamdisapa that her sister was making and reported them to her husband. Wamdisapa knew that a certain amount of the People would believe New Grass Woman and he understood that the longer they stayed near her influence, that more of the People would be swayed to her way of thinking. He returned to the camp after the cries of the geese left his ears. Shouting, he chased his women from their bed robes, and ordered them to begin packing. They were moving camp and they were leaving today. Soon half of the People were packing their belongings to follow Wamdisapa. The rest, due to New Grass Woman's urging, would stay behind to follow Tasagi.

Wamdisapa led his people south and to the east, instead of following their usual course which was to follow the *Inyaniake* river in a southwesterly direction until it converged with the Missouri

River. A few miles north from there is where they normally crossed and followed the big river north to the place of rendezvous with their western cousins.

But Wamdisapa had decided that they would not attend the rendezvous with their western cousins this year. He knew that many of the People from the western tribes would be expecting great stories about his powerful firestick gun and he didn't want to face having to explain that he had run out of the round lead balls, so he couldn't fire it any more. That would amuse the people, especially if New Grass Woman talked to them.

He suspected that, if for no other reason, Tasagi would lead the people who were following him to the rendezvous just to show that he was now a *Santee* leader. Wamdisapa knew that the key to the firestick gun lay with the white skinned men who came from the east. So he decided to lead his people east and try to make contact with them. If he could trade for more lead balls and more powder, he would try to conserve them. Then and only then would he attend the rendezvous the next summer.

With the snow gone and floodwaters in the rivers receded, traveling was easier. But their store of buffalo meat ran out three weeks after they left their winter camp and they had to hunt small game and forage for grubs, mice, and worms to eat.

Two days later, Sun At Night found a bear's den in a small hollow dug under the roots of a fallen *Wagachun* (cottonwood tree) on the banks of a small rocky river bed. He was able to pull three cubs from the den and club them before the young mother bear was aroused and charged out of the den. All of the men began throwing rocks at her and the camp dogs chased the small, foul-mooded creature for two miles down the riverbed until it finally turned at bay.

The black bear snarled and stood on her hind legs, her dugs dripping milk as she swiped her front paws at the dogs that were instinctively diving at her hind legs, trying to hamstring her. When the men from the village caught up, they surrounded the bear and began throwing a steady barrage of rocks at the bear, pummeling it unmercifully.

One of the dogs was hit in the spine with a poorly aimed rock and fell at the bear's feet. The bear quickly grabbed the yelping dog in its jaws and drove it to the ground crushing its rib cage. Two other dogs rushed in from behind and sank their teeth into the bear's hind legs just below its knees. The bear screamed in agony and roared with rage, spinning on its front legs trying to twist around snapping it jaws viciously at its tormenters! Sun At Night rushed in and buried a lance deep into the bear's chest. The mortally wounded animal screamed and reared to a standing position before toppling over backwards where it lay, a long, sorrowful moan of death escaping as the air left its lungs.

There was jubilation in the village that night. The much-needed meat was divided equally among all of the families. It wasn't a lot, and it was tough and stringy fare with little grease, because the she bear had only emerged from hibernation a few weeks before and had been suckling three cubs which kept her from fattening up this early in the spring. But the meat came at a good time for the People. It was rare to find a bear in this flat country and their good fortune at finding this one seemed to change their luck. Smaller game, berries and tubers became more plentiful and obtainable with each passing day as they moved south.

Early one morning in the *Moon when the Ponies Shed* Bright Morning Woman struggled to her feet by first rolling from her bed to her knees and then laboriously climbing to her feet. She felt bloated and unusually full and was on her way to leave the tipi and go relieve herself at the edge of camp. After taking only three steps, a hot flushing of water poured down her thighs and splashed across her feet.

A small cry of surprise escaped her lips and the first pain cramped its way across her lower stomach. Rain Dance Woman rose from her bed and took the girl by the shoulders. She guided her back to her bed and briskly ordered Wamdisapa to go tell Blue Nose that it was his daughter's time and that he should send his wives to help with the birthing. Knowing this would be a long day, she handed her own son, Pinched Cheeks, to her parents and hustled the old couple out of the tipi, instructing them to find another lactating mother to feed him.

Bright Morning lay on her bed of buffalo robes with Rain Dance Woman holding her hand, squeezing it tightly each time a spasm of pain came. She spoke reassuringly in low calming tones when the girl started to become excited.

"Rest little sister," she crooned when Bright Morning got through a pain and collapsed back. "All is well. Your mother will be here soon."

After her mother arrived, she took over talking soothingly to Bright Morning Woman, but as the hours droned on and the pains became incredible, worry spread across Catches Birds Woman's face. Morning Girl was so young! Not many girls were made to be women at this girl's tender age. In her mother's opinion she was not physically big enough to have a child. And the child in her womb appeared to be very large. This would be a difficult birth. She could see that. Also, because of the hungry winter, the girl had little reserve strength and was quite weak from the very onset of her ordeal. But though Bright Morning Woman was very frightened, she was determined to be as brave as the wife of the leader, Wamdisapa, should be. She vowed to not shout out the agony that was racking her small body. The vow was broken early, for when the wait between the pains became shorter and shorter and the severity of the pains increased, she had to scream!

Her labor lasted hours as, she was told by her mother, it does with many first birthings. Her strength ebbed and finally, she slept between each spasm, trying to replenish her exhausted body. Even though the naps lasted only three to five minutes, she began to dream. The dream was interrupted with each pain, but when she fell back to the bed, as it passed, she picked up her dream right where she had left off. The dream was about a mare in foal about to give birth.

*The mare's white hair was peppered with small black spots sprinkled across her lower belly and teats leading to larger, lighter red-brown spots over her ribs and flanks. The larger spots were the color of the red hair of the white man she had coupled with like a horse. She felt his hands holding her close and heard his voice whispering the soothing and calm words of endearment that she didn't need to understand to understand.*

Then a searing, tearing pain raced through her and she cried out in anguish, grunting and straining, fighting an overwhelming desire to push with all of her might, and thought she would soon be ripped in two.

When she fell back to dream again, the mare was there.

*It calmly lowered its head and cropped a mouthful of sweetgrass. It stood chewing the grass into a cud. Bright Morning Woman could see green colored drool forming on the horse's lips. It dropped to the ground in a long trail of slimy fluid. After a swallow, the mare again lowered her head and her dull, green stained teeth ripped another mouthful from the grass roots. Slowly, calmly, the cud was chewed, the green slobber formed on its lips and then finally, with a low grunt, the mare stepped backwards and spread all four legs to brace herself. She snorted, blowing green foam flecks and drool in all directions. She whinnied and her stomach muscles rippled across her ribs and with a great grunting groan passing her green stained teeth, she strained against the sudden pain and pressure.*

Bright Morning could feel the pain coming again, but put it aside in her mind. She wanted to hold on to this dream.

*A loud passing of gas sounded, followed by the emergence of the front hooves, nose, eyes and ears of a speckled colt that fairly slid from its mother's womb and landed with a plop on the ground. The mare, after seemingly looking deep into Bright Morning's eyes, turned slowly around and after one lick on the colt's head, began to devour the afterbirth.*

The most severe of all of her pains ended the dream for Bright Morning Woman. She rose unsteadily to her feet. Her mother and Rain Dance Woman tried to push her back to the bed, but she screamed at them to leave her alone.

"I know what I must do!" and she swung her hand as her mother reached out to support her shoulder. She waddled to the edge of the tipi floor to a spot where the grass had not yet been tread down. Suddenly calm, she felt no fear. She stood slightly bent over, her legs spread, trying to ease the pains.

Squatting low to the ground, groaning with effort, she balanced herself until the pain subsided. Blood and fluids drained down her legs to the ground and a small dirty pool formed between her feet. Rain Dance Woman tried to put the jacket from one of Wamdisapa's officer uniforms over the puddle, but Bright Morning woman angrily kicked it away and then squatted once again as another pain gripped her lower abdomen. She reached to the ground and tore out a handful of grass. Shoving it in her mouth, she chewed it until a muddy green slobber formed on her lips and her feverish, glazed eyes locked on another time and another place. She was the focus of her own dream. She had become the horse and drew on the animal's strength and as the horse in her dream, she chewed on her cud and she was calm.

When the final pains came, a moan, low and helpless and long lasting pushed from her insides and she puffed for air, thinking she would surely be turned inside out. She squatted so low with this last terrible pain that the baby's head at long last burst out and touched the ground. She stood straighter, grunting and straining with the effort of flexing her stomach muscles and the rest of the child followed, plopping out into the pool of muddy fluids at her feet. The landing jarred the child and he began to cry. Rain Dance Woman quickly snatched the baby boy from the ground and wrapped the squalling child in the uniform jacket.

Though the child had been born and his weak cries could be heard, the ordeal wasn't over for Bright Morning Woman. She was still locked somewhere between the dream world and real life. When her mother tried to coax the girl back to her bed, she pushed her away and continued to stand spread legged, resting her hands on her knees. Her breathing came in deep gasps of air that she swallowed noisily and blew back out of her nose, making a snorting sound. Her lower stomach muscles continued to surge and flex, finally pushing a bloody wad of afterbirth out. Feeling this final release, she turned in some confusion to look for her baby and reached to pick up the afterbirth. A quick panic came with the realization that the baby was not there. She looked wildly about and cried out, "Inkpaduta . . . where's my child?" and then she collapsed unconscious to the ground.

Her mother lifted her and put her to her bed. After covering her carefully, she turned to Rain Dance Woman and asked, "Inkpaduta?"

Rain Dance Woman had dried the child and walked over to where the afternoon light passed through the tipi door. Ignoring his indignant cries, she examined him and finally lifted him up and using one finger to open his mouth, guided her dripping nipple into his mouth and felt a warm relief when the child began to suckle. Bright Morning's mother walked over to look on and reached out a tentative hand to touch her grandson's head, tickling through the mass of light red hair that covered his crown. "Inkpaduta," she murmured.

"Inkpaduta," Rain Dance Woman repeated, shaking her head in agreement, adding, "She knew all along that the child would have red hair."

\*    \*    \*

Wamdisapa smiled thinking of his new son. The baby's skin was lighter in color than the skin of most *Dakotah* babies and his hair color also set him aside as being different. His eyes were dark, but were not coal black, like most of the People's. When he first saw the child, he felt a little disappointment upon knowing the boy's true father was the red haired whiteskin instead of himself. But a male child meant there would be another hunter in the tribe and another warrior for times of war. In the intervening weeks since his birth, the boy had been growing rapidly, nourished almost solely at the breast of Rain Dance Woman. Bright Morning Woman's milk had been slow to come and her supply had not been nearly enough to feed the ravenous baby. Newborn babies sometimes starved to death when their mothers couldn't make milk. It was lucky that Rain Dance Woman was still feeding her son, Pinched Cheeks, and had an ample supply for both children.

The red haired child was doing well. That was a good thing. It was the health of his young wife that caused Wamdisapa real concern. She had lain in her bed for several days after the birth and Wamdisapa had to delay moving the village to let her regain some of her strength. And even now, weeks later, after a day's travel, she was too exhausted to help Rain Dance Woman unpack and set up the tipi, when they stopped for the night. They traveled slowly to match her pace and Wamdisapa extended the stay at many camps to accommodate his young wife's need for rest. People were surprised that Wamdisapa showed such deference to this young girl. She was just his second wife.

But she was special to him. No one else knew it, but it had been *her* plan to trick the whiteskin out of his firestick gun. She had stood bravely facing his anger in the darkness outside of their tipi that long ago night and spoke calmly to him, laying out a plan she knew would work.

She understood by the way the young whiteskin had held her in his arms and whispered words she couldn't understand in her ear, that he loved her and would never let any harm come to her, if he could stop it. She was certain that the young whiteskin knew she had wanted his firestick gun for fulfilling his needs. And she was sure he felt bad for not giving her everything she asked for. So she spoke her plan. *She would follow the red-hair whiteskin into the water, with all of the people watching and ask again for his firestick gun. She told Wamdisapa to chase her and threaten to cut her nose off if she didn't get it.* The special part was that she knew that if she was wrong and the red-haired whiteskin didn't hand over the weapon, to save face in front of the People, *Wamdisapa would have to do it!*

For a woman, the girl had very strong medicine. She was wise beyond her years and she was incredibly brave. This was witnessed by Rain Dance Woman during the birth of the baby. At one point, the women were sure she was not strong enough to birth the child. She lay on the bed of robes in total exhaustion, barely breathing. Catches Birds Woman began wailing in grief, fearing the girl was about to fall into a sleep she wouldn't wake up from. Then the girl snorted through her nose and though in agonizing pain, stiffly climbed to her feet, squealing and striking out in anger when they tried to push her back to the bed.

"She whinnied like a horse twice," Rain Dance Woman whispered to Wamdisapa, "once before the child was born," her voice quavering with fear, "and once right after."

It had been a powerful dream, one filled with strong medicine that could not be ignored. Bright Morning Woman timidly described the dream to Wamdisapa. She recited, step by step, how the dream mare had shown her the way to rid her body of the child. She described in great detail, the color of the mare. It was white with spots the color of dried leaves running along its sides and over its back. But under its tail, where pink skin surrounded its vaginal opening, tiny black spots began and grew in size as they peppered down to her milk swollen bag and two large teats, encompassing them, leaving only one small red spot on the very tip of the right teat.

But it was the white face with a wisp of tawny red mane hanging on its forehead above bright blue eyes that gave the dream its real power! The white man father was watching through the mare's blue eyes! He was passing his strong medicine to the child and Wamdisapa knew this baby would also have strong medicine that would one day make him a leader of the People! It was clear to Wamdisapa that the dream was a powerful sign that called for a new name for Bright Morning Woman. The name also was clear.

They were camped in a copse of hardwood saplings on the banks of the *Wapsipinicon* River, deep in *Ioway* lands. It was a warm night with hardly any breeze and the people gathered around a large fire near the edge of camp. It was a happy time. While men often experienced name-changing events in their lives, it was rare when a woman was accorded the same honor. The women and children were laughing and chattering waiting for the ceremony to begin. They had heard of the strong medicine the girl experienced during the birth of her red-haired child and all were excited to hear her new name.

Bright Morning Woman appeared suddenly out of the growing darkness. Still showing the effects of a hard birth, she moved slowly, with little grace. She was totally naked, her body painted white. Rust brown spots of varying sizes reached from the nape of her neck, down her back and across her rump. Blue eyes were painted on her cheeks, just below her own eyes. Rain Dance Woman had taken special care to follow Bright Morning Woman's description of the mare's color. Small black spots, speckling her vaginal area, moved up her front torso, over her small sagging belly, growing in size until both breasts were painted completely black, except for the nipple on her right breast, which was painted red, like the mare's.

The girl moved further out nearer to the fire. She could feel its heat and worried that it could make the grease based paint run together, so she drifted away from the fire and started circling. She pawed the ground with her foot, snorted through her nose and whinnied and started a shuffling dance around the fire, snorting and whinnying in intermittent intervals.

As his wife danced to the immense pleasure of the assembled people, Wamdisapa stepped forward and related the story of his new son's birth as told to him by the woman who danced before them.

"The power of the horse dream can not be ignored," he said in finishing the story. "Her medicine has strengthened and she needs a new strong name to match it. From this day on, she will be known as Horse Woman With Spots!"

A great ululating cry of joy burst from the people as they joined Horse Woman With Spots dancing around the fire. Though still weak, the young mother danced with the other revelers in celebration of her new name deep into the night until the fire burned out.

Wamdisapa danced with the rest, but his mind was not at ease. He had not yet named the child. He knew that there was a correlation between the dream and what the child should be called. Naming the mother had been easy, but naming the child was not so simple. It was apparent from the dream that this child was special and thus, possessed strong medicine, even as an infant.

Wamdisapa didn't want to risk disturbing the boy's medicine by naming him wrong. He decided that until the message from the dream was better defined, the best course to follow would be to call the boy, Horse Woman's Child.

# Chapter 12
*Murder So Foul*

**T**here was a commotion at the far end of the camp as the people of Tasagi's family filed into the village. Tasagi was at their lead and just behind him walked New Grass Woman, proudly carrying her baby strapped to her back in a leather bag lined with goose down. The child's dark little face peeked bravely over his mother's shoulder. Piercing, coal black eyes, gleamed with inquisitiveness, rarely seen in one so young. The people crowded around to welcome Tasagi and his brothers and uncles back to the village after being separated from them for over three moons. Excitement rippled through the crowd as New Grass Woman pulled her child from the leather bag and held him high for everyone to inspect.

"The Buffalo Man's baby!" she shouted proudly as she spun in a circle with the child held high over her head so all could see him. Tight ringlets of black curls covered the child's head. His nose was broad, and his lips thick. "Buffalo Calf Boy is a child that will bring good luck!"

Wamdisapa saw the curly headed child and frowned. He had been wondering why Tasagi had led his people to find Wamdisapa's village. Now he knew. New Grass Woman was not content to merely have her husband be considered a main leader of the Wahpekute People, she was also obsessed with causing the downfall of Wamdisapa. He could read the people's thoughts and knew that many people, upon seeing Buffalo Calf Boy would consider Tasagi to be a very lucky man. And lucky men were considered good men to follow. In the back of their minds, the people were comparing Buffalo Calf Boy to Horse Woman's Child. Buffalo Calf Boy was dark skinned, strong, healthy, and bright eyed. Horse Woman's Child's skin was pale, and though, thanks to Rain Dance Woman, he was well fed and strong, he was smaller and his eyes were lighter and lacked the gleaming brightness of Buffalo Calf Boy's eyes.

Wamdisapa could not help but be impressed once again by the strong medicine that the white men possessed. Only two women in the Wahpekute band had become pregnant that year, and both had conceived while having sex with the men from the White Men's party. (To Wamdisapa, the Buffalo Man was just a dark skinned white man.) He allowed that the dark skinned baby would be a welcome addition to their band. But he was sure that Horse Woman's Child had stronger medicine.

Early the next morning, Wamdisapa rose from his bed and ordered his women to prepare to move the camp. He had reasoned that the only source for lead balls to shoot through his firestick-gun would be white men. They would travel further east to try to find some white men. He also wanted to see how much the arrival of Tasagi and his buffalo child might affect the peoples' loyalties. Disappointment lined his face when he saw that only about half of the people were packing after they saw his women getting ready to move. But he held his emotions in check and soon Tasagi's brother-in-law, Crow That Flies Away, came to complain about the village moving so soon after Tasagi's people had arrived.

"We have traveled a long and tiring journey to catch up with you Wamdisapa," the man whined. "We want to rest a few days and visit with our friends before moving on."

Wamdisapa showed great unconcern. "Stay and rest if you are too weak to travel," he answered with an exaggerated shrug of his shoulders.

Crow That Flies Away turned and stomped angrily back to Tasagi's tipi. It was with great relief that Wamdisapa saw New Grass Woman emerge from the lodge and begin to pack their belongings. The rest of the people also began preparing to move. But Wamdisapa knew that he had a very short time to win the people back, as their loyalty was waning.

They traveled down river for two days, stopping at night only to lay out the sleeping robes and sleep under the stars. At noon on the third day, he ordered a stop a short distance from a rolling river that fed into the Mississippi River. He told his women to set up their tipi. They would rest here for a couple of days. Tomorrow, he would scout the area for signs of their enemies, for they were in the land of the Sauk and Fox. If there were no signs of danger, they would move to the banks of the river, where he could watch the river for white men, while the people searched the shoals for clams and set out fishing nets.

This news excited the people. Everyone was tired of traveling and enjoyed the prospect of a long summer camp near the big river.

*   *   *

Wamdisapa growled angrily as he was awakened in the darkness the next morning. Horse Woman's Child was crying again! Horse Woman sat holding her child close, swaying slowly and singing soothingly to him. The child was hungry. She tried to nurse him and the hungry child aggressively latched on to his mother's offered nipple. Horse Woman winced in pain as the straining baby sucked hard for the warm milk his stomach craved. But no sweet milk trickled across his tongue. Horse Woman had no milk. An angry scream blew from the baby's lungs and he continued to cry, refusing Horse Woman's offerings of her other breast, which she knew was also dry.

It was strange to hear a child crying in a *Dakotah* village. Most *Dakotah* children were quiet by nature and if the inclination to fuss surfaced, the parents kept them satisfied by giving them what they wanted. Wamdisapa knew that the wailing child had probably already awakened the people in the tipis set up near his. It would be embarrassing in the morning if the people near them moved their tipis away. He knew that many people, outside of his circle of family and friends had already began whispering behind his back about this loud crying at night being a sign of the child's white blood. Wamdisapa would never admit to the public that the reason the child cried so much was because Horse Woman's milk had dried up. New Grass Woman had already guessed as much and spoke loudly about Horse Woman's bad medicine.

With an angry grunt, he ordered Rain Dance Woman to feed the child and considered the problem solved. But it was not a simple thing. Over the last few weeks, Horse Woman had grown more and more resentful of Rain Dance Woman's ability to feed not only her own child, but Horse Woman's Child too. Rain Dance Woman loved the light skinned baby. She had since that first time she had put him to nurse on the day he was born. She loved Horse Woman With Spots also, though sometimes she was jealous of the attention her husband gave to the pretty young girl. And she was especially jealous of the honor Wamdisapa had bestowed upon the girl by giving her a new name.

Her own son, Pinched Cheeks, only nursed in the mornings on most days now, because she had begun feeding the three year old by chewing up bits of meat and tubers and feeding the well chewed food to him off a horn spoon during the day. But her fantastic mammary glands seemed to produce a never-ending supply of milk and she had plenty to feed both children. Deep in her heart, she was glad to feed this hungry infant and felt sorry for poor Horse Woman With Spots, whose small-girl breasts seemed to produce little or no milk. But even with the love she felt inside for both the girl and the baby, she couldn't stop herself from giving Horse Woman a look of irritation when she stooped to take the whimpering child. She sat back and placed the boy's face near her breast, and felt a warm pleasure flow through her at his insistent tugging on her dripping nipple. Shortly, Pinched Cheeks crawled to her lap and nuzzled her other breast. With a small giggle, she put him to it. The sounds that the two boys made as both suckled and smacked in their feeding like two small puppies competing for the dugs at their mother's side, made Rain Dance Woman laugh in joy.

In the quiet of the dark tipi Horse Woman could hear the contented children at their breakfast. She could also hear the joy in Rain Dance Woman's heart through her giggles. Horse Woman felt ashamed. She could not even feed her own child. And she was hurt by the look of irritation from Rain Dance Woman. She was sure that the look had been more for show than for real, because she could see the sheer joy Rain Dance Woman was feeling while feeding the two boys. Somehow, that made it hurt all the more.

Slowly, Horse Woman rolled to her feet and left the confines of the tipi. She gathered some firewood in the sapling forest at the edge of camp and dropped an armful by the fire. She placed a bundle of kindling on the white coals in the bottom of the pit and laid a few larger sticks on top. She knew that the heat from the coals would soon start the kindling and the breakfast fire would be burning when she returned. She hadn't visited the sunrise since long before her light skinned, red haired son had been born and suddenly, the need to visit with the dust of her ancestors was strong.

She walked out from the village, ducking between the pole-like trees growing irregularly across the knoll they were camped on. The morning sky was warm and clear. Stars could still be seen on the western skyline, but on the rise to the east a soft light was beginning to show. Horse Woman shivered as she trudged up the rise and remembered how easy it had been to walk or even run up hills and down before the baby had begun growing in her stomach. She realized that the long hungry winter, followed by the birthing and the hard traveling since, had taken its toll on her health. She hadn't felt strong since before her child had been born. Just doing her chores around the camp always left her exhausted and ready to fall into her sleeping robes early each night. It saddened her to realize that she hadn't really even felt like playing with her child as of yet and resolved to change that.

Visiting the sunrise again would be a good start. This familiar act of walking out at dawn to perform her ritual of greeting her ancestors lent some solace to her weary soul. In fact, she thought, the exercise of walking up the hill suddenly felt good. Her joints loosened as the aching stiffness went away with the movement and her tired mind tried to shake the lethargy the recent weeks of inactivity had brought on.

She stopped and sniffed the wind. It came in a slight breeze from the south and carried a slight, unfamiliar odor. Her eyes searched the slowly lightening terrain for a clue as to the origin of the odor, but she could see nothing out of place and after only a few minutes, could not smell it any more. The sun rolled over the horizon in a breath-taking display of colors and light. The beautiful sunrise took her back to when she was still Bright Morning Girl and she strolled on, heading to the crest of the rise, feeling better than she had in months.

She followed the crest of the rise, walking into the breeze, stopping to sniff the air like a prairie wolf, searching for food. She realized she was getting farther from camp than usual, but the view from the top of the rise was intoxicating. The sun was full up and she could see for miles.

Looking down hill toward the river, she could see the thousands of trees lining its banks and the hills rolling up from it, covered in the buffalo grass that claimed the land. Excitedly, she thought about traveling on to the Grandmother of all Waters, where her husband had said they would set up the village and spend the summer. It was a big river and it had been many years since Wamdisapa had seen it. But he could remember its juicy clams found by wading in its sandbars and the abundant catch of horned fish that dried well in their smoky fires. She felt certain that a few weeks with plenty of good food to eat and time to rest would restore her strength and she would be able to feed her own son and make her husband proud.

Tiring, she walked to a rock protruding from the earth a quarter of the way down the far side of the rise out of sight from the camp and sat down to rest. After a few moments on the rock, she realized that she had wandered, while deep in thought, farther from camp than she had intended.

Standing to go back, she heard something moving in the grass behind her and turned to look. Was it a fox or a badger, or a mole or a rabbit? She saw nothing, but the odor she had smelled as she was walking up the rise, had returned and was much stronger than before. She sniffed again and again, trying to identify the musty smell that was remotely familiar, yet different. Hearing another sound, this time coming from the opposite direction she had heard the first sound, she turned to look again. But there was nothing to see. She breathed in deeply through her nose and with a start, recognized the smell. It was of human sweat, mixed with bear grease, charcoal and smoke. But it was not an entirely familiar scent. It was not the smell of a Wahpekute!

Hurriedly, she started walking back toward the top of the rise, heading back to the village. But before she had taken but a few steps, a boy, hardly as old as herself stood up out of the grass in front of her. His face was painted black, with red and yellow stripes reaching from his eyes to his chin. His upper torso was covered with charcoal and streaks of vermilion. His hair was tied in a knot on top of his head, held together with porcupine quills stuck through it from all directions. In his left hand, he held a bow. It was little more than a child's bow and he didn't even reach for the arrows he carried in a quiver strung over his shoulder. His right hand held a war club. It was a stout stick with a round rock lashed between the forked branches at its end. He raised it and shook it threateningly at Horse Woman.

Frightened, she turned to run away, only to see another similarly painted and armed boy rise up out of the tall grass to block her avenue of escape. Abruptly, she recognized the hairstyle the boys wore. They were Sauk, historic enemies of the Wahpekute people! Cut off from the village and too far out to shout for help, Horse Woman turned and ran away from the village into the grasslands leading away from the river!

The Sauki boys were like two young puppies, unsure of themselves and a little bit frightened by the situation they found themselves in. They stood and watched their quarry until she started to run. Then, like dogs after a rabbit, they chased her yipping with excitement! Running down hill hurt Horse Woman's stiffened shins and her ankles felt brittle. If this would have been a year earlier, she felt that she could have easily outrun the boys, as she had always been a very fast runner. But in her weakened condition, they gained on her rapidly. Each time she tried to turn in an arc that would take her in the direction back toward the village, one of the boys would sprint at an angle to get ahead of her, forcing the tiring girl to turn and go even farther from her safe haven.

Horse Woman skidded to a halt and then switched directions, running back on her own track as hard as her tired body would let her. The sudden change in direction fooled the boys and both slipped and fell when they tried to stop. Pumping her arms and driving her aching legs, she slipped between them as they slid down in the slippery dry grass. She heard their angry, little boy curses and it lifted her spirits and gave her the first hope she had felt since the Sauki boys had appeared. She had a long ways to go to the top of the ridge, where she would be back in sight of the village. The sun was full up now and maybe someone would be outside looking up at the sunrise on the ridge. It was her only chance and she drove her tired legs up the steady incline, telling her panicking mind that if she could just make the top, the run down the other side would be much easier.

She risked a look over her shoulder as she ran and saw that the bigger of the two boys was gaining rapidly. Suddenly, the ground seemed to come up and hit her in the face. Her right leg had stepped in an old badger hole. There was a loud snapping sound and Horse Woman hit the ground hard knocking the wind out of her lungs. Squealing with pain, she scrambled to a sitting position, and saw the jagged edge of her right shinbone protruding from the skin just below her knee. Excruciating pain blinded her with tears for an instant. But shaking her head, she blinked away the tears and bravely faced her tormentors.

"Sauki Dogs!" she screamed pulling the white man knife Wamdisapa had given her to carry at her waist. "Run home to your mothers before I cut off your man parts and feed them to the crows!"

The boys stood for a moment staring at their victim and glancing back and forth at each other, as if silently asking each other what they should do now? They couldn't understand the words she had screamed at them, but both understood her intent. The young woman sat defiantly facing them, pointing a long bladed knife at them. But she was gasping with pain. Her eyes kept rolling back in her head and it was apparent that she was fighting to remain conscious. Finally her hand holding the knife lost its grip and it fell to the ground. Instinctively, she dropped her hand to the ground, locking her elbow to help keep her body in a sitting position. The bigger of the two boys spoke, addressing her in his own tongue.

"I am called Water Boy," he grunted. "I am a strong Sauki warrior who fears nothing!" He stepped forward suddenly and without ceremony, swung his war club in a wide arc, smashing it into the wounded girl's face. She slammed back to the earth, spread-eagled, her legs and arms twitching and shuddering. Bravely, she raised her head once more looking at the boys through her left eye. Her right eye had been crushed by the blow from Water Boy's war club. With a gurgling moan her head dropped back to the earth, and her arms and legs jerked spasmodically. When her body went still, Horse Woman With Spots was dead.

# Chapter 13
## *Vengeance Vowed*

**W**ater Boy looked at his young cousin, Crow Egg Sucker. The younger boy's eyes were transfixed on the body of the dead girl. His face was red and Water Boy thought he could see tears forming in the corner of his eyes. He grunted loudly to get Crow Egg Sucker's attention and, puffing up his chest, Water Boy danced around the corpse singing a war song and waving his war club menacingly.

*This enemy I have found.*
*This enemy I have met on the field.*
*This enemy I have killed!*
*Aieeyi! Aieeyi! Aieeyi!*

Finishing his song of victory, he bent and took the girl's arm in both of his hands. Pulling hard, he dragged her away from the badger hole to more level ground leaving a short bloody trail in the tall grass. Glancing over his shoulder at his cousin, he cut the girl's clothing off and stood back to examine her naked body. Grinning suddenly, he elbowed Crow Egg Sucker in the ribs and giggled a nervous laugh. Reaching down, he cupped one of the small breasts in his hand and squeezed it tightly, jumping back in surprise to see a small sprinkle of milk spray from the nipple. This was not just some young girl who had wandered too far from camp dreaming of the young boys in her village. This was a woman and a mother! Water Boy felt proud. This woman would birth no more warriors to become enemies of the Sauk people. Water Boy picked up the knife the girl had dropped and using its sharp point, traced a circle around the top of the woman's head. Wrapping her long hair around his hand, he jerked in an upward motion. There was a tearing sound and then a soft pop, and the scalp came free from her head.

"Water Boy," Crow Egg Sucker hissed his first words since they had spotted the girl and decided to sneak up on her. "This was a

*Nadowwessioux* woman! Our enemies are camped just over the rise! I am frightened! We must hurry away from here!"

This spoken statement from his cousin summed up a situation that Water Boy hadn't planned on. They had left their Sauki town a half-day's travel to the south yesterday afternoon. They were in search of adventure and had decided to stay away from their home overnight, which would cause their mothers great concern, but would prove to their fathers that they were brave and able to take care of themselves. They were ready to become warriors!

The boys were anxious to prove that they were men worthy of helping to protect their women and children. They had set out on this adventure to prove that. But now, they were a long way from home with a band of enemies close at hand. Both boys felt the cold grasp of fear clutching in their stomachs.

With no further words, Water Boy and Crow Egg Sucker ran down the hill heading for the copse of trees they had camped in that night. When they entered the cover that the trees afforded them, they stopped and turned to look back up the hill to where the dead girl's body lay. There was no movement on the hill and they both stood, leaning against a tree to catch their breath. Small wisps of smoke could be seen rising from over the rise, which meant the *Nadowwessioux* village was coming awake and it wouldn't be long before the woman would be missed.

"Oh I wish we would have went to get our fathers last night when we saw the light from their fires," Crow Egg Sucker whispered in a hoarse, breathless voice. "I am tired from running already and I don't know if I can stay ahead of them if they chase us," he worried.

"We didn't know who they were last night," Water Boy answered. "They could have been a party of Fox hunters. Wouldn't we have looked silly if we brought our fathers out of town to attack our friends?"

"But what if they come after us?" Crow Egg Sucker whined. "I can not run as fast and as far as you can."

"How will they know which way to search for us?" Water Boy asked his frightened cousin. "We ran as light as foxes. The wind has straightened the grass where we stepped and they won't know if we went north or south." He held the longhaired scalp up in front of Crow Egg Sucker's face and shook it. "The sight of the dead woman will frighten them anyway. They will know when they find her dead body that the Sauk nation is aware that they are trespassing and they will turn to the west and run!"

"Are you sure Water Boy?" Crow Egg Sucker was near tears. He was only twelve years old and was small and weak for his age. Water

Boy had always thought that Crow Egg Sucker's mother had babied him too much because he was small. That was why he had talked his cousin into joining him on this adventure. But he could see that the frightened young boy would never be able to keep up with him, once he started on his journey to alert the men of their town about the *Nadowwessioux.* "Someone needs to watch our enemies so that we know which way they go after they find the girl," Water Boy reasoned. "Otherwise, they will get away back to the west with only this one girl's scalp being taken." He held out the scalp to Crow Egg Sucker. "Take this scalp and return to our fathers. Tell them what has happened here and bring them back. I will hide here and watch the *Nadowwessioux.* I will follow them and leave sign so our fathers will know which way they are traveling."

"But I can't run that far." Crow Egg Sucker shook his head in horror and refused to take the scalp. "I don't even know the way back to our town. What if I get lost and can't find it? What if it takes me two days to get back home? What if . . ."

"Then you stay here," Water Boy interrupted. "Hide behind one of these trees and watch to see what they do and which way they go."

"But I'm afraid to stay here alone."

"You are a man now." Water Boy slapped Crow Egg Sucker lightly across the face with the bloody scalp. "You helped kill this enemy! Be brave! Just hide and watch. I will run all the way back to our town and our fathers and the other warriors will run all the way back. We'll be back before the sun goes down. This is a great thing we have done! The people will sing our names around the fire at night! We will be given new names! We will be warriors!"

Crow Egg Sucker felt a bit braver just hearing Water Boy talk and before he could stop himself, he agreed to Water Boy's plan.

"I'll hide here and watch," he said in a quavering voice. "Just hurry back."

Water Boy didn't give him a chance to change his mind. Waving Horse Woman's scalp in a circle above his head, he took off running to the south as fast has his legs would carry him. Crow Egg Sucker stood watching him until the tall grass of the prairie hid him in the distance. He glanced up the hill and saw no movement, so he hunkered down behind the tree he was standing by. A half-hour later, he decided the tree wasn't big enough to hide him. He moved to another tree off to his right. But when he arrived at that tree, he found that it wasn't any bigger than his original tree. Noticing a bigger looking tree a few yards behind him, he walked back to it, but didn't like it either and decided to go back to his first tree. He thought of gathering some of the downed branches and laying them together and then hiding in them. A natural fear of retribution for the murder they had committed dominated his thoughts. He glanced up the hill and saw movement in the grass. Frightened, he began to cry and scurry back and forth between hiding places in a sudden panic. He knew he should get down out of sight and stay still, but after only a few moments in each hiding place, he was positive that he could be seen from up on the hill and he had to seek a better place to hide.

*   *   *

Wamdisapa left his tipi looking for Horse Woman. After the child's crying in the night again, he had decided to send her to the medicine man and have him try to coax a better supply of milk into her breasts. The medicine man would sing a milk-making song and rub her breasts with a paste made from mixing a mare's milk with cow buffalo bones ground into a fine powder. The man claimed that the songs and the paste had brought milk to every female he had used it on. Wamdisapa didn't believe in a lot of the powers the medicine man claimed to have, but he felt desperate. The people were gossiping about the crying baby, comparing him to the quiet Buffalo Calf Boy.

Upon stepping outside of his tipi, he forgot the medicine man and his incantations. There was something wrong in the camp, but he wasn't immediately sure what. There were other people out looking about the village, trying to figure out what was making the camp seem different?

The village seemed empty, much too quiet and void of activity. Wamdisapa was among the first to realize that it was the absence of most of the camp dogs that was making the village seem almost deserted. There were no dogs sitting under the meat drying racks waiting for a piece to drop in the wind. The packs of dogs that could usually be seen circumnavigating the camp searching for unprotected edibles were missing. There were no dogs snuffling around the cook fires or sitting by the tipis, hoping for a friendly handout. The only dogs in camp were the mothers with pups too young to leave.

The missing dogs drew Wamdisapa's attention away from the problem of his crying son. Camp dogs were important to the people. Many times dogs could sense the coming of bad weather. Often they picked up the scent of coming visitors. They kept the camp refuse cleaned up eating any little scrap that was dropped or thrown away. Sometimes the dogs found wounded or dying animals like buffalo with broken legs after stampeding through a prairie dog town. And on special occasions, or hard times, the dogs themselves could be feasted upon. For all of the dogs in the village to be gone at the same time, it had to mean something important.

Wamdisapa jogged to the top of the hill behind the village. He hoped to gain a vantage from which he could see in all directions. As he neared the top, he searched the surrounding area and thought he saw a slight movement in the trees way down by the river. He started down toward the river, following the crest of the ridge. Before going far, he heard the sounds of a dogfight. Growling, snarling and the snapping of teeth, the sounds of a pack of dogs jockeying for position over a kill, reached his ears.

Suddenly, he saw the pack and with a start, saw a smaller dog break loose from the teeming mass of fur and teeth, with a small piece of blood soaked clothing. With a cry of anger and anguish, Wamdisapa ran into the melee, swinging his war club viciously clearing the animals from the body he immediately recognized as that of his youngest wife. In a glance, he could read what had happened. He knew that the dogs hadn't killed her. It was obvious that her blood red baldpate shining in the early morning sunlight was a scalping and the smashed in remnant of her beautiful face was clearly caused by human hands.

Tears formed in Wamdisapa's eyes as he knelt by the girl's body. A sudden sense of real loss overcame him. This girl had been his favorite and in fact, she had been a favorite of everyone who knew her. He reached down and gently moved her arm, which one of the dogs had tugged back at an odd angle, to lie by her side. With shaking hands, he lifted her broken leg and examined it as though thinking about trying to pull it straight and set the bone. Tears streamed down his face and a silent sob shook his body. He heard a hail from the top of the rise and he stood and turned to see who had called. It was his friend, Sun At Night. Wamdisapa took two steps back toward his friend. The dogs had been standing at bay while he knelt by the body, sensed a change in his attention and dashed in for the body again. Wamdisapa spun back and with anger and grief coursing through his veins wielded his war club viciously, killing three of the animals before they could retreat.

He stood looking down at her broken and mauled body, and his emotions poured forth in a howl of anger and grief. Wamdisapa slashed his forearms and chest with his knife and began chanting a death song as he bent to lift her like a child. Cradling her tightly to his bleeding chest he carried her over the rise meeting Sun At Night and the two men walked side by side back down to the village. When they reached the village, word of Horse Woman's death spread quickly and Rain Dance Woman came running from the tipi screaming. She snatched the knife from Wamdisapa's belt and cut deeply to the bone around the first knuckle of her little finger on her left hand. Snapping the finger end over the knife blade, she threw the severed appendage in the fire pit and started to roughly chop her hair off with the same knife.

A wild keening commenced as Catches Birds Woman came running from Blue Nose's tipi. The woman dropped to her knees in front of Wamdisapa and began pulling out great fistfuls of her own hair! Many of the other women in the camp began crying and displaying their grief through self-mutilation as they wailed songs of grief and death. But none grieved so fervently as Rain Dance Woman. She had loved this young girl as if she had been her blood sister and felt guilt for the way she had treated Horse Woman that morning when Wamdisapa told her to nurse Horse Woman's Child.

With tears streaming down her face, she continued self-mutilation tearing chunks of her hair, leaving small bloody bald spots on her head and then slashed at her legs with the knife until blood flowed down her legs, soaking her moccasins.

Tasagi and his family didn't participate in the communal mourning for Horse Woman. They stood aside and watched. New Grass Woman refused to respect the dead woman with even a short death song. Instead, she drew Tasagi into their tipi and the two held a whispered conference.

"Tasagi, now it the time for you to take over as leader!" she hissed.

Her husband stood looking dully at her, his mind still on the mutilated body of his old friend's young wife.

"Wamdisapa can not think with his grief." She bent to lift Buffalo Calf Boy from his small bed and baring a breast, offered the child his breakfast. "I will feed this boy. While he eats, you must go about the village and speak to our friends. Tell them that we don't know who could have done this terrible thing to Wamdisapa's wife. Was it a lone warrior? Was it a small party of hunters, who may have sent for help from a nearby village and may soon return with a war party?"

Tasagi slowly shook his head in agreement. "It could have been *Ioway, Sauk, Fox, Winnebago*. We are in an unknown land with many enemies."

"We must leave," she whispered. "We should never have come here! It was a bad idea to travel here. Wamdisapa made a bad choice and now he has paid for it. Tell them!"

"I don't know if I should say that," Tasagi said. "It might make some people angry. Wamdisapa is a popular leader."

"All right," New Grass Woman hissed. "Don't say he made a mistake, but say that we are all in danger and we must go and go now! Tell them!"

120

She switched Buffalo Calf Boy to her other breast and began pushing Tasagi toward the tipi door. "Go. Go now. Tell them." As he ducked through the tipi door she added, "I will pack our things and we will leave. They will follow."

Tasagi walked quickly away from the tipi and starting with his relatives, began passing the word that he thought they were in great danger and should move the camp back to the west as soon as possible. He planted the seed of fear of a large war party catching them and soon, even those prostrate with their grief, stopped physically mourning and began packing their belongings.

Wamdisapa noticed that the group of people who had come to mourn with them had grown considerably smaller. Old Grandmother held Horse Woman's Child, who was frightened by all of the commotion and was crying. Pinched Cheeks too was frightened, and stood behind the old woman, burying his face in the fold of the trade blanket that she wore around her waist. Sun At Night and his family stood sadly by, his crying women had hacked their hair short and he had sliced through each ear lobe and stood with blood dripping from his pointed shoulders.

There were only a few people left, the rest were all packing their belongings and taking down their tipis. This disappointed Wamdisapa. He knew that they were dealing with an unknown enemy and that they needed to move the camp, so this enemy wouldn't know exactly where they were if they returned in force. He had already been thinking of where to go to set up camp that would be a better place to defend.

They had grieved long enough and loud enough to feel certain that Horse Woman's spirit had seen and heard. Her spirit would know that she had been loved. They would take her body with them and when they found a place of safety, Rain Dance Woman would dress her in her finest beaded clothing. They would suspend her body on a scaffold of poles or in the high branches of a tree high above the heavy earth. All of her worldly possessions, including her small bag of her ancestor's dust, some dried meat and fish, a boning knife and a hide scraper would be placed with her to help her on her journey in the spirit world. He knelt and spoke gently to Rain Dance Woman.

"You now are the mother to both of my sons. I'm counting on you to care for them both and raise them to be fine strong warriors. It is time to stop grieving and worry about keeping them safe. We must pack and move the camp."

Wamdisapa loaded Horse Woman's body onto a travois and helped Rain Dance Woman take down the tipi. Old Grandfather caught three of the big dogs and tied short travois poles to their backs for the light bundles. Horses would pull the tipi and the heavy articles. Rain Dance Woman strapped Pinched Cheeks and Horse Woman's Child into a buffalo hide bed on one of the travois. Both fussed and cried, but she knew that the motion from the horse's pace would soon rock them to sleep.

When all was ready, Wamdisapa turned to see that Tasagi and his family were leading and had headed up the rise. Wamdisapa shook his head in disgust. Tasagi had effectively thrown the entire village into a panic. He had the people following him up the rise until they reached the top and then angled toward the north, away from the scene of Horse Woman's death.

The rest of the village was packing and leaving in a rush to catch up. No one wanted to be left alone on this dangerous ground. It was far from an orderly exodus. The people were strung out for more than a mile along the very top of the ridge. Their silhouettes stuck out against the sky and anyone watching would know exactly which direction they were traveling. A smart leader would never expose his people by traveling on the top of a rise in the land. It was better to travel on the side hill, only sending a scout to the top occasionally to look for signs of an enemy.

Wamdisapa and his family were the last to leave the camp. Old Grandfather was leading the horse pulling Horse Woman's body. Old Grandmother led the horse pulling the tipi and Rain Dance Woman led the horse pulling their supplies and the children.

The dogs followed along, tethered by short ropes to the horses' tails. He pushed them to catch up with the caravan. When they neared the top of the rise, he turned them north to follow the rest. When they had traveled far enough for the curve of the hill to block the view of the trees by the river, where he had seen movement that morning while looking for the dogs, he told Rain Dance Woman to keep moving swiftly until they caught up with the rest of the people.

"I will catch up with you." He said and dropped over the side of the hill and circled back to where he could again see the trees by the river, just down the hill from where Horse Woman had been killed. Concealing himself in the tall grass, he crawled to the top of the rise and lay watching the copse of trees. He waited patiently and soon, he was rewarded by the sight of a human form emerging from the trees and heading up the hill toward him.

*   *   *

They came from the south and east, a powerful crew of men moving at a steady dogtrot that ate up the miles quickly. Their heads were shaved, leaving only a coxcomb or topknot or a roached mane, depending upon the wearer's preference. Whatever the style, the hair was heavily greased and colored with vermilion, yellow clay dye or blueweed, making it stand straight and tall. Gaudy feathers and shells decorated their colored hair, and bones and larger shells hung from their ears and protruded through holes in their noses. They were painted for war. Black and red paints made from roots and weeds and charcoal mixed with greasy fat covered their upper torsos. Perfect handprints of white clay decorated their backsides from shoulders to bare rumps. They were completely naked except for a narrow leather strap suspended from a thong tied around their waists, reaching between their legs and back up to the thong in the back, to protect their penis and testicles.

They were the "People of the Yellow Earth," the Sauk and the "People of the Red Earth," the Fox. Once two separate tribes with similar languages, they had made their homes in the upper Great Lakes region along the southern shores of Lake Huron. Through decades of warfare with the *Chippewa, Ottawa, Neutrals, Menominee and Potawatomie*, during the 18th century, both tribes were forced to migrate south and west across or around Lake Michigan and they settled in Wisconsin, spreading throughout the area into northern Illinois and eastern Minnesota, where they united into one tribe. Since their migration, their domain had been on the east side of the Mississippi River.

But over the past few years, new white skinned enemies called Americans had come from the east. They had fought the whites bitterly, but had finally realized the futility of continuing to war against the powerful Americans. Last year their leaders, including Keokuk, the Fox band leader, had signed a treaty ceding all Sauk and Fox lands in the *Illinois* country to the Americans and promising to move their towns to the *Ioway* side of the big river. It was believed that their enemies on this side of the river, the *Ioways, Winnebago, Omaha and Nadowwessioux* were less of a threat to their well being than the Americans.

Their towns of permanent houses, built of hewn planks neatly jointed and covered with bark were set in orderly streets. As they were a polygamous people, (a man might have as many as eight wives) each house was large enough for several families to live in comfortably. They were not nomads as was the culture of the tribes in this western land. They preferred to live in one place, venturing away only to hunt or to make war. They were a proud and fierce and sometimes a cruel natured people, a nature developed over centuries of warfare and hardship.

It was a war party of these men who now trotted swiftly across the grassy hillsides to the small river where Water Boy had left Crow Egg Sucker hiding in the trees eight hours before. They crossed the river holding their bows high to keep from getting the strings made of deer sinew from getting wet. Some men carried stone headed war clubs, some flint pointed spears. Nearly half of the men in the party were armed with rifles. The firearms had been obtained by trading with the English, who were anxious to help arm them against the Americans.

Water Boy guided the men to the spot where he had left Crow Egg Sucker that morning. Sees With The Eye Of A Hawk, their best tracker studied the area and pointed out several places where the boy had sat. Crow Egg Sucker had left a stick tied in the lower branches of a mulberry tree, pointing in the direction he had taken when he left the trees.

"It points up the ridge in the direction of where I killed the girl," Water Boy stated proudly.

Looking up the hill, they could see several buzzards circling and could hear the raucous cries of crows and other carrion birds. Undoubtedly, the cowardly *Nadowwessioux* in their hurry to escape had run off and left the body of the dead woman behind. Excitedly, the group of forty-three men and one boy left the grove of trees and started jogging up the hill. They were anxious to see if Water Boy had performed all of the handiwork of torturing the girl he had bragged to them about. His father was proud and ran faster, pushing ahead of the group. Not to be outdone, the other men picked up their pace and they raced up the hill.

The men ran past the bloodied grass where, the lagging behind Water Boy stopped, and over the crest of the hill where they came to a stumbling, ungraceful stop too.

Staring at them through empty eye sockets was the formless face of the child, Crow Egg Sucker. His head was stuck on a stake that had been driven into the ground just over the top of the rise from their line of sight at the bottom of the hill. His almost baby-like topknot had been ripped from his head and his ears and nose were gone. His headless body lay directly behind the stake. The arms and legs had been staked to the ground with rawhide thongs, the feet blackened by flames that had burned out in the small fire pit dug beneath them. Both hands were missing. Signs of his struggling against his bonds indicated that the burning of his feet and severing of his hands had happened while the boy was still alive. Deep cuts reaching down each leg from the hips to his knees flaying the flesh of his upper thighs to the bone was proof that the man who had performed this mutilation was indeed a *Nadowwessioux*.

Somberly the men began gathering up the pieces of the child and placing them on a blanket for transport home. They searched the grass finding fingers, joint-by-joint, scattered throughout the scene. Blood and gray matter had oozed from the head and congealed at the base of the stake. When Water Boy's father tried to gently remove the head from the stake, he had to pull hard and when it finally popped off, the mouth fell open and the boy's small penis and testicles dropped out on the ground.

Howls of anger and vows of revenge were shouted at the sky at the sight of this greatest of insults. When every part of the child that could be found was placed on the blanket, all of the men but Crow Egg Sucker's father and two of his uncles who would take the body home, fanned out, looking for sign of which direction the *Nadowwessioux* had taken. All the signs they found, including more pieces of fingers, indicated that the killer had headed due west. With Sees With The Eyes Of A Hawk leading, they stopped searching for sign and started a tireless dog trot toward the setting sun, confident of catching the murdering *Nadowwessioux* before it dropped below the far horizon.

\* \* \*

Wamdisapa had left a false trail to the west before turning north. He hoped the fast traveling Sauk and Fox warriors would be confused long enough to give his slow moving people time to hide their trail and escape. When he caught up with the people from his village, he took over leadership from Tasagi without argument. The blood covering his entire body was explanation enough as to why they had to move faster and smarter.

They traveled on the side hills where their silhouettes could not be seen from afar. They changed directions often with no pattern, sometimes doubling back, just after crossing a river and sometimes-redoubling back to go in the first direction again. Sun At Night lagged behind, watching their back trail for the Sauk and Fox warriors. They traveled into the darkness each night, stopping only to sleep and started in darkness each morning.

After two hard days, Wamdisapa called a halt in a hidden treeless valley. He told Rain Dance Woman to set up the tipi and passed the word that no fires were to be started. He sent scouts, led by Sun At Night to watch their back trail and instructed the women and children to rest.

Wamdisapa had regained the people's respect by avenging his wife's death and he had regained their confidence by turning Tasagi's panic led run-a-way into an orderly retreat. The people all felt that if the Sauk and Fox caught up with them, Wamdisapa would be ready for them and their fear began to leave. But Wamdisapa felt no joy at regaining the people's respect. He was still angry over the loss of his young girl wife and did not feel in his heart that she had yet been avenged.

In the days following the death of Horse Woman With Spots, Wamdisapa led his people in a desperate flight to escape the party of vengeful Sauk warriors. But the presence of the women and many small children, along with the large accumulation of their possessions that were too dear for them to leave behind, made it impossible for the Wahpekute people to outrun the determined force following them. Wamdisapa had known this from the beginning, but was determined to pick the ground where his people would stand and fight.

On the day it became evident that the Sauk war party would catch them, Wamdisapa encamped in the middle of a wide, flat plain rising slightly above the surrounding prairie.

The women, though exhausted from their headlong flight, set up the tipis and dug deep fire pits. The young men, who were itching to do battle, spent the rest of the day and evening in preparation for battle. They sang war songs and chanted prayers and boasted. Paint, black and red mixed to a thick paste, and yellow and white mixed a little thinner, colored their hair, faces and bodies in contrasting colors befitting each warrior's need to gain favor with his medicine god. Each man painted himself or asked for help from another warrior. Women were banned from participating in the preparation for war, for it was well known that a woman's touch could draw the strength from a man. There was also no food cooked in the village that night. It was proper to fast before doing battle.

The women gathered what wood and dried buffalo dung they could find before darkness made it unsafe to wander from the immediate village site and large fires were built in the center of the camp. The women and children formed a spectators' gallery outside the ring of fires and watched the warriors dance a dance of war in the openings between the fires. Each man declared his fearlessness of death through action and song, acting out his bravery and skill in battle to the beat of a hide covered drum and the chants and songs of the women. Late into the night the men jumped and gyrated, screamed and shrieked, and boasted and prayed for tomorrow would be a good day to die!

Soon after the sunrise the next morning, the Sauk warriors crawled in close to the Wahpekute village to size up their enemy. They were surprised to learn that the Wahpekute, with sixty-five warriors, actually outnumbered them. Wamdisapa's tactical retreat had successfully hidden the size of his village. When Sun At Night's guards spotted the sneaking enemies and raised the alarm, the courage of the Wahpekute warriors was raised tenfold to find their superiority in number. Some of the young men wanted to attack immediately. But Wamdisapa advised caution. He led fifty men at a slow walk toward the enemy force. Fifteen men stayed with the women and children and old men to protect them if another force of Sauk or their allies, the Fox showed up unexpectedly.

The Sauk warriors pulled back upon seeing Wamdisapa's warriors walking bravely at them. They bunched and began milling about, not sure what to do in the face of a superior force. The Wahpekute warriors were angry about running from these people for days and were anxious to recover some of their pride by defeating them soundly in battle. Wamdisapa could hardly contain his young men from rushing madly at the enemy. When his force had advanced to a point about fifty yards from the milling Sauk warriors, Wamdisapa unleashed an arrow and watched it fall short of the crowd of men by a few feet.

This brought a chorus of jeers and insults from the Sauks. Shouting, they drew aside their clouts and shook their privates at Wamdisapa and then turned around, bent over and showed him their bare rumps.

With a howl of anger, the younger Wahpekute warriors charged screaming at their enemies intending to meet the Sauks in terrible hand-to-hand combat! But the thunderous explosion of the Sauks' rifles stopped the charge before they had advanced half the distance between them. The Sauk shooters were not accomplished marksmen and none of the Wahpekute warriors were hit, but the barrage of near misses threw them into a panicked retreat. The sound of the gunfire reminded Wamdisapa of his own weapon lying useless without the lead balls, back in his wife's tipi.

He thought of how poor dead Horse Woman had helped him obtain the weapon and an uncontrollable anger surged through his body. He charged without fear, screaming an unintelligible war cry that caught both his enemies and friends by surprise. His anger driven legs covered the ground between them with incredible speed. Only two of the Sauks had reloaded their rifles, but the speed of his attack shocked them and both fired their weapons without taking aim. One shot hit the ground yards in front of the charging Wamdisapa, the other ball flew harmlessly over his head!

After the two shots were fired with no apparent harm coming to the rushing Wamdisapa, the rest of the Wahpekute warriors followed his charge, adding their war cries to his voice, raising a general din on the open prairie. The deafening noise of their screams and the swift, fearless charge by the *Nadowwessioux* leader into the face of their riflemen stunned the Sauks and they stood their ground for only a moment.

When the mass of painted, screaming warriors joined in charging at them, they turned and ran for their lives, leaving the battlefield without landing a single blow to avenge the death of little Crow Egg Sucker. But they would not forget this band of *Nadowwessioux*. Another time, when they were closer to home, less tired, and more evenly matched, they would face this enemy again. A day of retribution would come.

The battle was typical of many of the confrontations between two plains tribes before the introduction and proficiency in the use of firearms to their cultures. It had ended with no one on either side being injured or killed and though it had taken days in the build up, it had lasted only minutes. But in the minds of the Wahpekute, they had won a decisive battle. Their leader Wamdisapa had shown incredible bravery in the face of great danger and because of his bravery, they had chased their enemy from the field. That night, many of the camp dogs were killed and spitted over the cook fires. They feasted and danced and sang songs of victory extolling their great war leader Wamdisapa!

The next morning, Wamdisapa and Rain Dance Woman using tipi poles given to them by several of their friends, erected a scaffold at the top of the rise. The long grass waved in the wind, as they rolled the rank, decomposing body of Horse Woman With Spots in a warm sleeping robe and lifted her high onto the bed of the platform out of reach of the wolves that would be attracted to her ripening corpse. Clay pots, a knife, a bone needle, sinew, and a flesh scraper and the bag of her ancestors' dust were placed with her. These are the things she would need for her journey into the next life.

With a heavy heart and anger still seething in his soul, Wamdisapa, vowing vengeance in the future, led his people off, wending a path between the tall-grass marshes of east-central Iowa.

So began the blood feud between the *Wahpekute* of the *Santee Dakotah* tribes of southern Minnesota and northwestern Iowa and the Sauk and Fox nations that inhabited the eastern part of the state. It was a warfare between two peoples that would last for more than thirty years.

## Chapter 14
*Red End (1817)*

In the years following the death of Horse Woman, Wamdisapa's anger grew into a hatred for the Sauk that he could not control. He vowed vengeance against the entire Sauk and Fox nations and led his people on a nomadic path that kept them on the fringe of their enemy's lands. Leading war parties on forays deep in Sauk and Fox hunting grounds, he found many opportunities to slake his thirst for revenge.

As the months of battling turned into years of warfare, and season after season passed with unrelenting fighting, the life style of the *Wahpekute* people changed.

They no longer traveled to the west to hunt buffalo in the warm months preparing for the cold time. Instead, they stayed close to their enemies, hunting deer and elk and stealing from Sauk hunting parties after defeating them in battle.

In the winter months they traveled back to their traditional lands where they borrowed on the generosity of other *Santee* tribes. But as soon as the weather turned warm again, Wamdisapa led his band off to the southeast to battle the hated Sauk and Fox. Battle after battle, the war grew more heated and more violent. Gone were the days of posturing and slinging insults to prove bravery. Young men on both sides were careless in their desire to prove their courage and were wounded or killed. Oddly, with each death, the ranks of warriors swelled, for relatives and friends of the dead flocked to Wamdisapa's side, hoping for a chance for vengeance.

Wamdisapa's search for ball and powder was solved when his men overran a Sauk village, where five of the dead Sauk warriors were found to have rifles. He distributed the weapons to Sun At Night and four of his best warriors. From that point on, Wamdisapa's fighters became even more deadly. He lost his desire to deal with the day-to-day problems in the village and gave up his role as village Headman, choosing to be the War Leader instead. Tasagi, who somehow could not break away from Wamdisapa's influence and go off on his own, took up leading the women, children and old people while Wamdisapa was on the warpath and an uneasy truce between the two men was forged. Many of the people were relatives of the men fighting at Wamdisapa's side and they would only follow Tasagi as long as he led them to campsites on the fringes of the Sauk and Fox lands so they would be near to welcome their warriors home or mourn for them if they were lost.

The Sauk hunters ranged far from their villages, traveling up the rivers feeding into the Mississippi River. It seemed that the farther north and west they traveled the more game they found. The flesh of buffalo, deer and elk that they harvested, was cut up, wrapped in hides and loaded into canoes and floated back down the Iowa, Cedar and Wapsipinicon Rivers to their homes on the banks of the big river. These canoes, loaded with precious meat, became a favorite target for Wamdisapa and his men. It was along the banks and the lands in between these Iowa rivers that became the battlefields.

Wamdisapa chose when, where and how often his people would fight. He was a man of fierce conviction and a never-ending hatred, which grew with each year's passing. Because of Tasagi's reluctance to have the village near to danger, the fighting men found themselves on long journeys to fight and often went weeks without seeing their loved ones. As could be expected, many men grew tired of constant warring and chose to stay in the village and live the good life, watching their babies grow.

But Wamdisapa was a superior orator who had changed from a man simply seeking revenge into a man who loved war. He loved to fight. He craved the excitement, the danger and the blood. He loved to kill. With a blood lust equaled by few, his speeches about honor, revenge and glory always convinced more than enough warriors to go with him into battle each time he wanted to go.

And when his warriors returned in glory, waving the bloody topknots and roached manes of slain Sauk warriors, the men who had stayed behind could only watch the returned warriors sing and dance in celebration. They could only listen to the tales of glory and the praises heaped upon the fighters by their War chief and they felt shame and were sorry that they hadn't joined him.

When Wamdisapa next asked for volunteers to go on the warpath with him, many of these men remembered their shame and were the first to join his party.

Wamdisapa's preoccupation with war left Rain Dance Woman to raise his two sons almost all by herself. Wamdisapa helped only with the important things, like naming them and when they were old enough, he taught them to hunt and to fight. He named Horse Woman's child, Fallen Oak Leaf Boy, because the boy's hair was the deep, red-brown color that oak leaves turn when they first fall from the trees in *The Moon of the Falling Leaves*. He named Rain Dance Woman's son, Runs Fast Boy. Runs Fast Boy was tall and slender and moved with a grace and agility that could hardly be matched by his little brother.

Because of Rain Dance Woman's excellent mothering, sickness was unknown to either of the boys. In their first years, they breakfasted together on Rain Dance Woman's sweet breast milk and at other meals, feasted on foods she prepared and chewed to mush before feeding it to them to help them digest it. They played together in the day, and slept in the same robes cuddling the same mother at night. Because their father was off fighting the Sauk so often, the two brothers came to rely on one another, as they grew older and became all but inseparable. As the days and weeks and years passed, the bond between the two young boys and the woman who had in one way or another given each of them life, grew stronger and stronger.

When Runs Fast Boy was old enough, Rain Dance Woman allowed him to roam the village by himself. As soon as chubby Fallen Oak Leaf Boy was able to toddle after him, he followed.

As they roamed the village, the boys experienced a mixed reception from different segments of their society. The families of men who were on the warpath with their father, always treated both boys very well, often to the point of a young mother nursing the small red haired child if he indicated he was hungry while playing near her tipi. But the opposite treatment could be expected by the families of those who chose not to go to war, especially by anyone related to Tasagi.

The boys, born with the trust of the young, thought they would be treated well by all adults in the large village. But one day their travels took them close to the tipi of Tasagi. Buffalo Calf Boy was sitting outside the tipi, building miniature tipis with small sticks and scraps of deerskin. Buffalo Calf Boy had grown into a large child. Rolls of baby fat surrounded his middle and down his arms. His fingers were short and stubby. His legs were thin and quite long and looked too slender to support his body. Loose black curls spiraled off the top of his head hanging in his eyes and covering his ears, dangling nearly to his shoulders. His unkempt bushy hair, made his already large head look even bigger. Runs Fast Boy and Fallen Oak Leaf Boy stood across the fire pit from the large dark child and began chattering at him.

"What are you doing Buffalo Calf Boy," Runs Fast Boy asked, "playing with stick dolls?"

Buffalo Calf Boy didn't answer. He looked over his shoulder to see if his mother was near.

"Come and play with us instead of your stick dolls," Fallen Oak Leaf Boy said, adding, "or won't your mommy let you?"

Buffalo Calf Boy's eyes grew big, the whites of his eyes surrounding the small dark iris and pupils. He looked over his shoulder once again, then shook his head quickly.

"What's the matter?" Runs Fast Boy cried. "Are you too little?" And he laughed.

"Yeah, you're just as old as me," Fallen Oak Leaf Boy chimed in chuckling. "But maybe you're still just a little momma's baby. Maybe we should call you Buffalo Calf Baby!" Both boys convulsed with laughter as Buffalo Calf Boy, who was not used to interacting with other children, began crying.

Upon hearing the boys voices and Buffalo Calf Boy's crying, New Grass Woman emerged from the tipi with a buffalo tail whip. She chased after the two small boys, switching them across their bare legs as they ran. Fallen Oak Leaf Boy could not run as fast as his brother and caught the worst of the whipping.

This type of punishment was almost unheard of by the *Dakotah* People. Very seldom were children ever disciplined by words, let alone violence. Rain Dance Woman was irate with anger and marched to Tasagi's tipi demanding an explanation. New Grass Woman refused to come out of her tipi and face her sister. Instead, Tasagi was sent out to deal with Rain Dance Woman. He told her that New Grass Woman had come out of the tipi to find her sons beating Buffalo Calf Boy with sticks.

"Your boys are mean," Tasagi added. "They are undisciplined and need to show respect to their elders." He waggled his finger at Rain Dance Woman. "Keep your children away from this tipi and my son." Then he stepped close to Rain Dance Woman and muttered, "I can't guarantee the red haired one's safety if my wife catches him alone again. You know how she felt about his mother. She feels the same way about the kid." With this warning, he turned and walked back inside his tipi.

Rain Dance Woman took the boys home and spent many hours retelling to them the story of Fallen Oak Leaf Boy's mother and why New Grass Woman didn't like them. She warned them to watch out for the big woman, but did not tell them that they had to stay home. The sons of the mighty War Chief Wamdisapa would not cower in fear from anyone. Instead of keeping them home, she reminded them of New Grass Woman's hatred of them each day when they left. Runs Fast Boy and Fallen Oak Leaf Boy would not forget this treatment by

Tasagi and his wife. Their resentment of the village Headman and his wife grew each time their mother repeated the warning.

They were careful to keep their distance from Tasagi and New Grass Woman, but as the years passed and Buffalo Calf Boy started to wander the village with the other boys his age, the two never missed a chance to isolate him and abuse him harshly. Whenever they found him alone, away from his parents' protection, they picked at him, pulling his curly hair and pinching his ears. They tripped him and then kicked at his privates when he lay sprawled on the ground. They pelted him with dirt clods, and stones. Buffalo Calf Boy never showed any resistance. He passively fell to the ground crying, trying to protect his privates and face with his hands, or ran away in terror.

Soon, picking on the defenseless boy became a source of amusement for the two brothers. As they grew older, they became a team of bullies, always wrestling and fighting any boys in the village within two years either way of their ages. It wasn't long before they had established the village pecking order. Runs Fast Boy was the leader. Fallen Oak Leaf Boy was his first Lieutenant and a band of other youngsters, who wished to be on the side of the two mean brothers instead of one of their victims, followed their lead.

The mob ambled through the village boldly going anywhere except in the immediate area of Tasagi's tipi. Following their leaders' example, the gang had taken to terrorizing Buffalo Calf Boy at every chance they got. Soon Buffalo Calf Boy became a frightened boy who refused to leave his mother's side.

When Tasagi became aware of how the adolescent mob led by Wamdisapa's sons were treating Buffalo Calf Boy, he sought out Rain Dance Woman and ordered her to keep her children home and away from his son. When she asked the boys about their treatment of the dark skinned boy with the curly hair, they answered her truthfully, laughing delightedly as they described his facial expressions and clumsy attempts to escape their torment. They laughed even harder when she told them that Tasagi had come to ask her to keep them away from his son. When her boys laughed like this, she could never stay angry with them. Instead of punishing them, she merely entreated them to be careful and avoid making Tasagi angry enough to retaliate.

But Runs Fast Boy and Fallen Oak Leaf Boy were the War Chief's sons, and they felt in their hearts that their father was the true leader of the *Wahpekute* people. It was because of his leadership against the Sauk and Fox that the tribe had grown to almost triple the size it was when Fallen Oak Leaf Boy was born. All of the *Wahpekute* tribes had heard of the war with the Sauk and Fox nations and the men in the other villages who were eager to fight had moved their families to follow Wamdisapa, not that old *woman* Tasagi! The men who didn't want to join in the war had found their families living in small, isolated villages without enough men to protect themselves against even the Winnebago and before long, the peace lovers too, had come to live in Wamdisapa's village. With this attitude, the boys were bound for more trouble with Tasagi.

When Wamdisapa led a strong force of warriors out of the village one morning late in the summer, Runs Fast Boy was disappointed at his father's decision to leave him home again. He had lived for fifteen summers and felt it was time that his father recognized that he was a man and allow him to go with him to fight the Sauk. Chuckling with pride, Wamdisapa had shook his head "no," patted him on the shoulder and told him to wait two more summers. Then he could go on the warpath with him. Besides, Wamdisapa told him that the village was set up in an area unusually close to the Sauk hunting grounds, and he needed him and his brother to help protect the village in case an enemy war party should show up.

"How do you think I can leave your beautiful mother here, virtually unprotected? I can't count on Tasagi and his bunch of peace lovers to protect the women and children all by themselves, can I?" Wamdisapa asked and winked a conspiratorial wink at his sons. "But I know I can count on you two," he finished and led his warriors off to the southeast at a fast trot.

Tasagi was nervous about having the village set up in an area too close to the combat zone. As soon as Wamdisapa and his warriors left the village that morning, Tasagi ordered New Grass Woman to dismantle the tipi and pack their things. They would move the village to a safer location, many miles to the north and west. Wamdisapa and his warriors could come and find them when they returned.

When the word of Tasagi's plan to move the village reached Runs Fast Boy and Fallen Oak Leaf Boy, they were immediately angry. They complained bitterly to their mother.

"It is not right to move the village far away from our warriors when they go to battle our enemies," Runs Fast Boy stated. "What if they return with wounded men and need their women to tend their wounds?"

"What if father sends for reinforcements?" Fallen Oak Leaf Boy asked. "Tasagi never told him we were moving the village. Father told us he expected us to help protect the women and children. He expects us to be here when he returns," he said firmly.

Rain Dance Woman tried to calm her two angry sons by telling them that Tasagi had pulled this trick many times in the past.

"Right now, your father's mind is on war. When his mind turns to peace, he will come and find us no matter how far Tasagi leads us to hide."

But the boys didn't agree with her calm acceptance of Tasagi's betrayal. They ran from the tipi with angry cries. Several of their friends joined them as they raced through the village to Tasagi's tipi site. When they approached, the Headman was sitting on a boulder smoking his pipe. New Grass Woman and Buffalo Calf Boy had taken the tipi down and were in the process of packing their belongings. He stood and knocked his pipe out on the boulder, placing it in a leather bag that hung from his waist. He folded his arms in front of himself and spoke to the boys.

"What do you boys want? You should be helping your mothers pack your belongings."

Ignoring Tasagi, Runs Fast Boy and Fallen Oak Leaf Boy started shouting insults at Buffalo Calf Boy.

"Buffalo Calf Boy come and go hunting with us," Runs Fast Boy called. "What's that?" he held his hand to his ear as if listening to a response. "Oh, you can't go hunting. Is that because you have to help your mommy?"

New Grass Woman stopped what she was doing and turned to glare at them, but it didn't faze them.

"Buffalo Calf Boy, why are you working like a woman?" Runs Fast Boy asked.

"Go on you!" Tasagi shouted. "Get away! Go home and help your mothers," he ordered.

"He works like a woman," Fallen Oak Leaf Boy said, ignoring Tasagi, "because he has no man parts." He untied his clout string and dropped it, exposing his privates to Tasagi's entire family.

"Go!" Tasagi roared running at them.

The boys retreated, but stopped when Tasagi did.

"You boys go help your mothers pack now!" he ordered waggling his finger at them.

"You are a coward Tasagi," Runs Fast Boy stated. "We're going to leave, but only because you have no balls either. Just like your son." He tilted his chin up haughtily as Tasagi walked toward him. Deciding that he wouldn't back down, he added, "Your fat old woman with the milkless tits is more of a man than you are!"

A hush fell over the group of people that had gathered, drawn by the commotion. Tasagi was the village Headman and it was a grave insult this boy had spouted. Except for Fallen Oak Leaf Boy, Runs Fast Boy's cohorts all drew back as Tasagi walked up to stand toe to toe with him. Though healthy and strong for a boy of fifteen, Runs

Fast Boy was still no match for the man Tasagi. Tasagi flashed out his right hand striking Runs Fast Boy with the handle of his war club. The blow caught the boy across the forehead, dropping him to the ground. If it had been the stone end of his war club, the boy's brains would have stained the grass beneath him. As it was, Runs Fast Boy was just dazed for a moment and a small knot began to protrude from his forehead.

Tasagi looked down at the boy and appeared as if he were about to kick him, but thought better of it. He doubted if Wamdisapa would say much about him hitting the child after such an insult, but he didn't want to risk the War Chief's wrath by overdoing the punishment. He turned to walk away, ordering the boys to disperse and go home to help their families pack. But he had walked only a few steps when a clod of buffalo dung hit him in the back of the neck, raining a stinking whitish powder over his sweating body. He spun to see who had thrown it and another clod splattered against his chest. It was the younger brother, the one with the white blood, who was throwing the missiles.

Runs Fast Boy shook his head to clear it and scrambled to his feet. His legs were wobbly, but he found a stone and flung it at Tasagi. Bolstered by the courage of their leaders, several of the gang members picked up stones and dung and began throwing it at Tasagi. Tasagi started to run after them, but stopped. His shoulders sagged in defeat. He recognized that he would have to kill the two ring leaders to get them to stop throwing things at him and he knew that no matter how much he would have liked to kill these two trouble makers, the crowd of people who had gathered to watch would not tolerate him killing them.

"You will stay here!" Tasagi shouted in anger. His voice was quivering with rage and a fine spray of spittle flew from his mouth as he continued, "I will lead you no longer. You and your families are banned from my village."

At the sound of these harsh words, the boys stopped throwing stones and dung at Tasagi and looked at one another in confusion. As the village headman turned and stomped away, the crowd left to return to their own tipis leaving the gang of boys standing on the small knoll above Tasagi's campsite. They all looked to Runs Fast Boy as if to ask, "What now?"

"Your fathers are all on the warpath with my father," Runs Fast Boys stated calmly. "Go home and try to talk your mothers into staying here to wait for our fathers to return."

"But my mother is Tasagi's cousin," the smallest of their company, a boy of only ten summers said. "My mother is frightened in this land. I don't think she will wait for our fathers to return." His voice cracked and he began to cry. "I hope Tasagi will still let us travel with him."

Runs Fast Boy was a natural leader. He recognized the fact that if he pushed his agenda too strongly that he risked alienating some of is followers. "Just ask her to stay. If she refuses, help her pack." He placed his hand on the sniffling boy's shoulder. "I'm sure Tasagi will accept your mother. I'm sure it is only I and Fallen Oak Leaf Boy who are banned from his village." Then with pride rising in his voice he added, "We will wait here for our father to return, then we will see who is banned!"

Word of the confrontation and Tasagi's banning Wamdisapa's sons from his village spread quickly. Rain Dance Woman heard the news even before her two sons came ambling back to her tipi. She sat them both down inside the tipi and lectured them for acting so harshly toward the village headman. Both boys sat quietly taking their scolding with seemingly stoic resignation. Their eyes were lowered, but she could see their lips were turned up in small, half smiles of satisfaction. She knew that in their minds, they had taken a lot from Tasagi and his wife and were both glad to be rid of him, but being banned here in this hostile land was serious and she ended her admonishment with a question.

"What have you got to say for yourselves?"

"I know that throwing buffalo shit at the village headman is very disrespectful, Mother," Fallen Oak Leaf Boy stated gravely. "But," his voice changed from a serious tone to a giggle as he finished, "you should have seen the look on Tasagi's face when that clod of shit exploded all over his chest!" And both boys began giggling and rolling on the tipi floor, locked in a hysterical joviality that they hadn't displayed since they were young children. Before long, Rain Dance Woman joined in their laughing fit and soon all three were rolling on the floor, hugging one another, seemingly without a care in the world.

More than half of the village's tipis came down that afternoon and the majority of the people followed Tasagi's lead to the northwest. Most of those who stayed were families of the warriors who had followed Wamdisapa, leaving a village of woman and children and elderly people, protected by only young boys and old men.

\* \* \*

The men in the Sauk hunting party were elated. They had been hunting for many days, ranging far from the river in search of buffalo or elk. Their scouts crawled to the top of each rise and scanned the rolling grasslands hoping to sight a herd to hunt. After days of frustration at not finding their quarry, a man named Clam Shell Finder returned reporting that he had spied a mass of people moving carelessly along the top of the rises, where their silhouettes were easy to see. More scouts were sent out and immediately recognized the moving people as a large village of *Nadowwessioux*! The Sauk, realizing quickly that their party of forty warriors was not large enough to attack such a large band, they began back trailing, hoping to find stragglers that would be isolated and easy prey. Late in the day, they came upon a much smaller *Nadowwessioux* village and watched it until darkness fell. It appeared as if there were very few grown men in the village. It was a rich village with fine tipi hides, drying racks full of meat, scraped hides and many young women. The band of hunters retreated a few miles away and waited through the night with no fires.

In the predawn darkness, before the sun had peeked over the edge of the earth, the party of Sauk warriors tread softly over the damp morning grass to gain their positions for the attack. When the first streaks of light fell among the tipi tops, the men began a silent approach, hoping to get in close before the camp dogs winded them and warned the residents. They were attacking from the east, so that the rising sun would blind the *Nadowwessioux* when they tried to face their attackers. As the Sauk reached the first tipis, a sudden yipping and growling followed by a loud yelp of pain and a chorus of howling from the dogs raised the alarm and the Sauk warriors screamed their bloodcurdling war cries as they dashed madly into the unprotected *Dakotah* village.

Sun At Night's tipi was always set up on the extreme east end of the camp so that the white sun that was painted on the black background on the door of his tipi was the first to catch the sun each morning. The first to fall was the wife and three small daughters of Wamdisapa's captain. The pretty young woman and her babies were bludgeoned to death as they scrambled to rise from their sleeping robes. Many small children and their mothers died or were captured before any defense was mustered. Pandemonium broke out as the terrified screams of the *Wahpekute* women and children added to the din of the shouting attackers and barking dogs! Many mothers died, while trying to protect their children and the children died while crying in fear at the sight of their mother's being clubbed. Some people upon being awakened by the commotion, immediately escaped, running out onto the prairie, where they hid in the tall grass aided by the semi-darkness of dawn and survived the initial Sauk onslaught.

The small number of warriors left in the village and the young boys tried to mount a defense that would give the women, children and old people time to escape into the grasslands. As the first scream coming out of the darkness reached her ears, Rain Dance Woman, whose tipi was at the far west end of the camp, knew what was happening. She hastily aroused her old parents and hurried them out into the prairie. Her sons refused to follow her and she crept back close, hoping to convince them to join her in hiding. But Runs Fast Boy and Fallen Oak Leaf Boy, were armed with war clubs their father had helped them make and though just boys, they were warriors at heart. Runs Fast Boy also carried a trade knife his father had given him and Fallen Oak Leaf Boy carried a short handled flint headed spear.

Fighting as a team, they used a variation of tactics they had developed roaming the village as young children. Acting as a decoy, Runs Fast Boy duped a Sauk warrior into chasing him. Running just fast enough to stay out of the man's reach, he led him past Fallen Oak Leaf Boy who was lying on the ground, faking death. As the man passed Fallen Oak Leaf Boy, he quickly sat up and swung his war club with all of his might, hacking the man's kneecap and dropping him to the ground! Runs Fast Boy quickly clubbed the man's head.

The second Sauk they tried this maneuver on was no cannier than the first, but he was more agile and he dodged Fallen Oak Leaf Boy's swing, catching the blow on the side of his knee. The man hit the ground rolling and came to his feet swinging a white man's small ax! The ax blow was aimed at Runs Fast Boy's face, but Runs Fast Boy threw up his left hand just in time to block the ax's trajectory! The hatchet hit the boy's hand at the base of his fingers, cutting three of them off, sending them flying away in a rain of blood!

Stunned and in shock, Runs Fast Boy sat on the ground staring at his mangled hand. Rain Dance Woman stood up out of the grass and screamed as the limping Sauk stepped close to her wounded son and prepared to deliver a death-dealing blow with the hatchet. He swung the ax back as Rain Dance Woman screamed again and began running toward him, but before he could swing it forward, a searing pain fired through the base of his back! Then another pain, high on his shoulder made his arm go numb and he lost his grip on his hatchet.

Angrily, he turned around and saw a small, redheaded boy holding a short handled spear with blood dripping from its flint blade. With amazing speed, he grabbed Fallen Oak Leaf Boy expecting the child to try to pull away and run. Instead, the boy stepped inside his outstretched arm and drove the short handled spear in an upward thrust, deep into the soft part of his belly. The tall man spasmed and his arm clenched Fallen Oak Leaf Boy tightly to his chest, but the boy continued shoving the spear up, through his guts. A river of blood and entrails spilled out of the gaping wound, pouring over Fallen Oak Leaf Boy's head and face, drenching his body with the man's blood. Rain Dance Woman screamed again, thinking that part of the blood had to be her son's, but the Sauk's nerves finally released and he fell to the ground dead, leaving Fallen Oak Leaf Boy standing. Rain Dance Woman hurriedly ran to Fallen Oak Leaf Boy and led him over to Runs Fast Boy. Working together, they pulled her wounded son to his feet and then she pushed both boys before her, rushing them far out into the tall grass, where they hid until the carnage was over.

Wamdisapa and his men arrived at the devastated village two days later. All of the tipis were burnt. Not even the lodge poles could be saved. There was no food, clothing or extra hides. Everything of value was either destroyed or stolen. Many of his warriors' wives and children were dead or taken as slaves. Some were wounded. Some were still lost out on the prairie.

Many of the survivors had witnessed the bravery of Wamdisapa's sons. As they recounted to Wamdisapa the details of the fight the boys had waged in trying to protect the village, he swelled with pride. Both had killed an enemy in battle and could no longer be considered just boys. It was time to give them adult, warrior names. In honor of his wounded hand, he named Runs Fast Boy, Sidominadota (Two Fingers). And though Fallen Oak Leaf Boy was only twelve years old, for one so young to have defeated a man twice his size and strength in a fight to the death was powerful medicine to Wamdisapa.

He noticed that the dried blood from the Sauk warrior's stomach still encrusted the short handled spear the boy had killed him with. Its reddish-brown color closely matched the color of Fallen Oak Leaf Boy's hair. Stained by nature and stained by the blood of his enemy! This too was strong medicine! There was only one name for this warrior-child! It was the words his mother had uttered at his birth . . . Inkpaduta—*the red end!*

# PART TWO

## Chapter 15
### *The Long Hungry Winter*

**W**amdisapa was one of the few men out of his eighty remaining warriors, who had not lost any member of his family in the Sauk raid. Both of his sons and his wife and even his wife's ancient parents had escaped the attack by running out into the prairie to hide. The old couple had become confused and lost and had spent most of the first day circling farther and farther from the village, until young Inkpaduta found them and brought them back. By the end of the second day, all who were hiding in the prairie grass had been found or returned on their own.

Only eighteen women and thirty-seven children below the age of fourteen survived the massacre. There was much sadness and mourning, but their lives had to go on.

Wamdisapa had taken time to honor his sons with new names, but there was no time for ceremony. The dead ones had to be taken care of. There were no trees for miles from this killing ground, and since there were not even lodge poles that weren't burned or broken by the Sauk, there were no materials for the building of scaffolds. They would have to bury their dead in shallow graves scratched in the prairie sod using their bare hands and sharpened sticks. Everyone knew that the night prowlers would paw these dead women, children and old ones from their cold graves, and they felt great shame because of the poor sendoff to the next life they were giving their dear ones. As they buried their dead, sorrow filled their hearts, and they cried and cut their hair and slashed their arms and legs.

By the end of the third day, the burying of the dead was finished, and Wamdisapa had the people sift through the remains of the camp. But most of the items necessary to sustain life were either burned or stolen by the Sauk attackers. Tipi hides, lodge poles, robes, extra clothing, jerked meat, bladder bags and arrow shafts; all were damaged or carried away by the Sauk.

Everything that could be saved, larger pieces of burnt hides, charred poles, clay pots, and a few blankets and metal pots and pans that they had traded for, was piled in the middle of the camp. When the people were finished and everything that could be salvaged was on display in front of them, it became evident to all of the survivors, just how grave their situation was. They had no shelters, no extra clothing, no food supplies, no warm robes and the cold time was not far off.

Only a few of their travois horses had escaped the raiders, but most of the camp dogs returned on the second day after the Sauk raid. Several of the dogs were bludgeoned and cooked for the first meal the people had after the massacre. The next morning Wamdisapa led them away to the northwest toward the land of many lakes. If they kept moving, they could be there before winter came and find shelter among the many groves of trees they knew grow near the lakes. With luck, they would find other *Santee* tribes, the *Mdewakonton, Wahpetons*, or *Sissitons* as well as other *Wahpekute* villages wintering there.

It would be a long dangerous journey made even more perilous by the fact that they were poorly equipped. The women and children huddled together under the few blankets and robes they had salvaged from the wreckage of their village. Food was in short supply, and they had to travel from water source to water source because they had nothing that would hold water.

Rain Dance Woman's old parents traveled with them for only a few days before they came to her as she was helping to load one of the orphaned children onto a short-poled travois with three other small children. She would also pull the travois, as the hunters in their endless search for game were using the horses.

"The young ones who are left will need what food you can find," her mother reasoned with a gentle smile. "Our days of usefulness are long over and we have decided to stay here," the old woman stated firmly, expecting no argument.

Staying behind to die alone was a custom often followed by the elderly, when life no longer held meaning for them. Usually, their relatives left them with all the comforts they could muster to make their last days as easy as possible. Rain Dance Woman's anguish was that there was nothing to leave for them, and she knew that they would freeze, starve, or be killed by wolves.

Her father patted her hand and sat down by the fire pit crossing his legs. His back was slumped against the rising morning wind. His rheumy eyes surveyed the scene as Wamdisapa's people gathered their meager belongings and prepared to leave. "Gather some dung and wrap some grass logs, Woman," he ordered his wife, the pride of once again being in charge of his family, resonating in his voice. "This night will be a cold one." He watched as his daughter hugged her mother and smiled when she reached down to grasp his hand for a moment before she turned to follow her husband. He saw as the people trudged off, that they looked tired and defeated even though it was still morning, and knew that their journey would be long and their memories bitter.

Wamdisapa was a man torn. His strong desire for revenge pulled at him. But he knew that he had to lead his surviving people to safety. His certain knowledge that this tragedy would have been averted had Tasagi not split the village, wore on his soul. As he walked, Wamdisapa felt his anger growing with each step he took. Each time his left foot hit the ground, he swore to continue his vengeance against the Sauk. Each time his right foot touched the earth, he swore vengeance against Tasagi.

\*     \*     \*

By the time Wamdisapa's band arrived in the land of thousands of lakes, it was shrinking. Ten of his warriors, whose families had moved with Tasagi before the massacre, had grown impatient with the slow pace necessary for the starving women and children to keep going and chose to hurry ahead. As the weather changed from the cool nights during *The Moon When the Calves Grow Hair* to the even colder nights of *The Moon of the Changing Seasons* and food became even more scarce, five more of the elderly survivors being sick and exhausted, had elected to stay behind and die. Five of the youngest orphan children died. Not only weren't there enough mothers with milk at their breasts to feed them all, many of the mothers had barely enough food to keep themselves alive, and their milk stopped coming.

Wamdisapa pushed the people hard. He didn't wanted to get caught out on the open plains if an early winter storm came. He felt great relief after many weeks of traveling, when the landscape changed from a rolling grassy plain to one of evergreen trees and lakes. They pushed further into the North Country, looking for signs of their people. But after a full week of skirting around lakes and marshes searching for the *Mdewakonton* (The People of the Mystic Lake) Wamdisapa knew it was time to give up looking. The rest of the *Santee* must have decided to winter to the west and south, further away from their ancient enemies, the Ojibwa. The weather could soon turn cold, and it was time to prepare for it.

The land of lakes provided not only fresh water and a source of food in the fish that swam their waters, but a rough, hilly terrain with

145

stands of pine trees and numerous small groves of white birch. The tall, straight trunks of young birch trees made perfect lodge poles, but they had few hides to cover the poles as there had not been time to stretch and scrape the hides from the few deer and elk that the hunters had been able to kill on their journey.

The women had scraped the hides clean of flesh and smoked them over the night fires to preserve them before using them for robes to cover the children at night. Without tipi hides, they fashioned pole frames, lashing the slender rods together with narrow strips cut from the smoke-cured hides. They wove layers of pine boughs one on top of the other until the wind was blocked by the pine bough walls. The roofs were covered with more layers of pine boughs and thin sheets of white bark peeled from the larger birch trees. The *Wahpekute* had always been a nomadic people, whose homes were made of poles, covered with heavy animal skins that cut the cold wind and kept the snow out.

These semi-permanent structures were poorly built. The roofs leaked when it rained and during a snowmelt and the pine bough walls were drafty in a high wind. But this land had a large wood supply for warming fires that would help keep the cold away. The weeks of traveling with little food and no warm robes to protect them from the elements had weakened each individual. They would spend each day of the winter in a struggle against starvation, freezing cold temperatures, and sudden death.

A food supply and furs for making warm robes were necessary if the people were going to survive. Several of the men made barbed fish spears by trimming the many branches on pine tree saplings to short spikes near the sharpened end and fire hardening the spear by holding it over hot coals to cook out the sticky sap. By wading into the frigid shallows in the lakes these men were able to spear a supply of pike for an immediate food supply. They lived on fish soup for the first weeks in their new camp. But the cooling waters soon sent the fish into the deeper parts of the lake where the men couldn't follow, and their fish supply dwindled quickly.

The hunters, led by Wamdisapa and Sun At Night, searched for bear dens in the area, shortly after the first snows fell. The bravery of the younger men, Inkpaduta (Red End), Sidominadota (Two Fingers), Fetoatonka (Big Face), Kicking Dog and He Cries When He is Angry, was talked about for years after. Each time a bear den was found, one of these brave young warriors armed with only a stout spear, scrambled into the den to wake the animal by prodding and poking it. When the confused and angry bear charged after the boy, who fled back out of the den into the open, it was met by fifteen or twenty men with spears, rocks and clubs. The fatty, dark bear meat put life back into the starving people, but with one hundred twenty-three mouths to feed, the flesh was consumed and gone quickly. Hunger was constant. The heavily furred bearskins made warm sleeping robes for the women and children to huddle beneath at night, but had to double as robes for the hunters to wear, as there was not enough warm clothing. Heavy snows came early, adding to the people's misery.

One man returned to camp limping badly. His worn moccasins were not enough to keep his feet from freezing. Several of his toes turned black and shriveled up. He was in great pain and could not stand on his feet for weeks.

They had built their pole and bough lodges at the base of a hill, along the shore of a small, shallow lake in a valley that opened to the south following the winding path of a stream that fed from the lake. The low-lying ground along the stream provided some fodder for their remaining horses. The animals, whose tails had been stripped of long hair to make fishnets, had to paw through the snow searching for the dried grasses hidden beneath. The horses soon grew thin and bony. A gray-faced mare stepped in a hole on the stream bank. Thrown off balance, her other three hooves slipped on the frozen ground and she fell, breaking the leg. Wamdisapa ordered Sidominadota and Inkpaduta to slay the horse and the village ate for a few more days. Only a few camp dogs remained, the rest having been eaten and their hides made into moccasins to keep the hunters' feet from freezing.

Early in *The Moon of the Popping Trees* another snowstorm descended upon the valley. A herd of elk, sensing the coming storm sought refuge from its winds by leaving the ridges and open hilltops following a crooked trail, which wove between the stands of trees until they were deep in the valley out of the wind. Dark, heavy clouds came and dumped mountains of snow. Wild winds whipped across the land, piling high drifts in the protected areas. The elk yarded up in a copse of evergreens growing closely together so that their boughs intertwined forming a natural barrier, which afforded protection from the wind.

As the storm continued through the first night and continued into the second day, the apprehensive animals were anxious to keep moving, but soon found they were trapped in a natural amphitheater, surrounded by drifts higher than their heads. When the storm ended on the third day, the lead cow tried to break through the white walls surrounding them but the soft snow would not support her narrow hooves. She found herself floundering in the deep snow and had to turn back to the protected yard, where there was solid ground to support her weight. The nervous animals began milling about in a constant circle in a hopeless search for a path to freedom.

The cold temperatures and brisk winds during the storm kept even the bravest hunters in the village near the fires for three days. By the end of the blizzard, the people were desperately hungry. The young and the weak were the worst affected, their faces gaunt, their eyes glassy. It was with great excitement that the people heard Sun At Night's report that he had found a herd of elk yarded near the top of the valley only about a mile from their camp.

Grabbing their weapons, the men boiled from their lodges. The still swirling snow stung their unprotected faces as they wove a cautious path between the drifts as they climbed up the valley.

Following Sun At Night's instructions, the men approached the penned elk from two sides. A small party, led by Sun At Night, crept toward the animals with the wind at their backs. Their scent would carry to the nervous creatures and cause them to turn and look into the wind. Wamdisapa, leading a larger group of men, approached from the downwind side on snowshoes they had made from lashing cut saplings in a circle and webbed with strips of scrap rawhide, and took up positions near the edge of the amphitheater.

When everyone was in place, Sun At Night shot one of the cow elk with his rifle, hitting her in the rib cage. The explosion of the gun was the signal the men had waited for. Sun At Night's followers, screaming at the top of their lungs, rushed the elk, shooting arrows, jabbing with spears and swinging their war clubs! The attack panicked the elk herd and the animals turned and ran into the deep snow, only to become mired down. Wamdisapa and his men leapt upon the helplessly wallowing beasts with knives clubs and spears. Screaming like wild men, they hacked at the trapped elk until all were dead except for one wounded calf that had found its way back to the center of the amphitheater. It stood in the center, confused and frightened.

The hunters gathered around the kills and gutted one of the large cows. Everyone helped themselves to the steaming hot entrails. The starving men gorged themselves in minutes, building the strength they would need to haul these animals back to the village. With a full belly, a sudden sense of well-being and confidence grew within many of the young men. Inkpaduta was the first to see the wounded calf still standing in the center of the yard. It bleated pitifully, with blood dripping from its nose, where it had been struck with a club. With each snorted breath it took, a fine spray of blood spattered the snowy ground.

With a cry of delight, Inkpaduta rushed after the young elk. It whirled and ran into the deep snow, where it became bogged down. Everyone expected Inkpaduta to smash its head with his club, but was surprised to see the young man jump onto its back and slice one of its ears off. The animal began bleating in pain and bucked, throwing Inkpaduta off to a soft landing in the snow. Panic stricken, the young elk stumbled back into the yard and stood spread legged, exhausted from struggling in the snow. Sidominadota and a band of other young boys came running at the animal shouting with glee chasing the calf, jabbing it with spears and hacking at it with their knives as it began a stumbling retreat, tracing the circled path inside the snowdrifts. Blood spewed from a hundred wounds, none of which were lethal and it soon became apparent that the boys were not killing the animal, but torturing it.

Wamdisapa and some of the warriors gathered to watch the boys chase the calf. They laughed at its hopeless efforts to escape, pointing and shouting almost as loudly at the boys. The calf, stumbling in an irregular circle soon lost its other ear to Big Face, its short tail to Yellow Dog and a sizeable chunk of its nose was chopped off by the hatchet-wielding Sidominadota.

Inkpaduta slipped up behind the calf as it stood huffing for air, and cut the hamstring on its right hind leg. The calf began a three-legged shuffle desperately trying to escape, which brought gales of laughter from the young men. Another spear thrust cut the hamstring on its left hind leg and brought the animal down. It lay spread legged in the snow, its sides heaving in a labored effort to suck air into its lungs. Piteously, the agonized animal bleated out the misery of its body, sending a spray of blood and mucus from its torn nose and mouth. The boys, still giggling and jumping with their excitement, shouted as Inkpaduta jabbed a sharpened stick into the elk calf's eye.

While the other men watched and laughed, Sun At Night stood scowling. He disliked such things as torturing innocent, helpless creatures. The boys, he could forgive, for they were but children. But children who were not taught right from wrong, would grow up to be adults who didn't know right from wrong. It was one thing to torture an enemy to shame him and his relatives. It was something else to torture a helpless friend. The elk was their friend, a friend that would give up its life so that the starving Wahpekute people could survive this long cold winter. This calf did not deserve such shame!

With a grunt of anger, Sun At Night pushed his way through the crowd of men watching the hapless elk suffer its life away. Ungently, he shoved Inkpaduta back. The boy tripped and fell, landing on his rump in the snow. Anger filled Inkpaduta's young face and his hand grasp his knife handle as he jumped back to his feet. But Sun At Night jerked the stick from the elk's eye and in the same motion kicked out his foot, tripping Inkpaduta back to the ground! Before the boy could react, Sun At Night pushed the bloody stick close to Inkpaduta's face, stopping only when the point touched the skin of his cheek. The boy froze in unhidden fear. Silence surrounded the amphitheater broken only by the labored breathing of the dying elk calf. Wamdisapa and the rest of the men stood watching, shocked by Sun At Night's sudden action.

"Is this the way a warrior should show his bravery?" Sun At Night shouted in anger. "Is this the way the boy who kills Sauk warriors and chases bears from their dens, should act to show he is a brave man?"

Sun At Night was no longer looking at Inkpaduta. Instead his eyes scanned the circle of adults, finally landing to rest on the face of Wamdisapa.

"Is this the way your children should be taught? To shame our friends who feed us?" Standing, he threw the stick to the ground and swung his war club, striking the elk a savage blow between the eyes. The stone ball smashed the calf's skull, driving its head to the ground, where it lay finally dead and out of misery. Looking at Wamdisapa again, he somberly said, "This act of torturing a friend of our people will not go unpunished. It will be a long and hungry winter."

He looped a short rope around the dead elk calf's head and dragged it past the watching men, pulling it toward the village of starving women and children.

# Chapter 16
## *Feasting*

The winter proved to be as Sun At Night had predicted, a long and hungry time. The meat from the six cow elk and three yearling calves fed the one hundred and twenty-three people in Wamdisapa's village for only a few weeks. By the end of *The Moon of Frost in the Tipi,* the people were once again subsisting on a near starvation diet, boiling strips of elk hide with a powder made from grinding fire dried fish bones. The glutinous mass held little nutritional value but filled the void in their empty stomachs and kept those who ate it alive for at least one more day.

They were gaunt with hunger and became demoralized as people, starting with the very young and the very old, they began to die. The dying began with six children under the age of ten years who started coughing at night, developed fevers, and passed quickly. Three old ones, whose age was not known, froze to death when their night fires went out and they went out searching for more wood. Five hunters who left early one morning to search for game were caught in a sudden snowstorm and failed to return. Two other men disappeared while out on the lake checking fishnets that were set through a series of holes in the ice.

It was thought that one of the men must have slid through one of the large holes and slipped under the ice and drowned. No sign of him was ever found. The other man fell in and treaded water long enough to grasp the side of the hole where his wet hands froze to the ice. In his weakened state, he lacked the strength to pull himself out, and he was found the next day, frozen half in and half out of the water. These deaths occurred during the coldest and most hungry time of the winter, *The Moon of the Dark Red Calves.*

Wamdisapa heard rumors that one of the lost hunters had been found dead several miles from camp and was eaten by the men who found him. From then on, he ordered all of the bodies of the dead be piled with brush and burned.

It was *The Moon of the Snowblind* before there was a break in winter's grip on the land. The sun grew in strength, warming the temperatures and melting the snow. Along with the change in the temperature, came a change in their luck. An old timber buffalo bull, blinded by the sudden brightness of the sun glaring off the snowscape, came wandering along the lake shore one day and stumbled into the midst of the Wahpekute camp. The starving Indians quickly killed the beast, and an immediate feast of internal organs and intestines followed. A large fire was built and every drop of blood and shred of flesh and fat was consumed on the spot by the hungry people. Nothing was wasted, but by the time everyone had eaten their share, there was nothing left. For one night only, no one went to bed hungry.

The blind buffalo's medicine was strong, and as the warming weather melted the snow and lake ice, the fishermen began to catch more fish, and the deer that had disappeared during the cold time, returned. For a short time, the people had almost enough to eat and Wamdisapa started to relax his vigilance. But another problem soon drew his attention.

Two weeks after the buffalo wandered into camp, a young girl came running naked out of her father's lodge. Her father, a man called Lost Dog with five children who had survived the Sauk attack, was seen also without clothing, chasing after her with a small switch. When he caught the girl, he began slapping her with the stick as she cowered in the melting snow. Sun At Night was the first to intervene, grabbing Lost Dog by his long hair and jerking him backward until he lost his balance and fell to the ground. The angered Sun At Night stood over the now cowering man, threatening him with his war club. Some of Lost Dog's friends grabbed Sun At Night and held him until Wamdisapa arrived.

"Sun At Night," Wamdisapa asked. "What is going on? Why are these men holding you?"

"As I walked past this lodge, this naked young girl came running from it, screaming 'No Father! No!' and this naked man came chasing her shouting 'I'll teach you to say no to me!' and he began beating her with a switch." The tall, strongly muscled warrior shrugged himself loose from those who were holding him and stepped out to speak to the crowd of people who had gathered. "This man was going to rape his own daughter." And he added, "I think a man who would couple with his own daughter should be killed and his body cut up into little pieces and scattered in the snow for the wolves and foxes."

An angry murmur rose from the crowd at these strong uncompromising words from Sun At Night and the being inside Lost

Dog seemed to shrink. He could not hide his fear. He looked almost ready to run when Wamdisapa pushed through the crowd and stood facing the frightened man.

"Speak for yourself, Lost Dog," he commanded. "Is what Sun At Night says, true?"

Standing barefoot in the snow, wrapped only in a thin, tattered trade blanket someone handed him, Lost Dog began to talk. "The mother of my children died in the Sauk raid. She saved my children by rushing them off into the tall grass. She died when she returned to retrieve the child of Swamp Rat Woman, who had been killed by the Sauk." He stopped and drew a deep breath. He was shivering with cold and quaking with fear, but he licked his lips and drawing strength from the sound of his own voice continued, "I know the winter is long and cold, and we are all hungry. I know also that a man hungers for more than just food. I'm not so old that I don't still grow hard in the loins at the thought of a woman, and I have passed most of this winter without the comfort of a warm body next to mine at night." Growing braver from the reason of his words, Lost Dog walked around the circle of men, following the same path Sun At Night had walked.

"I need a mother for my younger children, to feed and care for them. I need a wife to cook for me and to scrape hides and make robes and to take down and put up my tipi when we again have skins for one. I need a wife to do all of these things for me. I have nothing to buy a new young wife with, even if there were any women available," he said evenly. With a sudden change in the tone of his voice, his head raised and pride filled the words coming from his mouth. "This daughter has been a mother to my younger children for this long cold winter. When there was food to cook, she cooked it for me and the little ones. And when there was no food, she kept them alive, when others around us were dying! She has sewn my moccasins and patched my leggings. She is young, but has also reached the age when her body can bring life to the muscle between a man's legs. She has acted as my wife in these many ways. So one night I asked her to join me in my bed robes and she came. In this way I made her my wife and she has been sharing my bed ever since!"

A rumble of voices from the men stopped him from speaking for a moment, but he held up his hand for silence and the crowd grew quiet.

"So you see, I was not raping my daughter," Lost Dog continued, "but beating my wife for refusing me. The girl is much like her mother was. There were times when she wanted me and there were times

153

when I had to beat her to make her lay down and spread her legs for me. How else do you think I ended up with so many living children?"

This question brought chuckles from some of Lost Dog's friends and a small smile played across Wamdisapa's lips.

But Sun At Night didn't think the question was funny. He was enraged by the injustice of the situation and he shouted above the voices of those talking. "We have many men, forty-five or fifty who are of marriageable age. And all eighteen of the women in this camp already have husbands. Some of the men have shared their wives with their friends, but that has still left many men without the attention of a woman." He stopped talking and his eyes sought contact with the eyes of other men who felt the same as he. "Now this man decides to take his own daughter, one of the few available females who could become the wife of any one of us, for his own wife."

At this, Lost Dog stepped forward again. "Who among you has two horses, or five finely tanned buffalo robes, or even a freshly killed deer and colored beads to buy my daughter with? Who can even offer me enough food to feed my other children for the next week?"

Suddenly, the crowd was quiet. Even the enraged Sun At Night could not answer his questions and all listened closely when Lost Dog spoke again. "I don't ask these questions to shame anyone. I am as poor as any of you, poorer, for I have five children." His hand reached out, palm up, as if begging as his eyes darted from face to face, asking for understanding.

"It is not right for a man to fuck his own daughter!" Sun At Night shouted in a desperately loud voice. "It is not right for a man to take his own daughter for a wife. A man should seek a wife from outside his own tipi."

Lost Dog turned to look directly into Sun At Night's eyes. His lips grew into a snarl as he looked at the man who would have him killed and feed his body to the wild beasts. "Can you tell me how I would buy a new young wife from outside my own tipi? Can you tell me that when the weather changes that you would not steal her from me and leave in the night with no payment?"

Sun At Night lunged at Lost Dog with murder in his eyes, but Wamdisapa and some of Lost Dogs friends grabbed him and held him! Sun At Night was a man who knew right from wrong, and he would never have done such a thing as steal a man's daughter. It angered him to find that everyone didn't know that. Wamdisapa knew that the men were waiting for a decision from him. As he struggled to hold his enraged friend, he spat his decision from between clenched teeth.

"The girl was his daughter. Now, she is his wife. He owns her as any of us own our wives and children and dogs." He placed his lips close to Sun At Night's ear and continued, "It is the only way, my friend. His daughter is his wife. When this cold winter is over, we will find women. If we can't find women we can buy, we will find women we can steal!" Upon hearing Wamdisapa's words, Sun At Night sagged back in defeat, and Wamdisapa released his hold on him. "Come back to my lodge old friend. Rain Dance Woman will bed with you. She is skilled at pleasing a man and drawing the hardness from his stone."

Another time, Sun At Night would have gladly accepted Wamdisapa's offer, for he liked Rain Dance Woman and had often heard Wamdisapa tell stories of her prowess under the sleeping robes. But he knew in his heart that it was not right for a man to cohabit with his own daughter. He was disappointed and angry that Wamdisapa refused to see the situation as he had. He jerked away from Wamdisapa's friendly hand and stepped back, a scowl on his face.

"I will not use your secondhand woman," he snarled. "Your people have lost more than just their possessions, they have lost their pride and dignity. And after the stories of this winter are told, they will have lost the respect of all people everywhere!" He calmed himself and spoke with sadness words of complete sincerity. "You may not be totally to blame for anything that has happened, Wamdisapa. But in times to come, it will be remembered that it was your sons who shamed themselves by torturing a friend elk, causing the medicine of the hoofed creatures of the woods to stay away from this place. It will be remembered that it was Wamdisapa's people who had to be burned so that they would not be devoured by their own relatives after they died. And it will be remembered that it was Wamdisapa who condoned a man's taking of his own daughter for a wife."

Sun At Night started to walk away, but stopped and turned to face his friend when he ended the friendship. "When the snow melts enough for me to travel, I will leave here and travel with you no more." He turned and walked back to his own lodge and ducked inside.

Wamdisapa was stunned by these words and angered by the accusations in them. Shouting loudly so that Sun At Night would hear him, he said, "From this day on, Lost Dog will be known as He Copulates With His Daughter, and this girl." He reached down to raise the young girl to her feet. "She will no longer be treated as a child, but will work with the women. She will be called, She Copulates

With Her Father. She will be his wife and he may do anything he wishes with her. He may sell her. He may beat her. He may use her in his bed." With those words, Wamdisapa stood facing Sun At Night's lodge. He Copulates With His Daughter took the girl by the hand and led her back to their lodge and the crowd began to disperse. But Wamdisapa stood looking after Sun At Night and felt a pang of sadness.

\* \* \*

Long before the flights of great honking geese began to appear in the sky or be heard in the night, Sun At Night left. With him went over half of the remaining warriors, eight of the married women and twenty of the children, and Wamdisapa understood how unpopular his decision to allow He Copulates With His Daughter to take his daughter for a wife was. At least, he reasoned, there were fewer mouths to feed. But he also realized that there were many less hunters to find food for the hungry people who remained.

They endured living in the wooden camp for three more weeks, catching fish and chewing on scraps of boiled hides. Finally, in *The Moon of the Red Grass Appearing*, Wamdisapa ordered Rain Dance Woman to prepare to move.

They traveled south and west, still hoping to find some Santee people. The long winter of near starvation, sickness, and constant cold left the people weak and there were many stragglers. There was little sign of game, as the land seemed to be almost void of all life. No animals scurried and no birds flew.

On the fourth morning of traveling, there was great excitement when one of the men reported seeing a deer running ahead. The men followed the animal's tracks until the trail disappeared in a half-frozen swampy marsh. That night, they camped on the edge of the swamp, tired and dejected.

In the morning, they tried to cross the marsh but soon found that the water was too deep, so they began skirting around it. At midmorning there was a loud cry of joy coming from the front of the caravan and everyone rushed to see what the cause of it was. Muskrat mounds could be seen dotting the shallow lake in front of them.

A large colony of the small furry rats inhabited the small lake and there were hundreds of the mud and reed dens within their sight. With clubs in hand, several men waded into the cold water and surrounded several of the mounds. Standing ready with their clubs raised, one man at each mound began chopping at the roof with a hatchet and then tore the top off with a long stick. Surprised muskrats came boiling out as each den was opened. The small, furry animals stopped, blinded by the sudden sunlight, and the men with clubs found them to be easy targets. Several men were kept busy just carrying armloads of dead rats back to the shore.

The women and older children hurriedly gathered firewood and started cooking fires. They skewered the animals by sticking a sharpened stick in the anal opening and shoving it through until it came out of the mouth. Hurriedly, they hung the soaking rats over the flaming fires. The tails, hanging down into the reaching flames, dried rapidly and burst into flames. The fire raced up the tails and immediately encompassed the furry bodies singeing them black. The cooking rat bodies swelled from the heat and burst sending juices into the coals, causing a sizzling sound and a burnt, musty odor.

Rain Dance Woman fetched one of the burnt rats from the fire and brought it to Wamdisapa. She placed the end of the stick on the ground, stepped on the animal's tail, pulled the stick out and handed the crispy carcass to Wamdisapa. Turning, she reached to the pile of wet rats and grasping one by the tail, started the sharpened end of the stick into the small opening beneath it and gave a mighty shove. There was a wet, sucking sound and suddenly the end of the stick appeared, coming out of the muskrat's mouth. She shoved her way through the people crowded around the fire where they were all trying to get one of the charred rats, and hung her rat over the flames.

Wamdisapa watched the people and recognized their hunger. He picked up the still sizzling rat Rain Dance Woman had delivered to him. Its stomach burst open, spilling the hot juicy intestines on his naked legs, making him howl in pain. But he was too hungry to wait for it to cool. Reaching his fingers inside, he grasped the handful of guts. Ignoring the burning of his fingers, he shoved the entrails into his mouth and swallowed.

Smacking his lips and chewing earnestly, he devoured the rest of the rat, stopping only to spit out small bones or charred lumps of skin with clumps of singed hair. Finishing, he threw the bones to the ground and signaled Rain Dance Woman to bring him another. He sat down and sighed, looking at the sorry sight of his people feasting on the stringy flesh of muskrats.

A sudden pain in his chest caused his eyes to water and he felt almost as if he would cry. Instead, his anger grew and he cursed the god who had brought him all of this bad luck!

With another curse, he made his decision. They would stay here and feed off of the muskrats until their strength returned. He still led thirty good warriors, thirty-two counting his sons. He decided that he would stop looking for their own people for help to recover what they had lost in the Sauk raid. Instead, when they were fit enough to travel and fit enough to fight, they would travel south again, back into the land of the Sauk.

There, they would take back what was taken from them. They would take horses and hides and weapons and . . . women!

## Chapter 17
### *The Refusal (1829)*

As the sun lowered in the afternoon sky, Wamdisapa sat on a knoll looking down over his village. Eighteen tipis were set in a crooked line along a shallow river that ran through the narrow valley. He watched the breeze rattling the silvery leaves of the *wagachun* trees that grew on the banks of the river, and he was content. In the years since the massacre of their village by the Sauk and the long cold winter, after which had left them destitute, his band had done well for themselves. Even with only thirty-two warriors, he had successfully led his people on a vengeful mission to collect a terrible payment in blood from the Sauk and Fox people. Twelve summers of fighting and stealing from those enemies and anyone else who didn't protect what they owned, had reclaimed, little by little, all of the properties that the Wahpekute band had lost. The warfare and thievery was necessary at first in order to quickly regain the things they needed to sustain life.

After they had enough robes, tipi hides, weapons, ponies and clothing to keep them alive and warm, it became evident that it was much easier to steal what they needed than it was to obtain it through the honest labor of hunting for food, and skinning and scraping and tanning the hides. Now, they hunted for food, only when they could find no one to take it from.

Wamdisapa had developed into a ruthless and crafty leader, never attacking unless his warriors outnumbered their foes and he was sure of victory. It was often necessary for Wamdisapa to lead his people deep into the lands of their enemies to find people who felt secure enough to live in small family units of three or four lodges, outside the protection of a large village. He and his scouts watched targeted villages for days, usually waiting until they observed most of the village men leave on hunting or trading trips, before his band of *Wahpekute* struck, killing anyone who didn't flee and stealing everything they could carry away. Wamdisapa expanded his list of enemies beyond the Sauk and Fox people to include villages of the less powerful Missouri, Ioway and Illinois Indians also.

Even though he was content with the way life was going now, Wamdisapa had a few regrets. In the old days, before the Sauk raid on their camp, when he led his warriors in great numbers against the hunting and war parties of men who presented a danger, the *Santee Dakotah* people considered him to be a great hunter and war leader. Then, he was a man to be listened to, a man to be respected. Now Tasagi's band of *Wahpekute* gossiped with other *Santee* people, suggesting that Wamdisapa's band preyed only upon the weak and the helpless. Tasagi spread the word that Wamdisapa killed when it was not necessary and took more than he needed. His reputation was that he was a man not to be trusted, a man to be watched, a thief and a murderer. Wamdisapa added this slight to his character to the list of reasons to kill Tasagi.

His desire for revenge against Tasagi had not been fulfilled because Tasagi had been a hard man to find over the years. Upon hearing the news of the Sauk massacre, Tasagi knew that Wamdisapa would blame him, and he feared Wamdisapa's vengeance. He immediately ordered camp to be broken and led his people far to the west. They stayed for several seasons living with the *Yankton* people avoiding all contact with the *Santee* lest his whereabouts become known by Wamdisapa.

But after a few years, Tasagi and his band did return to the *minne sota* country, taking up residence near a large concentration of villages by the falls on the *minne sota* river. Since hearing that Tasagi had returned from the west, Wamdisapa kept in contact with old friends living in the village by the falls. The large village was made up of people from all four *Santee* sects, a fact which Tasagi was sure would protect them from Wamdisapa's wrath.

Tasagi's awkward son had grown into a tall, dark skinned, strong man called Buffalo Calf Man. During their years in the west, New Grass Woman kept her son close and now, had even picked out a wife for him. Wamdisapa heard that Buffalo Calf Man's wife was a frail girl, who had been orphaned young. She was raised by her uncle, a man who was anxious to collect what payment he could from her prospective husband and equally anxious for her to move out of his tipi, as he had three other daughters.

This was a fact not missed by New Grass Woman when she was looking for a wife for her son. She not only had a husband and a son she could control, but a live-in slave woman to order around. Wamdisapa smiled thinking of Tasagi's plight, having to live with

New Grass Woman. He laughed out loud, thinking that killing the man would probably be doing him a favor.

Wamdisapa's sons had grown into fine brave warriors. Through the years of raiding, they competed with one another and were always anxious to be the first to enter a village to club down those who remained to resist. As the years passed, their interests expanded beyond warfare. Sidominadota was the first to marry. He met and was smitten by a beautiful Sissiton girl named Pretty Star Low In The Morning Sky at a rendezvous of the *Santee Dakotah* near the blue water lakes *Minnetanka and Okobooshi,* in the northern Ioway country. After a short, but old-fashioned courtship in which Sidominadota called to her each night with a wing bone flute, inviting her to visit him under his buffalo robe beyond the circled tipis, the girl responded. The next day, he and the girl's father negotiated a price including many whiteman goods stolen from the Sauk and Winnebago people, and the couple was married. As was the custom, Sidominadota lived with his wife's family in a *Sisseton* village north of the large *Santee* village on the *minne sota* river where Tasagi's people lived.

Inkpaduta too had taken a wife, the younger sister of She Copulates With Her Father. The girl hated her father and after marrying Inkpaduta she changed her name and chose to live with her husband instead of in her father's tipi. Hates Her Father was young, but had proven herself worthy of a warrior husband. She could carry a heavy load and was a very fast runner. As Inkpaduta was the first man to enter a village they were raiding, Hates Her Father was the first woman to follow the warriors and start pillaging for dried meat, blankets, robes, Whiteman kettles, and whatever else she perceived as valuable and could carry off. Her prowess at raiding a village was a source of great pride for Inkpaduta.

A smile played across Wamdisapa's lips as he thought of his youngest son, a tall, strong man who had started out life as a scrawny, pale skinned, malnourished infant. A lifestyle of almost constant warfare had assured that he was skilled in the ways of war. Inkpaduta had a quick mind and saw many things other men missed. He was slow to anger, but deadly when made mad. He had learned from his father the advantages of always being sure to have the upper hand before starting a battle and was good at judging when it was safe to fight and when it was prudent to run.

Wamdisapa's thoughts were interrupted when he observed Bent Leg Boy trudging up the rise to where he sat. The boy, dragging a misshapen leg, struggled to climb the knoll through the tall grass.

When he arrived at where Wamdisapa sat, he stopped and asked the whereabouts of Inkpaduta.

"My son it out hunting and won't be back before dark," Wamdisapa answered.

Genuine disappointment showed in the boy's eyes at Wamdisapa's words. Bent Leg Boy was a small child for being eleven winters old. He was the first and only child of He Copulates With His Daughter and She Copulates With Her Father. The boy was born with his right leg twisted and his right foot clubbed. The toes on his right foot were connected with web-like skin and curled tightly together. His right knee was malformed, causing the foot to turn out and the leg, from the knee down grew much shorter than his left leg.

He Copulates With His Daughter was ashamed of this boy with the twisted leg and had little to do with him. Many people thought that Bent Leg Boy's affliction was proof that Sun At Night had been right about it being wrong for a father to have sexual relations with his daughter. Wamdisapa, fearing that more people would abandon his village because of the crippled child, had counseled He Copulates With His Daughter to bash the child's head against a tree, when it was clear that the baby was deformed, only two days after his birth.

But She Copulates With Her Father heard of the plan and staunchly protected the child like a wild she-wolf, threatening He Copulates With His Daughter's life if he touched the child. He knew that if he carried out Wamdisapa's advice, that one day, his wife-daughter would kill him in his sleep. He reasoned also that few babies born with such an affliction would survive the hardships of life for long and decided it would be safer to let nature take its course. But She Copulates With Her Father spent every moment of every day and night providing for, and protecting the child. It was a credit to her motherhood that the boy had survived.

Bent Leg Boy worshipped Inkpaduta, his uncle through marriage. Inkpaduta had known the pains of being different. He had experienced the cruelty of children by being teased and tormented by his peers for having red hair and white blood. But he had been strong and healthy and had a big brother to help him cope with the others. Bent Leg Boy was not strong or healthy and had no one to watch his back. The plight of Bent Leg Boy struck a soft spot in his otherwise hard heart, and Inkpaduta took the boy under his wing and taught him the things that boys of his age should know.

The arrival of Bent Leg Boy on the knoll ruined Wamdisapa's mood of reverie and turned his mind to Sun At Night. His old friend had left this village in anger near the end of their bad winter. Now, only a week ago, Sun At Night and his new family had come to visit

Wamdisapa. Sun At Night had married a Teton woman. She was related to Crane Legs, a *Mdewakonton* whose village was set up with the other *Santee* villages on the river in *minne sota*. It had been a long time since Sun At Night had parted company with Wamdisapa, and he was anxious to mend the tear between them. Wamdisapa was glad, for he had missed his old comrade.

Sun At Night brought news. While he was camped in Crane Leg's village, a messenger arrived telling them that several *Santee* leaders had attended a white man council at a place called Fort Crawford which sat east of the Mississippi River at a French trading place called Prairie du Chien. At the council, the whites brokered a deal to buy a strip of land forty miles wide, reaching from the Upper Iowa River in the north, to the Des Moines River to the south, from the *Wahpekute* and *Mdewakonton* people.

The white soldiers explained that it was the Great White Father's desire that all of the tribes of the Sauk and Fox people move from their homes on the Illinois side of the Mississippi to lands in Iowa on the west side of the river. But many of those people were refusing to make the move because they were frightened by the continual warfare with the *Dakotah* people. Wamdisapa smiled at this revelation.

Therefore, this strip of land had been named the Neutral Strip by the whites. The *Dakotah* people were to live and stay to the north and west of the strip and the Sauk and Fox people were to live and stay to the south and east of the strip. Small branches of the greatly diminished Winnebago nation were going to be exiled from their homeland in Wisconsin to live in the Neutral Strip and act as a buffer between the warring *Dakotah* and their enemies the Sauk and Fox. Part of the deal agreed to by the *Santee* allowed the prime hunting grounds in the Neutral Strip to be used by all people to hunt for game, but specifically outlawed any and all warfare on the land owned by the white man.

"My friend," Sun At Night said softly, "it was Tasagi who represented the *Wahpekute* people in selling the land to the whites."

"Tasagi is playing a joke," Wamdisapa laughed. "A man can't own land! So how can he sell it?" He went on seriously, "The earth is the land of all men, and it can not be owned. If anything, the land holds dominance over men. Even birds need the land for bushes and tall grass and trees to grow from, giving them a place to rest their wings. Animals for food, clay for pots, water to drink, all of these come from the land. What right do the white men have to tell the *Dakotah* who they can fight and where they can hunt? Even Tasagi knows that one man cannot speak for another man. If the whites don't know this, they soon will!" Wamdisapa saw a painful expression crossing Sun At

163

Night's face upon hearing these words. Soon after their visit, his friend stood and patted Wamdisapa on the shoulder before bidding him farewell. He was taking his family back to the Tetons in the west, away from these white men and the problems they brought.

A few days later, a messenger arrived in Wamdisapa's village with a message from Tasagi himself. Tasagi's message implored Wamdisapa to bury his hard feelings toward him and join in a council where they would all sign a treaty to sell the white men the land they wanted. Each man who signed the treaty would be entitled to annuities to be paid by the whites which would feed and clothe his family forever!

"My Uncle, Tasagi," stated the messenger, "weeps with sorrow over what happened to our people twelve winters ago. He has lamented many times that if he had only known that the enemy was so close, he would have stayed and fought them off!"

Wamdisapa merely grunted at this statement.

"My Uncle, your brother-in-law, begs you to forgive him for the mistake he made those many years ago and wants to make up for the terrible losses that occurred then." The messenger grew nervous, as he saw the look on Wamdisapa's face, but continued on with the rehearsed speech. "The annuities the Whitemen have agreed to pay, will soon make you, Wamdisapa, a rich man, and your people will never want for the luxuries of life again."

A low growl escaped from Wamdisapa's mouth at these words, and he jumped to his feet.

"Tell your uncle that I will not attend this council," he stated firmly. "Tell him I will not sign a treaty selling something that is impossible to own. Also, tell him," he added, his voice cold, "that the White Man can not stop me from fighting and killing those who have wronged my people." He paused, and an ominous tone took over his voice. "Whether they be ancient enemies, or a friend who just made a mistake."

# Chapter 18
*The Challenge*

**W**amdisapa refused to change a way of life that had suited his people so well for the past dozen years, but all of the other *Mdewakonton* and *Wahpekute* bands attended the council and signed the treaty. For this act, the *Santee* were paid a cash amount of three cents per acre in the Neutral Ground, which they could spend at the stores in several Whiteman forts that had sprung up over the years and stretched across the boundaries of their lands. Those who signed would also be paid yearly annuities.

Wamdisapa knew his people would not be eligible to receive annuities, but he shrugged the thought of a yearly payment off, thinking he would never need it. It was Wamdisapa's opinion that any man who signed such a treaty was merely afraid to fight and take what he needed. He decided to send Tasagi a message and chose his son, Inkpaduta, to deliver it. He instructed Inkpaduta to wait until Tasagi and his son, Buffalo Calf Man, had left their village, before delivering the message to New Grass Woman to further add to the insult.

Inkpaduta rode to the large *Santee* encampment at the falls of the *mine sota* river. He camped outside the village, patiently watching for Tasagi and Buffalo Calf Man to leave, just as he had watched Sauk towns waiting for the warriors to leave before they attacked.

After a week, his patience paid off. Early in the morning on the eighth day of his wait, he saw Tasagi and his son mount their horses and lead a large contingent of men riding southeast, heading down the river. He quickly prepared himself and entered the village walking bold and proud. His step was slow and swaggering. His chin was upturned, lending an arrogant tilt to his head. Scorn filled his voice as he sang a song to tell all of the people who gathered to watch him come, the feelings of the true leader of the *Wahpekute* people, Wamdisapa.

*I am willing,*
*I will fight!*
*I am worthy.*
*I will fight!*
*I am brave,*
*I will fight!*

His hair, which was the red-brown color of dried oak leaves, instead of the intense black of a full blooded *Wahpekute* was parted down the middle. Bright vermilion colored the part in his hair and the bright red spilled out onto his forehead, circled his eyes and splashed across his nose. Heavily greased braids hung down over each ear. A single eagle feather skewered the knot at the end of each braid. As he stutter-stepped his dance to a beat heard only in his own mind, his swaying causing his braids to fly out from his head and the eagle feathers fluttered or soared from the wind of his motion. The lower half of his face, reaching down to include his neck and the top of his shoulders, was painted black to signify war and death. His chest was painted yellow for the sun and his buttocks were white for the moon.

*In the daylight,*
*I will fight!*
*In the darkness of night,*
*I will fight!*

Inkpaduta was completely naked except for leggings and moccasins. His penis and scrotum were painted white with red stripes. Aroused from the boldness of his act, his penis was erect and bounced with his step. His testicles hung loose, swaying with his motion. His leggings were decorated with beads and porcupine quills. Long strips of fringe danced down the backs of the leggings. Blue, yellow and red beads graced the tops of his moccasins and skunk tails, tied to the heels slid along, silently following his feet.

*If the day is hot,*
*I will fight!*
*If the day is cold,*
*I will fight!*

In his left hand, he carried a buffalo hide shield. It was painted with intricate designs and symbols depicting men at war. Small figures of men on horseback shooting bows and arrows and throwing spears had been painstakingly painted on the front of the shield. All of the enemy warriors were depicted in different poses of death. In his right hand, he held a long lance. The flinthead was chipped to a sharp point and painted red, representing the blood of his enemies. On the lance shaft, immediately under the red painted head, hung three scalps. Two were small tufts of hair, he had taken from Sauk warriors who had shaved or plucked their hair into a topknot and greased it to stand tall.

While impressive when on a living head, the two scalps were rather unspectacular when hanging from a scalp pole. But the third scalp was impressive and drew everyone's attention. People pointed and spoke quietly to one another or their mouths fell open in silent awe. Small children ran into their tipis and came back, dragging their parents to see the sensational scalp. The long, raven hair had been brushed to a visible softness and glistened in the sunshine. With each step Inkpaduta took, the long soft hair danced and waved.

Inkpaduta smiled inside, knowing the effect the special scalp had on people. It was the hair of an Ioway woman who had been a slave in a Sauk village.

When Inkpaduta and the other men of Wamdisapa's village attacked that village, it wasn't much of a battle. Most of the surprised Sauk women ran into the growing darkness to escape. Inkpaduta, leading the charge, met most of the resistance, clubbing one man and driving his knife deep into the neck of an old grandfather-man who stood up from his resting place to meet him. When she saw the old man fall, the young Ioway girl rushed at Inkpaduta, swinging a stickhandled hoe at him. He blocked her clumsy attempt and knocked her to the ground with his war club.

After all of the fighting was over, he returned to find the girl still alive, crawling aimlessly about on her hands and knees. He tipped her head back and saw that his club had smashed her face, destroying her eyes, nose and mouth. Knowing that her wounds were too extensive for her to live for long, he wrapped a strip of rawhide around her slender neck, and ignoring her struggles, strangled her. Her hair was long, clean and soft and it shined, even in the fading light. Carefully, he cut the scalp from her head. Trying to get all of her hair that he possibly could, he traced an oblong circle with his knife from her forehead around to just above her left ear to the nape of her neck, up and over her right ear and back to her forehead again. Then, wrapping the long hair around his hands and making tight fists with each, he placed his feet on the girl's shoulders and pulled carefully tearing the skin loose from her head, until it finally came free with a loud pop.

When Hates Her Father saw the scalp, she recognized it for the rare treasure it was and she scraped the head skin thin, cutting away all of the excess flesh and membrane. She rubbed it with salt and worked buffalo brains into the skin. She stretched it and chewed it, working it until the skin with the long beautiful black hair was soft and pliable as it dried. Then she brushed the tangles from the hair and combed it until it shone with a luster. Though the hair was connected to dead skin, it was beautifully alive and added to the power of Inkpaduta's medicine!

Shaking the lance in his right hand, making the scalps jump and dance, and fending off imaginary arrows and spear thrusts with the shield in his left-hand, Inkpaduta made his way through the long center street of the *Santee* encampment. Finally he came to the tipi he sought and stopped to finish his song.

*To fight our enemies is good!*
*Tasagi, why won't you fight?*
*To kill our enemies is good!*
*Tasagi, are you frightened?*
*To die in battle is good!*
*Tasagi, are you afraid to die?*

The people in the crowd that had formed were shocked at Inkpaduta's brazen boldness in delivering this insult to one of the respected leaders of a *Santee* clan. The arrogance of his actions and his song was shamelessly insolent.

But Inkpaduta's self assurance in delivering the insult impressed all who saw it. Hushed with expectation, they all waited for a response from the fat woman seated beside the tipi until the silence grew heavy. The sun was at its zenith, baking down on the waiting people with extreme heat.

New Grass Woman sat scowling at her painted tormentor. Rivulets of sweat ran from her shoulders over her fat, naked breasts making them glisten in the bright sunlight. Anger and fear made her breath come fast and her mouth grow dry. Grunting with effort, she struggled to her feet. Taking up a stick of firewood, she stepped toward Inkpaduta and swung the small club at him.

With the agility of a cat, he dodged the intended blow and laughed at her clumsy effort.

"You are too slow, Old Fat Woman!" he cried in delight, dodging another swing. She chased after him wildly swinging the stick again and again, but never coming close to the agile Inkpaduta. Soon she tired, making her stumbling gait and attempts to strike Inkpaduta even more futile. Finally, she fell to the ground in a heap, totally exhausted.

"You try to strike me, but I laugh!" Inkpaduta spat an exaggerated laugh as he walked to stand over her. He thrust his erect penis at her by flipping his hips in her direction, then turned and bending over, shook his white painted buttocks in her face.

New Grass Woman moaned and fell back flat on the ground, her lungs gasping for air. With each breath drawn, her pendulous breasts quivered as her laboring heart pounded in her chest. She stared at him through dull eyes as Inkpaduta stalked away in a broad circle, speaking now more to the crowd of people than her.

"Where are your men, Old Fat Woman?" he sneered, dipping his head toward where she lay. "Are they hiding because they are afraid to die? Where is the mighty Tasagi? Where is the man who would sell *Dakotah* lands and sell *Dakotah* pride to the whiteskins so that he will not have to fight his enemies anymore?"

Inkpaduta stopped his haughty march and glared down at the woman with hate lighting his eyes and began walking purposefully toward her. New Grass Woman, whimpering with fear, tried to back away, sliding her large rump across the rough ground, until he stood directly over her. She cringed in utter terror when with a flash of his arm, he drove the spearhead into the ground only inches from her head. The long black hair of the Ioway woman's scalp covered her face and she shook her head to clear it from her eyes.

Inkpaduta leaned down so that his face was only inches from New Grass Woman's and said, speaking slowly, "Tell Tasagi and Buffalo Calf Man that a warrior, who has killed many enemies and is not afraid to fight and die, awaits them!" He reached down and grasped a handful of hair from the Ioway woman's scalp and whipped it across New Grass Woman's face two stinging blows. "Tell them that a man who is not afraid awaits them!" With a final effort and a low grunt, Inkpaduta hissed, "Tell them that I await them." He bent low and glared directly into the stricken woman's eyes. "But tell them if they come to meet me . . . they come to die!"

With a wild roaring cry, Inkpaduta jerked the lance from the ground and turned on his heel. He began to laugh as he slowly, brazenly walked away.

His laughter continued all the way through the village, challenging anyone who took umbrage with his actions to do something about it. There were no takers. At the edge of the encampment, he swung up on the back of his spotted horse and rode away.

# Chapter 19
## *Infidelity, Retribution & Murder*

Sidominadota crept slowly through the brush along the creek on his hands and knees. The thorns on the gooseberry bushes grabbed at his skin and scratched deep, making small crooked furrows of red that bulbed into drops of blood at the end of each scratch before running in streaks across his arms and legs. Carefully, he moved his head lower and higher, dodging the whip like branches of the thorny bushes hanging level with his eyes. These same branches caught in his hair and gouged his ears making them burn and itch. But there was no pain or discomfort that could stop him from the mission he was undertaking. He had heard the whispered rumors. Now he would see for himself.

The sound of voices rising softly from the creek bank just beyond the brushy cover he was crawling through set his mind on fire. The quiet gurgle of water slowly dancing around rocks in the shallow streamed ahead of him, blended with soft mewling and low moans of passion. His hands parted the last clump of shallow grass and gooseberry bush branches and his eyes looked upon a scene that, though expected, was still startling to him. His wife, Pretty Star Low In The Morning Sky, sat astraddle a young *Sisseton* warrior named Young Bear Up In A Tree. The young man lay on his back on a buffalo robe spread in a small opening on the creek's bank. His eyes were closed and his hands reached up to fondle her breasts as she swayed back and forth and up and down, moaning with each thrust of her pelvis.

Sidominadota rolled to his back and squeezed his eyes tightly shut. Tears pushed their way through and slid down his cheeks. He loved Pretty Star Low In The Morning Sky. She was beautiful and he had paid the price for the right to be her husband. All of the riches: ponies, beads, shells, and buffalo robes that he had accumulated over the years of raiding with his father and brother had gone to her father for the right to marry her. He moved in with her family because he knew it would make her happy. He gave up on thoughts of riding south to join Wamdisapa for a summer season of raiding the Sauk. He changed his life for her and this was the thanks he got.

He almost panicked when he realized that the sounds from the clearing had stopped while he was lying there feeling sorry for himself. He listened, hoping that the couple hadn't detected his presence. Quiet whispers and soft giggles soon rewarded his straining ears. They did not know they were being watched. He rolled slowly back to his stomach as the sounds of lovemaking began again. His eyes focused on the sight before him and he blanched, growing sick inside with envy and anger. The fact that his beautiful young wife was cheating on him before his eyes revolted him, yet a kind of sick fascination wouldn't let him take his eyes off the passionate pair.

Pretty Star Low In The Morning Sky was now on her hands and knees in front of Young Bear Up In A Tree. He entered her from behind, grasping her shoulders with his hands. With each forward thrust of his hips, he pulled her back with his hands helping her find the rhythm of his motion. As his strokes became faster and his thrusts deeper, she frantically tried to keep pace with her lover, and soon her soft moans of passion changed to loud groans of pleasure and soft cries of ecstasy.

Young Bear Up In A Tree's back was wet with sweat and loud grunts of effort snorted through his lips. Sidominadota could stand it no longer! Without thinking, he jumped to his feet. The lovers, too far into their own world to hear, were oblivious to the noise he made. Sidominadota pulled the knife from his sheath and buried it into Young Bear Up In A Tree's back. The man gasped a feeble wheeze and fell forward across Pretty Star Low In The Morning Sky. The weight of his sudden collapse drove the girl forward smashing her face into the sandy soil.

"Not yet Young Bear, not yet!" she moaned urgently. "I'm not near the moment when our souls meet and join in wonderful bliss," she whispered, disappointment in her voice. Young Bear had never lost control and finished so soon before. Suddenly she was angry. "You are heavy. You are hurting me!" She struggled beneath his dead weight. "Get off!" she demanded, no longer whispering.

Sidominadota jerked his knife from Young Bear Up In A Tree's back. Hot blood flowed from the deep puncture wound and rolled down his side onto the struggling woman. When Pretty Star Low In The Morning Sky felt the blood pouring on to her, she panicked. Frantically, she bucked and rolled, trying to get out from under the dead weight of her lover's body. She succeeded only in rolling to her back, still pinned from the hips down. She froze when she saw

Sidominadota standing above her with a bloody knife in his hand. She screamed and fruitlessly pummeled Young Bear Up In A Tree's rib cage with frightened fists.

Sidominadota knelt down, grabbing her flailing arms and pinned them beneath his knees. He grasped her nose between his thumb and forefinger, brought the sharp edge of his knife to the top of her nose, deep between her eyes, and shoved the blade down toward her lips. The thick cartilage broke and cracked and when he pulled the appendage loose from her face, blood fairly squirted up at him.

Her screams of pain soon changed to gurgles, as her blood ran into her mouth and choked her. Coughing spasmodically, she tried again to roll from beneath Young Bear Up In A Tree. She struggled back and forth from side to side, growing weaker and weaker with each movement. Sidominadota had cut too deep. She would die. He watched her slowing struggles with uncaring eyes.

In the case of infidelity among the *Dakotah* people, tradition called for only a public accusation to the male lover by the cheated man and for him to cut only the soft tip off of an unfaithful wife's nose. Then he could have simply moved her possessions from the tipi and she would live her life as best she could marked for life as an adulterer who could not be trusted.

But Sidominadota in his rage had killed Young Bear Up In A Tree and then cut off Pretty Star Low In The Morning Sky's entire nose. It was still in his hand. He knew she would bleed to death or suffocate on her own blood. As he watched, her struggles became only a feeble wagging of her head. Gurgling screams and bubbly gasps for air as she tried to clear her windpipe marked the end.

When Pretty Star Low In The Morning Sky ceased all movement, he knew she was dead. He dispassionately placed the chunk of skin-covered cartilage that had been her nose in his medicine bag. He would rub it with salt and smoke it dry over a fire and carry it with him for the rest of his life.

Wading into the stream, he washed the blood from his hands and arms. Quickly then, he went to the pony herd and picked out five of his father-in-law's best horses. He threw war bridles around their lower jaws and tied them in a line, the lead horse to a stubby oak tree and each following horse to the tail of the horse in front of it. He had led stolen horses many times in this fashion.

Leaving the horses tied at the edge of the village, he went to his father-in-law's tipi to collect his personal property and weapons. Upon entering the lodge, he found Pretty Star Low In The Morning Sky's younger sister napping there. With no warning, he slapped her across the side of her head with a blow that knocked her out. Rolling the girl in a heavy robe, he carried her out to where he'd left the horses and threw the girl over the back of the second horse in line. He tied her hands to her feet under the horse's belly and passed another rope around her waist and up around the horse's neck to keep her from sliding and falling under the animal's hooves. Climbing aboard the lead horse, he rode off, heading due south. He kicked their pace to a trot, wasting no time, because he knew that as soon as what he had done was discovered, he would be followed!

Schooled from years of being chased by enemies, Sidominadota eluded the party of *Sisseton* warriors led by his father-in-law, on the third day out from the village. Leaving a false trail into a small southwesterly flowing river, he detoured back to the northeast across hard rocky ground where his horses left no tracks. When he was sure that he had lost his followers, he slowed his pace, taking time to make his young sister-in-law his wife.

At first she was reluctant to lie on her back and accept him. But she soon learned that if she resisted, he would beat her. She also learned quickly that if she gave in easily and participated vigorously when he wanted her, that he would treat her well. He named her Prettier Than Her Sister Woman and after a few weeks, the girl forgot about returning to her previous life and gratefully welcomed Sidominadota to her bed. By the time they rode into Wamdisapa's village, she considered herself to be Sidominadota's wife and wished for nothing else.

The arrival of the couple caused great excitement in Wamdisapa's village. Sidominadota's father-in-law, leading a large party of warriors had ridden directly to Wamdisapa's village after losing his trail two weeks before, thinking that Sidominadota would seek help from his father. But when he found that Sidominadota hadn't returned to his father the party rode off, vowing to return if they couldn't find Sidominadota and his youngest daughter in the *Wahpeton* villages to the west.

Wamdisapa was anxious for a showdown with Tasagi. Inkpaduta's insulting message had not been received well by his old foe, and Buffalo Calf Man had made certain threats of revenge. But neither of the men had made a move to carry the threats out. Wamdisapa and Inkpaduta were content to wait to lure Tasagi away from the safety of the large *Santee* village where they could kill him without fear of interference by the many warriors camped with him. The arrival of Sidominadota and his newly kidnapped wife changed their plans. They would wait no more for Tasagi. Wamdisapa ordered the camp struck and within the hour, his people were headed southeast, away from the danger of Sidominadota's angry father-in-law and his warriors.

*   *   *

As the seasons of the year passed, summer into fall, fall into winter, winter into spring, each leading into the effortless change of time, so moved Wamdisapa's band. From north to south, then west to east in an unpredictable, patternless wandering which crisscrossed the plains making it impossible for anyone who might have been following them to find them. With no thoughts of right and wrong, they dashed quickly and quietly into the Neutral Strip smashing, killing and stealing from whomever they encountered there. With a stroke of genius, Wamdisapa led his people out of the Strip to the south, deep into Sauk and Fox land as described in the signed treaty.

The move threw off the white soldiers sent from Fort Crawford, looking for renegade "Sioux." The commander of the white soldiers never thought the Sioux would try to escape by moving further into their enemies' land. When the troop returned empty handed, they asked Tasagi and Buffalo Calf Man where Wamdisapa and his people could have vanished to, but were answered with a mere shrug of the shoulders from both men.

When Wamdisapa's marauders struck a helpless town of Winnebagos in the Neutral Strip, wiping out most of the village, the survivors traveled to Fort Crawford for help. This time, Buffalo Calf Man volunteered to help track the hidden trail left by Wamdisapa.

For four days, the white soldiers, aided by the tracking skills of Buffalo Calf Man, trailed Wamdisapa and his raiders. It was only when Wamdisapa turned and led his people due west, traveling night and day in a desperate attempt to escape, that the whites, their exhausted horses near death, gave up and let them go.

When Wamdisapa was sure that the white soldiers had turned back, he circled his people to the north and back east, entering the Neutral Strip from the west end. There, among the hills along the Des Moines River, they waited. Sending out scouts for weeks, the people lived a quiet life in a camp with fires only made at night and then, only deep in the valley where the light could not be seen. When his scouts returned with news that they had spotted Tasagi's village, Wamdisapa knew that his old enemy had finally left the *Santee* encampment in *minne sota* to be closer to the Whiteman fort. Wamdisapa ordered his warriors to mount up. The women were left behind this time, because this would be a raid, not for foodstuffs, but for long overdue vengeance!

It took them two days of hard riding, but they rode into Tasagi's village fresh and ready for battle. The men in Tasagi's village emerged from their tipis carrying their weapons at the sound of the horses, but were confused when they saw, instead of enemies, other *Santee* warriors brandishing weapons as their horses circled, rearing and snorting. Dust from the ponies' unshod hooves floated thickly in the air stinging the men's nostrils and adding to the confusing sight. The men stood aside in small groups, watching Wamdisapa's warriors.

Wamdisapa was surprised that the men of Tasagi's village offered no resistance when his men rode up and down between the tipis, reaching down to fill their pack bags with dried meat from the racks sitting in the sun. Upon seeing a man he recognized, Wamdisapa rode his black pony over to the man and dismounted.

"Sits Down Dog," he said to the man. "Where is your Headman?"

"Tasagi is gone from camp," the man answered, adding, "He is visiting his brother who catches the fish with barbed horns on the side of its head, Bull Fish Eater."

Wamdisapa glared deeply into Sit Down Dog's eyes trying to read if the man was lying or telling the truth. He was greatly disappointed that Tasagi was gone when he had finally come for his revenge. Anger dripped from his voice as he began to berate the village men for following Tasagi.

"Why do the men of this village allow a Sauk town, our ancient enemies, to exist only a few hours ride to the south from here?" He walked to an opening where many men had gathered watching and continued, "To the east, the sun will rise tomorrow only three hours away on another camp of Fox hunters, who will be taking game that you might need to feed your families with in the cold time." His baleful eyes scanned the scattered men. He hawked dusty phlegm from his throat and spat it at Sits Down Dog's feet. "Or is it because you are not men, only frightened women? Are you afraid of the Sauk? Are you afraid of the Fox? Or, are you afraid that the whiteskins will disapprove and stop giving you presents?" An angry murmur began to rise from the ranks of Tasagi's warriors at these questions, but a hush fell over them at his next words, "It must be true. Why else would the son of Tasagi be leading the white soldiers on the trail of my people?"

"The Sauk and Fox people hunt in peace in the Neutral Strip because the treaty we signed with the whiteskins says they can." The answer came not from Sits Down Dog, but from Buffalo Calf Man, who stood in the shadow of a tipi to Wamdisapa's left. The tall, strongly muscled dark skinned young man with black curly hair stepped from the shadow and walked to face Wamdisapa. Inkpaduta and Sidominadota rode their horses up and stopped, flanking their father. Buffalo Calf Man continued, his voice low but clear, coming from deep within his chest. "I helped the whiteskins track you because they came to blame us and other innocent *Santee* for breaking the treaty." He glared angrily at Wamdisapa. "This we did not do. We kept our word. My father told them that it was cowardly outcasts who had committed the attacks in the Neutral Strip, and I helped them trail you to prove that we are men of our word." He stopped and looked around to see how many of his men were present and armed before continuing, "I trailed you, and I would have caught you if the whites hadn't grown tired and quit!"

These stinging words directed at his father made Inkpaduta nearly crazy with rage. He had ridden hard to get here, expecting to exact some revenge against Tasagi and now his son was taunting his father. Inkpaduta could contain his anger no longer.

"If you are so good at following a track, why didn't you find me after I challenged your old ugly mother one summer ago? I told her to tell you that I waited, and I did wait, but you are a woman and must be afraid to die!" Inkpaduta hissed the words from between his clenched teeth. His anger was seething from his every pore.

Buffalo Calf Man turned his eyes quickly to watch the man on horseback confronting him. He saw a man of medium to tall height, broad shoulders and a barrel chest. He was stocky and well muscled and sat on his horse comfortably. But what impressed Buffalo Calf Man the most about Inkpaduta was the wild light that shone in his eyes with his anger. Here was definitely a man to keep an eye on. Inkpaduta's words struck a tender spot in Buffalo Calf Man's mind. He had wanted to follow Inkpaduta that day last summer to answer his challenge and make him pay for insulting his mother. Tasagi had wanted to go too, but New Grass Woman, fearing treachery had forbid it.

"I am not afraid to die!" the dark skinned man shouted in pent up anger. He turned to face Wamdisapa again and spittle flew from his mouth into Wamdisapa's face as he shouted, "I fear no man, least of all men like you. Men who are very brave when it comes to insulting a defenseless woman. Men who kill women and children, just to steal food from them while their men are gone hunting."

At these words, Sidominadota kneed his horse closer and circled it to the left of Buffalo Calf Man. Buffalo Calf Man turned to watch this new threat and upon recognizing the man on the horse added, his voice filled with scorn, "I have no fear of a man who would kill his own kind by knifing him in the back. I do not fear a man who would kill his own wife and steal horses from his father-in-law and then kidnap his father-in-law's youngest daughter." His last words ended with a muffled groan as Inkpaduta thrust his spear into Buffalo Calf Man's left side. The stone head rammed between two ribs, smashing into his wildly pumping heart. Inkpaduta tried to pull the spear out to thrust again, but found it was imbedded. He rode close to Buffalo Calf Man and braced his foot on the dying man's shoulder, jerking upward with both hands. When the spear broke free, blood spewed from the wound splashing on Wamdisapa's feet.

Buffalo Calf Man, mesmerized from the shock of the unexpected blow, staggered a few steps backward and turned toward Wamdisapa. A look of disbelief crossed his face just before his eyes glassed over and he toppled to the ground. Tasagi's warriors and Wamdisapa's men stood in shocked silence watching as Buffalo Calf Man twitched twice and then lay still. A sudden cry of anger broke the quiet as Tasagi's men attacked Wamdisapa's followers, dragging one man from the back of his horse and bludgeoning him to death.

Wamdisapa's men were greatly outnumbered. They fought hard, swinging their war clubs and thrusting short spears as they tried to maneuver their horses away from the angry men of Tasagi's village. Being mounted and mobile worked to their advantage and Inkpaduta and Sidominadota were quick to call for a retreat. But Wamdisapa was afoot when the battle started and as he darted for his horse, Sits Down Dog followed him closely and when Wamdisapa vaulted onto his pony's back with a triumphant shout of glee on his lips, Sits Down Dog buried his sharp knife in Wamdisapa's lower stomach.

Fiery pain raced to his brain, and he instinctively clamped his legs tightly around the horse's ribs. His hands clenched into fists holding on to the horse's mane as it thundered in a panic out of the village following the rest of the running horses out over the open grasslands. Wamdisapa rode with no conscious thought while the blood from his veins mixed with the contents of his large intestines. After only a few miles, Wamdisapa lost all consciousness and his grip on the mane loosened. He slid slowly down his horse's side, falling under its pounding hooves and was trampled. He died there on the plains before his sons realized that he was missing.

# Chapter 20
## *Outcasts (1840)*

The seemingly trackless wilderness stretched out before the sergeant. He wondered where he had gone wrong. He left the ferry on the Iowa side of the big river across from Prairie du Chien and drove his team of mules due west for over five days looking for the crushed grass track that would lead him back to Fort Atkinson. Somehow, he had missed it and now he was hopelessly lost.

"Some Fort!" he griped out loud. "Miserable pile of cobblestones."

Right after snow melt that spring, his troop of soldiers had been dispatched to the farthest army outpost west of the Mississippi River where they had begun constructing a fortified facility. Fort Atkinson was named for their commanding officer. He was to direct them in building the fort. When finished, the plan was to have twenty-four buildings made of cobblestone, inside an eleven foot, nine inch tall log wall, to house the soldiers and their horses. After the stockade and buildings inside were finished, they would build additional buildings outside the wall as they were needed.

In May of that year, the army began the actual construction of the fort, locating it at the north end of the so-called, Neutral Zone, land that had been negotiated away from the Sioux a decade before. Originally, the Neutral Zone was intended only to be a buffer between the Sauk and Fox Indians, who were being forced west out of Illinois, and their ancient enemies, the Sioux. With the purchase of the Neutral Zone, the government brokered a peace between the two warring factions, except for a few renegade bands of outcast Sioux who continued to raid across the forty-mile wide strip of land. Now, in 1840 the government was forcing the Winnebago Indians to leave Wisconsin and was placing them in the Neutral Zone under the protection of the Army.

The soldiers stationed at Fort Atkinson were charged with keeping the Winnebagos in the Neutral Zone and protecting them from their ancient enemies; the Sioux, Sauk, Fox and Ioway tribes. As he looked around the barren countryside, the sergeant thought that building a fortress in this wilderness was a daunting enough task by itself, without having to keep wild Indians, bent on killing each other from fighting. He shook his head in frustration and idly scratched through his shirt at one of the pustulating sores that had appeared on his chest the day before.

He suddenly wished he had followed the example of the two privates who had been ordered to accompany him. The three had been sent by Fort Atkinson's doctor to take seven sick men back to Fort Crawford at Prairie du Chien. The doctor was pretty sure that the men had somehow contracted the pox. Two weeks before, the seven men had started complaining about a rash and were experiencing severe headaches and a fever.

At first, the doctor thought they were having a reaction to the tall nettle weeds the men were chopping out of a patch of ground where they were planning to build a granary. On the third day, the rash spread from their faces to the rest of their bodies and became raised bumps. On the fourth day, the bumps appeared to be filled with fluid. It was then that the sergeant and two privates had been charged with taking the men back to Wisconsin.

Early in the journey, the sick men only became sicker, with high temperatures and body aches making the bumpy ride, sitting four on the cot and three on the floor of the ambulance wagon, a living hell on wheels. At first, the sergeant tried to keep his distance. But as the sick men became weaker and weaker, it became necessary to help them get out of the ambulance wagon for their camp at night and back into the wagon to resume their journey each morning. Both privates deserted on the second day out from Fort Atkinson and the sergeant was left alone. On the fourth night, he didn't unload them. The seven lay moaning in the back of the wagon, too sick and weak to even try to get out of the wagon. On the fifth day, three of the men died. He buried them without noting their names. When he arrived at Fort Crawford a day later, the sores on the four survivors were beginning to scab over.

When the nature of his mission was realized by the Fort Crawford commanders, he was given a tent and four cots and ordered to drive a distance from the Fort before setting it up. He had stayed in the wagon by the tent for two more weeks, caring for the four survivors, feeding them the soup brought daily from the Fort and bringing copious amounts of fresh water for them to drink. Finally after the second week, he was glad to see the men slowly pull through the sickness and return to health though all four were terribly scarred from the pox sores.

Now, as the sergeant sat on the ambulance seat, he stared with despair at the sores that had begun popping up on his forearms. His head was aching, and he felt weak. He had the pox. He remembered the agony of the seven men he had escorted back to Fort Crawford. He could hear their moans of pain and cries for water. He could hear their teeth chattering and smell the sourness of men too weak to go relieve themselves.

He was lost and alone. Moving slowly, he crawled from the wagon seat to the pus-stained cot in the back. He felt a sudden chill from his fever and glanced at the burlap bag that he had stuffed the seven sick men's blankets into. Shaking his head, he sat on the cot and methodically loaded his cap and ball pistol. Shivering from the fever and his own fear, he laid back on the cot. He cocked the pistol, placed the barrel to his temple and pulled the trigger.

\*     \*     \*

It was the distant braying of mules that caught the *Wahpekute* band's attention. The animals' high-pitched ever-quickening brays reverberated with desperation from over the small hill the People were passing along the side of. Sidominadota led the men of the band to the top of the bluff to investigate. He could see down the clear grassy slope before them. A team of gray mules, hitched to a *wasichu* wagon, had wandered into a soupy marsh, looking for water to drink and had become bogged down by the wagon, which was slowly sinking in the mud. Its narrow, spoked wheels were not meant to traverse the bog that stretched across the lowland valley. Cattails lined the shore of the marsh. Stagnant water, covered with green slime and wiggling mosquito hatchlings, reached to the mules' knees. They stood where the weight of the sinking wagon had stopped them, about thirty feet into the marsh. Sidominadota could see a trail where the mule team had pulled the heavy vehicle on a crooked course leading down from the high ground on the bluff into the soggy lowlands. The weary mules dropped their muzzles into the torpid water. They snorted through their nostrils blowing a hole in the mass of floating green moss and tried to suck enough of the sluggish swamp water to slake their thirst.

The wagon's steel rimmed wheels cut deep ruts in the soft mud of the marsh and the heavy wagon had slowly settled to its axles in the muck as the mules stood stationary trying to drink. Upon finding only thick green ooze to drink, the animals, struggling and stumbling in their traces in the soft, seemingly bottomless mud were braying in frustration.

Desperation filled their voices as the dark, blue-black mud splashed across their bellies and up their flanks, staining the light gray coats of the matched pair.

Sidominadota sat on his horse listening to the stricken animals and watching the *wasichu* wagon. He had seen mules only a few times in his life, always from a distance, while observing the comings and goings of white men. He could not see a driver, and assumed that the mules had not been driven into the marsh on purpose, but his years of warfare had taught him to be wary of situations he was not familiar with. Finally, when one of the mules went down on its side, he decided it was time to act.

"Inkpaduta, take two men and cut the large headed horses from their tethers," he ordered, waving his two-fingered hand at his brother. "When you get them free, bring them around and we will tie ropes to the back of the wagon and have them pull it back out the way it went in."

Inkpaduta, followed closely by Man Who Makes A Crooked Wind As He Walks and a man called Snores When He Sleeps, slipped off his horse and sloshed through the muddy water. He directed Man Who Makes A Crooked Wind As He Walks to gather up the reins and stand in front of the mules, while he and Snores When He Sleeps carefully approached the thrashing mules. Nimbly dodging the flailing animals, the two men were soon successful in cutting the singletree loose from the wagon and both mules leaped from their muddy trap in surging jumps that knocked Man Who Makes A Crooked Wind As He Walks down. He stubbornly held onto the slippery reins and was dragged through the muddy water until he lost his grip and splashed to a sudden stop in the muck.

The women and children arrived just in time to see the sputtering Man Who Makes A Crooked Wind As He Walks climb to his feet. They laughed as he came up, caked in mud from head to toe and sputtering curses at the mules, where they stood trembling in the shade of a stunted pine tree. Sidominadota and Stands While The Bees Sting grabbed up the muddy driving reins and led the mules around to the back side of the wagon. They tied ropes to the singletree and tossed the other end of the ropes to Inkpaduta and Snores When He Sleeps, who tied them to the back axle. Sidominadota slapped the mules on the rumps with the reins, driving them away from the marsh pulling the wagon out of the bog backwards, and soon it stood on solid ground once again.

Inkpaduta was the first to climb into the wagon. He howled in surprise when he found that the *wasichu* driver was lying in the back of the high sided, covered wagon. The man was dead and was rank

182

with the smell of death. He was dressed in the blue uniform of a soldier. Inkpaduta saw a pistol lying on the floor of the wagon and noticed the black, dried blood on both sides of the man's head.

Gagging from the odor, Inkpaduta lifted the dead man off of the cot and dragged him to the back of the wagon. Bear hugging the heat-swollen corpse, he lifted it enough to clear the wagon's end gate and dumped the body over it. The dead white man hit the ground with a hollow thud, sprawled grotesquely with one arm bent under the body. Hates Her Father was the first woman to jump on the dead white man and stripped the corpse of its clothing.

The dead *wasichu* was wearing the blue coarse woven shirt and pants uniform of a soldier. The blue colored cloth of the white soldiers' uniforms was a favorite among the *Wahpekute* women. A general struggle occurred with all of the women trying to get a piece of the material. Soon the shirt was ripped into many pieces and everyone had a blue souvenir. The blue pants met a similar fate as the women, laughing and giggling, sliced long strips from the legs and tied headbands with long, trailing tails.

Rain Dance Woman was the first to notice that the dead man's body was covered with large sores that were fire red at the base but topped with yellow puss-oozing pimples. She drew back in alarm, but Hates Her Father laughed at her mother-in-law and turned her knife to the dead man. She scalped the corpse cutting just above where the ball had entered and exited and ran amongst the children waving the graying hair at them. The giggling children shrieked in terror and ran around in circles. Not to be outdone by her sister-in-law, Prettier Than Her Sister Woman used a hatchet to chop the man's head off. She sat it on a water barrel that was strapped to the side of the wagon and laughing loudly, pointed to the way dropping skin from the scalped forehead covered its eyes and how the cheeks hung in great jowls that puckered the lips.

Many of the rest of the women and some of the children joined in the laughter. They slashed deep cuts in the legs and arms and dragged the headless corpse to the edge of the marsh, where they scooped up handfuls of mud and plastered the sores on the torso with the sticky black substance.

"Mosquitoes won't bite you and maybe you wouldn't have sores all over your body, if you wear enough mud, you dumb *wasichu!*" She Copulates With Her Father cackled at the sight of the mud-caked body.

Inkpaduta searched through the inside of the wagon and found powder and ball to go with the soldier's pistol. There were several bolts of white cloth and bandage material stacked near the front along one side. There was a chest filled with small bottles across from the built-in cot with a tick mattress along the other side toward the back of the wagon. The Wahpekute were ignorant of the medicines stored in the bottles. He Copulates With His Daughter began sampling the ingredients of the bottles and retched at the taste of one marked "Cod Liver Oil."

The sight of the old man puking his stomach empty drew laughter from the rest of the people. He grew angry and smashed the rest of the bottles with his war club. Inkpaduta found five bottles with amber colored liquid under the seat boot. He was about to smash them as He Copulates With His Daughter was smashing the small bottles, when a cry from an old man called Sits In A Circle stayed his hand. Sits In A Circle told him that he was sure these bottles were *wasichu* firewater. He had sampled it ten summers before, when the *wasichu* had called a council to discuss buying *Santee* land and had provided all of the men drinks of this same colored firewater, before they voted. He couldn't remember how he had voted he said, but he remembered that the firewater tasted bad at first, but made him feel happy after only a few swallows.

Soon, the wagon was emptied of its meager contents. There were several narrow rolls of soft white cloth. A better find were seven woolen blankets that were stuffed in a burlap bag that was piled by the end gate. The blankets smelled bad and had yellow and red stains, but the women quickly shook them loose and draped them over their shoulders. They would wash them in the creek and squeeze them dry. The *wasichu* wool blankets were always warm to huddle under in the winter. Three long handled shovels were stashed under the bunk. A wooden mallet, a short handled ax, and a long coil of hemp rope, all would be useful.

Sidominadota's good feeling about the things they had found in the wagon was tempered with a nagging question of what the wagon was doing here, so far from the *wasichu* fort? It was at least a two-day ride from this swamp to where the soldiers were building their new fort. What the dead driver was doing so far away from the protection of the other soldiers puzzled him. But he was happy to have the many things they had found on the wagon and hoped that finding the wagon was a sign that their luck was changing.

He had been leading the band for the many years since his father was killed. He tried to emulate his father and lead as Wamdisapa would have, but it had been a hard job. It was widely known among the *Santee* tribes that he had killed his unfaithful wife and her lover. Some *Mdewakanton, Wahpeton,* and *Wahpekute* people felt that he might have been justified, even though killing an unfaithful spouse was not the way of their people. But he had to be ever watchful for his wife's people, the *Sissitons*. Pretty Star Low In The Morning Sky's father had sworn vengeance against him, and he knew that if the man or the people from his village ever caught up with him it would be a death sentence. Inkpaduta's killing of Buffalo Calf Man had turned many of the rest of the *Santee* against them. Again, there were many who were quick to state that Wamdisapa was killed in the same battle and thought it should be called even. But Tasagi, who had grown well respected from his dealings with the *wasichu* soldiers by helping to gain the annuity payments for land that was only marginally theirs to begin with, and his many followers still hunted them.

These thoughts rode heavy on Sidominadota's mind as they camped for the night in a copse of birch trees. He wished that he had strong medicine like his brother. Horse Woman's Child had been born with very strong medicine. Sidominadota recognized that. Everything that Inkpaduta did bespoke of his powers. He had killed Buffalo Calf Man, taking vengeance for the death of their father, even before he knew their father had been killed. Inkpaduta's wife, Hates Her Father had given birth to twin baby boys one year after Wamdisapa's death. A man who fathered twins was considered to have very powerful medicine, especially when they were male babies.

Two years later, another son was born and in two more years, Hates Her Father gave birth to a daughter and even now, her belly grew big again with a fifth child. Inkpaduta's prowess at fathering children, especially with two of them being twin boys was testimony to his strong medicine.

Wondering about the wagon once again, Sidominadota tipped one of the whiskey bottles to his lips. After downing three fiery swallows, he coughed until he gagged. Dizzily, he watched the world spinning around him and smiled to himself. Maybe their luck had changed.

# Chapter 21
## *Death Camp*

The hunting eagle soared high over the small lake. White feathers covering her head and neck gleamed in the early morning sun. Her wing and body feathers lay neatly in place, even though the updraft she rode was blowing hard. Her legs were tucked tight against her body. Her talon tipped toes, clenched into hard knots, lay hidden from the resistance of the wind by the long feathers of her belly. Her compact, graceful body rode the currents of the wind as if she weighed no more than a leaf.

Unlike a leaf blown in the wind, she was in complete control. A mere lift of her wing tips or shift of her gleaming white tail could change her altitude and direction in a fraction of a second. Exceptional eyesight allowed her to spot movement over land or water from hundreds of feet in the air, and while a scavenger by nature, she was a hunter at heart.

She soared low over the blue surface of the lake, watching the murky darkness for a flash of sunlight reflecting off the silvery scales of a white fish. With instincts inherited from generations of ancestors, she could not only judge the speed of her swimming quarry, but the depth at which it swam. Upon spotting the luminescent glow of a whitefish near the surface, she folded her wings and dove, hitting the water with an explosive force.

The fish, with instincts of its own, sensed the presence of danger as the big bird's shadow shot across its snout. Just before the eagle hit the water, the fish dove for the safety of an unreachable depth. The eagle's reaching talons stretched deep and speared into the slippery backed fish near its tail, and the supreme struggle for survival between the hunter and the hunted began.

With violent down strokes of her powerful wings, the eagle beat at the water, reaching to pull herself, and her catch from its depths. Again and again, she pumped her wings and lifted the fish with her legs until her body rose from the wet world. Slowly she broke contact with the surface and began to rise above it. The fish was a big one, heavier than she had anticipated and its weight threatened to pull her back until she finally struggled into the air.

The shock of the open air caused the stunned fish to struggle violently, jerking its head from side to side, twisting and flexing its body against her talons' grips. Suddenly, the fish's flesh clamped in one foot, ripped loose and the big bird was thrown off balance by the twisting fish. She spun and almost lost the air under her wings.

She began to lose altitude rapidly and finally had to release the grip with her other foot to keep from crashing back into the lake. The fish fell free, tumbling end over end until it splashed into the water, where it lay just below the surface for a short time, before sinking slowly into the deep.

Exhausted by the struggle, the regal bird doggedly beat her weary wings and climbed to a height where she could catch an updraft and glided for the tree line on the shore. Her nest stood stark against the sky and dwarfed even the tree she and her mate had built it in, three years before. They had returned to this same nest each spring adding to its size and bulk with twigs and small branches and tufts of swamp grass and cattail leaves. As she landed on the edge of the nest, her weight shook the tree and the three down-covered chicks hidden in the grasses and feathers of the nest came to life and started squawking in hunger, calling for food. She stepped gingerly toward them and instinctively tried to regurgitate her last meal, a striped gopher from two days before, but had no success. The hungry young ones continued their clamoring.

Her needle sharp eyes scanned the skyline and she saw the silhouette of her returning mate. He landed with food for their hungry nestlings. It was a scavenged catch with the flesh rotted to a sweet tenderness that pulled from the bones easily for the young eaglets. Their hunger satisfied, the downy eaglets huddled together in the center of the nest and fell asleep. Both adults ate what the young ones had left and knew that the quiet of their slumber would last only a few hours before the ravenous youngsters would be squawking to be fed again.

After resting through the hot afternoon, the male eagle stalked to the edge of the nest, crouched and sprang into the air. With only a few beats of his wings, he gained the altitude he sought and began circling in a wide arc out over the lake before crossing its shore. Leaving the lake, he flew due west until the raucous feeding call of thousands of crows faintly reached him. He shifted the angle of his wing tips and changed direction. Catching an updraft, he rode the wind current, flapping his wings only when necessary to keep altitude. His keen eyes searched the horizon and soon he saw circling buzzards dotting the sky, floating silently in ever shrinking circles until finally, one of the large scavengers dove to the ground and made a stumbling, running landing.

There were thousands of crows, all screaming their annoying "caw-caw—caw-caw-caw" over and over again. The noise was deafening to the eagle, which was used to quiet solitude. He circled low, surveying the scene. The ground was a writhing mass of black feathered crows, hopping from one pile of putrid flesh to another, pushing and shoving, each bird determined to get its share. Even the sky around him was filled with crows darting in and out and back and forth, some coming and some going, many circling and circling, looking to land and feast. All were screaming their incessant feeding call. The horizon was filled with increasing black dots, representing more crows that were homing in on the feeding calls of their brothers.

Deciding to land before any more competition arrived, the eagle glided gracefully to the ground. Hesitating only a second, he ran through the crowd of crows, brushing the smaller black birds aside with powerful strokes of his wings.

The crows were no match for his size and strength, and they retreated protesting loudly. With a short hop, he jumped on the prey he had spotted before landing, as if it were alive. Sinking his long talons into the soft flesh, he gripped it tightly and glared at the carrion birds surrounding him. The crows stood, their feathers ruffled, screaming their indignation at his thievery. Without further hesitation, the eagle sprang into the air, pulling at the sky with powerful strokes of his wings, and slowly climbed above the chaotic scene and headed back in the direction of the lake and his waiting mate and hungry offspring, arriving just in time for another feeding.

He feasted with them and then rested through the night. Early, with the rising of the sun, the male eagle was gone again, heading back to search out another easy catch, by stealing from the crows. His mate waited the long day for his return. She hunted the lake with little success and returned to the nest to do some housekeeping. She used her beak to shovel the refuse of the last feeding over the edge of the nest and glowered at the remains of the last catch he had brought back. It lay far below on the ground. Small white bones with bits of gristle still holding the joints together and thin strands of hair still attached to the empty eyed skull. A tattered blue and red blanket lay crumpled on the ground with the bones scattered across it, some on top, some beside.

The blanket had been the first part of her mate's catch rejected and shoved from the nest as it had no edible value. She had no comprehension of what the food he had brought back was, or where it had come from. But her babies were squawking to be fed once again and as the day passed into the evening, she could only wonder where her mate and gone, and why he hadn't returned.

\* \* \*

Hearing the baby crying, Rain Dance Woman struggled to her feet and waddled slowly to the tipi door. She pushed the door flap aside and peered out into the bright light of the afternoon sun. Heat waves rose from the ground, shimmering in the hot air, and she was sure that it was the odor that she could see rising from the corpses during the heat of the day. Nausea gripped her as the smell invaded her nostrils and she gagged, choking on the rancid odor. Inside the tipi with the flap closed and a small fire burning green plum branches with small amounts of tobacco, she could stand the smell. Going outside made her retch and lose anything that was in her stomach. But she had to go out. She also had to re-supply herself from the water in the creek and find more plum thickets. She had begun burning more plum branches as her supply of tobacco started dwindling. Once each day, she enjoyed a pipe of tobacco. It calmed her and the sweet burning taste helped mask the constant stench of death.

Gritting her teeth, the old woman bent and waddled through the tipi door into the bright sunlight. Holding her hand to her face, she tried to block part of the smell.

The sickness had come only two weeks after they had found the *wasichu* wagon. The women who had grabbed the blankets from the wagon and used them to sleep under were the first to develop the red rash of small red spots on their tongues and around their mouths. By the third day, the rash had spread to the rest of their bodies and the red spots became raised bumps. By that night, the women were all suffering a fever. By the next day, the infected women's' children all showed a rash on their faces and the women were sick enough that they could not move.

Not realizing what could be causing the sickness, Sidominadota directed them to set up the tipis for a permanent camp. They would rest here by a beaver pond on a dammed up stream and wait for the women to get better. On the fifth day, none of the women were any better and three more adults developed a rash on their faces. One of them was Inkpaduta. On the sixth day, one of the original sick women, died. Sidominadota didn't know what to do. As when he was a child, the thirty-eight year old war chief came to his mother when faced with a dilemma to ask for her guidance.

"It was the dead white soldier with the wagon," Rain Dance Woman told him. "The man had sores on his body. I told the women to let him lie. But they took his clothes and mutilated him. His medicine is angry and is taking revenge."

"How do we stop this mother?" Sidominadota asked, adding, "What do I do now?"

"Take the healthy people away," the old woman counseled. Rain Dance Woman had lived for over fifty winters. She had shrunk in size from a tall, slender beauty to a wizened old crone. Her back was bent from the years of hard labor toting and carrying her family's every possession. It had been a hard life. Her skin was wrinkled and dried from the sun and wind. Most of her teeth had fallen out. And her once milk laden breasts that had fed two growing boys at the same time, through their formative infant years, were now dried up sacks of skin that hung uselessly on her chest. But her mind was as sharp as ever and her love for her sons and her desire to help them succeed had not diminished. "Take the healthy people away," she stated again. "Take no one who shows signs of the rash with you. Let no one with any of the clothing or blankets from the *wasichu* wagon go with you."

"Where should I go?" Sidominadota felt like a small child again. He could lead his people into battle. He could raze an enemy camp and make all the right decisions when it came to out-running the pursuit of a more powerful enemy. But he had no idea how to lead his people away from this invisible and very powerful enemy.

"Go up river and up wind," Rain Dance Woman instructed. "Don't go so far that those who survive this sickness can not find you. But do not come back here. Only let those who show signs of the sickness come back. All healthy people must stay away," she stressed.

"What of you mother?" her eldest son asked. "You show no signs of the rash."

"I will stay with Horse Woman's Child," she stated flatly in a tone that indicated that she would hear no argument. She had lived in the same tipi with her adopted red-haired son since the day he was born. That would not change now.

Sidominadota's first move was to have the two gray mules killed. The two animals were led fifty yards up stream and shot in the head. Their great bodies became the first invitation for scavengers. Inkpaduta ordered his wife and children to follow his brother and instructed them to call Sidominadota husband and father, if he should not return from this death camp. Not wanting to chance that the sickness had invaded any of their possessions, the healthy people moved off, traveling up stream. They left most of the tipis standing and took only the clothes on their backs. They would start all over again.

Now, well into her second week in the death camp, Rain Dance Woman almost wished Sidominadota hadn't killed the mules. The dead had to be dragged away from the living. Otherwise, the night predators would come scavenging in amongst the tipis and there had been enough deaths to strain her small frame.

Slowly, she made her way in the direction of the squalling baby. The first few times she left Inkpaduta's tipi to drag the dead away, she tried avoiding the stench of the rotting dead by holding her breath as long as she could. That resulted in her having to take several deep breaths of the putrid air when her lungs ran out. Sucking the rotten odor deeply into her lungs made her sick and she heaved up her stomach, continuing to strain until she passed out. She had awakened barely in time to crawl back to her tipi before darkness and the wolves came. Since that time, she had learned not to try to keep from breathing, but to take short shallow breaths and to move slowly, lessening her need for great amounts of air.

The noise of the calling, fighting crows had become a common daily sound, as had the growls and snarls of the wolves at night. She had grown used to both and could live with them. But the crying babies, she could not grow used to. Each time a child's cry became never ending, it was a signal to her that the child's mother was dead.

Immediately, she was driven to do her grisly duty. Waddling slowly, dodging the fallen down remains of an empty tipi, she crossed the short distance to Long Leaf Woman's tipi. Long Leaf Woman's husband, Snores When He Sleeps, had come down with the disease the day after Inkpaduta. He had been one of the first to die, leaving his sick wife and baby to fend for themselves. Long Leaf Woman had begged the healthy people to take her child with them. They were leaving behind everything they owned in order to escape the sickness and no one wanted to chance taking in a baby whose mother and father were both sick.

Rain Dance Woman's tired eyes were drawn to the motion of a large eagle flying up from the dead grounds with a dead baby clutched tightly in its talons. It made her glad to see this. Surely, the child's spirit would be happy to see that its body would feed such a noble bird. After watching the eagle disappear on the horizon, she entered Long Leaf Woman's tipi and searched for the child. She found it wrapped tightly in a heavy fur robe. It was odd that the child hadn't died of the heat. Rain Dance Woman clucked her tongue in disgust. These young mothers knew nothing of raising children. A child must be wrapped warm at night and in the early morning to keep the night's damp chill from its little body. But in the heat of the afternoon, a child should be free of the confinement of warm robes and even of clothing of any sort. They should be allowed to run naked and free, to play with the wind and chase the butterflies.

As she unwrapped the crying child, she saw with dismay the angry red welts of the sickness. She left the baby lying naked on the robe, and when it quieted, took up Long Leaf Woman's heels, one in each hand. Struggling against the dead weight, she dragged the woman's body out into the sunlight. Putting her head down, she pulled like a horse dragging a travois, stopping to rest and vomit three times.

Finally, lightheaded and dizzy, she reached the dead grounds and she dropped Long Leaf Woman's legs, hearing the rigor-stiffened appendages hit the ground with two solid thuds. The crows and buzzards retreated only a few steps; they had grown used to the little woman who fed them. Shaking her head helplessly, Rain Dance Woman returned to Long Leaf Woman's tipi and picked up the screaming baby. Cooing softly to it, she carried the small male infant back outside and slowly trudged to where she had left his mother. Rain Dance Woman's soft voice and gently mothering calmed the child and it quieted and began nuzzling her breast.

A smile of memory cracked the old woman's lined face and a tear slid down her cheek. A second tear, and a third and fourth and then more, until a river of tears flooded her face, spilling from her chin onto the child. There were thirty dead *Wahpekute* lying with the mule carcasses on the creek bank without even the simple dignity of being buried safely against the ravages of scavengers. Suddenly she was very tired, and she slumped over the whimpering baby. Her body shook with silent sobs as she agonized over the realization that she would have to watch it die slowly from hunger, all the while letting it suffer from the terrible sores that were sure to come from the fiery rash that covered its face.

\*    \*    \*

His face itched and his head ached. The fever raged through his body, sending its fiery hot message to the end of each of his limbs. The rash appeared on the third day after the sudden violent fever began. Small red pimples grew on his face and forearms and spread rapidly to his upper arms and chest. A day or two later, blisters with gray pinpoint centers formed over the pimples. As the days passed, the blisters enlarged and filled with yellow pus. His face swelled until his eyelids were swollen shut and the itch and pain became agonizing.

Inkpaduta suffered. He was plagued, not only by the high fever and rash, but by vomiting and diarrhea. His back ached and pains shot through his head. His head, face and body itched and burned. He began scratching himself, digging and gouging with his fingernails until blood ran in rivulets from his face and shoulders. Rain Dance Woman rolled him onto his stomach and tied his hands behind his back to keep him from wounding himself further. She cried when he moaned with this new agony. When his temperature rose to its highest degree, he became delirious. In this unconscious state, his life began to pass before him in the form of dreams and death was only one less heartbeat away. During his delirium, the ordeal that his body was going through went unnoticed by his mind.

His first dream was more of a memory. It was something his conscious mind had not remembered before but now, in his fever induced dream, it was as real as it had been when it happened. It was a bump on the head. He was just a baby and his small soft head, a spot just above the temple, midway between his eye and ear, had received a bump from another head. The head was larger and harder. It was covered with a thick mantle of hair; long dark hair with short braids hanging down past large, flat ears. The bump was not a gentle little knock, but a rough, intentional butt. The head had the face of his brother when he was just a small child.

Mingling with the memory of the bumped heads was a memory of the swollen orbs of milk offered by their mother. He remembered how large and rock hard her breasts were when they were full after a night's sleep. Warm, sweet milk, always began dripping from her dark brown nipples as he or his brother began mewling with hunger, as she hurried about doing her morning chores before feeding them. Though it didn't show on the outside, inside, Inkpaduta was laughing at this memory. The jealousy between he and his brother as they both grew up suckling from the same mother at the same time, was now a fond memory.

His fever-heated mind next remembered the stories he had been told about his real father. A man with white skin and eyes the color of the sky and hair . . . the color of fire! The man was tall and strong and possessed powerful medicine. This dream was confusing for he knew his father. He was a squat man with dark skin and black hair that shined with bear fat grease. His eyes were black as night and shined also, especially when he was angry or speaking of making war on his enemies. A vision of dark father broke through the darkness that seemed to suddenly engulf him. His powerful body glistened with the bear grease and sweat. His long dark hair was twisted into tight braids, which were tied back behind his neck, out of the way. Vermilion colored the part on the top if his head. He was naked except for a snug clout hanging between his legs, and he was painted for war!

*A fire appeared from out of the darkness and Inkpaduta saw his dark father dance, circling the tipi twice, chanting a war song and brandishing his war club in one hand and the old firestick-gun he had tricked his white father out of, in the other. When he stopped dancing, his dark father was standing squarely in the fire. The flames seemed to grow up his feet and ankles and reached as high as the calves of his legs. He finished his war song and his weapons disappeared. He folded his arms across his chest and sat down, putting the fire out. His feet, legs and buttocks looked charred to Inkpaduta, his dark father's face showed no signs of pain.*

*"Hear my words, Horse Woman's Child," his dark father said calmly from his seat in the fire pit. "I will tell you of war and how to fight! Always know your enemy. Study him and look for his weaknesses. Never fight when your enemy is as strong as you are. Always wait until you out-number your enemy. Pick your battles and remember that one dead friend is harder to replace than one hundred enemies. You will always have enemies my son. You will not always have friends."*

*A flame grew from between his crossed legs and lit his dark father's face with a yellow glow that reflected red on the tipi walls. Anger glowed in his father's eyes and his figure started to fade away. Inkpaduta could still hear his voice. "Never trust the men with white skins! They are the beginning of the end for the Wahpekute! Watch them! Use them! Kill them!" The echoing voice was suddenly gone and the tipi was thrown into total darkness.*

*A horse thundered out of the darkness and stopped, rearing and snorting in the center of the tipi! It neighed and whinnied, shaking its head and stomping a front foot as if trying to get his attention. The horse stood, dipping its head up and down, while looking directly at him as if it were trying to tell him something. The light was poor at first and he could not see the horse well. As he watched the light grew, and he could make out the spots gracing the sides and rump of the mare. Finally, she stood calmly and looked deeply into his eyes. He could see a reflection of himself as a small child in those large brown eyes. As he stared at the animal, he saw a change come over her. Before his eyes, the horse's head and neck swirled in a puff of smoke and changed into the head and upper body of a young woman. Her hair was long, longer than most Wahpekute women kept their hair. The hair was brushed smooth and shone in the darkness. It played across her shoulders and tumbled down her chest, hiding the small breasts of a woman-child. The horse woman's arms reached out to him and her lips worked as she spoke, but he had never heard her voice and could hear nothing now. She lasted for only an instant and with the scream of a terrified horse, the woman disappeared and the long nose of a horse was back. The mare spun in a circle three times and with pounding hooves, ran off into the darkness.*

He shivered and felt cold. His true mother, Horse Woman With Spots, had just visited him. He knew it had been his mother for he had heard his birthing described many times. Because he was so large and she was so young and small, she had to change herself into a spotted horse to give birth to him! It was said that she was beautiful and that her medicine was very strong for a woman.

His fever broke soon after the visit from Horse Woman and slowly, his body began to revitalize. His memories left. Only occasionally would he think of them. But his dreams stayed with him and would guide him for the rest of his life. The dreams had created an inner strength bred of hate. The white skins were the cause of all of the evil that had befallen his people. Starting with the blood of the white skinned, red haired man, that mixed with the blood of his mother, creating him and ending with this horrible sickness, delivered to his people by another white skinned man, which was killing his village and had almost killed him. He would not die. He would live! He would live to kill the white skins!

He moaned from the pains in his aching body. His fever was leaving, but complete weakness flowed through him and he fell into a deep, dreamless sleep.

It was a long night for Rain Dance Woman. Horse Woman's Child had been tossing and turning and shouting out in his fever-induced coma for most of the night. Now, as morning time neared, he lay quiet and seemed to be sleeping comfortably. She yawned and bent to pick up Long Leaf Woman's child. Rain Dance Woman had held the child through the night, listening to its pitiful and ever-weakening cries of hunger and misery. Finally, as the light of morning came, she placed her hand over the sick child's nose and mouth and held it there, smothering the life out of it.

Weeping openly, she carried the infant to the dead ground searching for Long Leaf Woman's body. But during the night, the wolves had dragged the body away from where she had left it. She laid the child's body on the ground, away from the piles of rotting flesh, but couldn't bear to see it lying there alone. For just a moment, she would lie beside it and comfort it one last time. The old woman was weak from her own hunger and tired from a long sleepless night and worn thin by tragedy and hopelessness. She fell asleep on the ground with the dead baby still in her arms.

A short time later, she was awakened when she felt the dead child being torn from her arms. Fearing the wolves had come back, anger filled her soul and she pulled back on the child before her eyes opened to see the eagle trying to gain flight with this, the last of the dead children, clamped tightly in its talons. The little woman reached up and grabbed one of the feathered legs and reached for the other leg, just as the eagle released it grip on the baby's corpse and struck out at her, raking her shoulder with the sharp claw-like talons. The big bird beat Rain Dance Woman with its mighty wings and bit and pecked the little woman with its stout beak.

But in the end, she forced the bird to the ground and stood on its white head! Jerking and twisting with all of her might, she succeeded in breaking the regal bird's neck and pulling its head off. Releasing her hold on its feet, the headless eagle jumped and flopped, spewing blood over the sun burned grass of the dead grounds.

Rain Dance Woman struggled to drag the heavy bird back to the tipi. When alive, it had stood almost half as tall as she and the bruises that were appearing on her face, shoulders and chest proved the strength in its wings and legs. Her left arm was scraped and gouged where the bird's talons had raked her. Blood flowed from a hole on her upper thigh where the bird had attacked with its large hooked beak biting and pecking.

The wrinkled little woman chuckled with pride. It had been a war and she had won! She was wounded, but the bird was dead.

It was a great day! Proudly, she pulled the large feathers from its tail and wings. They were sacred and had to be saved. She carefully wrapped them in a piece of leather and hid them deep in a pile of her gear. She laid the body of the great bird in the coals of the fire and burned the feathers from its hide. While the feathers were scorching, she lugged water from the stream and filled a pot. Placing the pot on the hot coals, she chopped the charred carcass of the eagle into sections and dropped them, entrails and all, into the pot of water. As the water heated and boiled, she skimmed the scum and burnt feathers off and threw them away.

She fed Horse Woman's Child only the broth first. Until he grew stronger his aching insides would not be able to digest solid food. Soon, he would eat the flesh of the eagle and he would absorb the powerful bird's strong medicine. When he was strong enough, they would leave this place of death. They would fly on the wings of an eagle! They would search for Sidominadota and the rest of the village and find them, if any of them still lived.

Rain Dance Woman washed her wounds with hot water from the soup. She packed the open punctures with bear grease and covered that with mud from the creek to keep the flies from laying eggs in her flesh. She waddled over to where her son lay sleeping and felt his head with the back of her hand. His fever was gone! Smiling, she cut the rope she had tied his hands with to keep him from scratching and let him roll into a more comfortable position. After adding a few more sticks to the fire under the soup, she sat down and leaned back against her pile of buffalo robes. She felt confident for the first time since the sickness had befallen them. With a huge sigh, she closed her eyes and fell asleep.

# Chapter 22
## *Reunion*

**T**hree more weeks passed before Rain Dance Woman decreed Horse Woman's Child well enough to travel. The bodies of the people killed by the sickness had disappeared. Only bones, bleaching white in the bright sun remained, scattered in the tall grass by the scavengers of the day and the night. Gone, too, was the terrible stench of the rotting flesh. The skeletons of their tipis standing in a state of neglected disrepair were the only monuments to mark their passing. Inkpaduta had lost weight and was very weak. His usually ruddy skin was wan. Deep pockmarks covered all of his face except for his forehead and there were great channeled scars, gouged by his unconscious fingers, over his shoulders and chest. But his eyes were clear. The fever had not blinded him.

She began his recuperation by letting him sit inside the tipi for the first few days after the scabs fell off and his fever broke. Then she helped him stand and walk a short path around the fire pit. By the end of the first week, he was able to walk outside to relieve himself, but didn't much care for the smell outside of the tipi. She didn't bother telling him that it had been a lot worse while he slept.

During the second week, she led him on a path along the creek, skirting the dead grounds and had him help carry in armloads of firewood. Rain Dance Woman caught a large turtle at the edge of the beaver pond and, dodging its snapping mouth, dragged it back to the tipi. She was delighted to see Horse Woman's Child grab up the hand ax and chop its head off and then split the hard shell. Together they scooped out the turtle's entrails and cut the edible flesh from the ancient beast. The turtle kept them fed for three days. During the third week, Inkpaduta took his father's old rifle and hunted down the creek.

On his third day of hunting, he was lucky enough to see a sow raccoon with three almost fully-grown kits emerge from the tall grass on the bank and start searching in the shallow creek water for crayfish and clams. He shot the sow and carried her back to the tipi. That night as they ate the charred flesh of the raccoon, Rain Dance Woman announced that they would leave in search of his brother with the rising of the next sun.

Several weeks passed as Inkpaduta and Rain Dance Woman wandered the plains, searching in vain to find Sidominadota and the rest of the survivors. They found where Sidominadota and the people had camped only a few miles up the creek from the pox camp. Signs in the campsite indicated that they had lived there for about one full moon, before deciding that everyone in the pox camp must have died. Sidominadota had led his remaining people away from the creek angling in a northwesterly direction. Due to their long habits of not leaving signs for enemies to follow, Inkpaduta was not sure which direction his brother had taken.

Inkpaduta would have to follow his instincts. He knew that even though his band rarely stayed in one place for a long period of time, there was a pattern his father had followed and he suspected that his brother would do the same. In the spring and summer, Wamdisapa usually led the band to the south and east, through the Neutral Strip into the lands of the Sauk and Fox tribes, where they raided and became wealthy by taking what wasn't theirs.

When the cold time was coming, his father always led them back in the direction of their ancestral homelands north and west of the Neutral Strip. There, along the banks of the rivers and the shores of the lakes, groves of trees grew in abundance. The trees broke the wild winter winds that blew unhindered across the flat plains, providing protection from the weather and a source of fuel for fires to warm their lodges. It was there, in the land of lakes and rivers, that Inkpaduta hoped to find his brother and his family.

After conferring with Rain Dance Woman, they decided to abandon trying to track Sidominadota and headed for the last place they had wintered. He felt certain that by visiting the places they had spent their last few winters, they would find their people.

Early one morning as the pair followed a dried riverbed, they came upon an unconscious man prostrate on the rocky streambed. The man's body was crumpled over the rocky stream bottom. From the signs in the muddy ground, it was clear that the man's horse had floundered in the soft bottom and panicked. It had jumped back on the rocks, where it stumbled and fell, landing on the white man and rolling over on top of him. His legs were crushed, and his back was broken.

As they neared, the man's eyes opened and he moaned piteously. Inkpaduta loosened his war club with thoughts of putting the man out of his misery, but the white hunter spoke to them in a thirst-dried voice.

"Hold your weapon, my *Wahpekute* friend," he said in flawless *Dakotah*. "I am dead already, but there are some things I need to tell you."

"Let the man speak, Horse Woman's Child," Rain Dance Woman said reaching out to hold Inkpaduta's arm and stay his club. She had stopped using his adult name while he slept in his sickness and would address him by his childhood name forever more.

"My wife, Soft Winds Woman, was *Mdewakonton*, so I know your people," the white man said. "She caught the fever and died two years ago. She left me with two sons to raise alone," he explained, grimacing in pain. "They are good boys, and I left them at home in my cabin just a few miles down river," he continued, sobbing with pain from his efforts to speak. "They are young, and I'm very worried about them. It's been two days since my horse killed me. My back is broken, and I won't live much longer. But I've stayed alive hoping and praying to *Moneto* that someone would come along to save their lives." He spoke to Rain Dance Woman, his eyes pleading, "Please, good mother, go get my children and raise them as your own. Don't let them starve to death or let the wolves get them." His voice cracked, and he began crying. Then he turned his eyes to Inkpaduta. "My horse must have went home after it left me. You can have my horse! My rifle, shot and ball, dried meat and other supplies are all at my cabin. You can have them all! Just take care of my boys."

The man rattled on, nearly out of his head with pain and worry about his children. Suddenly, he stopped mumbling. His eyes cleared and he noticed the deep scars on Inkpaduta's face and he smiled at Inkpaduta.

"You've had the pox and survived. Your medicine is strong! You've defeated the *wasichu* disease. You will be a great leader of the people! Take my sons! Raise my sons!"

With one final deep breath, the man's eyes closed and a low moan escaped his lips as the air left his lungs for the final time. Rain Dance Woman had seen enough good people left to the scavengers. She began gathering rocks from the streambed and piled them on the body. Inkpaduta frowned at this inconvenience. A mission of mercy was not on his agenda. But he knew his mother couldn't be deterred from covering the dead man to protect the body from the wolves. With a deep sigh, he began helping her by picking up rocks and piling them over the dead white man.

They left the streambed and walked south along the bank through a rare forest of trees that spread up the slopes falling from the high prairie into the river valley. They found the white hunter's cabin sitting at the base of a high arching slope that rose steeply from the valley floor. The white man and his *Mdewakonton* wife had utilized the cliff-like face of the hill for the back wall of their cabin, building the sides and front out of logs and hides. There were no windows, only a hide covered door. The man's horse stood, still saddled, head down, at one corner of the building. A short lead rope was tied to a branch sticking from the side of the cabin.

As they approached, the horse lifted its head and whinnied a low welcome. At the sound, the hide door rippled and a small child, not more than seven years old emerged, lugging a long rifle. He stood, silent but resolutely on guard of the cabin and its contents. Inkpaduta stopped, but Rain Dance Woman continued walking toward the child. She began speaking to him in soothing tones, explaining that his father had sent them and that they meant he and his brother no harm. Her soft, *Dakotah* voice triggered the memory of the child who could still remember his Indian mother's tongue, and a longing for that mother welled over him as he dropped the weapon and ran to the old woman hugging her fiercely around the waist.

Inkpaduta rummaged around in the small cabin while Rain Dance Woman tended to the two boys. They were both starving, having not eaten since their father had left, and she fed them strips of smoked dried meat Inkpaduta found hanging high above their heads in the rafters under the pine pole and bark roof. He found a supply of powder and shot for the man's rifle, which was much newer than the ancient rifle his father had carried. Its barrel was not as rusted, but the dark wood stock was not as impressive as the cherry wood stock of Wamdisapa's rifle.

There were some blankets, a few buffalo hides, an ax, three flat wood plates and three horn spoons, and a leather-lined water bag. He pulled two of the longer poles from the roof and fashioned a travois, tying it to the saddle on the horse. He placed all of the goods on the travois and sat the two boys on the horse's back. Neither child had uttered a word to him since they had arrived and looked at his scarred face, showing fear on their own faces. Inkpaduta considered clubbing them, as he watched them sitting fearfully, but stoically, on the horse. As he laced their small legs to the saddle, it suddenly occurred to him that these boys were like him, half-breeds.

"How are they called?" Inkpaduta turned to his mother and asked. She had been talking softly with them and had gained their confidence.

"The older one is called Charley and the young one is Gunn," she answered, stumbling over the white man names.

\* \* \*

As they traveled almost due north over the next weeks, Inkpaduta considered changing their names, but decided against it. Their father had named them and a name given by a person's father should not be changed by anyone else. The young boys were an added burden, but their small faces and young voices seemed to lift Rain Dance Woman's spirits. She had felt depressed and fearful after these many long weeks of traveling, worrying that they might never find her older son and the rest of the band.

With the two young children to watch over, it seemed that her confidence returned. She started each day with a singing prayer to help them find the right trail. When the weather turned colder and snow began falling, Inkpaduta knew that if they didn't find their people soon, they would have to hold up for the winter. He was looking for a good place for them to camp the next day when they crossed a small hill and he spotted smoke filtering through the trees protecting the shores of a small lake.

Great joy filled his soul when he recognized one of the tipis as his brother's by the two-fingered hand that was painted on it over the door. He waited until Rain Dance Woman led the horse up behind him. The old woman looked down the slope in the direction he was pointing, and her eyes welled with tears.

"Who guards this camp from Sauk invaders?" Inkpaduta shouted down the hill, his breath steaming in the cold morning air.

The people in the village poured out of their warm tipis at the sound of the challenge. Ten men with spears and clubs and two with rifles spread out taking cover behind the trees to defend the village from the intruders. The women stood shyly, peeking around the tipi walls, looking up the hill. Suddenly, Hates Her Father screamed out with joy and began waddling up the hill toward the dark figures standing in the knee-deep snow. That voice! She knew that voice!

"Ink-pa-du-taaaa! Ink-paa-duuu-taaa!" she screamed as she struggled to hurry her pregnant body up the hill.

Inkpaduta trotted down the slippery slope to meet her and grabbed her in a mighty hug swinging her around in a full circle before placing her back on the ground. But the joy he felt was tempered when he saw the shock on her face. Upon seeing how badly the deep pox scars had disfigured his face, she pulled away from his embrace and started backing up the hill. Fear controlled her steps as she hurriedly tried to distance herself from him. But a strong arm suddenly encircled her shoulders and the raspy old voice of her mother-in-law spoke quietly in her ear.

"Don't fear your husband, my daughter," the old lady crooned. "He has defeated the *wasichu* disease as you can clearly see from the battle scars he carries on his face." Hates Her Father turned to look at Rain Dance Woman and saw her face clear of all blemishes other than those that her great age had given her. "Your husband's medicine is powerful." Rain Dance Woman continued speaking louder as most of the rest of the people from the village gathered around. "He wears the feathers of the white headed eagle and has feasted on its flesh. He brings a fine horse, a rifle, powder and ball and two young hunters, Charley and Gunn to join our people." She turned and pointed at the two small boys sitting calmly on the horse. All were smiling in happiness with this news. They listened intently as their leader's mother continued to speak. "Horse Woman's Child has gained great power from his battle with the white man disease and wears his battle scars proudly!" The wise old woman knew there would be many people frightened by the sight of his horribly scarred face. But she knew also that warriors who received wounds in battle were revered by the people and their scars were looked upon as badges of honor.

Hates Her Father pulled away from Rain Dance Woman and walked timidly back to Inkpaduta. Looking deeply into his eyes, she smiled and reached up to lightly run her hand over the rough pockmarks on his cheek. He smiled at her touch and was glad when his wife began leading him down the hill toward the village site. He glanced back at his surrogate mother and smiled as he nodded his head in silent thanks for her wisdom.

Two weeks later, Hates Her Father gave birth to another son. Unlike his older brothers and sister, who were born with dark skin and coal black hair and eyes, this small, squirming child was lighter skinned and had orange fuzz covering his head.

Inkpaduta didn't hesitate. "This child will be named Young Inkpaduta!"

With the birth of this child, Inkpaduta's power amongst his people was raised once again. His medicine was definitely strong. His twin sons, Fire Cloud and Roaring Cloud, were strong and healthy as was his third son, Rain Cloud and the orphan boys he had brought to bolster the village's number of male children. This latest child, another boy, along with his daughter, Little Raindrop, brought the total number of children attributed to his prowess to seven, almost half the number of children in the village. Many people began to wish that Inkpaduta was their leader rather than Sidominadota. But Inkpaduta was intensely loyal to his brother and refused to even consider taking the leadership role. Sidominadota was no fool. He recognized his brother's power and conferred with him about every important decision that had to be made.

\* \* \*

More changes in the world around them produced challenges for the brothers. Their reputation as troublemakers preceded them, and they were considered outcasts by most of the *Santee* nations. Because none of the band's men were accepted by the other tribes, they found it hard to find wives. They were forced to look outside the *Santee* tribes, to kidnap *Ioway, Winnebago* and sometimes even *Sauk* and *Fox* women, which created even more enemies for them to avoid in their ever shrinking world.

The coming of white traders began to shape the destiny of Sidominadota's band as well as the rest of the *Santee Dakotah* in the next few years. These white men, who brought goods to trade with the Indian people for furs, opened up the wilderness to a flood of a race of people hungry for land. Spurred on by the ideals of expansionism that had encompassed the country east of the Mississippi river, white settlers flowed over the Iowa territory like water bursting from a dam; rushing, crashing, rolling over the prairie. They searched out every nook and cranny and laid claim to it, heedless of the present occupants. The white skins were large, sturdy people, resourceful and self-reliant. They built societies that were totally different from the race of red men who had occupied the land for generations. Small farming and trading communities sprang up during these years. Some would die out, but others would grow to become major cities in the future. The immigration of white settlers was started by the white traders. Some were good men and some were bad men.

# Chapter 23
## *The Trader (1846)*

The white trader, Henry Lott, eyeballed the crossing from the driver's seat of his wagon. As a rule, a river ran deep between narrow banks and shallow between wide banks. The river's bed here stretched to nearly one hundred fifty feet wide. Both banks were low, making an easy access for horse and wagon on both sides. It had been a dry year, and the river was running low. Henry could see sun bleached rocks poking their pitted heads above the sluggish, gray-green water as it slowly swirled by. On the far side, a sand bar rose up out of the river and leveled off for twenty or thirty feet before rising up a gentle sloping bank.

"Waal, this is as good a place as any, I guess," he said to himself.

With a cluck of his tongue and a slap of the reins, he drove the single horse down into the dark water. The wagon was light. It bounced and jerked from side to side as its spoked wheels bumped across the rocky bottom. The horse went slow, picking its way across the rocks until it reached mid-current where the rocks stopped, the water level rose, and the muddy bottom sucked at its hooves. Feeling the slippery mud, the animal hurried its pace and lurched forward, jerking the wagon and almost unseating Henry.

"Whoa!" Henry shouted hauling back on the reins. "Damn ye fer a hard headed mule!"

He pulled the horse to a stop as the wagon rolled out of the muddy water and up onto the sandbar. Henry waited until the horse calmed down before jumping down off the wagon's seat. He hung a feed bag of oats over the horse's nose to keep it occupied and standing still, and walked to the back of the wagon. Lifting the tailgate from its slot, he dropped it to the sand at the edge of the water. With a grunt, he tugged a heavy cloth bag of flour from the wagon and let it drop onto the tailgate, where it tipped on its side and the mouth of the bag came open revealing mealworms wriggling in the white powder. Henry chuckled as he remembered how a white trapper had almost shot him when he tried to sell the mealy flour to him. Climbing into the wagon, he rolled a keg of trade whisky to the rear. He jumped back to the ground and carefully lowered the keg onto the sand beside the flour bag, making sure it sat with its bung up so none of the precious liquid would leak out.

This keg was a special concoction he had developed consisting of corn liquor that was not only diluted with river water and coal oil, but also contained a handful or two of black powder and a short measure of strychnine. The black powder colored the liquor, giving it the appearance that it had been aged in a charred keg. The right amount of strychnine made everyone who drank it sick enough to incapacitate them long enough for him to leave and be far away before they would be in any shape to follow. Of course, if he mixed too much of the poison in, or if any one individual drank too much of the keg, it would kill them.

Most white traders fed their Indian customers plenty of diluted whiskey to make them drunk and easy to cheat. But this time it was not on Henry's mind to cheat Chief Two Fingers by trading him worthless goods and trinkets for furs and buffalo hides. This time his plan was pure and simple thievery, and he needed the Indians to go down hard and stay down, if not forever, at least for a few days. The Army was abandoning Fort Atkinson and sending the troops stationed there to join with the troops fighting the war with Mexico. They needed horses, and Henry had lined up a buyer for any and all the horses he could supply. The two-fingered chief always had good horses and all Henry had to do was snatch the horses and lead them down to Pea's Point where the buyer said he would be waiting.

Hurriedly, Henry brushed his footprints from around the bag of flour and the whisky keg and climbed back into the wagon. Standing in the wagon, he studied the scene one final time. In his mind's eye, it looked as though when the horse lunged out of the water, the flour and whisky keg had slammed against the tailgate causing it to pop loose and all three had fallen unnoticed to the sandy edge of the river crossing.

With a short laugh, Henry climbed over the buckboard and onto the wagon seat. He slapped the horse with the reins and drove up out of the riverbed. The breeze picked up, and he turned his collar up to protect his neck from the cold. His eyes turned skyward, and he saw the dark gathering clouds. With any luck, it would snow before the day was out. He smiled to himself. Things were working out pretty good. A snowstorm would fit right into his plans. He drove the wagon for several miles down the river before stopping to unhitch the horse. In a few hours, he planned to saddle up and ride back to see if his trap had lured Chief Two Fingers and his band. He had cut their sign the day before and knew they would find his wagon tracks and follow them until they found him. He had traded with them before and knew that the two-fingered chief liked his whiskey. He was confident that the mealy flour and the keg of "fire water" was the perfect bait.

*     *     *

Inkpaduta was the first to follow the wagon's tracks to the river's edge. He could see that the wagon had crossed the river here and had lost part of its load on the other side. He studied the far bank and decided to wait for the rest of the band to join him before attempting to cross. He and his father had set up many ambushes at river crossings just like this one. He would use great care in checking the other bank before showing himself to any unfriendly fire from the other side.

When the rest of the band came up to the river crossing, Inkpaduta waved his arms directing some of the men up river from the crossing and some of the men down river. The warriors spread out along the low bank, taking cover in the dense underbrush. Most had rifles, and they looked down their barrels, aiming at the far bank. When all were in place, Inkpaduta, moving cautiously, waded out into the slow moving current. His sharp eyes watched the bank for any sign that might indicate danger. He was ready to dive to one side or the other, but as he entered the waist-deep water in the center of the river, nothing happened, and soon he walked out of the muddy water onto the sandbar. Ignoring the bag of flour and keg, he ran quickly for the cover of the underbrush on that side. He knew that if it were a trap, whoever had set it, might wait for him to stop and look at the abandoned goods on the river's edge. Or, they might wait until the rest of the people crossed and were examining the prize on the riverbank.

After searching the area surrounding the approach to the crossing, Inkpaduta found nothing suspicious. He followed the wagon's tracks for more than a half of a mile and found nothing to indicate that the driver ever realized that part of his cargo had fallen out at the river crossing. He returned to the crossing to find that the people, growing tired of waiting for him, had crossed. They discovered that the keg contained whiskey and one of the men immediately smashed the end of the keg. They were scooping their cupped hands into the dark liquid and were sucking it down. They howled with delight, even as they winced at the burning sensation of the firewater as it slid down their throats.

Most of the women were hurriedly scooping up the white powder to save it from the wet sand. Flour was something new that the white traders introduced to them over the past three years. They learned to add the white powder to pots of water that they boiled their meat in to make a thick, pasty gruel that filled their stomachs faster than the meat and water alone. The wiggling worms in the flour only added to its value as a food source and they were glad to see them.

Sidominadota called for an early camp to be set up on the sand bar. He and some of the other men were already reeling from the drink. He coaxed his wife, Prettier Than Her Sister, to stop helping with the flour and to come and drink of the Whiteman's firewater.

"Come woman," he commanded. "It burns your tongue and throat, but it makes your belly warm. It will warm our son and make him strong, so that when he is born, he will come out ready to fight!" He laughed as he patted her pregnant stomach and pulled her toward the keg of whiskey. Many of the other women dropped their flour bags and hurried to get their share of the whiskey before it was gone. Inkpaduta lowered his father's beloved rifle to the sand and bulled his way into the mob of men and women crowding around the keg. He wanted his share, too.

A light snow began falling on the people of Sidominadota's band. The adults, men and women, launched themselves into a night of merry making and debauchery that would find most of them passed out by sundown and the rest, soon after. Only the small children, who were left unattended to fend for themselves, would escape the sickness that the strychnine laced whiskey would cause their parents. It would not be just the usual hangover from drinking the Whiteman's firewater.

\* \* \*

Henry clucked softly to the *Wahpekute* horses as he crept slowly up to them. The animals had been hastily tied to the trees on the bank. He could hear the small children and babies crying. The falling snow was making them cold and no one had bothered to start a fire. He chuckled quietly to himself. It had been the perfect caper. The Indians had dropped everything when they saw the whiskey keg, as he knew they would. He gathered up the reins from seven good Indian ponies and untied the remaining five. He would lead the seven best and hope that the rest would just follow along.

Chuckling, he rode off slowly leading his prize. This was a good night's work. It was just after dark and it was snowing. If the snow kept up, it would soon cover his tracks and by morning, if any of the Indians woke up, they would probably think that the horses had wandered off and spend the next several days looking for them. He led the horses down river, heading for another crossing. He didn't look back and therefore, didn't see the hazel colored eyes of six-year-old Young Inkpaduta watching him lead the horses away. In the darkness, he also did not notice when the five horses he had turned loose stopped following him and was not aware that the eleven year old half-breed, Charley, was leading them back, one by one, to the sand bar camp.

*     *     *

Five days later and fifty miles east of the river crossing, Henry and his two sons, seventeen year old Simon and twelve year old Milton were sitting down to their supper table in his cabin in Webster County, when they heard their hound beller out a warning. Henry's wife dropped the pan of bacon and beans she was about to serve back on the pot-bellied stove she had heated it on, and crossed the room to peer out one of the rifle ports at the front of the cabin. She saw the hound rush out into the gathering dusk. A sudden gunshot silenced his baying with one last loud yelp of pain. At the sound of the shot, Henry and Simon jumped to their feet and saw to their rifles. Henry also lifted a short-barreled scattergun from pegs above the door and handed it to his wife.

"Aim it at the belly of the one in the middle," he said, adding, "It's loaded with horse shoe nails and won't carry far, but if they git in close, you'll bust two or three of the bastards and take the steam right out of 'em."

"Henry Lott," came a guttural call from the edge of the clearing. "Yoo come out."

"You come forward and be recognized," Henry answered, his voice steadier than his hands.

They could hear voices talking in the distance. The short, chopping syllables of a heathen tongue sent chills up Mrs. Lott's spine. Peeking through the narrow rifle ports, the family could see slight movements and finally, five figures moved out of the darkness in the trees and approached the cabin. When the men were close enough for Henry to recognize them, a low groan escaped his lips. He cursed himself for not mixing the strychnine stronger. Chief Two Fingers wasn't a bad sort. He had traded with him often and knew him to be as whiskey thirsty as any Indian. Because of the two-fingered chief's fondness for whiskey, it had always been easy to bilk him out of all of his band's furs for a few bottles of whiskey, a few blankets and some beads. It wasn't part of Henry's plan to answer to these Indians about the horses he had stolen from them. Everything would have been better if they would have just died right there by the river crossing.

It was Chief Two Finger's brother that Henry hated dealing with. He was a man with an ugly, scarred face and a mean disposition to go with his looks. He was also much smarter than most Indians Henry had dealt with. You couldn't win him over with a smile, a handshake, and a cup of whiskey. The man didn't seem too much impressed with the power of a whiteman. He didn't scare and couldn't be bullied, even when he was drunk. Henry shivered a little, knowing that the ugly one was not a man to be taken lightly.

"If trouble starts, I want both of you to shoot that ugly fucker on the far right and don't miss!" Henry growled to his wife and son. Mrs. Lott frowned at his use of bad language, but was too frightened to chastise her husband. "Milty," Henry said to his younger son, "you git over here and git ready to reload yer momma's scattergun."

"Lott! Come Out!" came the hail from outside again. Sidominadota stood boldly in front of the white trader's cabin. He and Inkpaduta had learned to speak the white man tongue as more white traders arrived in the area over the last few years. Charley, the oldest of the half-breed brothers helped them learn the basics. The rest they picked up from trading with the white men themselves. The blasphemous curses that sprinkled the unruly traders language was the easiest for them to learn.

"Goddamn yoo Lott, come out now!" Sidominadota shouted as his hand reached down to clutch at his aching stomach.

Henry slowly raised the latch on the door and signaled his wife and Simon to stick their weapons through the gun ports so the Indian would know that he was not alone. He had always found that a good showing of strength when dealing with Indians worked to his benefit. He stepped casually through the door and let the barrel of his rifle point at Sidominadota.

"Why, Chief Two Fingers, what brings you out on a cold night like this?" he smiled his most ingratiating smile, showing a toothy grin.

"Follow horse tracks," Sidominadota grimaced as another pain passed through his bowels. "Goddamn Lott, yoo shit-ass. Why yoo steal our horses?"

Henry noticed that of the five men standing before him, only the ugly one stood tall. The other four were slightly bent over with one hand on their bellies. Pain showed in their faces and he suddenly knew there would be no fight this night. Either the gunpowder or the receding strychnine was playing hell with their guts. And though these men were mad as hornets batted from their nest, they weren't going to attack without provocation. The realization made him bold.

"Don't know what yer talkin' about, Two Fingers," he lied as he shifted his eyes around the clearing, wondering if these were the only survivors well enough to track the horses or if there were more men hiding in the darkness.

"Shit, Lott!" Sidominadota growled angrily pointing behind the cabin. "Horses tied in woods!"

Henry silently cursed the government horse buyer for not showing up when he was supposed to. He had arrived home, to find that word had been sent that the buyer would be a day or two late. He cursed his luck at having the snow stop falling. It should have covered the horses' tracks, and he wouldn't be facing these angry men now! Bad luck all around! Now he was going to have to come up with a story to put these red men off his trail.

"Well I don't know where them horses come from," he said.

"Come from goddamn camp, Lott!" Sidominadota shouted, the anger showing through the pain in his eyes as yet another cramp passed through his bowels. "Follow tracks!" he added.

"I din't steal yer horses!" Henry answered in a weary voice. "I found 'em wanderin' free just a few miles up the river there and picked 'em up and brought 'em home." He made the mistake of looking down the line of men to see the smirking face of Inkpaduta and his confidence left as he finished lamely. "Figured someone would be along some day to claim 'em and, uh . . . I guess . . . ah, here you are." The steel gray glare in Inkpaduta's eyes sent a shiver down Henry's spine, and he felt compelled to change the subject from the horses.

"You got pelts?" he asked looking back to Sidominadota. "I got blankets, beads, bacon, flour, whiskey."

"No got gaddamn pelts, Lott," Inkpaduta spoke up from the end of the line. "No want blankets! No beads! No bacon! No goddamn whiskey! Got sore bellies from your whiskey!" He pointed his finger at Lott. "You steal horses!"

"I din't steal yer goddamn horses," Henry shouted, glancing at Inkpaduta, but turned quickly back to Sidominadota to try to change the subject again. "But you killed my goddamn dog!"

"You steal horses! My son saw you!" Inkpaduta shouted back, grabbing Henry's attention again. "No lie, we kill dog. Mebbe we kill yoo too, Henry Lott," he added in a calm voice.

At these words, the ominous sound of the firearms being cocked came from inside the cabin. Sidominadota looked at the men with him. Only Inkpaduta looked ready for a fight. The others were clutching their stomachs as the poisonous gas still held them in its grip. These men would hardly be able to defend themselves, let alone carry the fight against a fortified cabin. He held up his arm to stay his brother and spoke to Henry Lott.

"We take horses. We take dog. We not kill yoo." Sidominadota glared at the white trader and a deadly tone took over his voice. "Lott, yoo a shit-ass lie teller. We know dis. Yoo leave dis place. We come back in one moon. Yoo be gone from here," he ordered.

With these last words, Sidominadota turned on his heel and walked away, hoping he would not hear the sound of guns in the cabin exploding and feel the hot lead slam into his back. Three of his men turned with him, their only thought was to get back into the woods where they could bend over and relieve the agony in their stomachs. But Inkpaduta backed warily away with his rifle aimed squarely at Henry's stomach, watching for any movement that would betray treachery. Near the shadows of the trees, he stooped to lift the dead hound over his shoulder. They would feast on the creature this night and hope that the magic of dog flesh might drive the sickness from them.

Henry Lott was confident that the Indians had no idea that he had actually poisoned them. Often the Indians became sick from drinking too much whiskey that was not poisoned. The unscrupulous traders of the time had no qualms about taking advantage of drunken Indians to enrich themselves. He knew too that in a short time, the hangovers and stomachaches would go away and their thirst for whiskey would return. Many Indians sold their souls for a drink of the whiteman's firewater, and this knowledge led Henry Lott to laugh off Sidominadota's warning to leave. He told his wife that there was nothing to worry about. They would stay in their cabin here north of Pea's Point. In the spring, he would find Chief Two Fingers and patch up his hard feelings with a bottle of good whiskey.

## Chapter 24
*Milton Lott*

As the month of November came to a close, the weather turned colder and snow fell. There was not great amounts of it all at one time, but there was enough that Simon had to scoop a path to the outhouse and the pile of firewood. When the mercury in the thermometer dropped to below zero, the family stayed in the cabin around the potbellied cook stove. At night, they stayed in their beds, covered with every blanket they owned, plus two buffalo hides Henry had traded bacon, beads and dried beans to the Indians for. Simon and Milton shared a tick mattress on the floor as close to the stove as they dared to be. It was their job to stoke the fire and feed the stove each morning and to feed the stove at night when it burned down and the cabin began to cool off. When the temperature got cold enough, it was often the sound of the frozen trees popping outside that woke them and told them it was time to feed the stove.

Because of the cold, the Lotts didn't go far from the cabin. Simon and Milton braved the cold each morning to empty the night's privy pail and carry in enough firewood to get them through the day. The boys performed the same tasks again each evening, just as the sun lowered into the trees west of their clearing. Even these chores left the family in close quarters for long hours of the day and night, and they all began to get cabin fever. Arguments broke out between the two boys about whose turn it was to empty the pail and whose turn it was to carry the firewood. As the long days inside passed into the third week without much of a break, the adult Lotts found their differences too. They argued most often about the warning that the two-fingered chief had given them. Mrs. Lott worried that the month was about up. She wanted to pack up their belongings and leave, even if it was just to move into Pea's Point for the rest of the winter.

"Oh ma! We ain't goin' nowar." Henry would not budge. "Ol' Two Fingers forgot about them horses soon as his belly stopped achin'.

Them Injuns ain't gonna bother us none. 'Specially in this kind o' weather!

"I don't know," the woman countered. "He looked pretty serious to me."

"Naw. He was just bein' prideful," Henry stated. "If'n he'd a jist tucked tail and walked away, the rest of them boys of his might quit follerin' him and start follerin' that ugly bastard of a brother of his. A pity on us all if that ever happens!" An involuntary shiver raced up Henry's spine at the thought of the two fingered chief's pox-scarred brother.

The argument went on, day after day until on December 15, when there was a break in the cold weather. The temperature rose above zero for the first time in over twenty days. Henry and Simon escaped the cabin and went out hunting, bringing back a small doe. They butchered it, and the family enjoyed fresh meat for the first time since the onslaught of cold weather had confined them to the cabin. On the sixteenth, Simon left the cabin with an ax and returned shortly with a small pine tree. It was the first hint of the season to come for Milton. Christmas was soon to be upon them, and the warming of the weather raised everyone's spirits.

On December 17, Henry left to go to the settlement. The boys and their mother decorated the tree stringing garlands made of dried cornhusks cut into shapes of animals, and dried fruits. She tied small candles to the long-needled tree branches. The boys strung long ropes of brightly colored trade beads and tied them to the branches with ribbons of colorful cloth.

When they were finished, they stood back to admire their beautiful tree. Finally, they lit the candles to see them shine and spent the rest of the day reading stories from the Bible and listening to their mother tell them about how though Christmas trees were not popular in America, that her parents had brought the custom from Germany to their home in Pennsylvania when she was just a small child. It was her goal to pass this tradition on to her children.

Henry returned from Pea's Point carrying gifts and placed them under the tree. It was plenty early before Christmas, but he wanted to be ready in case the weather turned foul again. Milton was excited, for under the tree, there was a long package, wrapped in oilcloth. He was sure that it was a squirrel rifle he had been wanting. Simon was sure that he was going to get a new skinning knife. He had broken the blade on his while he helped his father butcher the doe. Their mother could tell by the gleam in Henry's eye that he had a surprise for her hidden somewhere too.

Through most of the year, Henry was not an easy man to live with, but at Christmas time, he became generous and kind. That night, the family feasted on tender doe haunch and apple and wild plum preserves spread on slices of bread baked that afternoon. With their stomachs full and their sweet tooths satisfied, they sang Christmas carols and felt good for the first time in weeks. As they prepared for bed, Henry announced that he would be going to Pea's Point in the morning. With Christmas only one week away, he wanted to be well supplied with good whiskey, cane sugar, peppermints, coffee and flour, just in case the weather turned cold again. He would need help carrying the dry goods, so he would take Simon along.

With thoughts of the most holy of celebrations putting smiles on their faces and a peaceful feeling in their hearts, they fell asleep happy and content. All thoughts of an Indian threat were forgotten.

In the morning, Milton stoked the fire and fed the stove several sticks of firewood. He shivered from the draft left by his father and brother as they opened the cabin door and left on their trek to the settlement. As soon as the flames rose in the stove, Milton rushed across the cold dirt floor and jumped under the blankets of his parents' bed. Snuggling up to his mother's warm body, he fell back to sleep.

\* \* \*

The noise seemed to come from a long ways off. The pounding shook the entire cabin, but it didn't wake Milton from his deep sleep. It was his mother's sudden cry that brought him to a sitting position on the bed.

"Indians! Milton get dressed!" she cried as she tried to climb out of the bed and pull her clothes on at the same time.

Milton jumped from the bed and quickly pulled on his britches. He had only one shoe on when the pounding on the door stopped. He had just slipped his other shoe on, when a loud crash from the wooden hasps that held the bar in place split as the door flew open! A draft of cold air blew into the cabin and his mother screamed! She stood half-dressed in her linsey-woolsey dress, clutching her heavy woolen nightgown to her bosom, trying to hide her state of undress from the men who had just smashed the door and barged into the cabin.

The eight men were dressed in buckskin pants and shirts with animal hides and trade blankets draped around their shoulders. They stood with wolfish grins, looking at his mother. She stood in place, not making an attempt to continue dressing or moving in any way. A look of complete terror was frozen on her face. Milton tore his eyes away from his mother and glanced at the men. It was the Indian chief Two Fingers with several members of his band, including his ugly faced brother. The ugly one laughed loudly and said something to the others in their own tongue, and they all joined him in laughing at his joke. One of them swung the door, which still hung by its leather hinges, shut to keep the outside cold from coming in.

"Where Lott?" the two-fingered chief asked Milton's mother. When she didn't answer, he strode forward and jerked the woolen gown from her hands. The act ripped open the front of her dress, for a moment, baring her breasts to the eyes of the men. She quickly grabbed the torn material and wrapped it back around to cover her front. But the men in the room had seen her and they laughed as she frantically gathered the edges of the torn cloth. Fear and the sudden chill in the room caused her to shiver and her nipples to grow hard and protrude, raising bumps in the thin cloth covering them.

"Where Lott?" Sidominadota shouted again, but the woman didn't answer.

"Pea's Point—he went to Pea's Point!" Milton answered for his terrified mother.

At the sound of his voice, Sidominadota spun to face Milton. He slapped him across the face. The blow knocked him to the floor and made his ears ring. Milton was only partially aware that his mother had screamed and ran to him as he lay on the dirt floor, waiting for his head to clear. She bent and reached to help him stand and pulled him to her bare chest, hugging her arms protectively around him. Fear and exertion caused her breath to come in great draughts and she began to hyperventilate.

"This one is a little old to still be on the tit!" Sidominadota said in *Dakotah*, pointing at the boy's head buried between his mother's heaving breasts as she clutched him tightly. The rest of the men laughed at his joke. "Henry Lott tried to steal our horses and is not our friend any more," he continued. "So, as in the old days, we'll take what we want from our enemies!" He swung his deformed hand in a wide arc around the interior of the cabin and ended with his thumb pointing directly at Mrs. Lott.

Systematically, the men began ransacking the cabin. The brightly decorated evergreen tree was an odd sight. They had never seen a tree inside a cabin before and wondered at the significance of it. Upon seeing the packages lying under it, they quickly tossed it on the cook stove. The green needles quickly dried from the stove's heat and burst into tiny bursts of fire. Soon the entire tree flared into flames and for a few minutes, Milton was afraid the entire cabin would catch on fire. But the Indians laughed and danced around the stove shouting as they dodged the shooting heat. Like large children, they made a game out of trying to push one another into the fire. The tree burned out quickly, and they soon returned their attention to destroying the inside of the cabin.

One of the younger men cried out in surprise when he tore the oilskin from Milton's squirrel rifle and then added it to the growing pile of valuables near the door. Milton's heart sank at the sight of his Christmas present being tossed on top of the pile along with his father's scattergun and bags of powder and shot. The quartered doe, clay jars of preserves and all of their blankets and robes made the pile grow.

They broke the furniture and smashed the coal oil lamps. The Lotts' bed mattress and pillows were slashed with knives and their stuffing of feathers and leaves were spread wildly around the darkened room. When the house was in shambles, with nothing left to steal or destroy, one of Inkpaduta's twin sons, Roaring Cloud, jerked Milton from his mother's side and struck him, knocking the young boy to the floor. He began beating the child with a stick of firewood as Milton cried out, covering his head with his arms and rolled back and forth on the floor dodging the relentless blows.

Suddenly, his mother's scream rent the air and she attacked the young Indian, hitting him with fists of fury! He dropped the stick and grappled with the woman. Grabbing her around the waist with one arm, he tangled his other hand in her hair and jerked her head back bending Mrs. Lott over backwards. In desperation, she struck at his face with claw-like fingers, and he released his grip on her, staggering back with blood flowing down his cheeks!

This injury brought roars of laughter from the rest of the men. Ignoring them, she rushed at Roaring Cloud intending to gouge his eyes, but the pox scarred Inkpaduta grabbed her by the hair and with a quick jerk on the back of her dress, tore it from her body. He threw her to the floor where she lay stunned after bumping her head on the hard earthen floor.

Inkpaduta stood for a moment looking at the naked woman. Then with a short shake of his head, he made up his mind. Pulling her roughly to her feet, he shoved her over to Simon and Milton's tick bed on the floor of the cabin.

"We will take all that Henry Lott has," he said, pointing at the semi-conscious woman. He untied the rope belt of his own leather britches. "I will be first."

Sidominadota picked Milton up from the floor and pushed him out of the door.

"Go find Lott," he ordered, switching to English, and gave the boy another shove.

Milton stood for a moment, staring at the wild man standing in his father's cabin doorway. He could see vague movements in the darkened interior of the cabin and could hear all of the men shouting inside the cabin and hear his mother's feeble cries as she struggled with her tormentors.

"Go!" Sidominadota shouted pointing toward the timber along the river.

Milton turned and ran for the river. He had to find help if he was going to save his mother's life. He knew Pea's Point was down river, but he didn't know how far. He and his brother had taken a canoe to Pea's Point during the spring flood and it hadn't seem to take very long to get there by water. He jogged down the frozen river with no fear of falling through the ice. As he ran, he tried not to think of his mother and the things that were happening to her inside the cabin. He wanted only to think of finding his father and returning in time to run the Indians off!

His father and his brother and he—they would run the stinking redskins off and kick their asses as they did it! They would be sorry that they had hit him and they would be sorry for the things they were doing to his mother, too!

Milton had been pushed from the cabin dressed only in his night shirt, britches and shoes on a day the temperature hovered above zero, but below freezing. In his excitement that morning, he had forgotten to pull on some warm socks. Socks would have felt good. His feet were already cold. In fact, so were his face and hands, and just about everything was cold. Everything except his chest. His chest was hot; it was hot from the inside out. His lungs were burning from sucking in the freezing air as he ran. His lungs hurt. He had to stop and catch his breath. His nose was running and his eyes were watering tears. He wiped his face with the sleeve of his nightshirt.

After a short rest, he started out again at a walk. Pea's Point wasn't so far, but he couldn't run all the way there, not in this cold weather. As he walked, he looked for different landmarks that might give him a hint as to how far he had come. He recognized a hollow tree that he and Simon had smoked a fat old coon out of during the summer. He was disappointed to see that he had traveled such a short distance from home. His ears were burning with cold and the mucus draining from his nose froze. He couldn't feel his upper lip. His shoes, filled with snow then melted, and his feet were now beginning to freeze. His hands had little feeling. His sweat-soaked nightshirt soon froze to him. Doggedly, he trekked on.

After only a few more miles, he suddenly felt tired and was frightened by the thought that he might not find his father in time. He began to cry, the tears freezing to his face.

"Papa, where are you?" he shouted in anguish. He listened for an answer, but there was none.

He kept walking, pushing himself beyond any believable endurance. Up and down the snow piles on the river, back and forth with the meandering course of a slow moving stream. Many miles passed his short legs, but not many as a crow flies. He was nowhere near his destination. He stopped, panting, his chest heaving with the effort to keep breathing the stifling cold air. But only small amounts of the burning oxygen filtered through his swollen throat to his belabored lungs.

"Papa, Mama needs you!" he squealed, but his cry was weak. This time he couldn't hear his own voice because ice balls had formed in his ears. His vision was cloudy. He could only see shadows. Exhaustion and the cold were taking a terrible toll on the young boy's body. He stumbled and fell, only to rise and push on. He fell three more times, after the last of which he lacked the strength to rise again. He began crawling, his small voice crying with unintelligible sobs of despair.

Finally, mercifully, the snow pile felt soft and warm to his depleted body. He had no conscious thought to rest, but finally his adrenaline-driven strength had given out. Milton Lott would not move under his own power again. There was no one there to hear the last indignant whisper to pass from beneath his frozen upper lip.

"Papa, they took my gun."

\*    \*    \*

Henry and Simon were returning shortly after Milton had run for the river. They traveled slowly, walking their horses. Henry was worried that his wife would smell the cheap perfume of the woman at the Pea's Point Tavern. He had had a good run of luck at the cards and had won some extra money. The woman was willing, and Henry felt that he deserved a Christmas present too. So after swearing Simon to secrecy, he accompanied the woman back to her room in the rear of the Tavern.

Simon was in no hurry either. He was worried that his mother would smell whiskey on his breath. His father had given him part of a bottle and told him to stay in the Tavern until he got back. It was a bribe to keep him quiet about the woman. He knew that, but he didn't know what he would do if his mother smelled the whiskey and started questioning him. When they topped the rise in front of the cabin clearing, Henry spotted some of the Indians leaving the cabin. They were heading in the direction of the shed where he kept his trade goods, wagon and harness. He pulled Simon to a stop and turned their horses around.

"We got to go get help," he whispered.

"But what about Ma and Milty?" Simon asked.

"They's too many of the vermin fer you and me ta handle on our own," Henry hissed. "We'll go back ta the settlement and git some help. Then we'll run them bastards off. Ma and Milty'll be fine."

They rode their horses hard back the way they had come, through the timber, never going near the river as the river route was too full of curves doubling the distance. When they returned from Pea's Point, several armed men who were itching for a fight accompanied them. But they were too late. Sidominadota and his band had left, leaving Henry's wife inside the cabin, where she sat, still naked, staring blindly at the now cold cook stove. She had been beaten severely and raped by all eight of the Indians. None of the white men who accompanied Henry was a doctor, but they did their best to patch her up and wrapped her in their jackets. At first, Henry was afraid the Indians had taken Milton with them, but one of the men found fresh tracks leading to the river.

After sending his wife back to Pea's Point with two of the men, Henry, Simon and the rest started following Milton's tracks. They found him several miles down the river. He lay in a snow bank, curled in a ball, as if in his last minutes he was trying to keep warm.

They lifted his stiff body and took turns carrying it back to the cabin. Milton's mother died in Pea's Point two weeks later. Henry figured it was just as well because after her experience with the Indians, he knew that her mind would never be right again. He allowed that she had been a good woman, maybe even too good for the likes of her husband.

Even though Henry Lott hadn't been a good husband, he went wild with grief for a brief time that winter. He drank large amounts of whiskey and tried to assuage the guilt he felt by fighting any man who looked cross-eyed at him. He stayed the rest of the winter at Pea's Point, moving in with the woman at the rear of the Tavern. He lived with her trying to drink his grief away. That spring, he married the woman and tried to start his life over. But ever present on his mind was the oath of vengeance that he had sworn over the graves of his son and wife. One day, Chief Two Fingers would pay!

# Chapter 25
## Annuity Day (1846)

After the army and the white traders like Henry Lott opened the Iowa territory, white settlers were quick to follow. On December 28, 1846, ten days after the death of Milton Lott, the Iowa Territory became the twenty-ninth state in the union.

The Mississippi River in the east and the Missouri and Big Sioux Rivers in the west bordered the new state. Its southern border was the Missouri State line. Its northern border was trimmed down from the Minnesota Territory to a straight line stretching from a point in the Dakota Territory, just below the west turning bend on the Big Sioux River running east across low lying swamps and marshlands and rolling prairie land to the rocky hills leading back to the Mississippi River in the east.

By the end of 1846, fifty thousand white people had populated the eastern half of the state. Only a few adventurous trappers and traders had pushed west of the Des Moines River. Sidominadota and Inkpaduta feared a strong reprisal from the whites around Pea's Point and led their band to safety by going west and north. They didn't stop in the traditional *Santee* land in Southern Minnesota, but continued to the land of their cousins the *Yanktons* and *Tetons* in the heart of the *Dakotah* lands. The lifestyle of these western tribes was almost too primitive for the *Wahpekutes*, who over the years had grown increasingly dependent upon trade with the white men. Flour, metal pots, beads, colorful cloth, and whiskey were almost non-existent in the western lands. There were no steel traps, and there was nothing to trap on the high prairie anyway. They expended the last of their powder and shot hunting buffalo, and they found that they had lost many of the hunting skills still used by their wilder cousins. Soon after, Sidominadota brought his people back to the eastern door of the *Dakotah* nation.

Using buffalo hides for barter, they were able to replenish their supply of shot and powder, cloth and needles, steel knives and hatchets. For the next several years, they traveled a circuit that led them away from large villages and brought them into contact with only those they could steal from and those few whom they could trust. It was in 1852, on the northern swing of their yearly journey that they met up with their uncle, Black Otter. They were surprised to find Black Otter's village near the *minne sota* river. Black Otter was glad to find his brother's sons. They were *Wahpekutes,* and he was sure they would appreciate his complaints.

"We are the People Who Shoot Among the Leaves," he said, using the ancient translation for *Wahpekute.* "We have lived among the trees along the great Father of All Waters (Mississippi River) for generations. I knew where to set my fish traps and where to hunt deer and bear at our home on the big river. I am lost here in this strange land." The old man slumped as he sat by the fire pit. He was older even than their father would have been had he lived. Deep wrinkles covered his face and his long hair, greased with bear fat, hung in gray tails across his shoulders. He reached into the pouch at his side and retrieved a twist of tobacco. He shaved off enough to fill his pipe bowl and carefully placed the twist back in his pouch. Placing the end of a burning stick from the fire in the bowl, he sucked on the pipe stem, drawing the flame into the tobacco and soon fragrant smoke rolled out of his mouth around the stem. After several deep puffs, he handed the pipe to Sidominadota and said, with regret in his voice, "I will probably die here, far from my home."

"If you are unhappy here Uncle, why do you stay here?" Sidominadota asked before placing the pipe stem between his lips. It had been a long time since Sidominadota had smoked real white man tobacco, and he savored it, listening to his uncle's answer, before passing the pipe to Inkpaduta.

"Little Crow, the *Mdewakonton,* and a man called Wabasha and some Missionary Indians from the northern tribes traveled to the rising sun to see the Great White Father. When they came back, they told us we had to move here to these reservation lands. They said they had sold all of the *Santee* lands except for here on this *minne sota* river.

"Sold the land!" Inkpaduta exclaimed. "How can land be sold? It cannot be owned, so it can not be sold." It was the argument his father had stated when the *Santee* led by Tasagi had sold the Neutral Strip to the whites twenty years before. He reached down and scraped up a handful of dirt from between his feet. "You can only own what you can pick up and carry away with you." He shook the handful of dirt at his uncle. "You can't own the land you walk on. It owns you." Suddenly, a huge grin appeared on his face. "Little Crow must have

224

taken a pouch full of dirt to the Great White Father and handed it to him and said, 'This land is your land.' He has played a great joke on the whites!" he cried, laughing wildly.

"If it was a joke, why did he tell me to move my family here?" Black Otter asked, swinging his arm in a wide arc indicating his tipis. "And why are the whites paying us great amounts of their gold?" he asked as he pulled a bag full of gold coins from the pouch where he kept his tobacco twist.

At the sight of the gold, both brothers gasped in surprise! Over the years of trading with white traders, they had learned the value of the white man's money. Envy filled both brothers. After taking his turn puffing the pipe, Inkpaduta handed it back to Black Otter. A crafty look came into Inkpaduta's eyes, and he signaled Sidominadota to sit back.

"Where did you get this white man money, Uncle?" he asked.

"From the agent at the Lower Agency," the old man stated, explaining, "It is at a place called Redwood Falls on this little river."

"Uncle," Inkpaduta interrupted, "Give us this money. Tomorrow you can go get more."

"No—No, I can't." The old man shook his head. "They made the payments today, and they said that if I come back next year, I will be given money again."

Black Otter smiled and patted his medicine bag, saying, "This is my money. I can buy many things from the white traders at the agency. They have good tobacco, you know. It is the only good thing about moving here."

"We will go to the agency and get our money!" Sidominadota said jumping to his feet.

"Too late! You are too late," the old man cackled as he tried to rise quickly with his nephews. "They made the payments at the Redwood Agency today. Tomorrow, they will make the payments up river at the Yellow Medicine Agency. The *Wahpeton* and *Sisseton* have always lived there. They are happy with this sale of *Santee* land. You can try to get your money there," he said as he watched Sidominadota and Inkpaduta walk away into the growing dusk without a word of farewell. Turning back to his fire, he shook his head and chuckled to himself. His brother's sons had always been of a different sort.

It was a full night's ride to the Yellow Medicine Agency. The brothers stopped by their camp to gather their warriors and rode out that night to travel to the Upper Agency. When the sun had risen above the trees the next morning, Inkpaduta, along with his twin sons, Roaring Cloud and Fire Cloud, stood among the loose circle of *Wahpeton* and *Sisseton* surrounding the Agent in the yard in front of the Yellow Medicine Agency cabin. The white agent, John McAfee, sat at a crude table made of rough-hewn planks. Seated at his side was army Lieutenant Melvin Gibson. His interpreter, a man called Sits With The His Back To The Wind, stood at his other elbow. The interpreter was a crafty man who was always trying to improve his social standing by being close to the men in power. A well-armed troop of infantry soldiers stood quietly in the shade of a nearby grove of oak trees. The soldiers' bright blue uniforms and fancy hats and their rifles that had long knives attached to the ends of the barrels impressed the assembled *Santee.*

Sidominadota, Big Face and Man Who Makes A Crooked Wind As He Walks stood a short distance from Inkpaduta. The half-breed brothers, Charlie and Gunn, were farther back in the growing crowd. The men of Sidominadota's band fell in to line as they watched the men of their cousin tribes advance to the agent's table one at a time. The agent handed each man before him a quill pen and asked his name. Sits With His Back To The Wind repeated each man's name, changing it to English words and the agent wrote it in his black-bound ledger. Each man made a mark by his name and in turn received a small bag of gold coins.

It was the *Moon of Making Fat,* and the sun was hot. Beads of perspiration developed on the waiting men's faces and dark spots grew under the arms of the dark suit worn by the agent. The waiting men hoped for a breeze to cool them as the morning wore on. When it was Inkpaduta's turn at the front of the line, he stepped forward eagerly and stated his name.

"Inkpaduta."

"Red End." Sits With His Back To The Wind translated the name to English and the white agent wrote down the name and handed Inkpaduta the pen. But before he could bend to make his mark on the paper and receive the money, a voice from the back of the crowd rang out coldly in the hot sun.

"Wait, this man deserves no payment!"

Everyone turned to see who had spoken, and the agent pulled the bag of coins back and stood, craning his neck to see around Inkpaduta. It was Tasagi, who stood and walked slowly to the front. He was an old man, but his voice was strong, and he moved with a grace belying his age.

"This man's father refused to sign the first treaty when the whites bought the Neutral Strip. Wamdisapa wanted no part of it!" Tasagi's eyes burned with hatred as he neared the Agent's table. "Wamdisapa and his sons, these two men," he paused to point out Inkpaduta and Sidominadota, "continued to fight the Sauk and the white soldiers and even our own people in the Neutral Strip. After they broke the treaty, they fled to the west. And when Buffalo Calf Man tried to stop them, they killed my son, a *Wahpekute*."

Tasagi's accusations aroused the rest of the people and even before he had finished speaking, another man stepped forward and pointed his finger at Sidominadota shouting, "This man killed my daughter and stole my second daughter!" Sidominadota recognized Pretty Star Low In The Morning Sky's father. "I haven't seen her since. He probably killed her too!"

"He also killed my son!" shouted Younger Bear Up A Tree's father from the back of the line. All of the Upper Agency warriors pulled their weapons and began to surge toward Sidominadota and Inkpaduta.

"But Buffalo Calf Man killed my father!" Inkpaduta bellowed as more shouts of anger rose from the crowd.

"And Pretty Star Low In The Morning Sky was fucking Younger Bear Up A Tree!" Sidominadota yelled above the rising din as the men of his village drew their weapons and crouched together in a small circle facing the surrounding mob of Sisseton, Wahpeton and a few Wahpekutes, followers of Tasagi, who had moved to the Upper Agency to be nearer to the missionaries.

McAfee, listening with one ear to Sits With His Back To The Wind's interpretation of what was happening, saw that the situation was about to deteriorate into open warfare. It wouldn't look good on his record to have any kind of armed conflict on Annuity Payment Day, and he acted quickly.

"Gibson, get your men in there and keep these people separated!" he ordered, and then boldly marched into the crowd of men, rudely pushing people out of his way and shouting, "Calm down! Everybody calm down! We will work this out." Sits With His Back To The Wind followed him closely, shouting his interpretation.

The blue clad soldiers double-stepped into the mob and formed a loose circle around Sidominadota and his people. Not understanding what the confrontation was all about and not knowing which faction would threaten more danger to the troop, Gibson order the men to alternate every other man with his bayonet pointed in toward the *Wahpekutes* and the next out toward the Upper Agency Indians. They lowered their rifles and pointed their bayonets at stomach level forming a lethal two-sided circle. With the soldiers in control, a sudden silence filled the agency yard.

"These men are outlaws," Tasagi said, facing McAfee. "They have never signed a treaty and have never abided by the agreements made by our people." He raised a shaking hand and pointed it at Inkpaduta, adding, "They have killed many of our own people and for this, they are considered outcasts! Do you think we would say this about our own *Santee* brothers if it weren't true?" His voice cracked with emotion as he finished. "You should kill these men, right here!"

Only the low mumble of the interpreter, explaining the details to Agent McAfee could be heard in the silence that followed Tasagi's speech. But the men with Sidominadota and Inkpaduta tightened their grips on their knives and war clubs, preparing to sell their lives dearly. McAfee signaled for Gibson to come near. The two held a whispered conversation.

"We can't kill these Indians," McAfee said, "but we can't give them any money, either."

Gibson shook his head in agreement. But, as he watched the growing discontent on the faces of the Upper Agency Indians, he knew they had to do something and do it fast. "You're right John, we can't kill them. So we had better send them on their way fast, because before long these Yella Medicine Injuns are goin' to take matters in their own hands. And I don't want to chance losin' any of my boys just tryin' to keep these gut-bags from killin' each other." McAfee frowned at Gibson's remarks but knew that he was right. He turned back to the crowd and dragging his suddenly reluctant interpreter with him, stepped through the ring of soldiers and faced Sidominadota.

"Because of the crimes you have committed in your society," he said, speaking loud and slow to let Sits With His Back To The Wind interpret in an equally loud voice so that all could hear. "You are here-by banished from this agency and must never come here again on pain of death." He hoped that the idle threat to kill these *Wahpekute* if they came again would pacify those demanding their deaths now. "You have been named as outcasts by your own people and must live by the circumstances of your own actions. You do not qualify for annuity payments and are not welcome here." He stopped and when the interpreter had caught up, he finished, pointing south. "Leave here in safety now. But do not return!"

With their weapons still gripped tightly and their eyes glowering with hatred, the outcasts moved solemnly away. They mounted their horses and returned to their camp by the Lower Agency.

Once again, fearing reprisals from the relatives of the people they had killed, Sidominadota announced that he would lead his people to the west. But the lure of the riches to be obtained by living near the agency took some of his people who had relatives living at the Redwood Agency. They moved in with their relatives and hoped that after a year's time, they would be accepted as part of the agency's populace and would be able to collect their share of the annuity payments.

This same attraction brought the brothers back to the Lower Agency each year to try to obtain an annuity payment. But Tasagi, anticipating their plan to mix in with the rest of the crowd and get paid, was always present to announce loudly that they were outcasts.

Each year, the white agent heard Tasagi's accusations and ordered them away. They tried three years in a row and were thwarted by Tasagi each year. With each year's failure, a few more of their people left to join with the agency tribes. By 1855, only direct relatives of Inkpaduta and Sidominadota and a few people with no other relatives were left to follow the brothers, and they became truly an outlaw band, stealing from anyone not strong enough to stop them. A long festering hatred for Tasagi grew in their hearts and each brother renewed his sworn vengeance for their father's nemesis.

## Chapter 26
### *1855 – Revenge!*

**I**t was the *Moon of the Red Grass Appearing,* two moons before annuity payment time. The spring night was warm. Water stood in puddles along the narrow wagon path that led from the agency into Tasagi's village. Tasagi sat beside his tipi, listening to the night birds and pondering the problems of his newfound religion. Two years before, his wife New Grass Woman had died. Shortly after her death, he bought two young sisters and married them both. He was an old man with many needs, and he wanted two wives to take care of him. When the white missionary, the Right Reverend Ezra Conover, found out that he had two wives, the white holy man made Tasagi promise to get rid of one of them.

"God will spate the man with multiple wives from his kingdom in heaven, as the water falls over the cliffs, delivering him to hell below!" the Right Reverend Conover stated, shaking his finger in Tasagi's face. "Rid thyself of this sinful existence or regret the consequences, brother Abner," he warned, using the English name he had given Tasagi.

As he thought about the problem, Tasagi wondered why the Whiteman God cared how many wives he had. The sisters didn't mind sharing their wifely duties. But the Right Reverend was adamant. One had to go. Which? The fat one could cook and was warm and comfortable to snuggle with under the sleeping robes. The thin one did most of the other chores including carrying water from the agency well and sweeping out the tipi. She could massage the aches from his old bones better than her larger sister. She also made him feel young again when she climbed naked under the robes with him.

Making one of them leave was a problem that he really hated to face up to. Tasagi thought about leaving the agency and taking both of his wives with him. There were only two other men and their wives left of those who had followed him when he moved to the Yellow Medicine Agency, hoping to learn more about the Whiteman God from the missionary stationed there. All of his other followers had become disillusioned with the Right Reverend's stringent teachings and moved back to the Redwood Agency to be with the other *Wahpekute* people who lived there. But Tasagi was not unhappy here. Reverend Conover had shown him a new way to happiness through the ghost of the Whiteman God's son. It was a strange religion to him, but he could hear the total belief and confidence in Ezra Conover's voice each time the man preached a sermon. And he could see the sincerity in his eyes and could feel the heat of his passion! So, he decided, he would send one of his wives home to live with her parents. Then maybe in a few weeks, he would sneak her back and hope that the good reverend wouldn't notice her return.

The spring sun dipped below the trees on the western edge of his village clearing. Tasagi added more wood to his fire and sat back pondering his problems. He could hear his wives whispering in worried voices inside the tipi. They were upset by their impending separation, and he could hear it in their voices.

As he listened, hoping to get a hint as to which of the two would be least upset if she were sent home, another sound came to his ear. Horses, their hooves muffled by the soft earth, but sucking up in the spring mud as they walked slowly on the rutted wagon path leading from the agency clearing two miles away. Light from the sun was almost gone and Tasagi stood, peering into the gathering darkness. But the light from his fire had stolen his ability to see into the dimness outside of its radiance. He could hear that the horses had separated and circled around his clearing, surrounding the three tipis. A sudden fear ran its course through his body, causing his voice to shake as he cried a warning, which brought the other two men from their tipis to stand beside him.

These two men were younger than Tasagi, but were far past their prime years also. They held their war clubs, but left them hanging at their sides as the visitors entered the area lit by the camp's fires. Inkpaduta and Sidominadota and twelve of their men surrounded the three old men and stood silently glaring at Tasagi.

"What do you want?" Tasagi asked, gaining control of the tremor in his voice.

When no one answered, Tasagi frantically looked around the circle of men, hoping to see a friendly face. But all he saw was hatred. Realizing the gravity of the situation, he dropped his own war club and reached to take the weapons from his two compatriots. Taking their hands in his, he began reciting a prayer the Right Reverend Ezra Conover led them in each Sunday.

"Our Father who live in heaven

Sacred be your name on ground as it is in heaven.
Your Kingdom–land where you live
Your wishes be done on ground and in heaven."

Sweat began to pour off the old man as he struggled to remember the words in the white man's tongue. His antagonists stood quietly listening to him, waiting for him to finish. Tension grew in his voice as he struggled on. He was disappointed that the peace that the missionary had promised him would accompany the saying of the prayer did not come. But he continued on hoping something good would come of it.

"Give us today our food and forgive us for doing wrong things.
And we will forgive people who do wrong things to us.
Don't lead us down the wrong path, and protect us from evil men.
For Yours is the Kingdom–land where you live–
The strength and happiness forever and ever! Amen!"

When he was finished, Tasagi felt a brief moment of pride at being able to remember it as well as he had without prompting from the missionary. It was a confusing prayer for him because he couldn't distinguish between which were words of the actual prayer and which were words of explanation of what the prayer meant. He knew he had little time left, and just to be on the safe side, in case the missionary was wrong about the Whiteman God loving his *Wahpekute* children just like his white children, he sang his death song–a prayer to his own god, whom he hoped was a good friend to the Whiteman God.

*"One above who makes the sun rise,*
*Hear me!*
*Soon I'll pass through the mists of time.*
*Hear me!*
*I am a brave man and a good hunter,*
*Hear me!*
*Take me to where the great herds have gone,*
*Hear me!*
*I will fill your lodge with tongues and livers,*
*Hear me!*
*No person will go hungry,*
*Hear me!*

Tasagi's two friends joined him in singing their own death songs as Inkpaduta stepped forward, grabbing Tasagi's right hand in the steel grip of his left hand. With an angry smile, he shoved his knife in an upward thrust into Tasagi's chest, just below his left nipple. Tasagi

233

collapsed into Inkpaduta, a low moan escaping his lips. The move was so quick that the other men seemed for a moment, not to notice.

But as Inkpaduta stepped back, letting Tasagi's body fall, the other two men stopped their songs and stood staring blankly at him. Before they could make a grab for their war clubs, Inkpaduta's twin sons Roaring Cloud and Fire Cloud, bashed the back of their skulls with their war clubs and the two men fell forward, landing on Tasagi's body. Moving quickly, Sidominadota lead the rest of the men. They entered the three tipis and quickly killed the four women they found in them. There would be no witnesses to point their finger at the two brothers. Their camp was over a hundred miles south of this place. They had traveled at night, hiding by day for many days to get to the Yellow Medicine Agency. They would return to their village the same secretive manner, and no one would know they were even in the area when Tasagi's village was wiped out!

The outcasts quickly ransacked the tipis, taking anything of value. Three bales of prime furs were loaded on a packhorse, and they fled into the growing darkness. Moving south, the band traveled only under the cover of night and hid in heavily timbered valleys with fireless camps during the daylight hours.

Near noon on the third day, they arrived in their village on the *Inyaniake* River sixty miles south of the northern border of the new state, Iowa. The brothers huddled in council that night and made plans to strengthen their alibi by moving even further from the crime scene.

Sidominadota decided not to flee to the west as they had in the past, when there was a chance they might be the targets for retribution. It was only two moons until it would be annuity time, and Sidominadota reasoned that since it had been Tasagi who had blocked their application for annuity each year, they would be suspected of the murder. But, he also knew that if they didn't show up as usual, at the Redwood Agency on annuity day, their absence might be construed by some as proof that they had killed Tasagi and were afraid to show their faces around the Agency. In order to look innocent of the crime, they would show up as usual and act surprised when Tasagi wasn't there.

Tasagi's furs presented a problem. The brothers knew that it would be a bad idea to bring the furs they had stolen from Tasagi with them to trade with the white traders at the Agency. It would be possible for one of Tasagi's friends to recognize the bales if they saw them up close.

Inkpaduta suggested taking them to a white man who lived several days south on this same *Inyaniake* River. His name was

Curtis Lamb, and the brothers had met him two years before, in 1853, when he had been with a group of twenty-five whites who were building cabins for a small settlement they were calling Smithland along this same river they called The Little Sioux.

Curtis Lamb was a good man, who treated them with respect. He spent time trying to learn their language and tried to teach the brother's the white tongue called English. They liked and trusted him. Twice before, when they delivered furs they had trapped to him, he had acted as their agent and sold the furs ninety miles further to the south at a place called Kanesville. He had always paid them a fair price and took little for his services.

While sitting around the fire that night, the two brothers hatched a plan that they hoped would prove as an alibi, should they be openly accused of killing Tasagi. They would split up. Inkpaduta would lead most of the village south to Curtis Lamb's land and ask him to sell Tasagi's furs for them. Sidominadota would take his family east. They would spend the next month gathering honey from hollow trees. His mother, Rain Dance Woman, was old and tired and had few teeth remaining. It had been years since she had tasted the wonderful, sticky, sweet taste of honey, and she had been begging Sidominadota to take her to a place where she remembered there had always been an abundance of bee trees. Inkpaduta's youngest son asked to go with his uncle and help with the honey gathering and was granted permission.

The next day they struck their camp, and as the sun started to go down, both groups, after promising to meet again at the Redwood Agency in two moons, moved off into the gathering darkness. They traveled at night, hiding by day until they reached their destinations. Their presence in two different areas so far from Tasagi's village would be a foolproof alibi. It seemed like such a perfect plan.

*     *     *

It was early in the *Moon When the Ponies Shed* and the wild flowers of spring covered the rolling prairie. After traveling far to the south along the river, the honey hunters stopped and set up their tipi in an area the white residents called Humboldt County, not far from the settlement of Fort Dodge, Iowa. It was a simple thing to find the bee trees. Young Inkpaduta and the women stood on the edge of the trees along the river watching the flight pattern of the bees as they left the flowers on the prairie and flew back to the timber, laden with nectar. It took several hours of trailing the fast flying insects as they lost sight of them often. But slowly the general direction the bees were flying was found. Each time the bees they were following disappeared, they had only to wait for more bees to come along. Continuing this process they slowly worked closer and closer to the bees' nest and finally spotted the hollow tree where the bees were depositing their precious cargo.

Each time a bee tree was found, Sidominadota covered his body with a thick layer of mud scraped from the river bottom. He plugged his ears and nose with rolled up *wagachun* tree leaves, covered with more mud to keep the bees from crawling in. He approached the tree with a hand ax and chopped a hole at the lowest hollow point below the bees' entry hole.

A similarly mud-coated Young Inkpaduta brought him a smoking torch, which he placed in the hole. The smoke and heat drove the insects from their sanctuary. They boiled out into the daylight and attacked Sidominadota viciously. But the dried mud protected him from all but a few of the bees while he calmly fed green leaves to the several fires he had built around the honey tree. Thick smoke filled the air forcing the bees to retreat. After several hours of keeping them at bay with the smoking fires, the bees gave up and it was safe to harvest the honey.

Sidominadota chopped the tree down and then split its hollow shell. The women filled reed baskets with dripping honeycombs. After returning to their camp, they squeezed the sweet liquid from the combs, storing the honey in buffalo bladders. The combs were then boiled in water until they melted, then strained through a cloth, leaving wads of beeswax, which they used to waterproof their moccasins and leggings.

It was pleasant work, which lent a tasty addition to their diet, and the family lingered for weeks in the area. The white population in Humboldt County had grown over the past two years and Sidominadota often met white men traveling on the river or walking across the land. There were men who farmed nearby, and Rain Dance Woman and her daughter-in-law visited their cabins often, begging for flour, salt, coffee and tobacco. Most of the whites they met were friendly and didn't seem to mind sharing the land with this small family of Indians. The men smiled and shook hands with Sidominadota and laughed at his clumsy attempts to speak English.

At the cabins, the women found the white people to be generous and tolerant, if not friendly.

With fewer and fewer Indian people living in the state each year, news that the two-fingered chief and his family were living in Humboldt County traveled down river to Fort Dodge. Henry Lott had moved from Pea's Point, closer to Fort Dodge, where he still tried to make a living by cheating his customers, Indians or whites. When he heard that Sidominadota was in Humboldt County, it awakened the hatred he felt for the two-fingered chief. He left the tavern he was in when he heard the news and rode directly to the cabin he shared with his son, Simon. Simon, now a grown man in his mid-twenties had become his father's trading partner with even fewer scruples. After a short discussion over a bottle of whiskey, the two renewed their vows of vengeance against the hated chief. The next morning, they saddled their horses and rode north with several bottles of trade whiskey in search of the two-fingered chief's camp.

Since it was Sidominadota's intention to be seen two hundred miles from the site of Tasagi's village that spring, the Lotts had no trouble finding his camp. Sidominadota was not happy to see Henry Lott and his son sitting on their horses in front of his tipi. It had been almost nine years since he and Inkpaduta had raped Henry's wife and ransacked his cabin. These were acts Sidominadota didn't think a man would forgive. He was surprised to see Henry Lott smiling and hear his friendly words of greeting.

"Two Fingers, my old friend," Henry shouted as he climbed down from his horse. "I heard you was in the neighborhood and had to come to see if you have furs to trade."

"No furs, Lott," Sidominadota answered holding his scattergun across his chest, ready to swing it to aim at either of the Lotts if they showed any threat. But neither of the men reached for a weapon or stopped smiling.

"Wal, then let's jest sit and have us a friendly drink then," Henry said pulling two bottles of whiskey from his saddlebags. He pulled the cork with his teeth and tipped the bottle to his mouth taking a long swallow. Sidominadota's mistrust faded at seeing Henry drink from the bottle and then reach it out, offering it to him. He gruffly warned his wife and mother and Young Inkpaduta to stay inside and keep the children with them and quickly grabbed the offered bottle and drank deeply from it.

Henry, Simon and Sidominadota sat around the fire pit by the tipi, passing the whiskey around. The Indian didn't notice that after the first few passings, the white men only pretended to drink at their turn. Sidominadota was soon drunk. The men talked and joked and by the time the whiskey was half gone, the conversation turned to the scarcity of game in the area. Sidominadota quickly agreed, telling them that he was having a hard time keeping his family fed, adding that he had sent his women to beg for food from the area farmers. He told them that his family was all packed and ready to move.

The next day, they were planning to leave and go back to the northwest where there was more game. By this time, Sidominadota's judgment was not good, and his ears perked up when Henry casually remarked that he had heard that there was a herd of elk, grazing in a nearby meadow.

"Me and the boy here, was on our way to hunt them elks, when we run across yer camp," Henry expounded. "An I sez ta Simon, 'Boy it jest wouldn't be right to go kill them elks without letting my ol' friend Two-Fingers come get his share, too!'"

The drunken Sidominadota was quick to respond. He jumped unsteadily to his feet grabbing his rifle. Without saying a word to the women, the three mounted their horses and rode off to the west. After only going two miles, they came to a small hill with a narrow game path leading around the sidehill. Indicating that the elk should be just over the rise, the Lotts pulled back and allowed Sidominadota to take the lead. Eager to be the first to see the animals, Sidominadota kicked his horse to the front of the column and rode ahead, not noticing that the Lotts dropped back, letting him get twenty feet ahead of them. He didn't look back and never saw the father and son raising their rifles to aim at the center of his back.

Two terrible blasts sounded, but Sidominadota never heard them. Two fifty-caliber balls struck him squarely between the shoulder blades, knocking him from his horse. He struck the ground, landing on his face. With a grunt, he rolled slowly over and was surprised to see Henry Lott standing over him, calmly reloading his rifle. Understanding finally seeped through his whiskey soaked brain. He wanted to move, to dodge and roll away from the Lotts and their guns, but all of the strength had left his body, and his arms and legs felt as numb as his brain.

With wide eyes, he could only watch as both Lotts walked slowly toward him, take aim at his stomach and shoot him twice more. The pain of death coursed through his body, but a small chuckle escaped his lips. His alcohol-fogged brain had turned to the elk that were supposed to be on the other side of the rise. He took some comfort with the thought that the Lotts had probably scared them away with all of the noisy gunfire, and they wouldn't have any meat either. A lopsided smile grew on his lips as he died.

With a whoop of victory, Henry Lott rolled the dead Indian out of his bloody blanket and pulled the band that had held Sidominadota's long hair in place from his head. Simon rifled through Sidominadota's medicine bag and was disappointed to find nothing other than some small bones, strange shaped rocks and a dried bird's foot. He threw the contents to the ground in disgust. Then with a wicked laugh, Henry drew his knife and severed Sidominadota's head from his body. Holding it high by the hair, he shook the head at the sky, a vicious cry of triumph on his lips. But his vengeance was not yet complete. He wrapped the head in a burlap bag and tied it to his saddle. Mounting Sidominadota's horse, he pulled the dead Indian's bloody blankets around himself and pressed his headband down over his own forehead.

Henry rode back to Sidominadota's camp, with Simon following at a distance, leading his father's horse. When Henry approached the lone tipi, Prettier Than Her Sister Woman and Rain Dance Woman mistook the blanket-clad rider to be Sidominadota and they ran out to greet him. Their surprise was complete when he rode hard at them and swung his rifle like a club, first striking Rain Dance Woman and then Prettier Than Her Sister Woman.

Rain Dance Woman's old body was severely injured. She lay on the ground, stunned with one leg broken as it was bent under her body when she fell. The wind was gone from her lungs, and her mind went dizzy. Through half-dead eyes, she watched as Simon Lott rode up to join his father. She heard them laughing and saw them slapping Prettier Than Her Sister Woman back to consciousness. She could hear the younger woman's screams as the two white men ripped her clothing from her body and forced her to the ground, where they took turns raping her.

Prettier Than Her Sister Woman fought them, and they beat her more and laughed at her distress. When finally, both had satisfied themselves, they allowed the wounded woman to gain her feet. She stumbled crookedly toward the tipi, crying out to her children and Young Inkpaduta, telling them to run and hide, but her words were suddenly stopped, when a blast in the back knocked her to the ground, ending her life.

"Damn ya boy!" Henry cursed his son, who stood with Sidominadota's own scattergun still smoking in his hands. "I wasn't done fuckin' that bitch!" Then with another curse, he turned his attention to Rain Dance Woman, who stared at him through unmoving eyes as he raised his gun butt above her head and crushed her skull with the butt of his rifle. Simon ripped through the door of the tipi and entered, exiting almost immediately carrying two screaming young children, holding them each aloft by one foot.

The squalling children reminded Henry of chickens that were about to have their heads chopped off before they are butchered. He pulled his knife from his belt and holding each child by its short braided hair, slit their throats in turn, silencing their terrified screams.

Suddenly subdued from their blood lust, the two men dragged the bodies of the women inside the tip and threw the children on top of them. They piled everything in the tipi on them and using embers from the fire started a blaze that soon engulfed the tipi. It was only as they watched the rising blaze that Simon voiced the thought that had been on both of their minds since the excitement of the slaughter had passed.

"What about his ugly brother, Paw? Where do ya spose he is?"

Fear invaded Henry Lott's soul. He turned and looked about the darkening sky. His hands began to tremble and sweat broke out on his forehead even though the evening was cool. Wasting no further time, the two men mounted their horses and raced away from the smoldering tipi containing the bodies of the murdered women and children. They rode south, stopping only to impale Sidominadota's head on a stake on the courthouse lawn of the Webster County Seat in Homer and traveled directly to their cabin. In the morning the father and son quickly packed together all of their belongings, loaded their wagon and headed west. They had decided that the only safe place for them was California.

*     *     *

Young Inkpaduta carried Sidominadota's youngest child, a son, on his hip as he had seen the child's mother do. He struggled on, mile after mile, day after day, carrying the small child. Each night, he fed him by chewing bits of meat into a soft mash and spooning it into the child's mouth with his fingers. The child was always hungry and not used to such food, but the dried meat was all Young Inkpaduta had. He had snatched a handful of the meat as he slid out the hole he cut in the back of the tipi just before Simon Lott burst through the flap door.

He knew there was no hope for the adults. After hearing the scattergun blast, he peeked through the flap door and saw his aunt writhing in agony on the ground in front of the tipi and watched Henry Lott smashing his gun butt into his grandmother's head. There was no sign of his uncle and he was sure that wasn't good news.

After laying the child in the reeds by the river, Young Inkpaduta returned to the camp, hoping to rescue the other children. But when he arrived, the tipi was already in flames and the Lotts had ridden away. He tried to rescue his weapons and more food from the burning tipi, but the flames were too hot, and he could smell the burning flesh of his relatives inside. Shaking his head sadly, he returned to pick up the child and headed west. He would find his father. His father would know what to do. Just before dark, seven days later, he stumbled into his father's camp on the *Inyaniake* River. It was a sad reunion.

After hearing his son's tale of the murder of his brother's family and his mother, Inkpaduta led his band east.

Arriving in Humboldt County, he learned the details of his brother's murder and that Henry Lott had impaled Sidominadota's head on a stake. The white residents had buried the body, and they told him his brother's head had disappeared. Anger ridden, Inkpaduta spent days searching Humboldt County, looking for Henry Lott and was so bold in his searching of the settlers' cabins that the residents of the county grew alarmed. An armed patrol of volunteers rode out looking for the pox-scarred chief. But the wary Inkpaduta escaped up river and headed for the Lower Agency in Minnesota.

His mood was ugly, and they were a somber group that arrived at the Redwood Agency on Annuity Day. When word of the murder of his brother and mother circulated the agency population, many men who had planned to ask him about the death of Tasagi, changed their minds. When he stepped forward to draw the payment for fifteen adult males and their families, no one questioned his right to the money.

# Chapter 27
*Settlers (1856)*

**A**mbrose Mead followed close behind his two companions as they rode through the belly-high prairie grass. Mead bought the horses they were riding back in Cedar Falls. Having left his home in Ohio, he was traveling west in search of good farm ground. Ambrose found that he was a little bit afraid of the vastness of this prairie land and was glad when he met two brothers traveling west with the same intentions as his in mind. It would be easy for a man traveling alone to become lost, die, and never be heard from again. Three men were safer than one alone, especially in Indian country. The warnings about Indians from the man he bought the horses from played over and over in his mind as he rode.

"Watch 'em!" the man had said. "They'll steal ya blind in the wink of an eye! Watch yer horses. Watch yer blankets and yer salt, sugar and coffee. They'll take yer boots, yer hat, even yer dirty socks," the man had said as he walked over and placed his hand on Ambrose's shoulder, adding, "But most of all, watch yer gun. That's what they want the most and if'n they get yer gun away from ya, watch out fer yer life!"

Ambrose took the man's advice to heart. He considered it his lucky day when he bumped into Gust and Jacob Kirchner, and they accepted his invitation to join him in traveling west. They were both big men and well-armed men, too. Gust's shoulders were broad and his chest a barrel. At twenty-seven years old, he was in his prime. He was tall and strong with muscles that rippled across his shoulders.

When Gust was twelve years old, his parents had packed up his sisters, baby brother and him and moved the family to America from Bavaria in Germany. As a young boy, John Agustin (Gust), worked hard on the rock bed farm in New York State, where his father chose to settle.

When a young man in his early twenties, he grew tired of the farming life, and gold fever drew him to California. But the wild life in the gold fields didn't appeal to him, and after only a short try at prospecting, Gust Kirchner realized that farming was what he wanted to do. He resolved not to farm the rocky country in upstate New York that his father had been fighting for the past fifteen years.

He read about a place called Iowa in one of the pamphlets that circulated around the gold fields. RICH DARK SOIL, the pamphlet had read, COME TO IOWA! PRAIRIE SOD LOAM – ENOUGH SPACE TO MOVE AROUND – LAND TO SETTLE – LANDS TO FARM! It seemed to shout off the page at him. IOWA – IOWA – IOWA!

Upon returning to New York, Gust convinced his father that the new state of Iowa was where they should go.

His brother Jacob was much younger and not quite as burly as Gust. But at only seventeen years old, he already had a reputation of being a tough, gritty young man. The boys at school learned fast to never pick a fight with Jacob Kirchner. He was mild mannered and never started a fight, but he never backed down. And if someone started a fight with him, he was always there at the end, to finish it. Jake had also grown up working his father's rocky farm and had the reputation of being a hard worker. Because of his reputation, the first lad the neighbors around their New York farm tried to hire was Jacob Kirchner. Jake's strength of character and his ability to take care of himself convinced his father, Christian, to send the young boy to help his older brother search for a new home for the family in the wilderness.

The three men rode west at a steady, but leisurely pace, following their noses for they had no map. Several people in Cedar Falls were talking about the Spirit Lake country on the northern border in the far western part of the state. It was a land filled with beautiful lakes and fair soil. Wild fowl and fur bearing animals were supposed to be plentiful. Hunting and trapping would both supplement their diets and give them a way to make money by taking and trading furs. It sounded wonderful, and the three riders were excited to find the Spirit Lake. But in the middle of the fourth day out from Cedar Falls, the trio met a man who changed their minds.

The wind was blowing hard into their faces, stinging their eyes with needle-like blasts of cold rainwater. Jacob, who was in the lead, spotted a horse, ground-hitched with its rear facing the wind, in a shallow depression on the flat prairie. A hide covered lean-to set up with the opening facing away from the wind sat on the far side of the hollow. They rode slowly up to it, but before they could dismount, a short man dressed almost entirely in animal skins burst from the shelter, aiming a buffalo gun at them.

244

"Slowly, Pilgrims, slowly!" the man shouted over the wind. Squinting, he held his head at an odd angle. "Mine eyes be poorly anymore on accounta' getting' the snow blindness once't ta offen," he shouted as he circled behind the Kirchners and Mead, sniffing noisily through his nose, "but I'm not a man ta be trifled with!" he added, moving around them until he stood facing them in front of his lean-to once again. After a moment, he seemed satisfied, and he walked close enough to poke the long barrel of his rifle into Gust's stomach and asked, "Be that hair sproutin' on yer face, Pilgrim?"

"Ja, I vear a beard," Gust answered, a bit of German accent creeping into his voice.

"Aha-ha-ha-ha-ha!" the old man cackled. "I knowed ya twern't redskins! Ya don't stink enough for to be Injuns! Git yerselves down boys!" As the three men climbed down from the horses, the man held his hand out as a blind man might, in the general direction of Gust's huge frame.

"People call me Snow-Blind Charlie Snook." He shook hands with Ambrose and Jacob, without even waiting to hear their names. "Ain't had me a good visit with a white man in a coon's age. C'mon, share my tent."

As the three travelers sat out the storm in Snow-Blind Charlie Snook's lean-to, he told them about his long life of hunting and trapping on the plains. He wasn't completely blind; he was quick to tell them, he could see shadows and some bright colors. He had recognized that they had homespun clothing but was always careful because, with all of the Indian traders spreading across the wilderness, more and more Indians were wearing brightly colored, "white man" clothing. Charlie told them that there were very few white settlers that had come this far west and the farther west they went, the fewer white people there would be.

"I could tell ya twern't Injuns when I got a good smell of ya," he explained. "I got me a good sniffer!" Snow-Blind Charlie Snook boasted to them. "Ya don't smell like buffler fat and fire ash. That's what Injuns smell like on accounta that's what they make their paints from. Rotten stuff it is." He scratched his head vigorously, chasing lice down his long, stringy hair, which hung to his shoulders. "I make you boys ta be farmers on accounta ya smell like dirt."

"That's right, we're heading for the Spirit Lake country to find ground that would be good for farming," Ambrose Mead answered.

"Aha-ha-ha-ha! Told ya I had a good sniffer!" the old trapper cackled. "But you boys be green, green as grass. Spirit Lake ain't the best farmin' ground. It be sportin' country. It be good fer catchin' fish and shootin' elk, and I've even heard there might be a buffler or two up that way. But I doubt it Pilgrims. I doubt it richly! One thang more thets up thar is Injuns aha-ha-ha-ha! The closer up to the Minnesota territory you get, the more Injuns ya gonna see."

"But we'll need the fish and the elk and buffalo for food. That's fresh meat Charlie!" young Jacob cried out in defense of the land he had been dreaming about ever since this adventure had started.

"Waugh!" the old man scoffed. "There be elk and deer all over this country right here. An' what do ya think is in them rivers ya been wadin' them horses through? Fish boy! An ya don't need no boat ta go after 'em with. As far as buffler goes, what do you think made this holler, we be sittin' in? It's a buffler waller!" The old man hawked his throat clear and spat out the open side of the lean-to. His milky eyes took a sincere glow, and his voice changed to a low, liquid flow of words.

"I were a farmer onc't, boys. I know good ground when I seen it. Wished I would of stayed at farmin'. But my feet itched, and the huntin' and trappin' was too easy. Now I'm old and blind as a bat and ya can see what I got . . .nothin' but a head full of stories." He cleared his throat and spat again and sat staring at the falling rain for a moment. "Were I to want a piece of ground to farm," he continued his voice mellow in his reverie, "I know right where it would be." He pulled the ramrod from his buffalo rifle and scratched out a rude map on the trampled dirt floor of his lean-to. "I would want my farm to sit on the river bottom near the river us whites call the Little Sioux. The Injuns call it, *Inyaniake.* The river is a good water source. Thar's timber on the south side of the valley I'm thinkin' of, and the soil all along it will grow anythin' ya want to grow. That be where I'd go, if'n I was ta be a farmer," he added as he sat back on the pile of robes.

The four men sat discussing the land and the possibilities until it grew dark. With a steady drizzle beating on the lean-to roof, they fell sound asleep and dreamed of the days to come.

In the morning, the Kirchners and Ambrose Mead left Snow Blind Charlie Snook. Following his directions, they traveled west looking for the river he had described as a wild, meandering stream.

Three days later, they angled their direction to the northwest and ambled over a rolling plain. There were many cattail marshes in the low lands between the rises.

On the fourth day, they rode down hill into a wide sweeping valley and for the first time saw the Little Sioux River. Trees grew sparsely along its banks, and they followed the winding course until they came to a stretch of the river valley that ran generally east and west. On the west end, just before the river jogged to the north, a long grove of trees grew on the high bluffs rising from the south bank. They pitched their camp and spent the next day exploring up and down the river. They found no buffalo, but there were deer and elk tracks along the muddy riverbank, and they flushed several flocks of ducks as they walked along the river. Gust took a spade from their pack and trekked a short distance above the flood plain. He turned over several spades full of the grassy sod. Grasping two handfuls of the rich black loam, he crumbled the dark soil and watched it fall slowly back to the bed of thick grass between his feet. His eyes surveyed the horizon of the hilltops surrounding the valley. There was timber for building a cabin, wild game and fish, rich soil and plenty of room to move around in. This was a good place.

\* \* \*

Inkpaduta's twin sons, Roaring Cloud and Fire Cloud, had grown to full manhood. Each had taken a wife and started a family. With each passing year, Inkpaduta found himself relying more and more upon them in the decision making process for the people. He consulted with them before deciding where to lead the band and when to move from one of their seasonal haunts to another. Often, one of the boys made the decision of which man should scout ahead and who should trail behind to guard their back trail.

The population of Inkpaduta's band had shrunk to an all-time low. There were very few people left from the time when his father, or even his brother, was still alive. His sons and himself, Big Face, Man Who Makes A Crooked Wind As He Walks and the half-breed brothers, Charley and Gunn, were the only men of the old times left. Other men who had joined the band in the last year were His Mysterious Father, Old Man, Putting On As He Walks, His Great Gun, One Leg and Inkpaduta's son-in-law, Rattling.

Most were misfits that had been kicked out of other bands for one reason or another. They were accepted in Inkpaduta's band because they agreed to follow his lead with no questions asked. Of the fourteen men in the band, nine were married. There were no unmarried women left since Rattling had married Inkpaduta's daughter the year before. There were eleven children, ranging in age from nine months to ten years.

The band made its living as it had under Wamdisapa and Sidominadota's leadership, stealing from enemies and friends alike. Because of this, the band's reputation among their own people suffered, and they found that they were unwelcome in most villages they entered. But with the coming of the white population came another, even easier way to get what they needed to live. The whites were found to be soft hearted and stupid. Many times, the women and children of the band got food by standing by a white man's wagon or outside the door of his cabin and holding out their hands, begging for something to eat. If this failed, a mother had only to pinch her baby on the butt hard enough to make it cry and say in pidgin English, "Pease—food—hungy!"

Almost always, they were given enough food to carry some back to the village and feed the men, too. Also, the whites were trusting and careless. It was much easier to steal from them than from other Indians. Many whites were afraid of Inkpaduta and his men and offered little if any resistance when they entered a cabin and took what they wanted. Even though, after the killings of his brother and mother last year, Inkpaduta blamed and hated the white skinned people, he had to admit that the influx of white settlers had made life easier for his people.

They wintered in the central part of the state on the Des Moines River, begging from and stealing from the settlers near Fort Dodge. With the coming of spring, Inkpaduta ordered their camp broke and was leading his people back to the agencies in Minnesota. Annuity time was approaching and with last year's success, he was sure of getting his share again. It was about midday, warm and sunny, when Roaring Cloud came down from a rise in the land and reported that he had spotted a lone tipi sitting under a tall cottonwood tree. There was no sign of more tipis or people.

Inkpaduta rode with his sons to investigate. They approached the tipi cautiously, never knowing what kind of a reception they would receive. As they neared, Inkpaduta exclaimed and pointed at the tipi. He knew the paintings on this tipi's walls! There was a painting of men killing a bear with rocks and bows and arrows and clubs. There was a picture beside it of several dead elk laying in a snowy yard of trees. Another picture showed human stick figures, huddled below high snow banks, depicting a long hungry winter.

There were several more paintings encircling the base of the tipi. None of the others meant anything to Inkpaduta except the last one that rose high above the others. It was a bright yellow sun, high in a black, starless night sky. These pictures on the tipi told the story of the owner's life. It was the tipi of a famous warrior and good friend of his father's, Sun At Night. He was awed that the old man could still be living.

Inkpaduta rudely burst through the tipi door without coughing to announce himself. Inside, he saw Sun At Night, a mere rack of bones, lying naked on a bed of buffalo robes. The old man's skin was wrinkled and shrunken, making his hips, knees and elbows look unnaturally swollen. Close by the old man's side, crouched a young warrior. The boy clutched a war club in one hand and a trade knife in the other. He stood as the intruders entered, prepared to go down fighting. Roaring Cloud swung his short-barreled shotgun to bear on the boy's middle and thumbed the hammer back. A stern look and a monosyllable grunt from Inkpaduta caused him to lower the hammer, but he kept the gun aimed at the young man's stomach.

"It is all right, Grandson," Sun At Night said in a low, scratchy voice. "This is the son of a good friend of mine."

"You've grown old and look ready to die," Inkpaduta answered with no friendliness in his voice. He had not liked Sun At Night since that day long ago when the man stopped him and Sidominadota from torturing the wounded elk calf.

Sun At Night laughed a weak laugh. "You haven't changed, Red-Haired One. Your face is badly scarred, and I wouldn't have recognized you except for the color of your hair and the hate in your voice."

Sun At Night's eyes were good. The only light in the tipi came from the door opening, and Inkpaduta kept his hair greased, making it look almost as dark as the rest of the *Wahpekute* people. He had hated the color of his hair since he was a small child and most people couldn't see the red in it in good light.

"This one should have left you to die alone," Inkpaduta said, gesturing toward the young warrior at Sun At Night's side.

"This is as I told him," Sun At Night answered, but added with a smile, "But he could not leave me and snuck back before the rest of the village was one day gone. He has sworn to stay until I die. It has been over a week and still I cannot pass into my last hunt."

"My father and brother are both dead," Inkpaduta stated flatly.

"That news saddens my heart," the old man stated solemnly, but brightened saying, "But it also makes me happy to know that your father, my good friend, and I shall be hunting together again soon. Even your brother will be glad to see me, for at the last hunt, all old hatreds are forgotten." Sun At Night coughed and tried to spit thick phlegm from his mouth. But he lacked the strength and had to swallow it back down. He licked his dry, cracked lips and called for water in a thick voice. His grandson dropped his weapons and knelt to tip a water-filled gourd to his grandfather's lips. After drinking, Sun At Night sighed heavily and slowly climbed to his feet and stood facing Inkpaduta.

"Inkpaduta, I know that you don't like me, and we are not friends," he stated. "But I have a request for you, and I ask you to do it to honor the friendship between your father and me." He smiled wistfully and continued, "It will not be hard."

"What do you want, old man?" Inkpaduta asked rubbing his pock-marked cheek with his thumb, a habit he had when angry or agitated.

"My grandson, Brave Bull, has danced to the sun, as you can see by the scars on his chest. He is a brave and able warrior." Sun At Night turned his head to look at the young man and love shone in his wet eyes. "But his family—my daughter and her husband—were taken by the white man sickness that caused the scars on your face," he said, pointing a finger at Inkpaduta. "He is young to be all on his own this far from his people. He has an uncle, his father's brother, who is an *Hunkpapas* named Sitting Bull. It is said among the western *Dakotah* that one day he will be a great man."

"What is it you want?" Inkpaduta asked impatiently.

"I'm asking you to take Brave Bull to his uncle after I am gone to my last hunt," Sun At Night said, getting to the point. "He is not used to the ways of the *Santee,* and there are too many white men here."

Inkpaduta glanced at the young man but could read nothing in his face. He looked proud and strong. The boy would be a good addition to his village if he could adapt to their life style. If the boy couldn't, and became a problem, he could kill him and save making a trip to the west, Inkpaduta reasoned.

He shook his head in the affirmative saying, "I will do as you ask, Old Man. I will take Brave Bull with me. But it will be many moons before I will be traveling to the western lands. He will have to be content to live with us until I lead him there."

"Fine, fine," the old man said softly, "he will wait until you are ready to go west and help your village as long as you promise to do as I have asked. But there is one more thing I must ask you to do," Sun At Night added.

"What is that?" Inkpaduta asked, a suspicious look on his face.

"Brave Bull has sworn not to leave me until I am dead," Sun At Night said, glancing at his grandson once again. "I seem to be finding it hard to die, so I want you to kill me," he added calmly.

The statement shocked even Inkpaduta. Brave Bull quickly retrieved his weapons from the floor and stepped between his grandfather and Inkpaduta and raised his war club threateningly. But a feeble hand raised up to rest on his shoulder.

"Leave this tipi, son of my daughter. Go and wait with the men of Inkpaduta's village. Follow this man, and he will take you to your home and let your mind rest easy knowing that I will be where I want to be, with my old friend, Wamdisapa," Sun At Night said, adding, "You have honored your pledge. Now I ask you to let me go quickly to my last hunt. I am tired of this life."

The tense readiness left the boy's shoulders, and they sagged in defeat as tears came to his eyes. He turned to face his grandfather and grasped the old man's bony shoulders in both hands as he looked intently into his eyes. Then without a word, Brave Bull stepped between Roaring Cloud and Fire Cloud and left the tipi.

Inkpaduta offered Sun At Night another drink from the water gourd. The ancient warrior sucked some of the brackish water into his mouth and swallowed it, sighing heavily. Then with a short nod of his head in thanks, he turned and kneeled, facing away from Inkpaduta. After glancing at both of his sons, Inkpaduta gripped his war club in both hands and raised it high over his head, before crashing it down with all of his strength on the base of Sun At Night's skull, driving the withered old man's body violently to the ground, where it lay kicking for a few minutes until his life was totally gone.

At Inkpaduta's directions, Fire Cloud and Young Inkpaduta wrapped Sun At Night's body in one of the buffalo robes and dragged it out of the tipi. Fire Cloud sent Old Man to summon the women to build a scaffold, using the poles and hides from Sun At Night's tipi. The section of the painted tipi wall with Sun At Night's symbol painted on it was lashed to the poles as a platform and his body was laid to rest on it high above the prairie floor. Inkpaduta's old wife, Hates Her Father, tore a lock of her scraggly hair from her head and tossed it under the scaffold and chanted a death song under her breath.

"*Hoka-Hay*—It is a good day for a warrior to die!" Brave Bull shouted as he used his trade knife to chop off the end of his little finger at the first joint and let the nubbin fall to the earth under the scaffold. "*Moneto* help your warrior succeed in this final hunt!" he added quietly. With only these two acts of mourning, the rest of Sun At Night's possessions were packed on a travois, and the people of Inkpaduta's band left the old warrior with his god.

# Chapter 28
## *The Bear Face (1856)*

**I**nkpaduta led his people on a meandering route across the western half of the state. He had agreed to take Brave Bull to his uncle with the *Hunkpapas*, but that was a long journey. The trip west would have to wait until after annuity time. When they reached the *Inyaniake* River, they turned to follow its course north. He liked traveling along the wide valley cut through eons of time by the water of the *Inyaniake* as it meandered a crooked course to the northeast. Deer, elk and small game were plentiful all along the river, especially near the groves of tall hardwood trees. Walnut, ash, elm and oak grew in scattered pockets in protected valleys along its course. Late in the afternoon, at a place where the land sloped gently uphill before the river turned east and the lay of the land on the south side grew hilly with steep approaches to the water, Inkpaduta told the women to set up the tipis. It would be a good place to stop and rest the people before crossing and heading north to the agencies on the *minne sota* river. He wanted to arrive at the Lower Agency in time for payment day and planned to travel fast from this camp to the agency.

The next morning, the hunters left the village searching for elk or deer sign. It would be good to dry some meat for the trip, and this rest stop would be their last opportunity to do so before trekking north. By mid-morning, all of the hunters had returned except Charley and Gunn. The women were busy cutting up the meat from three deer that the men brought in.

When the half-breed brothers returned, they excitedly reported that they had spotted two white men on the north end of a long grove of trees in the valley about three miles east of the *Wahpekute* camp. The men had started building a cabin and had dug up a patch of flat ground. From what the brothers could tell watching from their vantage point near the summit of the hill, the white men were living in a tent pitched near the cabin foundation. They saw several hand tools including axes, hammers, and saws, leaning against the foundation, but there was no sign of horses to steal.

Inkpaduta decided to visit the whites to see if they had anything of value. Knowing that many whites were frightened by Indians, he took only a small party including: Roaring Cloud, Fire Cloud, Charley, Gunn and Brave Bull. He invited Brave Bull along to see how the young man handled himself around white men. He was curious to see how he would react if they decided to kill them and take their belongings. The six Indians approached from the west and watched the white men as they labored. Looking down from the top of the ridge, they could see the beginnings of a log house. Foundation rocks had been dug into the ground at four corners and several eight-inch thick logs, ten to twelve feet long, had been trimmed of branches and pulled from the grove of trees to the south. The logs were stacked in an even pile, waiting to be notched.

"The big one is a Bear Face," Gunn whispered to Brave Bull and pointed through the grass at the big man with a beard. Brave Bull was impressed. He hadn't seen a man with a beard before. The Indians waited until it seemed both men were busy before they slipped quietly into the camp. All six *Wahpekutes* were only a few feet from where the two whites worked at trimming and notching the logs, before they were discovered.

"Gust, look behind ya!" the younger of the two men cried.

As the big bearded man turned slowly, his hands holding his ax handle loosely, Inkpaduta watched him closely. He saw surprise, but no fear in the man's eyes. Even the younger man showed no signs of being afraid. Inkpaduta had surprised other white men by sneaking into their camps before. They had always shown fear in some way: a short cry, fast talk or by running for their weapons. But not these men, they showed no fear. The Bear Face even began walking toward them, his hand outstretched, a smile on his face. Confidence and bravery seemed to shine from this man.

Inkpaduta didn't know for sure what to do. He respected bravery above all else, but he also feared brave men. For an instant, he considered ordering his men to shoot these whites and kill them while they were unarmed. But the moment passed, as the younger of the two casually stooped and picked up his rifle.

Inkpaduta's eyes turned to a venison roast hanging from a spit over an even bed of hardwood coals in the fire pit. He pointed at the roast and then back to his own mouth.

"Eat–hungy–want eat," he stated in his best English.

"Ja, we will share our meal with you," the bigger of the two men said, adding, "It will be just a short while before it is cooked done."

Without waiting, Roaring Cloud skewered the roast with his skinning knife and pulled it from the spit. He dropped the meat on a stump and cut a large chunk from it. The other Indians rushed forward and cut chunks from the bleeding roast and quickly devoured the meat. Blood ran down their faces, over their chins and dripped onto their chests. Neither white man made a move to take a share of the meat and soon it was gone. Inkpaduta pulled a long stemmed pipe from his pack and held it out toward the white men.

"Smoke? Got baccy?"

"Ja, I've got tobacco," the big bearded man answered again. He tipped his head toward the younger of the two whites and said, "Jacob, get the tobacco out of the tent. We will smoke with our guests."

Jacob, carrying his rifle, ducked into the tent and returned with a twist of tobacco they had purchased back in Cedar Falls. They had been told that Indians expected to smoke when they met up with whites and were friendlier if tobacco was provided for them. Inkpaduta considered killing these men again, but saw a third white man approaching from the trees. He was riding a horse and had a rifle resting across his lap.

Ambrose Mead had staked out a place for his cabin about a mile south and east from the Kirchners, at the other end of Long Grove, as they had began calling the south bank of the river. His fear of being alone had dissipated during the few weeks since he and the Kirchner brothers arrived in the peaceful river valley.

Having grown adventurous since his fear left, he had taken a trip up river and came across a hunter named Abner Bell. Bell had arrived on the Little Sioux River with his sister and her husband, a man named Weaver, and a family named Totten. The group chose a spot about ten miles east where the river narrowed and flowed fast over rocks and deadfall trees. After sharing a pipe and a good long gab with Bell, Ambrose returned to his cabin site to feed his horses. He kept the horses penned in the thickest part of the grove to keep them out of sight as a precaution against wandering bands of Indians. He was anxious to visit the Kirchner boys to let them know about the newcomers to the area. It was especially important because the three men had discussed at length the dangers of bringing women into this wilderness.

But now with the arrival of the Weaver and Totten women, it was apparent that it must be safe. He was excited to tell Gust and Jake because the brothers had promised that as soon as their cabin was built, they would be ready to return east to fetch their family.

Ambrose was waiting to accompany them back to Cedar Falls to bring his wife and good friends the Taylors to help build his cabin.

A cold chill ran up his spine upon seeing the Indians as he rode out of the trees into the Kirchner clearing. The Indians were standing in a semi-circle, facing Gust and Jacob and as Ambrose pulled his horse to a stop, he could feel the tension in the air. He had no idea that his sudden appearance had probably just saved the Kirchners' lives. Not knowing what to do, he sat on his horse and watched as Gust, moving forward, instinctively picked out the Indian leader. He reached out and shook Inkpaduta's hand with a friendly smile on his face. Inkpaduta felt the strength in the big white man's grip and read the strength of character in Gust's eyes as he raised his own to look at the bearded man's face. Slowly he pulled the long stemmed pipe from the bag on his belt, deciding that under the circumstances, it would be best to make this a friendly visit.

"Smoke?" he asked again, holding the pipe high, a broken toothed grin split his face as he looked at the twist of tobacco in Jake's hand. He had a plug of tobacco himself, but had learned long ago not to use his own when there was a chance to use someone else's.

The old Indian stuffed the pipe bowl with shards of tobacco cut from the twist and sat on a stump. Fire Cloud drew a small ember from the fire and placed it into the packed bowl and as Inkpaduta drew on the stem, the tension in the air seemed to leave. Ambrose climbed down from his horse and since the Indians had eaten the entire roast, Gust told Jake to build up the fire and spit another roast.

The Indian men sat circling the fire, watching the meat cook and sizzle as Gust, Jake and Ambrose smoked the pipe with the old leader of the Indians. After they had smoked two bowlfuls of the pipe dry, they spent the afternoon talking. By using a mixture of hand signs and pidgin English, it was possible to communicate. It was pleasant and friendly. Gust had a knack for telling stories that even the red men could understand. He told jokes and laughed long and hard at both his own stories and those the Indians related, whether he understood them or not.

When the venison was scorched but still bloody, the Indians began feasting, each man using his knife to cut his own chunk of the meat. Gust treated the red men with a jar of molasses brought all the way from New York State in his backpack. The Indians loved the thick sweet syrup and poured it on the bloody meat as they wolfed down large bites, barely bothering to chew. After the meat and molasses were gone, the men sat around the fire, burping and belching and moaning in discomfort. It was a warm afternoon, and some of the Indians napped.

256

Late in the afternoon, Roaring Cloud and Fire Cloud woke feeling good. They wrestled with one another, grunting and straining. Roaring Cloud, being the stronger of the two, soon pinned his brother and then gave him a bite on the ear before letting him up. In his mid-twenties, he was healthy and strong and was very proud of himself. After laughing at Fire Cloud, who was holding his bleeding ear, he chased after Charley and Gunn. But the half-breed brothers were both too smart and too fast for him to catch. With a mischievous grin, Roaring Cloud pounced upon Brave Bull as the boy sat listening to Inkpaduta talk with the three white men.

Roaring Cloud liked to set the pecking order in the band by physically showing his superiority. He was mean and usually insulted the men he beat with a bite on the ear or neck. He dared not jump Inkpaduta because he knew that his father would kill him without a second's hesitation.

But periodically, he picked a fight with Fire Cloud, Young Inkpaduta, Rattling or any other man in the band he thought might challenge him to be second in command. Attacked from behind and taken by surprise, young Brave Bull was driven to the ground, his face smashed violently into the deep green grass and held there, while Roaring Cloud chewed on both of his ears. When Roaring Cloud finally let the young man up, blood ran from both of his ear lobes and his nose.

Roaring Cloud was still not satisfied.

"Are there no men here?" he shouted as he pranced around the clearing, grinning from ear to ear. "It seems I have only women to fight." He was feeling strong and invincible and decided that he would show his father how to handle these white men. Speaking in *Dakotah*, as he boasted, he told Charley and Gunn to get ready to snatch the white men's guns.

As he walked behind the Bear Face, with cat-like quickness, Roaring Cloud jumped on Gust Kirchner's back. His plan was to drive the white man's face into the ground as he had done to Brave Bull. But the thick set German was not so easily handled. Gust rolled to his side, as he felt Roaring Cloud's weight come crashing into him. Then with the agility of a much smaller man, the Bear Face twisted from Roaring Cloud's grip and reversed the advantage, locking his arms around Roaring Cloud's waist. Roaring Cloud felt the vise-like squeeze around his waist and banged at Gust's head with open hands and pulled at the white man's beard and head hair. But Gust retained his hold around the Indian's waist and struggled to his feet, lifting Roaring Cloud off the ground. He held Roaring Cloud there, helpless as a babe and began to laugh as if this were all in fun.

It was not fun to Roaring Cloud. He wanted to best the white man and steal their guns from them. Adding to his anger at being held helplessly off the ground was the fact that he could see that Charley and Gunn had failed to grab the white men's weapons. Ambrose Mead and Jacob Kirchner stood firmly planted on either side of their rifles and it became apparent to Roaring Cloud that these whites were not as careless and carefree as he had thought, when he decided to make this challenge. The smug look on Inkpaduta's face told him that his father hadn't overlooked the readiness of the white men, and was slightly amused that he had.

Angered and embarrassed by his inability to break the Bear Face's hold on his waist, Roaring Cloud drew his knife from his belt and in a slashing motion, cut the lobe off of Gust Kirchner's left ear!

Grunting in surprise and pain, Gust threw Roaring Cloud to the ground where he landed so hard that the knife flew from his hand. As quick as a cat, the big Bear Face sprung on Roaring Cloud, wrapping his muscle knotted arms around the Indian's middle from behind, picked him off the ground again and began to squeeze. As he squeezed, he began shaking the hapless Roaring Cloud and the harder he squeezed, the harder he shook the man. His rippling biceps flexed and bulged until the seams of his homespun shirt exploded with an audible ripping sound.

The blood flowing freely down Gust's neck from his wounded ear soon mixed with blood that began coming from Roaring Clouds nose and ears, and the Indian started to lose consciousness.

Expecting trouble, Jacob and Ambrose reached for their rifles and the four younger Indians stood, tense and excited. Only Inkpaduta still sat, calmly watching the fight. He knew that though the numbers were in his favor, the odds were not good if these white men decided to fight them. In the heat of the afternoon, the breeze had fallen, and the valley had grown quiet, except for the heavy breathing and grunting of Gust and Roaring Cloud. Suddenly, the quiet was broken by the soft popping sound of Roaring Cloud's ribs cracking and his high-pitched scream of pain!

Roaring Cloud collapsed into semi-consciousness, and Gust dropped him like a rag doll. His anger drained away, and he walked to the canteen of water hanging on the woodpile. Taking a long swig from it, he walked over to where Roaring Cloud lay grimacing on the ground, handed it to him and walked calmly over to sit by Inkpaduta.

"That one is a good wrestler," he said with a grin to the pox-scarred old man.

"Humph." Inkpaduta grunted with a twinkle of humor in his eye. Maybe it was good that Roaring Cloud had been taken down a notch or two. His son had been getting a little high minded and hard to handle lately. He decided to act as if nothing had happened. Ignoring Gust's try at diplomacy, he asked, "Mabe got wisky? Got baccy, mabe give?"

Smiling, Gust reached to his pack and pulled the twist of tobacco they had used from earlier and handed it to the old man. "No whisky," was all he said. Inkpaduta frowned at this response, but took the tobacco. He stood and walked away up the hill.

"We go," he said over his shoulder. Fire Cloud and Gunn helped Roaring Cloud to his feet and supported the injured man as they fell in line to follow Inkpaduta.

# PART THREE

"**H**e was oafish and sullen and kept to himself. He was a little under six feet tall, heavy-set and powerful and in the neighborhood of sixty years old. His face was horribly pockmarked and his hair was red." – Elijah Adam's description of Inkpaduta after the incidents at Smithland, Iowa, in early 1857.

# Chapter 29
*Smithland*

The blue water lake is crystal clear. Its shoreline is irregular, with wide bays of shallow waters along its western shores, which belie the secrets of the great depths of the main part of the lake. The *Santee* call the lake *Minnetanka* (Big Water). On the east end of *Minnetanka*, a peninsula from the north and one from the south form a narrows. Calm, narrow bays lead to the east and swing to the north of the deep *Minnetanka*. The water loses its crystal clearness and changes to a dull green. The depth of this eastern lake is not as extreme, and vegetation growing from the muddy bottom gains enough sunlight to flourish. The *Santee* call this lake, *Okobooshi* (a place of rushes.)

Tangled brambles of spiked briars and gooseberry and sharp grass interlace the ground on the edge of the lakes. Tall stands of oak, elm, and birch trees grow in intermingled groves back from the shores. The waters teem with fish, frogs and turtles. Rushes are in abundance, gracing the shorelines with a garnishment that waves and rustles with the gentlest of breezes. Chubby cattails bulge on sturdy stems, poking their fuzzy green pestles skyward. Ducks, geese and swans nest in the cover of the rushes and swim in loose formations over the calm bays.

To the north of *Okobooshi,* there is another lake. It is the biggest lake of the three. It is a wide lake with a large, hatchet-head shaped bay stretching to the east near the northern end. Its regular shorelines are smooth, and sand beaches stretch down the western shore. Groves of trees and thickets of plum and gooseberries flourish along its shores. Fish and fowl also live in this lake. It is a dark lake, its water more of a slate color than the blue water lakes to the south. Its shoreline lacks the configuration of *Minnetanka* and *Okobooshi* with fewer bays and no narrows. The water in the lake is shallow compared to the great depths of *Minnetanka*, and is easily riled. Even just a slight wind can make the water rise in angry waves with white tips, rising and curling and slapping down. *Santee* legends tell of many who have lost their lives while trying to canoe across this wide lake. The lake is called *minnewakan* (water of spirits) and is considered to be a sacred place.

The *Santee* people have roamed the shores of these lakes for generations of time. The lakes were a favorite wintering place, because they were a source of fresh water teeming with fish. And the lands between were home for herds of wild game in the trees and undergrowth that also provided the people with a fuel source for their fires and protection from the wild winter winds.

White hunters and trappers discovered the lakes years before the territory had become a state, but it was in July of 1856 that the first white settlers came to the area. Four men from Redwing, Minnesota: Bert Snyder, Carl and William Granger and Dr. I. H. Harriott, arrived from the north. They built their cabin on the north-side peninsula reaching down to the narrows connecting *Minnetanka* (West Okoboji) and *Okobooshi* (East Okoboji.) The four entrepreneurs formed The Redwing Company. It was their intention to form a community at these lakes that would rival the settlement of Springfield (the future city of Jackson), which was twenty miles north, in the Minnesota Territory.

Springfield residents boasted of not only having several scattered cabins in that area, they also had a small general supply store owned and operated by the Woods brothers. The Redwing Company members believed that the wild beauty and natural resources that the lakes offered would soon draw many more settlers and they felt certain that any business they chose to follow would thrive.

Proving their prediction, a farmer named James Mattock, his wife and five children arrived that summer and staked out a claim on the southern peninsula, directly across the narrows from the Redwing Company. Mattock brought chickens, pigs, oxen and a milk cow. Seeds for planting corn, pumpkins, squash and snap beans were in his larder, and after building a cabin for his family and shelter for his livestock, he had only to wait for the next spring to plow and plant. He was anxious to put his hands in the soil.

About a mile south along the shoreline of West Okoboji, Rowland Gardner chose to build his cabin. Gardner was forty-two years old and had spent most of his life moving from one place to another. He was a restless man who never seemed to be satisfied with the job he held or the area he lived in. His wife, Mary Francis, held the family together through the trials of constantly pulling up roots barely set, with a strong faith in the Lord. She read from the scriptures to three of their four children, Eliza, Abby and little Rowland. Each meal was begun with thanks to the Lord.

Their eldest daughter, Mary and her husband Harvey Luce, had accompanied the Gardners when her father decided to move west. Since winter was close upon them, the Luces, with their two small children, took up residence in the Gardner cabin. Harvey had entertained the thought of becoming a preacher in his younger days and shared the Gardners' strong religious beliefs. The Gardners and Luces looked toward a bright future, believing that the strength of their faith would help to pull them through the long cold winter to come.

Joe Howe, his wife and six children, ranging in age from nine years to twenty-three years, came to the lakes hoping to spread out and farm in a big way. He picked an open, rolling plain on the east side of Okoboji for their farmstead. Joe and his sons built their cabin on the south end of a large grove of trees, overlooking fields of waving grassland.

They had brought a boar and a sow, a coop of chickens and a pair of mules. Joe planned for his sons to branch out from the start. He would give them this new land, and the family would claim more and more land. His daughters were not left out of the plan. His oldest daughter's husband, Alvin Noble and Alvin's good friend, Joseph Thatcher and his wife, had taken up land a mile to the north of Joe's cabin on the north end of the same grove of trees.

The Nobles and the Thatchers each had only one child and for the first year, they planned to share the same cabin. Alvin and Joseph's good friend, Morris Markham, followed along with them to see the country and decided to stay on, living in a lean-to he built onto the south side of their cabin. Morris was a trapper and hunter with little interest in farming. He promised to keep the cabin in meat through the winter.

Far to the north on the west side of Spirit Lake (*minnewakan*) is where William and Margaret Ann Marble decided to build their cabin in a copse of trees that would protect their home from the winter winds. They were newly married and had no children. For several weeks after arriving at the lake, the young couple thought that they were the only white settlers in the area. It was only when the hunter, Morris Markham, came upon their cabin early in the fall that they found out about the rest of the white community spreading south around the lakes.

The summer of 1856 was a time of westward movement and settlement of the white population in Iowa. By the end of the fall, these six cabins were well established in the lakes region, and before the cold weather arrived, three more men arrived, looking for a good place to bring their families in the spring.

Bad weather caused the men to decide to wait until spring to leave. Robert Clark took up residence with the Gardners. Joseph Harshman lived with the men in the Redwing Company cabin, and Robert Mathieson was invited to stay with the Mattocks. The winter promised to be a long, cold one. But all of the settlers in the lakes area were filled with hope and confidence. They built cabins, hunted the game, fished the waters and prepared the soil for tilling in the spring.

As the rumors said, this land around these northwestern lakes seemed to be a possible paradise. After that first pleasant summer and fall, the settlers had great hopes of building their lives to a fruitful existence in the wilderness.

Settlement along the Little Sioux River (*Inyaniake*) was in full swing in the summer of 1856 also. The river meanders a curving course from its beginning in southwestern Minnesota. It passes on the west side of the Iowa lakes on its way to join up with the Missouri River on Iowa's western border.

Twenty miles south of the Gardner cabin, George and Isaiah Gillett put up their cabins, a barn and a sleigh shed on the hilltop above the Little Sioux floodplain. Their cabins sat about one-quarter mile apart, both bordering the grove of trees that blanketed the hillside south of the river's bank. George's wife was an excellent cook and Isaiah took most of his meals with his brother and sister-in-law. He planned to bring his own wife to "Gillett's Grove" in the spring.

At a place the residents were calling Sioux Rapids, the Weavers and Tottens built their cabins and settled in. Mrs. Weaver's brother, Abner Bell, talked about the heavy coats the squirrels were growing and predicted a long cold winter. Bell built no cabin. He would sleep on a pallet in the Weaver's cabin and pay his way by hunting meat for them.

Gust and Jake Kirchner left their partly finished cabin and the garden they had planted as summer arrived and returned to Dubuque in June. Gust took a train from Dubuque back to New York State. He would return with the rest of the family as soon as he could. He gave Jacob their meager supply of money and instructed him to take odd jobs to earn more and to start securing the supplies the family would need for their return trip to their new home on the Little Sioux River.

There were twelve Kirchners in all: Gust's father, Christian and his mother, Magdalena and eight more children younger than Jacob. When they arrived in Dubuque from New York, they were packed in covered wagons. Teams of slow moving but sturdy oxen drew the wagons, containing the children too small to walk, and all of their worldly goods.

It was a difficult task to move a family as large as the Kirchners over the hills and through the valleys in the eastern part of the state and then across the wide prairies to the west, dodging low and insect infested swamps. They traveled for days on end in the heat of the hot summer sun, without a tree for shade in sight. It took six weeks for them to travel from Dubuque to the cabin site on the Little Sioux. They arrived in time to finish building their cabin by the end of September.

When the cabin was finished, the family moved into it and Gust and Jake took one of the wagons, this time drawn by a team of horses, back to Cedar Falls to buy supplies for the winter. When they returned, they brought the James Bicknell family with them. The Bicknells had only one grown daughter, and James had little chance of raising a cabin before the cold winter arrived. While Jacob and Gust were gone for supplies, it had become evident to the rest of the family that the cabin the boys had built in the spring was not nearly large enough. Christian Kirchner sold their claim and cabin to the Bicknells for $260. The Kirchners moved back across to the north side of the river and quickly erected a larger, more suitable cabin at the base of bluffs running north up out of the valley near where a good spring of drinking water gushed from the ground.

By this time, Ambrose Mead had returned with his family and shortly after, more people began to find their way to the valley the people were referring to as Long Grove: the Williams, the Frinks, the Shoots, the Taylors and the Watermans. All families of varying sizes, they spread up and down the river to build their cabins before the cold weather came. The Taylors moved in with the Meads, helping to finish Ambrose's cabin.

Hannibal House Waterman moved the farthest west, three and one-half miles down river from the Kirchner cabin. He built his cabin at the beginning of the plain on the top of the hill that rose up on the south side of the river. It was his dream to start a town and name it after himself. He felt he had found the perfect site, and all the while he worked on the cabin, he told his wife, Hanna, and his daughter, Emily, about his plans for the fine town they would live in.

Waterman Town would become the first town in O'Brien County, for they had passed out of Clay County only one and one-half miles west of the Kirchner place. In contrast, the Kirchners having no desire for a town to be named after them, called the small, spread out, community that grew from their early settling place, Long Grove.

Soon, it would be named Peterson, the first incorporated town in Clay County.

The settling of western Iowa continued at a fast pace with nine more cabins going up on the Little Sioux River at a place called Cherokee. Here and there along the river, isolated cabins sprang up during the summer of 1856. Far to the south, a wagon train of over twenty people led by Elijah Adams arrived at Smithland, swelling the population of that community to more than fifty white people.

\* \* \*

The sudden influx of hundreds of white settlers didn't go unnoticed by Inkpaduta and his people. The summer of 1856 was a long and disappointing time for Inkpaduta. The band traveled to the agencies in Minnesota at annuity payment time, expecting, because of their success the year before, to collect their share of annuity payments at the reservation again. But because of the presence of a full company of white soldiers in full strength, Inkpaduta's old enemies in the other *Santee* tribes spoke out against him. Even the *Wahpekute* leaders present refused to speak in favor of sharing some of the annuity money with Inkpaduta's people. The new agent refused him his payment making it clear that he should not try to collect again because he would not be likely to forget the ugly, pock-marked face of Inkpaduta.

Inkpaduta's frustration was complete. He could see that his people were considered outcasts and would never be accepted openly by any of the *Santee* tribes. His sons wanted to cause trouble, but Inkpaduta, recognizing the strength of the Army troops, led them away with their hands empty. They traveled south, back into northwest Iowa and camped for weeks on the north shore of *minnewakan.*

The men of the band ranged far in their hunting and reported each new white settler's cabin in the area to Inkpaduta. His frustration grew. He hated the thought of sharing this land around the lakes with the white settlers and was angry at the whites for coming to this land that had been his camping ground for decades, but didn't know what to do about it.

To add to his disappointment, he awoke one morning to find that Charley had left the band. Gunn said that his brother had grown bored with life in this small band and was heading back north to look for a woman. Life in Inkpaduta's band made it difficult for the men to find wives. Inkpaduta's twin sons, Roaring Cloud and Fire Cloud, had been lucky a few years before and found *Mdewakanton* women whose families were eager to sell their daughters into marriage. Each

268

was expecting to gain a hunter to help provide for their family unit. But both families were disappointed when their new son-in-law ignored custom, and took their daughters and grandchildren to follow Inkpaduta.

Inkpaduta's third son, Rain Cloud, took his wife from a half-breed trader, after clubbing the man to death in a drunken brawl. The mixed-blood woman was unhappy with her fate and was quiet and uncommunicative most of the time. Even after two years with the band, she smiled only when tending her young son, born to her and Rain Cloud.

A young *Wahpekute* man named Rattling married Inkpaduta's daughter, Beaded Hair Woman, and had joined the band only the year before. Beaded Hair Woman was the last female of marriageable age in the band. Because there were no women of marriageable age that weren't already married, the men in Inkpaduta's band had to find wives from other sources. Inkpaduta's reputation always made it difficult to find women with parents who were willing to let their daughters marry into his village.

After their treatment at the agency on annuity day, Charley decided that if he wanted a wife, he would have to disassociate himself from Inkpaduta's band. Inkpaduta was worried that more of the young men might leave to look for wives. He decided that it was time to fulfill his promise to return Brave Bull to his uncle in the west.

They packed the camp and moved west the next day. They searched the rolling grasslands west and north of the Missouri River for weeks, but could not find the *Hunkpapa* village of Sitting Bull. Winter came early, and the wild northwest winds blasted across the wide-open prairies unimpeded by hills or forests. The temperature dropped and stinging snow flew in the wind. It was the *Moon of the Changing Seasons,* and Inkpaduta could read the future in the clouds.

It would be a long, cold winter, with deep snow and hard blowing winds. Inkpaduta had not expected an extended stay in the west, unless they were welcomed into Sitting Bull's village and invited to stay. But without finding the *Hunkpapas,* the band had only a small supply of dried meat and was poorly prepared with only a few warm robes and worn trade blankets to spend a harsh winter on the open prairies.

There were only sixteen men of hunting age left in Inkpaduta's band with nine women and nine children to feed. The rolling, snow covered prairie was vast, and the hunters had little success bringing in enough meat to keep the babies from crying from hunger at night. Inkpaduta gave up looking for the *Hunkpapas* and led his people back to the south and east. Travel conditions were tough, as the people found themselves trudging through ever deepening snow and suffering from colder temperatures with each passing day.

When they came upon the north bank of the Missouri River, they followed it east until they came to the white settlement called Sioux City. Inkpaduta skirted around the frontier community, crossing the Big Sioux River several miles up stream from where it entered the Missouri. He decided that they would travel east to Smithland where the white man Curtis Lamb lived. Lamb had acted as their agent in selling furs in Kanesville the year before, and Inkpaduta was confident that the man would allow them to camp along the *Inyaniake* River on his land. He thought that if he asked, Curtis Lamb might be willing to extend him a line of credit with the traders, so he could get his people supplies for the winter.

At about noon on the second day after crossing the river at Sioux City, Inkpaduta and his band approached Curtis Lamb's cabin and were shocked to find that the one white man who had befriended Inkpaduta and gained his trust by treating his people fairly, was gone. Upon the arrival in Smithland of a wagon train that summer, Curtis took advantage of the situation and rented his farm to one of the newcomers, Mr. Livermore, and moved to Sioux City. He hadn't mentioned his friendship with the Indians and Livermore met the bedraggled band of starving Indians with an unsympathetic eye. He called his two hired men, and the three threatened Inkpaduta's people with shotguns and ordered them off the property. Livermore had no time to deal with a bunch of dirty Indians.

Confused by the absence of Curtis Lamb and angered by Livermore's actions, Inkpaduta could only lead his people away from the cabin and the shotguns.

They crossed the boundary of Livermore's property onto the land recently purchased by Elijah Adams. Adams' two young sons, Wallace and Harry, who were digging tunnels in the deep-banked snow saw the Indians first, and they ran home to tell their father. Elijah hurried out to meet with Inkpaduta. His reception of the Indians was the opposite of Livermore's. He welcomed them to find shelter upon his land and felt pity for their decrepit state. Sending Wallace and Harry to fetch a small gift of coffee and tobacco, he presented them to Inkpaduta. It was the tenth day of December on the white man's calendar near the middle of the *Dakotah Moon of the Popping Trees*. It would be a long, cold winter for the poorly equipped Indians.

Inkpaduta ordered the camp set up on the south side of a small copse of trees in a hollow near the river. There were only seven tipis. One housed the seven bachelors, and the nine married couples and their children shared the other six tipis. The weather continued to be fiercely cold, but they were protected from the wind by the trees, which also provided them with a good source of fuel for their fires.

Soon, the women in the band found that the people in the area were easy to beg from and even easier to steal from. They took corn from the cribs and an occasional pig or calf from the farthest-reaching cabins. Several dogs that roamed freely away from the farmsteads of their owners, found their way to the *Wahpekute* cook pots.

The Smithland residents became angry when they discovered the Indians were stealing their corn and killing their dogs. In retaliation, they stopped giving food to the Indian women when they came begging. Many of the young men from the surrounding community quickly formed a militia of volunteers and were determined to put a stop to the thievery. They were ready to act but talked to Elijah Adams first, demanding that he tell the Indians to leave the area. Adams refused, saying that making them move in the dead of winter just wouldn't be Christian. Instead, he visited Inkpaduta and made the Indian leader understand that his people had to quit stealing corn from the cribs and that they had to stop killing the settlers' dogs and domestic animals, or leave.

Inkpaduta solemnly promised that his people would quit taking corn from the cribs and that they would only hunt wild animals from that point on. Adams left satisfied that the problem was solved, but Inkpaduta knew that it was going to be a long winter and wondered how long he could keep his hungry people from starving, if they didn't steal from the whites.

\*    \*    \*

The frontier mercantile in Smithland was a split-log building. Its walls were built high in the front and low in the back, making the roof slanted to allow rain and melting snow to run off the back. The split wood shingles were only partly successful, and on days when the sun shone brightly, melting some of the snow on the roof, pots and pans had to be set out to catch the dripping leaks. The convenience of glass hadn't reached this far west, and the building's single hide-covered window was shuttered tightly against the winter cold. It was dark in the room, the only light coming from two coal oil lamps, one hanging over a square table, the other sitting on a long low counter. Behind the counter were shelves with trade goods. Hammers, axes, spades and shovels hung along the other walls. A small keg of short nails, with one end only slightly smaller than the other, sat on the end of the counter. There were bags of flour and cane sugar and coffee beans, and a pot-bellied stove, forged in New York and shipped to the river port of Dubuque from whence it was all hauled across the prairie to Smithland on the same wagon. The cold winter made the stove the main attraction in the mercantile. Everyone else in the area still depended on their fireplaces for both heating their homes and cooking their food. Heat radiated from the stove's rounded body, sending warmth to even the farthest reaches of the room.

O. B. Smith, the owner of the small mercantile business, sat basking in the warmth of his stove, staring up at the stovepipe chimney. He shook his head in disgust. He had burned too much sapwood already this winter. Burning green wood caused the inside of the chimney pipe to be coated with an oily, black build-up which,could catch on fire, causing the pipe to glow red from the heat, a sign that he knew meant the hot pipe could cause his roof to catch fire. He would have to cool the stove and clean the stovepipe soon.

He glanced at his friend, John Howe, who had come to spend this cold winter day drinking corn mash and playing cards in the warmth of the mercantile building. With no wind blowing outside, it was quiet and warm in the building, and the two men, who sat sipping their corn mash from tin cups, drowsed in the early afternoon. They had shared a good dinner of beef pie, and now, the clear liquor burned in their bellies and made their heads swim.

Suddenly, the silence of the afternoon was broken, and both men sat up in their straight-backed chairs. At first they thought they were hearing the high-pitched chattering of a gaggle of geese slowly circling near the town. But soon, the high-pitched voices could be recognized as the sound of young women's laughter ringing through the still air like hundreds of small bells, all ringing at the same time. John Howe stood and walked to the heavy plank door and opened it a crack.

"What the hell?" he said peering out into the bright sunlight. "Hey O. B., come take a look at this."

It was a bright crisp day early in *The Moon of Frost in the Tipi*. The three young women trudging through the knee-deep snow were in a light-hearted mood. Even Rain Cloud's wife, Trader's Slave Woman, felt happy. She usually was not happy. Living with these *Wahpekute* people had been a hard life for her. Her husband was mean, and he treated her more as a slave than a wife, as her name signified. She cooked his meat, mended his clothes, packed his possessions, struck his tipi and carried the load piled high on her back. When he used her under his robes at night, he was rough, slapping her hard even when she didn't resist. It was only after she had given him a boy child that he quit beating her almost every night.

When the white man called Adams warned them against stealing from the settlers, Inkpaduta issued orders to stop killing domestic animals and to stop taking corn from the white men's cribs. The men hunted far up and down the river for elk and deer, but had very poor luck, bringing back only one small deer and an occasional turkey.

The people had been hungry for the past two weeks, but today they would eat. Trader's Slave Woman, walking ahead of her sisters-in-law, Beaded Hair Woman and Worn Moccasin Woman, on their return trip from a begging expedition to cabins on the far side of Smithland, stumbled into a deep snow drift and found stalks with unpicked ears of corn buried under the snow. This unpicked corn was an important find. It was obvious that the white men didn't want the corn, or they wouldn't have left it on the stalks. Trader's Slave Woman and her two sister-in-laws spent the morning digging down through the drifted snow in the field and harvesting one bag of the unpicked corn each.

It had been a fun morning. Worn Moccasin Woman filled her bag first and spent time teasing the other two about being slow. She was married to Fire Cloud and knew he would be pleased with the find. Fire Cloud was the most even-tempered of Inkpaduta's sons and treated her with tenderness and respect. She was very glad that Roaring Cloud's fat wife, Afraid of Her Husband Woman, wasn't there. Afraid of Her Husband Woman was lazy and moved very slowly, except when she was dodging Roaring Cloud when he chased her, beating her with the handle of his war club.

Beaded Hair Woman filled her bag last. She was Inkpaduta's only daughter and was favored by her father. By marrying Rattling, she had brought another warrior into the band. Rattling was a tall, good looking young man from another *Wahpekute* village. He had dismissed the reputation of her father and brothers and fallen for the grace and beauty of Inkpaduta's young daughter, who always had colorful beads strung in her hair. Beaded Hair Woman was the only woman in the band to befriend Trader's Slave Woman. She was quick to praise Trader's Slave Woman for finding the unpicked corn and told her that she would make sure her father knew who had found it.

The three young women, trudging through the snow while lugging the bags of corn over their shoulders, decided to take a short cut through the white village. As they walked, they joked and laughed and made plans to return to the unpicked patch to get more corn to feed their hungry families. Their light, singing voices carried far across the snow-covered land. As the three women approached the town from the south, they walked right through the center of the small huddle of cabins.

The deep snow made the walking hard, causing them to breath hard, making their voices jump with their efforts as they spoke, sounding even more unintelligible to the listening white men.

Smith, who had joined Howe at the door of the mercantile, threw the door wide open, letting a blast of cold air rush into the building.

"Lookee at that O. B.," John Howe whispered as if the women could hear. "Them girls can't be over fourteen-fifteen year old!" He grinned a wide grin. "They be wild lookin' don't they?" He leaned closer to Smith and whispered again. "I bet they'd be plenty wild under a heavy blanket on a soft feather tick. Haw haw haw!"

"Yer old woman hear ya talkin' like that Howe, she'll gut ya out and feed ya to the hogs!" O. B. Smith answered, laughing. Then he pointed asking, "What's that they be carryin'?"

"I dunno," John Howe muttered and stepped out the door, feeling the cold air surround him. The Indian women were straight out in front of the store. They stopped and stared at Howe as he walked toward them. "What's that you squaws got there?" O. B. Smith followed Howe and pointed at the bags they carried.

Instant terror gripped the young women. They had never been talked to by white men before. When begging, they always had only women to contend with. These men were big and gruff, and they looked even bigger as they pulled on their winter coats while they walked toward them. The three girls froze with fear.

"Let's see what's in yer bag there, Missy," O. B. said, reaching to take the bag of corn from Worn Moccasin Woman. "Why I do believe these little red niggers been stealin' agin, John," O. B. added as he wrenched the top of the bag open to reveal the ears of corn.

"I think these little cuties should be punished proper fer stealin', O. B.," Howe answered, adding, "Else there won't be a crib with a cob o' corn left in it come spring!"

Shaking his head in agreement, Smith walked back to the mercantile and returned with two cattle switches and handed one to Howe. Trader's Slave Woman knew what was coming, for she had felt willow switches at work before.

"Run! Run!" she screamed, and the three young girls took off as fast as they could go, while still lugging their heavy bags of corn. The men kept up with them easily in the deep snow, striking them repeatedly with the switches across the backs, shoulders and rumps.

The blows were stinging, bruising swipes that brought whimpers of pain from the girls. Tears rolled down their cheeks. Beaded Hair Woman was the first to drop her bag of corn. Without the burden to carry, the strong young woman easily outdistanced the men. Upon seeing her sister-in-law getting away, Worn Moccasin Woman soon dropped her bag and ran ahead also. But Trader's Slave Woman refused to drop her corn. She trudged on as John Howe and O. B. Smith concentrated their efforts on her while the other two escaped. It was only after she reached the edge of the *Wahpekute* camp that the two men stopped and turned back heading for the warmth of the mercantile.

Both men were perspiring from their efforts, and when they came to the spot where the two girls had dropped their bags of corn, they walked on leaving the corn lay in the snow. There wasn't enough there to bother with. Both of the men were very proud of the fact that they had taught the thieving "bitches" a lesson and were anxious to relate their story at the militia meeting that night.

That night, while the militia met, cattle on the farm of Jim Kirby and Eli Floyd were driven from their pens, killed and left to lie in the forest. Inkpaduta wanted revenge for the beating of his three daughters, but he didn't want any evidence in the camp that could prove that his people had killed the cattle. Two days passed and so far, no one had come to accuse them of killing the cattle. The people were starving, and many of the young men were grumbling about the dead cattle as being meat that was available and just going to waste. But Inkpaduta was sure that the whites were waiting by the carcasses to catch them coming back for the meat and wouldn't allow them to go after it. He was beginning to be concerned that the men might ignore his orders and fall into a trap he was sure the militia had set, when Roaring Cloud returned to the camp with the news that he had sighted a herd of elk.

The elk were yarded up in a small stand of trees only a short distance up river from their camp. It was a large herd and if they worked the hunt right, they could kill enough meat to last them for the rest of the winter, and the white men could sit there and watch the dead cattle get eaten by coyotes!

The band of hunters moved out with a new confidence in their step. Fire Cloud, Young Inkpaduta, Rattling, Old Man, Big Face and Man Who Makes A Crooked Wind As He Walks were going to circle down-wind of the herd and get into position to shoot them as they tried to escape when they winded the other hunters approaching from the up-wind direction.

Before they covered half the distance, a dog ran out from a nearby cabin, barking and growling. It was a big, black and white beast with long, thick fur. It ran through the herd of elk yipping and nipping at the animal's heels. At first, the elk milled about nervously, reluctant to leave the yard. One cow launched a kick, catching the dog in the rib cage, sending it flying. But the kick did little to deter the dog, and it came back dodging and barking, biting the hind legs of the elk until the herd finally broke from their cover and ran for the river. The frightened animals crossed over the slippery ice and disappeared in the trees on the other side. The dog stopped at the river's edge, tired and happy. His tongue hung out and his tail wagged. At the sound of a sharp whistle, the dog turned and trotted for home, ignoring the Indians who had been only able to stand helplessly by and watch as the dog chased their food supply for the winter off.

Jonathon Leach had heard his dog barking and followed the sound of his large pet, wondering what he was barking at. When the barking stopped, he whistled and soon saw the big black and white animal trotting toward him. He never saw the Indians, until he heard the gunshot! His beloved pet yelped once and rolled over and over from the impact of the ball hitting him. Jonathon looked in the direction of the gunshot and saw Young Inkpaduta standing only a few feet from him, with smoke curling from the barrel of his rifle.

In a rage, Leach rushed the young Indian and knocked him to the ground. Young Inkpaduta jumped back to his feet, only to be knocked down again by a blow to the face. When he hit the snow-covered ground for the second time, Leach began kicking him in the stomach and chest, rolling the younger, smaller Indian over and over. Leach wanted to keep kicking the Indian who had shot his dog, but a sixth sense warned him, and he looked up to see the rest of the wild men converging on him! He turned on his heel and ran for town where he would find plenty of help to avenge the death of his dog.

Inkpaduta and Roaring Cloud lifted the badly beaten Young Inkpaduta to his feet and the men helped him limp back to their camp. Fire Cloud brought along the only meat they had found for days, the black and white dog. They would eat it, but even so, it would be another hungry night.

Just before dusk, the Smithland Militia came. There were over twenty well-armed men surrounding the camp, aiming an array of rifles and shotguns at the people of Inkpaduta's village. One man, who wore a tattered army uniform, spoke for all of the rest. He demanded that they bring out all of their firearms. The tipis were searched. The militia left them their bows and arrows and war clubs, but all of their guns were taken.

Inkpaduta didn't know the man in the uniform but had little recourse but to listen as he told them that it was the militia's mission to relocate Inkpaduta's people. He instructed them to pack their belongings and be ready to move in the morning. There was a reservation down across the big river at Omaha where they would be accepted. He instructed them to go there, adding that Inkpaduta's men could reclaim their guns the next day, when they moved through town on the way to the Omaha reservation. Then, with no more fanfare, carrying the *Wahpekute* band's guns with them, the Smithland Militia returned to town feeling safe now that the savages had been disarmed.

Feeling vulnerable without their firearms, along with not fully understanding what the white man in uniform had said, caused Inkpaduta to fear treachery from the militia. Soon after the white men left the dark camp, he sent Roaring Cloud and Fire Cloud to follow them and watch the trail leading from town. He put the women to striking the tipis and packing their belongings. The preparation to leave took only two hours and with Roaring Cloud leading, the people moved off into the cold night's darkness like silent shadows in the snow.

Inkpaduta waited behind and scooped snow on the fire at his feet. He stood for a few minutes looking over the empty camp. Seven dark tipi circles stood out against the snow-white landscape. He sniffed the soft breeze and his eyes turned to the garbage heap where they had pitched the refuse accumulated during their short stay. It had been his hope to stay in this sheltered area a while longer, at least until the weather changed and became more suitable for travel. But now, they could not. His mouth set in a grim line. He had made up his mind about white people. He would no longer think of them as curiosities that could be counted on as benefactors during hungry times. From now on, he would treat them as he had always secretly thought they should be treated; as victims to be preyed upon, as the wolf preys on the rabbit!

Inkpaduta and his band moved out that night. But they didn't move south toward the Omaha reservation. They trekked north, up the *Inyaniake* River. They were going home to the land of the blue water lakes.

# Chapter 30
## *Up the Inyaniake – Waterman*

**S**eventeen-year-old Jacob Kirchner had to concentrate to put one foot ahead of the other, as he struggled through the deep snow drift. One blizzard after another had blasted the frontier with the most severe winter in memory. Arctic cold winds swept down from the north, whipping twenty-seven inches of snow into drifts that rose as high as the cabin roofs. More snow was expected, as it was only the middle of December.

His laboring through the deep snow made him breathe hard though his mouth, and the freezing cold air scorched his lungs. His chest was beginning to burn with each breath. He could feel a painful strain in his back muscles caused by the weight of the heavy pack he carried. Heaving the pack upward, he tried to shift the straps farther out on his aching shoulders. Gritting his teeth with effort, he struggled on, fighting his way through the deep snow. With the tree line in sight, he stopped to catch his breath. In the silent air, Jake could hear muffled calls behind him. Abner Bell and Bell's brother-in-law, Mr. Weaver, followed in the trail he was breaking through the drift. He was sure that if they kept going at a steady pace they could probably make it to Weaver's cabin before nightfall. Wishing that the two men would just keep up, he groaned as he heard the muffled cry from behind. It was apparent that the two men had stopped to rest again.

Over a week and a half ago, Jacob, driving a team of oxen pulling a sled, picked up Bell and Weaver at the Sioux Rapids settlement. The Sioux Rapids men, with their own team of oxen, joined Jacob on a trip to Fort Dodge for supplies. The winter was going to be a long one and supplies for the settlers on the Little Sioux River were already running short. The sun was shining on the day they left, and it was hoped that the lull in the winter storms would last long enough for the men to return before another blizzard hit. That hope had proven to be a fruitless one. Long, deep snowdrifts were difficult for the oxen to pull even the empty sleds through on the journey to Fort Dodge. On the return trip, with sleds laden with supplies, a fresh blizzard dumped several more inches of snow, and the howling winds blew the trail they had broken on the way to Fort Dodge shut. Yet the men and animals moved steadily, stubbornly on into the heart of the storm.

A second storm started to blow just as they reached the Lizard River. The wind and snow caused visibility to be shorter than a few yards, and the men decided to turn back, returning to a settler's cabin on the Lizard to wait for the wind to fall. While there, it was decided to leave the weakest team of oxen and one sled with the farmer. They pressed on the next day, only to have another blizzard force them back once again. The blowing snow was freezing in the oxen's nostrils, making it hard for the laboring beasts to breathe.

The next day, the men decided to leave the oxen and sleds and carry what they could in packs on their backs. They had no money to pay for the oxen's keep, but brokered a deal with the farmer allowing him to use what supplies he needed from the sleds in payment for taking care of the oxen until they returned for them. None of the men could guess how long that might be.

The three men started out on foot to cover the many miles to their homes on the Little Sioux. Each man carried a pack stuffed with as many supplies as he could heft. It was a long, cold trail with deep drifts to plow through. At first they took turns leading, the man in front breaking a trail through the drifts for the other two to follow.

But soon it was apparent that the younger, stronger Jacob Kirchner was better suited to break trail for the two older men. Bell and Weaver were grunting with their efforts and sweating profusely, even though the temperature was far below freezing. The two men soon lightened their loads by dumping part of their supplies. Jacob watched and shook his head in dismay, wishing that he could carry what they were leaving, for he had hungry brothers and sisters at home.

The wind blew through that first day out from the farm where they had left the oxen and their supplies, but at least it didn't snow. They camped that night huddled together around a roaring campfire in a grove of elm and hickory trees.

When they awakened the next morning, their legs were cramped with cold and ached from their efforts of the day before. Without taking the time to rebuild the fire, the three men started off as soon as it was light. Each ate a dried biscuit for breakfast and washed it down by eating handfuls of snow. They made good time by following the ridgelines at the top of the rises where the wind had blown the snow away. But by mid-afternoon, they came to a drift that stretched for miles across their path, and Jacob knew they couldn't circle around it. He started plowing through the deep drift, heading for a tree line that marked the river's edge, one hundred yards away. It was when he was nearing the trees that he heard Bell and Weaver calling his name. Ignoring their muffled calls, he struggled on through the drift to the edge of the tree line and finished breaking through the drift. He stood close to the riverbank and Jacob determined that because of their detours around the drifts, they had struck the Little Sioux River up river from Sioux Rapids. If he was correct, they would now only need to follow its frozen course down river until they came to Weaver's cabin.

Both men were still calling him from somewhere back in the drift. He shrugged his shoulders out of the pack straps and lowered it to the ground, setting it beside a large cottonwood tree. His back muscles shuddered, and a shiver ran up his spine as he slowly plodded back into the drift. He found both of the men lying in the snow where they had fallen in exhaustion.

"Me and Weaver been talkin', Jake Boy," the woodsman, Abner Bell, said as Jacob reached them. "This snow is too damned deep, and we be too damned tired ta get up agin."

"Come on Ab," Jacob answered, "Get up and keep movin'. You know lying in this snow will only make you colder."

"Now don't you start tellin' me what ta do!" Bell answered angrily. "I been in the woods a sight longer than yew, and I know when I'm through!"

"You figger you're through too, Mr. Weaver?" Jacob asked, looking at the other man.

"Abner says maybe if we lay up for an hour or so, we'll get our strength back, and we'll be able to walk out of this drift," Weaver answered, not looking Jacob in the face.

"Weaver, you know as well as I do, that if you two lie in this snow for an hour, your legs will be froze up for certain and you won't even be able to walk on good ground let alone bust through this drift!" Jacob shouted in exasperation.

"Maybe he's right, Abner," Weaver said, glancing sideways at his wife's brother.

"Wal then yew just get up and let that young fool walk ya ta death!" Bell shouted angrily. "Yew go on, Jake Boy, but yew can leave me cause I ain't goin' nowhar till I'm damn good and damn ready!"

Jacob didn't answer immediately. He knew that more shouting would accomplish nothing. Instead, he pulled the horse pistol from his belt and methodically charged the cylinder, capped it and turned it so it would rest beneath the hammer when he thumbed it back.

281

"Watcha doin' there boy?" Bell asked looking at the gun.

"Come on, Mr. Weaver," Jacob said, ignoring Bell's question as he reached out his left hand to pull Weaver to his feet. Then he turned to Abner Bell. "We been havin' wolves follow us all day. I figure they're just waiting for a straggler to fall behind."

"You sure?" Weaver asked, turning in a short circle to look down their back trail. "Are there wolves back there?"

"Aw fer Christ's sake Weaver, the boy's just tryin' ta scare ya," Bell answered, smirking. "Truth is, Ol' Mister Jake Boy is probably scared to go on all by his own self."

"You got me all wrong, Ab," Jacob answered. "I'll leave you behind for the wolves. Fact is I'll leave you both, if that's what you want." He looked at Weaver and then back into the satisfied grin on Abner Bell's face. "But I'll not leave a living human being as wolf bait. I couldn't live with myself if I was to do that."

He raised the horse pistol, aiming it at Abner Bell's face and thumbed back the hammer. Without another word, Abner Bell rose to his feet and shouldered his pack. Slowly, methodically, on already cold stiffened legs, he began plodding along Jacob's trail through the drift. With a fearful glance at Jacob, Weaver stumbled along after. Neither man slowed down or called out for help again, and they arrived at Weaver's cabin just before dark that night. Jacob Kirchner had saved their lives by threatening to kill them.

\*     \*     \*

Hannibal House Waterman rested on his cornhusk mattress watching the fire in its place and reflecting on the days of his life. At his side, his wife, Hannah, was curled close to him for warmth. Just on the other side of her, encircled by her mother's arms was their ten-year-old daughter, Emily. In the fire's dim light, he could see Hank Meyers toss and turn on his cot built on the far wall.

Hank was their hired man, and though he only had one arm, he could work as good as most men with two arms. But the one Hannibal liked to watch in the firelight was Injun Charley. The man was curled up on the floor in front of the fireplace with the two hounds. Hannibal House thought it was amazing just how much like the hounds the Indian was. The man used his sense of smell, taking anything strange to him to his nose and sniffing it just like a dog would. If the smell didn't offend him, he'd eat it, again, just like the hounds. He chuckled, remembering when Hannah had handed Injun Charley a bar of lye soap. The poor boy sniffed it, and sure enough took a bite out of it before anybody could stop him! Then, not wanting to offend Hannah, he chewed it up and swallowed it! Injun Charley had disappeared for a few days after that, and Hannibal House had commented to Hank that he bet ol' Injun Charley had himself one bad case of the screamin' shits!

Hannibal House Waterman liked Injun Charley. The young man had shown up shortly after the Watermans arrived at the site on the hill above the Little Sioux River three-and-a-half miles west of Long Grove. He was friendly and anxious to help as Hannibal House and Hank Meyers began building the cabin. Injun Charley didn't talk much, probably because he didn't know much English. He had merely stated that his name was Charley and that he was from "up north," and hadn't said much else since he arrived.

He took an immediate liking to Emily and especially enjoyed teaching her how to set snare traps and how to break a hole in the river ice to fish through. He helped the girl with her chores, carrying in firewood and caring for the few chickens the foxes hadn't killed. With hunting as poor as it had been, some of the chickens were considered expendable. But they were determined to save the cock and three hens to start their flock with in the spring. Hannah taught Emily her book-learning in the evenings by the firelight, and Injun Charley had taken such an interest, that she was trying to teach him too. The Indian was picking up a little more English, but really had no interest in the books.

Hannibal House Waterman sighed in satisfaction. It was a good life here, and he was anxious for the weather to straighten out. It was the middle of February, and spring could be just around the corner, if it would just quit snowing! Finally, with visions of spring plowing in his mind's eye, Hannibal House rolled over and snuggled up against his wife's backside. Slipping his arm under the goose feather blanket, his hand found her warm soft breast and held it gently as he fell into a deeply contented sleep.

Just before dawn, Hannibal House heard Injun Charley rise from the heavy rug he shared with the hounds in front of the fireplace. The man stoked the coals and threw on more wood. It was cold in the dark cabin. Donning a heavy buffalo skin coat, Charley unlatched the door and walked out into the freezing morning air. Hannibal House smiled to himself. Whenever Injun Charley left before dawn, it meant there would be fresh meat for the evening meal. It might be a turkey, a quail, a rabbit or even a pike he pulled through a hole in the ice on the river. Meat was scarce, and Hannibal House fell back to sleep dreaming about a nice fat deer haunch sizzling over the coals in the fire pit.

Two hours later, the family woke, and they sat down to their breakfast. Hank Meyers was teasing little Emily, trying to get her to eat her bowl of oat mush, when the cabin door suddenly burst open from a hard blow that shattered the latch! An Indian stepped in, but it wasn't Injun Charley. This man's face was hideously painted with black greasy paint covering from below his nose down to his throat. His eyes were circled with red and yellow and more black covered his forehead and reached back into his hairline. Pox scars, too deep to be hidden by the paint, lent his face an ugly, evil countenance and his crooked, yellow teeth showed in an angry scowl as he stood above the cowering Waterman family.

As more painted Indians pushed into the cabin, gun shots, followed by the thump of large bodies striking the ground, came from outside.

"They done shot the oxen, H. H.," Hank Meyers cried as Hannibal House jumped to his feet and faced the ugly Indian. Hank stood also, helping Emily off her stool and stood with his hand protectively on her small shoulder.

"What is it ye be wantin'?" Hannibal House shouted at the Indian leader. His hand was gripping the chair back so tightly his skin showed white around the knuckles, but there was no fear in his voice.

The Indian didn't answer. His eyes wandered about the room, searching its contents carefully, finally coming to rest on Hannibal's rifle leaning in the corner by his bed. More Indians pushed into the room, some were women, carrying chickens with their necks already wrung. Great chunks of bleeding red meat, still steaming from the cold air, were carried in and spitted over the fireplace. Red hair from one of the oxen's hides singed and burnt, giving the cooking meat a bad smell. The Indians hadn't bothered to skin the ox. They just chopped large chunks from the hindquarters. The rest of the women and the few men who weren't in the cabin, slit both oxen's stomachs open and dragged out the intestines and liver, gobbling up the steaming entrails, and thin slivers sliced from the liver before the cold air could cool them. Several men cupped their hands and drank the salty blood pooled in the animals' body cavities as the blood ran down their forearms and dripped from their elbows.

"What is it ye want?" Hannibal asked again. He had been watching the Indians through the open door from where he still stood by his table and was clearly shocked by the suddenness of the attack on his home.

But the Indian leader ignored his question again and shouted orders as the men began turning over boxes and crates Hannah used to store many of their worldly goods. The contents were dumped on the floor and stepped on and the crates were filled with the Waterman's winter supply of flour and dried beans. More of the

Indians from outside pushed through the door and began helping to ransack the interior of the cabin. Blood dripped from their chins and colored their chests and forearms.

The press of bodies in the small cabin pushed Hank Meyers and Emily to the back wall of the cabin. Hank held his arm protectively around Emily, pulling her to the wall, out of the way of the Indian men as they paced around the room, pushing and shoving anyone in their way. Hank moved slowly along the wall until he came to a small summer door Waterman had cut in the north wall of the cabin for use when the weather was warm. Hank knew that there was no good coming from these Indians, and he felt a panic coming. The Indians had already taken up the shotgun H. H. kept by the front door, and they had pulled all of the butcher knives from the cupboard. As far as he could see, the family was defenseless.

One of the Indian men skewered an oxen roast from the fire with a long-bladed knife and flopped it in the middle of the table. Blood ran from the burnt, but yet still raw meat, and the hungry Indians went after it like hungry dogs. They chopped off chunks and held them to their mouths with their bare hands, tearing at the meat with their teeth, smacking their lips and grinning as the hot juices mixed with the paint on their faces and dripped from their chins. When the half-cooked meat was all gone, the Indians wiped their hands and faces on their blankets and some of the women began filing out the door. Young Inkpaduta picked up Hannibal House's rifle and started for the door with it.

"No!" Hannibal House shouted and stepped forward grasping the weapon by the barrel. "Ye'll not be stealin' me rifle!"

At the sound of the white man's cry and the sudden movement to grab the rifle, Inkpaduta raised his tomahawk and struck Hannibal House Waterman on the back of the head! Waterman crumpled to the floor like a felled tree from the blow. Hank Meyers could stand no more. With the sight of his employer being tomahawked, Hank grabbed Emily and pulled her through the small back door and the pair started running away from the cabin! The deep snow was hard to run in and Hank knew that if the Indians chased after them it would not be long before they were caught. Emily tired quickly, and Hank tried to carry her.

They had only run about one hundred yards from the cabin into the trees when Emily fell. Hank pulled her to her feet and hefted her over his shoulder, but the girl was too heavy for the one armed man to carry very far. In desperation, Hank sat Emily down in the snow beside a scrub oak and gravely told her to, "Stay put till I come back."

Hank Meyers then changed directions and ran east, heading for the three-mile distant Kirchner cabin at Long Grove.

Charley was returning to the cabin with two wild turkeys for Hannah to butcher, when he saw Fire Cloud and Roaring Cloud coming out of the cabin. He hailed them as they started to follow Hank's tracks and asked them what was going on. They were so surprised to see him after the many months since he had left that they forgot about chasing after Hank and Emily and summoned Inkpaduta.

Inkpaduta charged from the cabin, his eyes still angry until he saw Charley standing with his twin sons by the split rail fence. "It is good to see you, my long lost adopted son!" he said reaching out to grasp the younger man by the shoulder.

"I'm glad to have found you too, Old Father," Charley answered. "I had no luck finding a wife, and I've been searching for my people since before the cold season started. I thought you would be camped for the winter on the shores of *minnewakan*. When I didn't find you there, I started following the *Inyaniake* until I found these people. They took me in and treated me well. It was cold weather, and they let me stay in the warmth of their cabin."

Inkpaduta told him that they were angry with this white man for trying to stop them from taking what they wanted. This was the first white man to resist them since they had left Smithland. While traveling up the *Inyaniake* river, they stopped at all of the isolated cabins, killed the livestock and took whatever they wanted from the frightened people living in the cabins. Most of the white people stood meekly by or cowered in fear, letting them take what they wanted without interfering. This man had shown little fear and had even tried to stop them.

"We will kill the men and take the woman and girl," Inkpaduta said, adding with a malicious grin, "you can take the woman and we will give the girl to Big Face."

Charley thought fast. He liked Hannibal House Waterman. The man, his wife and daughter had taken him into their home and treated him like a member of their family. But he knew that Inkpaduta would care little about how good the white family had treated him. It would take more than his own consideration for the Watermans to save their lives.

"But, Old Father, there are many white people living just to the east of here. The hired man has run to warn them," he said, pointing to Hank Meyers running tracks. "It might be better to leave this man and in a few days after they are no longer afraid, visit the other cabins and take what we want from them. If we kill this man and take his women, they will band together and fort up, and we will not be able to steal from them without a fight."

Inkpaduta thought about Charley's words and could see good sense in them. Reluctantly he shook his head in agreement. "You are right, my adopted son. We will leave these people and visit the others in a few days." He looked at Roaring Cloud and said, "Tell the others we are leaving now. Tell them to leave the man and his women." The old leader walked away following their own tracks leading back to their campsite from the night before. They would stay there for a few days and watch this cabin to see how the other whites in the area reacted to what had happened here.

When little Emily got cold from sitting in the snow behind the tree, she slowly, fearfully, wandered back to the cabin. Carefully, she squeezed her head through the back door that Hank had left ajar when they ran out, and her small eyes could see that the Indians were gone.

Her mother was crouched on the floor tending to her father. The flat side of the tomahawk had struck Hannibal House, leaving a large lump on the back of his head. With a mighty effort and help from Hannah, Hannibal House was able to climb to his feet and stumble unsteadily over to the bed. After he was lying on the bed, Hannah ran outside and packed snow in a small blanket. She brought the cold bundle in and put it under his swollen head. Then she quickly bolted the door and put more wood on the fireplace. Beckoning to Emily, she pulled the back door closed also, and barricaded it by propping the legs from the broken chairs against it. As the fire grew and a dull glow of light filtered through the dark cabin, Hannah picked up her straw broom and began to sweep up the mess left by their visitors.

It was three hours later, shortly after noon, when Gust and Jacob Kirchner, accompanied by men named Shoots and Taylor and a reluctant Hank Meyers arrived at the Waterman cabin. Hank was surprised and more than a little embarrassed to find the Watermans all alive and well. He had been sure that H. H. had been killed and expected that Hannah and Emily had been kidnapped. He was a very happy man to find them all alive.

After Hank had arrived spreading the alarm, Gust and Jacob visited each of their nearby neighbors, asking them to come to the Kirchner cabin to stay for the next few days. There was strength in numbers and they could face the Indian threat together. Gust offered to help them move down to the Kirchner cabin for a few days.

"Naw," the proud and stubborn H. H. Waterman said, shaking his head. "The Watermans will stay in Waterman. Ain't no red devils gonna run us out of our own home!" he growled.

The Kirchners, Mr. Shoot and Mr. Taylor all tried to talk Hannibal House Waterman into joining them just for a few days, but Waterman still refused to go with them.

"Thankee fer yer concern, but we'll be just fine. Them red men took about all I got fer 'em ta take." He gestured toward the carcasses of the oxen and the mule. "I doubt if they'll be back. But we best save what we can of it. Hank, if'n yer gonna stay here with us, git ta skinning out what's left of them dead critters. We might as well hang some meat on the roof so the coyotes and wolves cain't git it." He shook Gust's hand then and warned, "You all better hurry on back to yer own families. If'n you got livestock, them heathens will probably be after it."

As H. H. and Hank began skinning the mutilated animals, the men from Long Grove took his advice and started walking back to their homes, following the trail in the snow they had made when they came. The two men finished skinning and cutting up what was salvageable from the dead animals. The Indians had eaten or carried off most of the hindquarters and the front legs off of both oxen and the mule. The rib cages, necks and heads of the animals were left and would provide the family with enough meat to make soup for most of the rest of the winter. If they used it sparingly and had any luck hunting at all, Hannibal House thought they could make it through till spring.

It was nearly dark by the time they finished securing the supply of salvaged meat, wrapped it in the animal's hides, and lifted the bundles onto the roof of the cabin. H. H. and Hank entered the cabin and sat down for a sampling of the soup they would be eating for the rest of the winter. Both men were impressed by how Hannah and Emily had cleaned up the inside of the cabin. When the soup was gone, the Waterman's climbed into their bed and Hank wrapped up in a scrap of blanket the Indians had missed on the floor in front of the fire place. His cot had been broken and burned by the Indians. They would have to build a new one.

Soon after they were all down, Hannibal House heard a faint scratching at the door. He leapt from the bed, grabbing a length of wood to use for a club and stood at the door, growling, "Who's out thar?"

"Injun Charley," came a low-pitched answer.

H. H. opened the door a crack and peeked out. Upon seeing Charley, he opened the door wide enough to let the man in and slammed it closed, bolting it all in the same motion! He turned to see Charley grinning at him, while holding out his rifle and bag of powder and shot.

"My gun!" Waterman reached out to clutch it. "Howdja get a holt of my gun, Charley?"

"Stole it," was the man's simple explanation. Charley had decided to not leave his friend defenseless; even though he knew Inkpaduta would be angry when he found out the gun had been returned. He turned to the door and grunted, "Go now."

"Wait now, Charley. Go where?" H. H. asked, adding, "Stay the night. Them Injuns killed the hounds, but you can curl up with Ol' Hank by the fire ta stay warm fer the night."

Charley glanced at Hank and shook his head. He had seen Hank running though the snow after dropping little Emily and had no desire to share a sleeping spot with him. He knew too, that Inkpaduta wouldn't hesitate to come back, if he thought Charley had tricked him. He shook his head.

"Go now," Charley said, and turned to unbolt the door.

"Wait!" H. H. cried reaching out to place a hand on Charley's shoulder. When he was sure the man would stand, he placed his rifle on the table and removed a small leather pouch from around his neck. Opening it, he emptied the contents into his hand. Two silver dollar coins were all that was left.

"I don't know fer sure what you did today, but I know ya did me a service," he said placing the coins in Charley's hand. "Take this fer all yer troubles."

Charley glanced at the coins for a moment. He knew little of the white man's money system, but knew that Inkpaduta liked white man money. Maybe the coins would help to cool Inkpaduta's anger at having lost the fine rifle of Hannibal House Waterman. Charley glanced at H. H. for only a second and then turned to the door and walked out into the dark night.

# Chapter 31
*Up the Inyaniake – Long Grove*

Inkpaduta sat outside of his tipi, watching the flickering flames of his low-burning campfire. After leaving the camp west of the Waterman cabin, he led his people to this spot only about four miles east and down into the river valley. Here they were sheltered from the wind and could camp with a good wood supply. As the night grew darker and the cold of the night settled in, the other people of the village had all gone seeking the warmth of their robes.

As the stars began to appear through the bare winter tree branches, he threw more sticks on the fire and leaned back against a tree stump. It was going to be a cold night. The heat from his fire felt good. He pulled his robe up around his shoulders and leaned back against a tree stump. Dozing while staring into the flames of the fire put him in a pensive mood, and his mind began drifting.

Though he didn't know exactly how old he was, he thought that he had probably already lived longer than his father had lived. He could remember the good days, when he was a small boy and his father, Wamdisapa, was the leader of a large *Wahpekute* band. Hundreds of warriors followed his father because they thought of him as the best leader in the tribe.

Now, those who followed Inkpaduta did so only because none of the other bands would accept them in their villages. His people were a difficult bunch to lead, he reflected. His twin sons were sometimes the hardest to control of them all, as both were always vying for power. Sometimes even the women of the band were problems. They were jealous of one another and quarrels between them often led to hair pulling fights. The bachelors in the band were often angry with the married men for not sharing their wives with them. But the married men had little to share, for most of their women still had small children suckling at their breasts and wouldn't allow even their husbands the pleasures of having sexual intercourse with them.

Inkpaduta understood the frustration and pent up anxiety for the want of a woman that the bachelors felt. His own wife, Hates Her Father, had grown old, and though she was still a good worker, was a particularly unsatisfying sex partner. He tried bedding with each of his daughters-in-law, but each in turn had shown little interest in the act. They were merely performing a reluctant duty to their husband's father and exhibited no pleasure themselves. Only Trader's Slave Woman had provided him with any excitement, and that was only because she had fought him and he had had to slap her into submission. Adding to his dissatisfaction, his sons expected payment or other concessions for the favor of using their wives. He decided that his son's wives weren't worth the problems using them caused. Like the bachelors, he needed to find a new woman, from outside the band.

He thought of the woman Charley called Hannah Waterman. She was a plump, young woman, who looked soft and very appealing. When he had told Charley that he could have her, in his heart, Inkpaduta wanted to kill her man and take the young woman for himself. The bachelors could have fought over the little girl. But he was glad that he had followed Charley's advice to leave the family. There were other whites to steal from in this valley. The very stump he leaned against was a proof that. Roaring Cloud and Fire Cloud had scouted the valley while the women set up camp. The tree from that stump was surely used to build one of the six cabins his sons reported seeing in the valley. Last spring there had been only the cabin that the Bear Face was building. The sudden influx of white people living on the *Inyaniake* bothered Inkpaduta. There was getting to be too many white people.

He held the two silver coins Charley gave him after stealing Waterman's rifle. He wasn't angry with Charley for taking the gun anymore. He had another gun and would get more tomorrow morning. The silver coins were valuable because he could buy whiskey with silver. Licking his lips at the thought of the fiery liquid, he heard a dog barking across the river and glanced in the direction of a dark cabin silhouetted in the snow at the base of the treeless hill on the far side of the open valley. It was a bigger cabin than the Bear Face's cabin. Bear Face's cabin was on this side of the river, and they visited it yesterday. Bear Face was not there, so they searched the cabin finding only a short bag of flour and a small crock of beans.

Inkpaduta grunted as he stood and walked to the edge of the fire's light. He waited for his eyes to adjust to the dark away from his fire, and he looked across the valley to the cabin at the base of the hill. In the bright moonlight, he could make out the log walls and could see the movement of the dog, as it ranged back and forth in the snow in front of the cabin barking incessantly. Grunting, he reached into his pants and pulled his penis into the cold air. As he urinated in the snow, leaving a dark patch, he wondered why the white people in the cabin didn't kill that annoying dog and boil it for breakfast. In the morning, he would visit that cabin and he would make that dog breakfast! He laughed to himself at this thought. Come morning, they would visit that cabin and take the dog, the oxen, flour, beans, guns and powder and if everything looked right, maybe even some women. Smiling to himself, he turned and went back to his tipi.

\*   \*   \*

The people in the cabin on the north side of the valley could hear their dog barking too. They knew what was causing it to bark. The dog didn't like the fact that the Indians had seen fit to set up their camp so close to their cabin. The campfires of the Indian camp could be seen through the darkness. Every one in the cabin was apprehensive about what the next day would bring. There were twenty people huddled in a semi-circle around the fireplace. Twelve were Kirchners and the rest were Shoots, Frinks, and Bicknells. They all listened carefully as Christian Kirchner, the patriarch of the family, spoke.

"Gust says dae Indians speak some English, so to keep dem off guard, ven dae Indians come ve vill speak to one another only in Cherman," he said in heavily accented English adding, "If ya can't speak Cherman, keep your mout shut." He smiled after giving this order and the rest of the people chuckled at his attempt at levity. They were all frightened from what they had heard happened at the Waterman cabin, and the tension in the room was accelerated by the barking dog outside. The Bicknells, Shoots and Frinks had moved into the Kirchner Cabin on the day they heard about the incident at Waterman.

After five days without seeing any Indians, they were about ready to return to their own homes. But as soon as the Indians were spotted moving into the valley earlier that day, their thoughts of returning to their own cabins were forgotten. They spent most of the afternoon hiding most of their supplies. Gust warned them to leave something unhidden for the Indians to find. Otherwise he was sure they would keep searching until they found everything. It would be a long sleepless night for the inhabitants of the Kirchner cabin. Their fears were summed up in Christian Kirchner's last directive:

"Ve vill let dem take whatever dae vant and treat dem as friends until . . . " He paused and held up one finger. "Dey touch one of the vimmen. Den, ve vill fight dem until ve are dead."

The morning dawned bright and cold, finding most of the people in the cabin still awake. They had finally brought the barking dog inside, but the animal refused to lie down, standing by the door whining instead. Only young Jacob slept well. He rose early and hobbled across the floor to take his turn at the peephole in the door. He had spent most of three weeks in bed with frostbitten feet after his trip to Fort Dodge with Abner Bell and Mr. Weaver a month earlier. He and Gust, Bicknell and Shoots volunteered to keep watch of the Indian camp through the peephole in the door, so that they would not be surprised if the Indians came visiting. Everyone would stay inside that day and pray that the Indians would move on and leave them alone.

But as the sun rose high in the sky and the hour of noon approached, a warning cry from Mr. Shoots, whose turn it was at the peephole, told them to be ready. Gust took over at the peephole and watched the Indians approach. When they were near the cabin, Gust opened the door and walked boldly out with a smile of welcome on his face. The dog squeezed out with him and began barking ferociously. A gunshot rang out echoing off the hillsides and Magdalena Kirchner screamed, thinking the Indians had shot her eldest son! But Gust quickly opened the door and walked back in. He was smiling and speaking in German.

"The dog. It was only the dog, Mama," he said still smiling largely.

He turned back out and closed the door again and still smiling advanced to meet the Indians. There were eight men and three women. The men were painted in various shades of yellow, red, white and black. The women were not painted. All of them were wrapped in robes and blankets. Each man was armed with a club and five of them also carried guns. One of the women immediately picked up the dead dog, slung it over her shoulder and started back across the flat river bottom ground hurriedly walking toward the Indian camp.

It took only a minute for Gust to see the deep pox scars on Inkpaduta's face for him to recognize the man. "Welcome, welcome," Gust said over and over as he walked toward the Indians and spent time thoroughly shaking each man's hand. The snow had drifted high and was approaching the height of the cabin's roof on the southeast side of the cabin. The cold had been bitter for weeks and a dead ox lay frozen where it died two weeks before, in a small pen on the west side of the cabin. At a gruff command from Inkpaduta, the remaining two women pulled axes from beneath their blankets robes and began hacking at the frozen ox corpse, chopping large chunks of frozen meat from its hind quarters.

With an unfriendly glare, Inkpaduta pushed past Gust and walked into the cabin. He stopped in the doorway for a moment to let his eyes accustom themselves to the darkness of the interior. Surprise flickered across his face when he saw how many people there were in the cabin. For the first time, he was uncertain about what to do. He had thought that the Bear Face lived across the river in the cabin that they had ransacked yesterday. But the man was here now and acted like this was his cabin. There were also many more people here than he expected to find. Many of them were armed men whose eyes looked at him without fear. He was confused, too, because these people spoke to one another in a different white language than what he was used to hearing. A slow dread began to push its way into Inkpaduta's mind.

"Mamma, Pappa, we have guests," Gust said in German, adding, "Make them feel welcome but watch their every move."

Rain Cloud, Fire Cloud, Roaring Cloud and Young Inkpaduta pushed past their father and immediately began snooping through the chests and cabinets, looking for anything that might catch their fancy. Rattling, Gunn and Big Face took up positions near the door and stared with stone faces at the white women huddled near the back wall of the cabin. Worn Moccasin Woman and Beaded Hair Woman skewered chunks of the frozen ox meat and leaned it over the flames in the fireplace. Fire Cloud discovered three poorly hidden bags of flour and dried beans. He ordered the two women to take them back to the camp as Afraid of Her Husband had done with the dog. They shouldered the bags and walked quickly out of the cabin.

When the frozen ox meat had warmed enough for the blood to begin dripping into the flames, Inkpaduta ordered Magdelena to fetch it to the table. The older woman looked to Gust in wonder, because she didn't understand the pock- marked Indian's words.

"Put the meat on the table, mamma." Gust told her, and grasping a potholder to protect her hands from the hot skewer, she carried the meat to the table and plopped it in the center. All eight Indian men rushed to the table and began tearing at the meat, chewing and swallowing as fast as they could.

Gust placed a jar of molasses on the table and removed the lid. Roaring Cloud poured the thick sweet liquid over a chunk of bloody meat and howled with delight over the taste of it. Soon they were all covering the meat with molasses and a chorus of approving grunts followed each time they swallowed it down. Finally, as they smacked their lips and belched with satisfaction, they wolfed the very last morsel of the sweetened meat.

Inkpaduta stood and looked about the cabin. He ignored the white people sitting in clusters staring back at him. His men had left the interior of the cabin in shambles. There were tipped over boxes and chests. Blankets, clothing and broken furniture were strewn helter-skelter across the large, one-room cabin. Even though his women had taken flour and beans and the barking dog, and each of his men was gathering up armloads to carry with them, Inkpaduta was disappointed with what they found. He knew that the people of this cabin had more supplies and suspected that they had hidden their food. This angered him. But there were seven armed men in this cabin, and he had never forgotten the lessons his father taught him about not fighting a battle if he had a chance to lose.

He turned to his men and with a silly grin on his grease smeared face he said, "We will go now. Take whatever you can get without causing a fight." He walked up to the Bear Face and shook his hand, as he pointed at the molasses jar and shaking his head up and down stated in exaggerated English, "Gooood! Gooood!" Then he walked out the door

Slowly, the rest of his men filed toward the door also, each carrying an armload of clothing, blankets or goods. But the last man, Gunn, was empty-handed and as he neared the door, he reached out as quickly as a bee sting and snatched the rifle from Jacob Kirchner's hands and ran for the river.

With an angry shout, Jacob started to chase after him. It was his favorite rifle; he had carved the stock from walnut and fit it perfectly to his shoulder and eye. But Gust, fearing a bloody fight, called Jacob back, and all the young man could do was watch as the Indians ran laughing across the snow-covered ground. All in all, the people who had forted up in the Kirchner cabin felt pretty lucky. They just hoped the Indians wouldn't return.

The next day they were gratified to see the *Wahpekute* band pack up their camp and move to the east. Gust and Jacob decided to follow to see where and how far the Indians would move. As it turned out, they didn't go far, setting up camp again near Ambrose Mead's cabin only about a mile up river from the Kirchners. Gust and Jacob decided to go to Mead's cabin and try to help the people there if the Indians came to visit. The two brothers were cutting through the trees just north of the Mead cabin, when they came across the Indians lined up across their path. They stopped stock-still, out numbered and out-gunned.

Roaring Cloud and Fire Cloud approached Gust, shouting and pointing back in the direction they had come from. It was clear that they didn't like being followed and were warning the two white men to go back. Gust smiled and pointed toward the Mead cabin saying in English, "Just going to help my friend Mead patch on his cabin. We mean you no harm."

Roaring Cloud angrily pulled his knife and held it at Gust's chin. He hadn't forgotten the embarrassing beating the Bear Face had dealt him last spring and decided now to frighten the white man. With quick circular motions, he swished the sharp blade past Gust's face and around his ears, ending the display by slowly passing the knife across in front of Gust's throat.

He was disappointed to see the smile still on the Bear Face's lips, but also noted the friendly light in the man's eyes had changed. There was no fear in the eyes, only anger. The thought crossed Roaring Cloud's mind that he should step back and shoot this man, who showed no fear, but he knew that he should be prepared to die also, for this man would not go down without a fight. At the sound of a commotion, Roaring Cloud glanced to his left and saw Gunn jostling and pushing Jacob Kirchner back away from the scene. The young half-breed finally threw Jacob's rifle, that he had stolen the day before on the trail, and was shoving Jacob toward it, shouting the only English he knew, "Go gawddamit Go!"

"Gust!" Jacob shouted as he picked the rifle up. "We ain't gonna do much good down here. There's too many of 'em."

Without answering, Gust Kirchner turned his glaring eyes from Roaring Cloud's face to check on his little brother's position. He could see that Jacob was right. There were just too many of them for the two brothers to handle by themselves.

He was filled with regret. He wished Mead and Taylor had heeded his invitation to come and fort up in the Kirchner cabin like the Shoots, Frinks and Bicknells, after what had happened at the Waterman place. But they had chosen to go it alone and now that is what they would have to do. He glanced back at Roaring Cloud and an angry sneer crossed his face.

Boldly, he turned his broad back totally unafraid and walked back up the trail. Roaring Cloud brought his gun to his shoulder and aimed it at the Bear Face's back. He had killed many men before who were stupid enough to turn their back on him, but before he could pull the trigger a sudden fear flowed through him. It was as if the Bear Face was daring him to shoot and was totally unafraid. A certain dread of failure overcame Roaring Cloud, and he dropped his rifle from his shoulder and watched the Kirchner brothers walk away.

When Inkpaduta heard of the confrontation, he praised his son for not shooting the Bear Face. The sound of the gunshot would have undoubtedly warned the people in the cabin they were approaching.

Still, he worried about interference from the Bear Face. He sent Brave Bull to watch with orders to come running if he saw a force from the Bear Face's cabin coming. Without preamble, Inkpaduta opened the door to the Mead cabin, and he and his warriors walked in. Inside, they quickly disarmed the two grown men present, and Charley and Gunn held them at bay by aiming shotguns at them.

Roaring Cloud circled the table and grabbed the younger of the two grown women, Mrs. Taylor, around the waist. She started to scream, but a dirty hand quickly smothered it over her mouth. He dragged her out of the door! Her husband, shouting angrily tried to pursue, but was clubbed unconscious by Gunn. On seeing his mother dragged off and his father beaten to the ground, the young Taylor boy ran to follow his mother.

Young Inkpaduta picked the small boy up and threw him into the open fire pit under the smoke hole at the east end of the room. The boy's nightshirt burst into flames, and he screamed in pain and fear. He bolted from the pit a flaming torch, which threatened to catch the interior of the cabin on fire. Ambrose Mead quickly caught the child and smothered the flames. His wife hurriedly started to treat the burns by smearing them with lard and wrapping them with clean cloths.

While the Mead's were preoccupied with helping the small Taylor child, Young Inkpaduta grabbed their eldest daughter, Harriet, and dragged her from the cabin. Big Face snatched their youngest daughter, Emma and carried her screaming from the cabin. Mrs. Taylor and Harriet, after struggling briefly, seemed to accept their fate and went along quietly. But little Emma fought hard, screaming and kicking at her captor, scratching at his eyes and biting his hand if he tried to put it over her mouth.

Big Face tried to spank the young girl, which only caused her to fight much harder. Finally, he grew tired of the struggle and let her go. The young girl raced back to the cabin and covered her head with a blanket. The Meads spent that night by caring for the young Taylor boy and his father. Taylor regained consciousness, but couldn't stand. They worried about their daughter, Harriet, and Mrs. Taylor, but knew that there was nothing they could do to help them.

In Inkpaduta's camp, Mrs. Taylor and Harriet were shoved into the bachelor's tipi. Roaring Cloud and Inkpaduta were the first to enter. Inkpaduta took young Harriet and Roaring Cloud slapped Mrs. Taylor hard across the face. She fell to the ground, but got back up. He raised his hand to slap her again, but she reached up and began unbuttoning her shirt.

"Just do what they want ya ta do, Harriet," the Taylor woman advised to her fellow captive. "Otherwise, they'll jest beat ya ta death and do it anyway."

It was a long night. Each man in the village took at least one turn at raping the white women. In the morning, Hates Her Father entered the tipi and shouted at the two white women pointing at their clothes and then pointing at the door of the tipi. They soon understood that they were to get dressed and leave. Feeling lucky to be released and not kept as slaves, the two quickly dressed and ran back to their cabin. Mrs. Taylor was devastated by the sight of her son wrapped in white cloth and her husband still not able to rise from the bed Ambrose and his wife had put him in. Harriet sat by the table and stared at the flames in the fire pit, not talking, just barely acknowledging her mother's hugs.

It was mid-afternoon when Inkpaduta and his sons returned. Roaring Cloud and Fire Cloud pushed Ambrose to the floor and pulled Taylor from the bed, shoving him to the floor beside Ambrose. The two men sat staring dully up the barrels of the Indians' rifles as Inkpaduta and Young Inkpaduta pushed Harriet and Mrs. Taylor out the door again.

They led the woman and girl back to their camp. Charley and Brave Bull were ordered to watch the cabin to make sure no one attempted to run to the Kirchner cabin for help. For Harriet Mead and Mrs. Taylor, it was another long night, but both lacked the will to fight and they accepted their fate once again.

At sunup, the same old woman came in and ordered them to dress and leave. The two women trudged back to their cabin, worn out from lack of sleep, bruised and sore, but otherwise, physically unharmed. Wrapping their arms around one another, they walked the last few steps to the cabin and entered, hoping to feel safe in the confines of their home. But even though the Indians broke camp and moved off before the sun had risen above the trees, neither would ever feel safe again.

# Chapter 32
## *Up The Inyaniake – Gillett's Grove*

As his people moved up river that morning, Inkpaduta was glad that he had found a way to make the men in his band happy again. His warriors were angry about the way the whites had treated them in Smithland. They had been vocally complaining about not retaliating ever since they left their camp on Elijah Adams' farm some sixty miles down river. Roaring Cloud even went so far as to suggest to some of the other men, that maybe his father was afraid of the white men. He was careful to keep his comments to himself when Inkpaduta was in hearing distance. But he had made it known amongst the men that, in his opinion, stealing from the whites and pushing them around just wasn't enough.

Now, as they rode through the trees toward the rising sun, Inkpaduta could sense a much lighter mood in the men. It seemed that stealing the white women, using them to ease their sexual desires and then letting them return to their men, was an insult to the white men that met with Roaring Cloud's approval.

Inkpaduta decided that when conditions were right, they would continue to take white women to use for a night or two. He insisted though, that they only kidnap women whose men could easily be overwhelmed without risking a fight. The Bear Face's cabin, with seven armed men present, had been too well defended. He was sure that if they had tried to take any of their women, there would have been a fight, and some of his men would have been killed. But the second cabin, with only two armed but very frightened men to protect the women, had been a perfect situation for them.

Later that day, as they came to the Weaver and Totten cabins, he found they had the same advantage. Weaver and Totten tried to resist, but they were disarmed and beaten unconscious. Rain Cloud, Old Man and Puts On As He Walks slipped up on Abner Bell as the hunter was returning to the Weaver cabin and captured him. They dragged the struggling man to a tree growing by itself on the edge of an open field, tied him to the tree and beat him with their war clubs until he hung limply in his bonds. Mrs. Weaver and Mrs. Totten were afforded the same treatment as Harriet Mead and Mrs. Taylor. Both women tried to fight their rapists off, only to be severely beaten before being forced to submit to the warriors' desires. In the morning, the Indians struck camp and rode off up river again, leaving Mrs. Weaver and Mrs. Totten to find their way back to their cabins.

A few days later, twenty miles up river, the band came across the cabins of George and Isaiah Gillett. When they burst into the cabin, Inkpaduta immediately saw that even though there were only two men present, it would be dangerous to try to take their woman. Both of the Gillett brothers stood back with shotguns in their hands and knives and tomahawks at their belts. He also saw a gray light in their eyes and a grimness about their mouths that reminded him of the look in the Bear Face's eyes after Roaring Cloud had cut off part of his ear during the wrestling contest last spring. Something in that look said that if you asked for trouble, these men would give it to you.

"These men will kill you if you touch that woman," Inkpaduta warned in his own language as he sat at the table and shouted in English, "Food, bring food!" His men sat at the table also and began pounding it with their war clubs shouting "Food—eat—hungy!" over and over again.

At a nod from her husband, Mrs. Gillett quickly set some meat and beans on the table. She was a plump, smiling woman who sang softly as she sliced a fresh loaf of bread and placed it on the table. Even with Inkpaduta's stern warning, most of his men looked hungrily at George Gillett's wife. She was a comely young woman with pleasant features including a friendly face, large breasts and a full, rounded rump.

After shoveling the hot bean meal into their mouths and gobbling the offered meat, the Indian men stood up from the table and began to carefully snoop around the cabin, hoping that the white men would let their guard down. But as soon as they stood up from the table, the woman retreated to the corner of the cabin and stood behind the two well-armed white men. Big Face and Putting On As He Walks were grumbling in low voices about wanting this woman to keep. They wanted to kill these white men and take the woman. But the threat of the Gilletts' shotguns at close quarters was too real. Inkpaduta ordered them to leave, pushing the two men out the door before walking out himself. They went back to their camp, two miles up river and settled in for the night.

An hour before dawn, Putting On As He Walks slipped out of the bachelor's tipi and hurried back down river to the Gillett cabin. He was a young man who until recent days had never had sex. After his experiences, first with Harriet Mead, then Mrs. Taylor and the Weaver and Totten women, he felt like he knew what he wanted, and since he was a man, he would take what he wanted. He wanted the Gillett woman. He had begged Inkpaduta to take all of the men back and kill the two white men, so that he could have this woman. But the old man refused, stating that the two white men were too well armed to take the chance. He wanted no trouble with them. Putting On As He Walks thought that maybe Roaring Cloud had been right when he said that Inkpaduta was afraid of white men. He decided that if Inkpaduta was afraid to take the woman, that he would just take her by himself.

The dawn broke with dark snow clouds in the sky, and a cold northwest wind that promised a storm was on its way. The young Indian stood at the edge of the timber and watched the Gillett cabin until he saw both of the white men leave. One of the men with a short length of rope looped around his shoulder carried a rifle, walked down the hill behind the cabin, and headed down river. The other man with a bucket and small ax in one hand and a shotgun in the other walked past Putting On As He Walks hiding behind a tree, and down the slope leading to the river. When he reached the middle of the sloping hill, he passed from the Indian's sight.

Putting On As He Walks waited no longer. He dashed to the house and burst through the door, finding the woman standing by the fireplace, dressed in only a nightshirt and long woolen stockings. She screamed at the sight of him. Dumping the oatcakes she was frying in a heavy iron skillet, she raised it threateningly and backed away, screaming even louder.

Putting On As He Walks spoke to her in a soothing voice in his own language. But his calm, friendly voice did little to calm her. She continued to scream louder and louder. He thought that after the men left, it would be a simple matter to snatch this woman. He planned to drag her to the low-built outbuilding where the white men kept their horse. He had even envisioned in his mind his triumphant return to Inkpaduta's village with both a stolen woman and a stolen horse! But it all depended upon him acting fast.

He rushed at the woman dodging the heavy fry pan she threw at him. Laughing at her futile effort to scare him off, he ran to the other side of the table. She was quicker than he anticipated, and he had to hurry to block her from escaping out the door. He hoped that she would grow tired of screaming, but her screams seemed to be growing louder and louder as she ran back and forth across the room keeping the big table between them.

303

He tried to talk to her again, to tell her that he was not there to hurt her. He wanted only to take her with him, so he could bed her. He promised that he wouldn't share her with the rest of the men. She would be his and only his. Nothing he said seemed to calm the woman down. But she was tiring and began slowing down. He was finally able to slip around the table before she could circle it, and he had her trapped on the fireplace end of the cabin. The woman backed toward the fireplace as he advanced toward her. But he pulled up when she picked up a black iron rod that was used to stoke the fire and began swinging it at him.

Putting On As He Walks hesitated. He hadn't planned for trying to capture the woman if she was armed and in a mood to fight. He noticed that the woman's face was not the sweet smiling face she had yesterday. It was a snarling, angry face that she wore today. He wondered which face she wore most often. Her constant screaming hadn't slowed any and now each time he took a step toward her, she swung the rod at him, or stabbed at him with it. Angrily, he considered shooting the woman, but knew that the sound of a gunshot would probably bring her men back. And if he killed her, they would probably track him to the village and trouble would surely break out.

Putting On As He Walks stopped chasing the woman and started thinking about the situation he was in. While lying in his robes with an erection from thinking about her the night before, he had made the decision to kidnap her. But now it seemed that maybe Inkpaduta was right when he said there were more white women who could be taken much easier than this one. He had a sudden change of heart and decided to abandon the idea of kidnapping this woman even more quickly than he had made the decision to kidnap her.

He backed slowly, cautiously, away from her, watching the pointed stoking rod in her hand. When he neared the open door, he turned and ran through it out into the snowy clearing in front of the cabin. Before he could even turn toward the river, a sudden impact struck him in the left side knocking him to the ground. As his body landed in the snow, he heard the sound of a shotgun blast register in his brain.

George Gillett stood only ten feet away at the corner of the cabin. Smoke curled up from the dark muzzle of his scattergun. He had heard his wife's screams and ran back up the hill expecting that maybe a wolf was after the livestock again. But as he rounded the wall of the cabin, the Indian burst out of the cabin and in the same instant he realized that his wife wasn't screaming any more.

Expecting the worst, he pulled the shotgun to his shoulder and shot the Indian where he stood. The nine heavy balls in his buckshot load didn't spread much in the short distance traveled before striking the man in the rib cage of his left side.

Blood flowed freely from the wounds, turning the white snow a dark crimson. Putting On As He Walks struggled to a sitting position, and he reached with his right hand to feel the damage to his left side. His eyes riveted to the bloody holes, as he watched his life's blood drain into the snow. A low cry escaped his lips, and he fell back into the snow, rolling over and moaning deep in his chest. Spasmodic jerks shook his body twice and then he was still, dead as a stone.

Mrs. Gillett ran from the cabin and embraced her husband. They stood for several minutes holding one another, staring dumbly at the steam rising from the body of the dead Indian. A shout from the edge of the trees broke their trance, and Isaiah came running from the woods. He had heard the shot as he neared his own cabin and expecting trouble, came running the entire quarter of a mile distance.

Sudden fear gripped all three Gilletts. They didn't know how far away the Indians had camped. If Isaiah had heard the shot clearly from his cabin, it was possible the sound had reached the Indian camp. If that was the case, it probably wouldn't be long before the ugly old leader of the band missed the dead boy lying here in their yard. If the old man put two and two together, the Gilletts reasoned that they could be under attack in the matter of an hour.

They panicked! George and Isaiah grabbed Putting On As He Walks by the feet and dragged him south of the clearing to a huge fallen tree. The ancient windfall was hollow and had been a home for raccoons, foxes and even a bear. Now it would be a good place to hide the body. After stuffing the young Indian's body into the hollow tree, the brothers returned to the cabin and realized that hiding the body would do little good. The bloody trail they left while dragging the body to the hollow tree was easily seen.

The realization that they couldn't wipe out the blood trail good enough to fool the Indians increased their panic. They knew that if the Indians came looking for this young man, they would find him and there would be trouble. They were outnumbered and knew that they wouldn't have a chance. Without further waste of time, they hitched their horse to the sleigh and packed food, warm clothing and ammunition. Shortly before noon, with a light snow beginning to fall and the skies threatening more snow, the Gilletts climbed on the sleigh and they headed south and east. Expecting that since they had killed an Indian, there would be a war coming, they headed for Fort Dodge as fast as the horse could pull them.

\*   \*   \*

It was mid-afternoon before the other bachelors missed Putting On As He Walks. They told Inkpaduta that he wasn't anywhere around the camp and that the falling snow had covered his tracks. Inkpaduta suspected where the young man had gone and led the men to the Gillett cabin. Scavengers had already pulled the body from the hollow tree and had begun feasting on it by the time the *Wahpekute* found it. Circling turkey buzzards and the feeding cry of crows led them to the body. Foxes had chewed away the trade blanket and buckskin clothing. Their sharp teeth had made short work of the freezing flesh of his left leg and the crows and buzzards had been at work on his face and eyes.

The women were summoned, and they cleaned his body and sadly wrapped it in the boy's thin robe. Big Face and Old Man, both relatives of Putting On As He Walks, hoisted him onto a platform of branches lashed in a fork of a tall tree not far from where his body had been hidden by the white men. Several of the women cut their hair and keened for the dead boy, praying for his safe journey to his next life.

Anger grew in Inkpaduta as he stood staring up at the body. He had warned the young men to forget the woman. But Putting On As He Walks hadn't heeded his warning, and now he was dead.

They searched the Gillett buildings taking all food and supplies the white people had left behind. Then, Inkpaduta ordered the cabins and outbuildings to be set on fire. As the blaze started burning up the side of the wall, the Indians walked off to the north without watching the buildings burn. The falling wet snow put the fires out quickly.

Inkpaduta's people returned to their campsite and sadly settled in for another long, cold night. Inkpaduta slept restlessly. He dreamed—

*His birth mother appeared from out of the darkness. Spotted Horse Woman stood facing him from the edge of the ring of fire light. He recognized her because her body was that of a white horse covered with large brown and small black spots, and her head and upper torso was that of a young woman. Long dark hair hung loosely over her shoulders, tickling the small, upturned breasts of a young girl. Her face was clear and beautiful, but she was crying. Her tears streamed down from her wide set, coal black eyes as water on her cheeks, but they changed to sparks of fire when they fell to the ground around her hooves. A sudden wind blew at her feet, whipping the sparks into the air where they formed glowing shapes of his loved ones who had passed into the next life.*

First, his Indian father, Wamdisapa grew from the sparks and took a place next to Spotted Horse Woman. Inkpaduta could see Wamdisapa's lips moving in a low chant but could not hear the words. Rain Dance Woman rose from the sparks, and then, Sidominadota formed from the tears, and the three began a circle. Soon Sidominadota's wives and children and then Sun At Night joined the circle. All of them were chanting soundlessly with Wamdisapa. His mother continued to cry, and the tears continued to stream down her pretty face, and the sparks blew before the cold wind. The circle continued to grow, including everyone he had ever known that had died. There were all of the people, men, women and children, who had died from the pox, when he had survived. Even his enemies, men that he had killed himself; Tasagi, Buffalo Calf Man, and New Grass Woman, all were mourned by his crying mother.

Suddenly, his mother stopped crying. Her large eyes filled with fear, and she turned to look into the darkness. A dim figure with no facial features slowly emerged into the shadows just outside the firelight. Inkpaduta recognized the red hair and light colored skin as well as the fancy rifle with the cherry-red stock. His white father advanced toward the ring of light causing the circle of people to spread apart and let him through. He stopped and stood looking at Inkpaduta through eyes that shone red on his blurred face. The man began laughing a loud, joyless, cruel laugh.

Spotted Horse Woman began crying again as Inkpaduta's living relatives began filing into the ring of firelight: Hates Her Father, Roaring Cloud, Thunder Cloud, Rain Cloud, Beaded Hair Woman, Young Inkpaduta, Afraid of Her Husband, Worn Moccasin Woman, Trader's Slave Woman, each of his grandchildren, and Charley and Gunn. All were painted black, the color of death. The last person he saw enter the sphere of firelight was himself. The laughing of his white father had grown louder and louder with each person who squeezed into the circle of light, but the laughing suddenly stopped, and all he could hear was the moaning of those on the outer rim of the circle. Their moans became screams of pain and terror as the flames burnt lower and lower, and the light faded slowly throwing more and more of his people into the eternal darkness!

Inkpaduta woke in a cold sweat. He sat up and threw the blankets from him. His thoughts ran wild until he gained control, and he knew what the dream was telling him. The white men were slowly killing his people off and would continue to do so until all of the *Wahpekute* were gone.

As he sat thinking of the dream, he suddenly knew what Wamdisapa had been chanting—*Kill the white man—Kill them all—Kill the white men—Kill them all!*

They would break camp in the morning and travel to the northern lakes: *Minnewakan, Minnetanka, and Okobooshi.* When they arrived there, he knew what he must do.

# Chapter 33
## *Blood in the Snow*

**R**oland Gardner rose early from his bed and packed a bag with a change of clothing and two wool blankets. It was March, but the cold weather still held. Snow fell almost every other day adding to the huge drifts from the early part of the winter. Poor hunting along with the visitations by small bands of ravenous Indians had put the settlers in the Lakes Region in grave danger of running out of food if spring didn't come soon.

Occasionally, it was necessary for them to make the eighty mile trip back to Fort Dodge to re-supply themselves, and with their food supply dwindling, Gardner had decided to make the trip.

His wife and eldest daughter were preparing a breakfast of oat mush while he packed. He heard his son-in-law, Harvey Luce, calling their houseguest, Mr. Clark, and the children for breakfast. He carried his pack over to set it by the door, before sitting down at the table. He was just beginning to say grace when there came a loud pounding on the door. Harvey jumped up to open it. They were expecting some of the other settlers to be bringing letters for Rowland to carry to Fort Dodge where he could post them. Harvey's disappointment couldn't have been more complete when he saw an Indian, dressed in rags, standing in the open doorway. The man rubbed his stomach and made the motions of putting food in his mouth.

"Hungy–jib food–hungy," the Indian stated in a whining voice.

"Invite him in, Harvey," Mary Francis Gardner instructed her son-in-law. "We haven't much left, but we will share what we have with the needy."

He Who Makes A Crooked Wind As He Walks hobbled into the room and seated himself on Harvey's stool. He hungrily grabbed up the bowl of oatmeal and started shoveling the hot mush into his mouth. Rowland continued with his prayer of thanks, while the rest of the Gardners and Luces bowed their heads.

Mr. Clark watched the Indian eat, and an uncomfortable feeling came over him. This Indian was eating like he knew there wouldn't be enough to go around.

Even before Rowland finished his prayer, the door flew open and several more Indian men, women and children pushed into the cabin. They wore no paint, and though they all appeared to be as beggarly poor as the first Indian, they were wrapped in bright trade blankets to protect them from the cold. Without speaking, the group pushed and shoved trying to get to the food on the table. The press of unwashed bodies soon had all of the white people moved back from the table. Harvey, Rowland and Mr. Clark looked at one-another and shrugged their shoulders in helplessness. They could only watch as the starving Indians quickly devoured the meager breakfast meant for themselves.

When the pan of oatmeal on the table was gone, the Indian men spread out in the room and began snooping though everything. Some let their blankets fall, for it was warm in the cabin and the three white men were astonished to see an array of weapons, ranging from knives and clubs to short barreled shotguns that had been concealed beneath the colorful garments. There were fifteen Indian men, six women and five children in the cabin with the Gardners, the Luces and Mr. Clark.

Inkpaduta stood by the door. He watched Rowland Gardner, hoping the man would walk away from his rifle. Roaring Cloud and Fire Cloud took a similar position near Harvey Luce and Mr. Clark. The rest of the men and women were busy trying to draw the attention of the white men, so Inkpaduta and his sons could grab their rifles away from them.

"Mr. Gardner," Clark called over the noise in the cabin. "Be on your guard!" I think these redskins are sizin' us up, just waitin' to get the jump on us!"

"Hold now, Clark!" Roland Gardner answered, excitement making the pitch of his voice high. "Let's hope you are wrong. We'll let them take whatever they want and pray that they soon leave."

A faint smile formed on Inkpaduta's lips, for he understood enough English to get the drift of what the two white men had said. He nodded his head in approval as his women bundled up warm, heavy blankets, and the men took a supply of lead balls and powder. There was little food in the cabin, but they took every morsel they could find.

Seeing that almost everything of value in the cabin had been gathered, Roaring Cloud suddenly shoved the barrel of his shotgun at Harvey Luce's face and tried to thumb back the hammer.

Harvey was a stout young man and grabbed the barrel, pushing it away as he tried to wrench the weapon out of the Indian's hands.

Roaring Cloud shouted in anger, and Young Inkpaduta entered the scuffle, pushing Harvey back against the wall, while Roaring Cloud tried to regain control of his shotgun!

A loud pounding on the door brought all activity to a standstill. Inkpaduta shouted a warning at Roaring Cloud and Young Inkpaduta to stop, and everyone in the room turned their eyes to the door. Rowland opened the door and stepped out. Bertell Snyder and Dr. I. H. Harriott from the Redwing cabin had trudged over with letters for Rowland to mail in Fort Dodge. Rowland was frightened and sweat was pouring from him. Steam rose from his body in the cold morning air. He stepped from the cabin door, pulling the Redwing men with him.

"Thank God you showed up!" he cried, trying to keep his excited voice down, but fear was causing him to talk fast and loud. "Something is going on here! These Indians have moved in and are taking everything we have! Mr. Clark thinks they mean us harm! One of them even looked as though he was going to shoot Harvey, but Harvey grabbed his gun and they was wrestlin' over it just when you two started poundin' on the door!"

"Aw now, Rowland, you know how these people act—like they own everything." Bert Snyder said in answer to Rowland's fears. "We all been through it a time or two this winter. Just calm down."

"But these Indians are different!" Gardner cried. "They are more pushy than usual and are taking things no other Indians took before."

"Calm it down, Gardner." It was the stern voice of Dr. Harriott. "Indians respect bravery and if you show them you're scared, they walk all over you." He glanced in the open door and could see part of the throng of sweating bodies inside. "Besides, they have brought women and children with them. I assure you that they mean you no harm. They wouldn't take a chance on getting their women or babies hurt."

This statement did seem to reassure Rowland Gardner, but the vision of his son-in-law struggling with two wild Indians wouldn't completely leave his mind.

"Just the same, you two go warn the rest of the people that these are some mean Indians," he stated with deep conviction in his voice. "We have the largest cabin here. I think that everyone should bring their food and ammunition here. We'll fort up in this cabin until these people leave the area. I think it is a good idea. I think we should do it," he pleaded.

Upon hearing this, Inkpaduta walked out of the cabin flanked by Roaring Cloud and Fire Cloud. All three wore friendly smiles on their faces. Inkpaduta shook hands with both white men and spouted a string of his best English to impress them.

"Gawddammit–cold as hell–sumbichin' cold!" he shouted, laughing. He reached out a hand and touched a green scarf Dr. Harriott was wearing around his neck. "You trade?" he asked holding out a grimy leather pouch that had colorful beadwork on the flap.

Dr. Harriott grinned broadly, pulled the green scarf from around his neck, and held it out. Inkpaduta grabbed it and handed over the pouch. The smile on Inkpaduta's ugly face as he wrapped the warm scarf around his neck was infectious.

"Good gawdammit trade!" He beamed and ran back into the cabin to show off his prize.

Both Snyder and Harriott laughed at what little it took to mollify these primitive people.

"Ya see Gardner, he's the biggest, meanest looking Indian I've ever seen, but you give him what he wants, and he's as harmless as a child," Dr. Harriott said as he watched Inkpaduta showing the scarf to one of the old women inside the cabin.

"But he didn't act this way until you two came," Gardner countered. "He just stared around all haughty and mad-like." But his argument fell on deaf ears.

"You just hold a tight rein and keep your wits about ya," Bert Snyder advised. "By and by, they'll get their fill of white food and leave ya' be."

"Will you still be going to Fort Dodge?" Dr. Harriott asked, adding, "Or shall we take our letters back with us?"

"I'll not be leaving until I'm sure these people have left the area." Gardner answered. "Leave them with me if you want and in a few days, I'll make the trip," he added reaching to take the small packet of letters, a worried expression still on his face. His voice cracked with the tension building within him as he went on, "Please, for the sake of our Lord, don't make light of what's happening here today! These red men are up to no good. I know it! I fear for the safety of our entire community, not just myself!"

Snyder and Harriott merely looked at Rowland Gardner. Neither man knew what to say to calm the man's fears, for neither of them felt the situation was as dire as he painted it. Snyder looked at Harriott, and they shook their heads in agreement. It was time to leave.

"Well, we've got to go, Gardner," Dr. Harriott said.

"We'll be back tomorrow to help you repair any damage these rascals do," Bert Snyder offered with a small smile. It seemed to him that Gardner always had had trouble coping with the Indians.

"Please do as I asked! Warn the others. Tell them about the situation here and tell them to bring enough food and ammunition to fort up for a few days," Rowland Gardner begged again as the two men walked off to the northeast, toward the lake. He didn't hear them chuckling together at his discomfort.

Inkpaduta heard Gardner's pleas for the two white men to warn the rest of the whites and decided to change his plans. He pulled Charley and Gunn aside and told them to follow the two white men. He wanted to know if they were going to go to the other cabins and warn the people there, as this white man asked them to do. The two half-breed brothers ducked out the door as Rowland came back in. Inkpaduta saw that all three white men were back on their guard. Their guns were held at the ready. The chance for surprise had passed, and he knew that there was a good chance that some of his people would be hurt if they tried to take the cabin now. He was worried about what would happen if the two men who had just left spread the warning, like this man asked them to. He wanted no fight with a large, well armed and forted up group. It was time to pull back and wait.

With a shout, he ordered his people to get ready to leave. This cabin was alert for trouble. They would leave it and come back later. There were four brace of oxen and three milk cows penned up near the cabin. They drove the animals ahead of them, shooting one of the beasts every few feet until all eleven lay dead in the snow.

As they watched the Indians leave their cabin, the Gardners, Luces, and Mr. Clark felt that their prayers had been answered, but as they watched their livestock being slaughtered, they were confused as to what the Indians' intentions had really been. Was this slaying of the animals enough to quench the red men's thirst for blood? They barred the door, and all but Clark knelt to say a prayer of thanks and a prayer of hope for the future.

Clark stood watching through the peep hole and saw Inkpaduta's pox scarred face turn to look back at the cabin. He felt a chill run up and down his spine and bowed his head in a private prayer that he would never see the ugly Indian again.

\*   \*   \*

It was mid-afternoon when Charley and Gunn returned to the Indian camp to report that they had scouted the entire area and visited the clearings around four more cabins. Harriott and Snyder went straight back to their own cabin without warning anyone. They had also observed that the cabins built on either side of the narrows between *Okobooshi* and *Minnetanka* had the most men living in them. For this reason, Inkpaduta decided to raid them first. He sent ten men with Roaring Cloud in charge, to surround the Granger cabin, which housed the four men of the Redwing Company.

Roaring Cloud, Brave Bull, Big Face and Young Inkpaduta crossed the narrow ice field quickly and hid close to the cabin, aiming their weapons at the door. Rain Cloud, Rattling and His Great Gun hid in the trees on the north peninsula, while Charley, Gunn, and His Mysterious Father took up positions on the south peninsula. When they had the cabin and the path crossing between the peninsulas covered, they settled down and waited for the sound of gunfire to begin.

Inkpaduta, Fire Cloud, He Who Makes A Crooked Wind As He Walks, One Leg, and Old Man crept quietly up on the clearing around the Mattock cabin on the south peninsula. There were three white men, a woman and two children cutting, stacking and carrying wood to the cabin. Inkpaduta was glad to see that none of the white men had their weapons close at hand.

Two of the men were swinging broad, double bladed axes to split large logs of firewood into manageable pieces. The children were busy picking up the pieces and stacking them in small piles. The other man and the woman were picking up the piles and carrying them into the cabin. Inkpaduta waited until the woman was on her way to the cabin and the man was bending to pick up another load. As the axes rang in the cold clear air, he took aim and squeezed the trigger of his rifle.

"Kill them!" he shouted, as was the chant of his Indian father in the dream. "Kill them! Kill them!"

The other four men with him fired before the sound of his shot had quieted and all five hit their target. The four adult white people fell dead and the two children were hit by a shotgun blast fired by Old Man. One child, a tawny headed girl, had taken most of the force and lay dead, her face blown away. The younger boy was shot in the legs and lay screaming as he struggled to pull himself toward the cabin door. Inkpaduta quickly reloaded and shot the child again, killing him. There were screams from within the cabin, and he heard the bar being dropped across the door as silence briefly covered the clearing.

\* \* \*

Carl Granger was sick, and even though Doc Harriott had mixed medicines and poured a gallon of fish oil down him over the last few days, it hadn't seemed to help much to relieve the stomach cramps that kept him sweating from the knots of pain gripping his lower abdomen.

Today he felt a little better and had dressed, eaten a little, and was sitting by the fireplace. As he and his two friends sat enjoying the warmth of the fire, the sound of gunfire from across the narrows came to their ears. Harriott and Snyder glanced at one another and jumped to their feet, grabbed their weapons and ran out the door hurrying down the path leading to the Mattock cabin.

"Wait," Carl Granger cried. "I'll come too!"

Roaring Cloud and Young Inkpaduta followed Harriott and Snyder, keeping hidden behind trees. They knew there was another white man inside the cabin for they had heard him calling after Harriott and Snyder. Brave Bull and Big Face stayed back to wait for him to come out of the cabin.

Granger struggled into his heavy coat, the exertion triggering a cramp that doubled him over. But as soon as the pain subsided, he took up his shotgun and walked out the door. Just as he crossed the threshold, a hot pain slammed into his belly, knocking him to the ground and his shotgun flew from his hands.

His first thought was of the stomach cramps, but in the same instant, the loud explosion of a gun blast reached his ears, and he knew he had been shot. He could only lay and watch his blood turn the snow around him red. Through shocked eyes, he saw a horribly painted Indian standing over him. He saw his own broad ax that he always left by the wood pile being raised and watched as the heavy blade came crashing down, striking him just above the bridge of the nose, cleaving his head in two!

Gleefully, Brave Bull lifted the top of Carl Granger's head by the hair and shook it. He would skin the skull and scrape out the brains. It would make a handsome bowl. Big Face was not happy. He shot this white man, and it was only because he stopped to reload that Brave Bull was able to count coup by being the first to touch the enemy while he was still alive. Not wanting to cause trouble, Brave Bull quickly traced a circle around the crown of the half-head and carefully pulling and cutting, removed the scalp from it. He handed the scalp to Big Face, keeping the skullcap for himself. Big Face grunted his satisfaction, and the two turned to join the rest of the warriors across the narrows.

Harriott and Snyder rushed across the ice of the narrows. So hurried were they as they ran through the crunching snow, that they didn't hear the gun blast behind them and weren't aware that they were being followed. They slowed their pace as they entered the trees on the south side and crept steadily toward the Mattock cabin. Both men were silently cursing themselves for not heeding Rowland Gardner's warning. It was heavy on their minds that if they had just stopped to warn the Mattocks on their way home, this may not be happening.

The two men stopped in the last row of trees by the clearing. They could see the bodies of four adults and two children lying grotesquely as they had fallen.

"Damnation!" Bert Snyder whispered hoarsely, wondering where the murderers were. "Where are they Doc?"

Moving his head from side to side, Harriott looked through the trees. He could see no sign of the Indians. He didn't answer Snyder. Silently, he cursed himself again. This time it was for not bringing his doctor's bag along. Maybe he could still help those people lying in the clearing. He could hear crying coming from inside the cabin.

"I think they must be gone, Doc," Bert said in a loud whisper. "I'm goin' in!" and he left the cover of his tree moving out into the clearing.

Before he had traveled more than twenty feet, a shot rang out from behind Dr. Harriott. Bert Snyder spun around, and then was slammed to the earth when he was struck by a shotgun blast. The stricken man started to sit up, but fell back, with blood spewing from his mouth. He screamed a last time and died.

Harriott turned at the sounds of the shots and saw at least five Indians creeping up on him. He took a hurried aim and fired! His ball struck His Mysterious Father low in the side. Knowing that the white man's gun was empty, the rest of the Indians rushed toward him before he could reload.

The terrified doctor, finding himself surrounded by twelve painted wild men, wished once again that he had believed what Gardner was trying to tell them that morning. He felt like a bobcat, surrounded by a pack of wolves.

The Indians laughed and shouted in excitement, each time the doctor swung his empty rifle at them, trying to keep them at bay. But while Rattling was jabbing at him with his short spear, His Great Gun snuck up behind and swiped the hat off of his head. Slowly, the harried doctor backed himself against a tree to keep them from coming up behind him. He couldn't reload his gun. Every time he tried, an Indian jabbed him with a spear or swung at him with a club.

He was bleeding from a dozen small wounds. Suddenly, Gunn ran forward and aimed his rifle straight at Harriott's face. Tears of fear fled down his cheeks, as he silently prayed for the ball to take his life quickly.

His prayer was not answered. Gunn had purposely left the ball out, loading his rifle with powder only. The burning black powder blasted from the barrel in a cloud of burning smoke, striking Harriott in the face and chest, imbedding in his skin where it burned and sizzled. Harriott screamed, clutching his face with one hand, but still waving his empty gun with the other. He swung the rifle blindly, hitting a tree and breaking it's stock as it was jolted from his hand. He was blind from the burning powder blast in his eyes, but he broke from the tree, running, insane with pain and fear.

He tripped and fell to the ground. He tried to rise, but Roaring Cloud struck him with his war club on the back of the legs just above the ankles. A sickening crack sounded as the bones broke. Harriott's screams of agony seemed to excite the rest of the Indians, and they all began beating him with their clubs or gun barrels. Soon, several bones in his body were broken and he was bleeding from the ears, nose and mouth. He died slowly, alone in the snow.

The Indians left the dead doctor and gathered with Inkpaduta in the clearing by the cabin. Inkpaduta sent Young Inkpaduta to watch the trail leading to the Gardner cabin. He didn't want to be surprised by the men from that cabin. Charley and Brave Bull went to fetch the women and children from where they had been left waiting in a small grove of trees a short distance to the south. The horses and dogs were still packed and ready to move. Inkpaduta had instructed them to be ready to flee in case the attack went bad.

While waiting for the women to come, the rest of the men amused themselves by mutilating the bodies of the dead whites in the Mattock clearing. They removed the scalps from each corpse and stripped off any clothing that they wanted. Old Man and One Leg fought over a bright red dress the Mattock woman was wearing. They tugged and pulled on it until it ripped in two and each stood holding their own piece of the garment. Big Face helped His Mysterious Father move to a sitting position at the base of a large oak tree. The rifle ball had passed through the fleshy part of his side, leaving a clean hole and hitting nothing vital. Big Face packed the bleeding holes with strips of cloth torn from one of the white men's shirts. He pushed his wounded friend back to a reclining position and then rolled him onto his side, banking snow up around the wound, hoping the cold would slow the bleeding.

The rest of the men were pulling the bodies into an uneven line to put them on display for the women when Young Inkpaduta rushed into the clearing shouting that two men had left the Gardner Cabin and were trying to circle to the east around this clearing.

"Kill them," Inkpaduta ordered and all but he, His Mysterious Father, and Old Man ran off to find the two white men.

\*   \*   \*

In the Gardner cabin, it had been decided that since no one had arrived to fort up with them, that Dr. Harriott and Bert Snyder had not spread the alarm as Rowland had begged them to do. Rowland felt it was his Christian duty to warn the others, even if the men of the Redwing Company didn't feel it was theirs. So he decided that Harvey and Mr. Clark should at least warn the Mattock cabin that there was trouble and ask them to come and fort up in the Gardner cabin.

Luce and Clark were walking through the trees for the Mattock cabin when they heard gunfire coming from that direction. Instinctively, they took cover huddling behind a broad evergreen tree. Indecision plagued them.

"What do we do?" Mr. Clark asked.

"I dunno," Luce answered.

"Go back?"

"I dunno."

"Go on?"

"I don't know!" Harvey Luce answered desperately.

As sudden as the gunshots had begun, they ended. The following silence was ominous for the two frightened men.

"They must all be dead," Clark observed.

"I 'spose," Luce agreed.

"There'd still be shootin' if they was still alive!" Clark stated.

"Unless they're forted up in the cabin and the Indians are hidin' in the trees," Luce argued.

The thought brought chills to their already shaking bodies. They were silent for a few minutes, listening as each peered around the tree in the direction of the Mattock cabin, even though both knew they were too far from there to see anything.

"Ain't much we can do for the Mattocks, even if they are still alive, being's there is only the two of us," Harvey Luce reasoned. He was starting to get cold and knew that sitting there was doing no one any good.

"What should we do then," Mr. Clark asked. "Head back to the cabin and fort up?"

Harvey Luce was in a quandary. He knew that his father-in-law expected them do the right thing, but he wasn't sure what that would be. The smart thing would be to go back to the cabin and protect themselves. But Rowland Gardner's strong conviction that they needed to help others in times of need overruled his common sense.

"It seems they be headin' away from us. They took practically everything we had this morning," Harvey reasoned.

"That's true," Mr. Clark was eager to agree. "You know it is! They'll probably take what ever they can from the Mattocks and then head right on over to the Redwing boys, or go on to the Howes and Thatchers."

"The Redwingers are close enough that they know what's goin' on," Harvey said. "Maybe we better head on over to the Howes and warn them." After looking back in the direction of the safety of their own cabin, Mr. Clark finally shook his head in agreement. It would be the right thing to do. With noble thoughts of helping their neighbors, they began walking south and east following a wide berth around the Mattock cabin site.

Young Inkpaduta had spotted Luce and Clark when they changed direction to bypass the Mattock cabin. Roaring Cloud, who was leading the war party after Young Inkpaduta raised the alarm, guessed their intention and set his pace and course to meet up with them at the outlet on the south end of the lake. His men were in position before the two white men arrived. All ten Indians raised their guns and fired when their quarry came into range. Five rifle balls hit Harvey Luce, slamming his body into the snow on his face! There was no life left in him.

Mr. Clark was struck by only one ball through the shoulder and some buckshot in the rump from His Great Gun's shotgun. He was spun around but did not fall down and kept running, still hoping to make it to the Howe cabin, which was still miles in the distance.

His Great Gun reloaded and sprinted to catch up to the running white man. He stopped and fired again from such a close range that the shot didn't spread. The main load struck Clark in the forearm, knocking his rifle from his grasp. But the grievously wounded man trudged on in the deep snow, his pace slow and clumsy. He could feel blood running down his legs from the wounds in his rump, and his arm was on fire. Pain from his wounds spurred him on, his breath coming in slow, wrenching sobs.

Rattling was the first to catch up with him. He swung his war club, hitting Clark in the back. The force of the blow knocked him down. Clark quickly rolled over to face his tormentors, kicking his feet and swinging his good arm at them. They surrounded him and dodged his flailing feet, laughing and shouting.

Fire Cloud jumped in from behind and lifted the wounded man to his feet. He gave him a shove, sending him into the circle of laughing men, who continued to shove the bleeding man around the circle until an opening was made and Roaring Cloud shouted in his face, pointing toward the dead body of Harvey Luce.

"Run and join the blood of your brother!"

Before Clark could take a step, a slashing motion of Roaring Cloud's tomahawk hamstrung him, and he fell screaming. He rolled in the snow, clutching at his wounded leg, crying in agony. Laughing, the Indians stripped the clothes from his body. Slowly, they tortured him, slicing with knives and chopping with tomahawks, until the snow was splattered red for yards in every direction. Their excitement grew with each of his screams until finally, Roaring Cloud chopped his head off and gave it a kick. Several of the young men also kicked the head until it was far up the lake.

When they arrived back at the Mattock cabin, the women were setting up camp in the clearing. Crying and whimpering could still be heard coming from inside the cabin. Roaring Cloud led the way to the cabin door, intending to batter it down and enter the cabin. But Inkpaduta called him away. They would save the cabin for later. Now, he wanted to go back to the Gardner cabin. There was one armed man there who had to be taken care of before dark. He didn't want to chance having the man creep up on their camp at night. He also didn't want to give the Gardners time to escape. He was afraid that under the cover of darkness, they might circle around their camp and make it to the cabins on the east side of the lake.

Inkpaduta, his four sons, Rattling, His Great Gun, and He Who Makes A Crooked Wind As He Walks started off for the Gardner cabin late in the afternoon. As an added incentive, at the Gardner cabin, there was a young, yellow haired girl, and they were all anxious to touch the odd colored hair to see if it was warm like fire, as Old Man claimed was the way of such hair.

As Inkpaduta and his party left the clearing, Afraid of Her Husband wandered to the back of the Mattock cabin. She wasn't able to keep her mind from the crying and whimpering coming from inside. The constant grieving sounds plagued her and were beginning to make her angry. There was a pile of brush, trimmings from big trees dragged in and cut up for firewood stacked a short distance from the cabin. She began dragging brush from the pile and stacking it against the cabin walls. Beaded Hair Woman and Corn Stalk Woman began helping her and soon three of the cabin walls were stacked high with kindling brush. Trader's Slave Woman and Worn Moccasin Woman stood together watching. They knew what was about to happen, and fear and sadness filled their eyes.

Afraid of Her Husband hurried to the fire pit burning near her tipi. She scooped up a load of coals in a small metal pot and brought them back to the base of the back wall. Laying tiny twigs in a crisscross pattern over the coals, she knelt and carefully, blowing slow and steady on the coals, coaxed a tiny flame, which she fed small twigs, one at a time until the fire grew large enough to catch the brush laying against the wall.

320

With a cry of delight, Afraid of Her Husband and the other women jumped back and ran around to the front of the cabin. Each grabbed sharpened sticks and took positions near the door of the cabin.

Screams of a woman and small children soon could be heard coming from inside the cabin. The men who remained in camp gathered together at the edge of the clearing to watch as the flames growing from the back wall of the building began licking at the shake-shingled roof and moved around to encompass the sidewalls. The hysterical screaming coming from inside the cabin reached a desperate pitch, and the Indian women heard the sound of the bar being removed from the door. Ignoring the growing heat, the women stepped closer, waiting for the door to open.

When it opened, a tremendous billowing of dark smoke escaped through the door into their faces. Coughing, they started to pull back, but held their ground when a large white woman stumbled through the door. She carried a small child in her arms and dragged a small boy behind her. Tears streamed down her face, making rivulets on her soot darkened cheeks. Half blind from the smoke, she tried to run along the front wall of the cabin. Hates Her Father Woman and Beaded Hair Woman stopped her by jabbing her with their sharpened stick-spears. Turning, she tried to run the other way around the cabin, but was turned back by the stick-spears of Afraid of Her Husband Woman and Sick From Her Babies Woman.

The child the woman was carrying and the little boy she was dragging were screaming in terror. Sick From Her Babies Woman stopped stabbing the woman and began jabbing at the children. Hesitating for only a moment in front of the cabin door, the large white woman began wailing in protest, screaming unintelligibly at the Indian women. They stepped back in surprise and lowered their stick-spears. She glared at them fiercely as her eyes swept past them to the bodies of her husband and friends, lying dead and mutilated in the snow.

Trader's Slave Woman was surprised that the other women stood back. It appeared that they would let the woman escape the fire. She knew a little English and tried to coax the wounded white woman away from the cabin. "Come," she beckoned.

Suddenly, with a loud keening cry the woman stumbled back through the dark door of the burning cabin. She tripped and fell, losing her grip on the small boy. Frantically, she searched through the choking smoke, but could not find him. The sound of his cries were drowned out as the roaring of the burning building grew in crescendo.

She sat hugging the small child to her bosom, praying a prayer that was not answered as the roof of the cabin fell in on her.

The heat from the fire chased the Indian women back from the door as it engulfed the roof and the front side of the building. They could no longer hear the screams from within, as the rush of flames gathered speed that roared in a hot wind away from the inferno. Large floaters of glowing ash rose with the black smoke on the heated wind escaping from the cold, snowy earth, only to cool and fall back to the ground, turning the white snow gray. Pools of melted snow formed a ring around the burning cabin.

There was a sudden crash as the main beam holding the roof up burnt through and fell in. A cloud of sooty ash and smoke billowed high into the air above the cabin site. Watching the towering smoke, the men became nervous. If the settlers on the east side of the lake saw the huge smoke cloud, they would surely take warning. They knew that Inkpaduta would be angry if that happened.

# Chapter 34
## *Blood Lust*

**N**ow that the killing had started, Inkpaduta knew that there was no stopping it. His young men were excited by the experience and felt that finally, they were proving themselves as men. They had been angry about the white settlers moving into their homelands for a long time now and considered that it was now time to begin ridding their country of white people. White men were their enemies. Therefore, it was the *Wahpekutes'* right to kill them and take their weapons, food, blankets and even their women!

With these feelings, he and his men returned to the Gardner clearing and stood in the trees on the edge, watching the cabin. The young men were anxious to attack, excitement shone in their eyes and even Inkpaduta could feel the blood coursing quickly through his veins. But caution told him not to enter the open ground and chance getting shot by the last living white man on the south end of the lakes. Suddenly, the cabin door opened, and he saw Rowland Gardner walk out into the late afternoon light. The man was unarmed! With a wave of his arm, Inkpaduta signaled his warriors, and they moved en mass out of the cover of the trees. When Rowland Gardner saw the Indians emerge from the trees, he turned and hurried into the cabin.

"There are eight or nine Indians coming!" he cried to his wife and daughters, slamming the cabin door shut. He checked the loads in the two guns left in the house and laid them on the table. Moving to barricade the door, he declared, "While they are killing us, I will kill a few of them!"

"Now Rowland, we don't know their intention," argued his wife, Mary Francis. "Maybe they are only wanting food." She was a deeply religious woman and could not bear the thought of confrontation.

"But why haven't the boys returned?" he asked, broaching the subject they had been afraid to bring up before.

"Maybe they went on to the Howes. It would take them a long time to get there and I can't imagine Mrs. Howe allowing them to leave on a cold day like this without first filling their stomachs with something warm." She stood before him, her eyes imploring him to listen to her convictions. "We've prayed for Harvey and Mr. Clark's safe return, and I believe the Lord will bring them home at any minute. Dear Rowland," she begged, "if we must die, then let us die innocent of shedding another human's blood."

"But Mama, what if you're wrong?" her daughter, Mary Luce asked. She handed baby Amanda to her sister Abbie who was sitting in a rocking chair beside the fireplace. She walked to the table and stood gripping the back of a chair so tightly that her knuckles turned white. Her eyes were red-rimmed from crying, and her normally young face had aged from an afternoon of worrying about her husband.

"We can't think that way," her mother said, adding, "We must trust in the Lord." She turned her head from her husband and looked at the two young boys playing with stick dolls on the floor in front of the fireplace. Her youngest child and her oldest grandchild were only months apart in age. A soft smile played across her lips. Seeing the two boys playing without a care in the world gave her reassurance that everything would be all right. She was calm now, calmer than she had been all day. Her faith came to rescue her from worry and fear. "The Indians have always responded to kindness."

The door burst open and Inkpaduta, leading his men into the cabin, strode deliberately up to Rowland Gardner. He noticed with pleasure that, though two rifles lay on the table, the white man was still unarmed.

"You gib flour now!" he demanded.

Rowland Gardner glanced out of the corner of his eye at his wife and saw a reassuring nod. He turned to walk to the flour bin at the back of the kitchen area.

Inkpaduta followed him closely. As they neared the bin, the pox scarred Indian raised his rifle and shot Gardner in the back. The stricken man fell to the floor and rolled onto his right side. His eyes searched wildly about the cabin, but he died before seeing his wife and daughters one last time.

There was a short moment of shocked silence as Inkpaduta lowered his smoking gun and turned to look at Mary Francis Gardner's disbelieving face. Screams of terror erupted from Mary Luce as she tried to run to her fallen father, but Roaring Cloud grabbed her by the hair and dragged her toward the door. Mary Francis began wailing in anger and fear as she realized what had happened and tried to run to her husband. Inkpaduta swung the butt of his rifle, striking the woman in the chest, knocking her back into the arms of One Leg, who with the help of Rain Cloud dragged her out the door.

Young Albert Luce and his uncle, little Rowland Gardner, jumped up from their play and stood, one on either side of Abbie, who was too shocked to move and still sat in the rocking chair, rocking the baby. The two little boys clutched her arms, crying and screaming with fright.

Mary Francis Gardner was wild with grief and anger at these men who had reduced her unquestioning faith in the Lord to mere wishful thinking. She struggled with One Leg and Rain Cloud as they pulled her out of the cabin into the clearing. Jerking a hand loose from Rain Cloud's grip, she clubbed One Leg in the face, knocking him to the ground, and she ran back toward the cabin door screaming for Abbie to run! Rain Cloud caught her before she could enter the cabin and dragged her back to where One Leg sat in the snow, holding his bloody nose.

One Leg was angry. He knocked Mary Francis to the ground and using his knife, cut the tendons just above her heels to prevent her from running again. While she sat in shock, clutching at her severely wounded legs, he wound her long hair in his left hand and traced a circle in the top of her head with the point of his knife. Jerking violently upward, he tore the scalp from the top of her head and watched her writhing in agony in the snow.

Mary Luce couldn't hear her mother's moans. Roaring Cloud, Fire Cloud and Rattling ripped the clothes from her body and pushed her down in the snow. Young Inkpaduta stood by, watching and waiting. One after another, they took turns raping the helpless woman. She struggled and fought, screaming and crying until she was exhausted. Finally accepting her fate, she was only slightly aware of the cold snow against her bare backside as she lay back and let the men finish.

When Young Inkpaduta had taken his turn and stood, pulling his buckskin pants up, Mary Luce rolled to her side and saw her mother's fate. Mary Francis had climbed to her hands and knees and began crawling in a broad circle, leaving a crimson trail in the snow. Mary Luce could hear her mother's agonized moans, and she tried to climb to her feet to go to her. Upon seeing Mary start to rise, Young Inkpaduta took his war club from his belt and swinging the weapon with all of his might, struck her on the side of the head, caving her face in and killing her instantly. Clumsily, he cut the scalp from her smashed head.

Inside the cabin, Inkpaduta and One Who Makes a Crooked Wind As He Walks stood contemplating the two little boys who were weeping piteously and clutching to the yellow haired girl in the rocking chair. The boys reminded Inkpaduta of how Charley and Gunn had looked when he and Rain Dance Woman found them. They had grown to be vital citizens of his band. But these boys were different. They had no Indian blood. And times were different, too. There was seldom enough food now, to even feed the children they already had. Inkpaduta knew that he had to make a decision. Roaring Cloud and Fire Cloud came into the cabin and looked at their father questioningly.

"Save the Yellow Hair," he said, pointing at Abbie Gardner. "Kill the rest."

The two little boys buried their faces in Abbie's shoulders, hiding their eyes from the horror they had already witnessed. Their screams had quieted to frightened whimpers, but they found full voice again when Roaring Cloud pulled little Albert Luce away from his aunt's side. Carrying the child by one arm, he went to the firewood box and pulled out a hefty stick of wood. Changing his grip to the back of Albert's neck, he held the boy for a moment contemplating him, like a man thinking about clubbing a fat rabbit.

With a sudden downward swoop of his arm, he hit the small child on the back of the head, popping the top of his skull off. Roaring Cloud carried the quivering body of Albert Luce to the door and threw it out into the snow, where One Leg kicked it toward the body of his now dead grandmother.

Roaring Cloud returned and clubbed little Rowland Gardner where he stood, still clutching Abbie. The small boy stiffened for a second, then collapsed to the floor. Fire Cloud pulled him from the cabin by one foot and deposited him by Albert's body. The cold air revived Rowland, and he began crying. Rattling struck him with his gun barrel, silencing the child's crying, and Young Inkpaduta smashed the life from the boy with his war club.

Abbie hadn't left the rocking chair. She sat dry eyed and quiet, still holding the baby tightly in her arms. She was praying that death would come quickly for her. When Roaring Cloud came back and reached for baby Amanda, Abbie pulled her away trying to shield the baby with her own body. Angrily, Roaring Cloud hit Abbie with the back of his hand. The blow loosened her teeth, and she lost her grip on Amanda. The baby fell to the floor and started crying.

Roaring Cloud snatched the infant from the floor and carried her outside, ignoring her piercing screams. He approached a large oak tree near the clearing edge and began swinging the infant by the feet. Amanda's screams grew louder and louder until they were cut short when her head struck the tree trunk, bashing the life from her.

Roaring Cloud stepped away from the tree and flung the lifeless body in the general direction of the other bodies in the clearing.

Inkpaduta roughly tied Abbie's hands together and pushed the young girl out the door into the darkening light of the dying afternoon. She stood, trying not to look at the grizzly sight of her dead family, lying naked and bloody in the cold winter's snow. Rain Cloud and Fire Cloud ransacked the interior of the cabin and carried everything of value, including Rowland's still loaded guns and the rest of the flour out to pack it up for the trek back to their camp.

As the sun finally set on this day of death and destruction, they walked off into the growing gloom and approached Mattock's cabin clearing shortly after dark. Abbie was roughly pushed into one of the tipis, where she sat shivering with cold and fear. Large chunks of meat cut from the Mattocks' dead ox were sizzling over coals raked from the burnt cabin, and the men of Inkpaduta's village feasted and danced celebrating the fact that they were finally striking back at the white man.

One by one, each of the men of the village visited the yellow haired captive and raped her. At first Abbie tried to fight them off, but each time she was battered and out-powered, and after the overly rough Roaring Cloud was finished with her she was too tired and frightened to resist the rest. Late that night, the tipi filled with men women and children, and soon all but Abbie were sound asleep.

As the sun rose the next morning, Inkpaduta kicked his men from their beds. Two more cabins stood on the east side of *Okobooshi,* and there were more whites to be killed. Using charcoal scraped from the burnt skeleton of the Mattock cabin, mixed with bear grease, the warriors painted their faces black and moved off to the east in the early morning light.

Their yellow-haired captive shivered with cold and fear as she peeked through the flap door on the tipi she sat alone in, clutching a thin blanket. Her clothes had been ripped from her body the night before and not given back. Crying most of the night, she slept little, dozing shortly before dawn. The noise of the men rolling out of their sleeping robes awakened her, but she feigned sleep until everyone else left the tipi. As she watched the men sneak off in the direction of the Howe cabin, she saw one of the woman approaching, carrying a small pot. She let the flap fall shut and slipped across the tipi to the other side and sat clutching the blanket in front of her naked body. Thinking they were bringing her food, she decided that though she was suddenly hungry, she would decline food. She would rather starve to death than go through another night like the last one.

When the flap opened, three women entered, one old, one middle-aged and one younger. It was not food they brought in the pot. Hates Her Father Woman carried the pot with the remnants of the charcoal black paint the men used to paint their faces. Afraid of Her Husband Woman pushed Abbie roughly to the ground and pulled the blanket away.

"This one was a virgin," Hates Her Father Woman said, pointing to the small trickle of blood dried between Abbie's legs. "But she's not any more," she added laughing.

"When Father said to darken her hair, did he mean that hair too?" Beaded Hair Woman snickered pointing at the small patch of light colored hair, just starting to grow on the young girl's pubis.

All three women laughed at the joke as Afraid of Her Husband Woman began rubbing the sooty black substance into Abbie's face and shoulders. Hates Her Father Woman held out the pot and Beaded Hair Woman began working the black grease into Abbie's hair to darken it. They dressed her in a worn leather dress and braided her darkened hair into a common *Wahpekute* fashion. Inkpaduta had left orders that the captive should be disguised to look like a member of their village. They would be traveling north into Minnesota and a yellow-haired girl traveling with them would look out of place and cause people to ask questions.

After her arms, legs, face and hair were darkened by the sticky black grease, Hates Her Father Woman ordered Abbie to gather firewood. The leather clothes chafed her skin and the thin moccasins did little to keep her feet warm as she trudged around the campsite seeking burnable wood. Some of the other women and older children followed her, cutting off any thoughts of escape. Several of the women stopped her and touched her greasy blackened hair, trying to see the yellow it was supposed to be. Others switched her with stinging blows with sticks, as was the proper treatment for a slave. Only Trader's Slave Woman and Worn Moccasin Woman watched the young girl with pity in their hearts.

* * *

Joe Howe trudged through the deep snow in the direction of the Gardner cabin. He knew that Rowland was planning a trip to Fort Dodge and wanted to ask him to keep an eye out for Joseph Thatcher. Thatcher had gone to Shippley earlier in the week and hadn't returned. Joe's son-in-law, Alvin Noble, shared a cabin with Thatcher and his wife. The young people were worried that maybe Joseph had been caught in a snowstorm. Joe was going to ask Gardner to tell Thatcher to hurry home if he saw him.

Lost in his own thoughts, Joe didn't see the Indians until he was directly upon them. When he did see them, not knowing anything of the preceding day's happenings, he raised his hand in friendship. With laughs and smiles, Inkpaduta led the band out of the trees and stepped up to Joe offering to shake his hand, which he knew was the white man custom. When Joe took the offered hand, he found his hand held in a vice-like clench that would not let go. Inkpaduta shook his hand vigorously, pulling Joe toward him, while Fire Cloud came up behind Joe and buried his knife in Howe's back

Joe tried to pull away, reaching with his left hand at the sudden pain in his back. But Inkpaduta's grip was like a steel trap, and he spun on his heel leading the mortally wounded man in a stumbling circle. Finally, Joe Howe stopped trying to get away and stood still, listening to the Indians laughing at his predicament. His eyes searched the blackened faces surrounding him and only then did he realize what was actually happening. With a roar of anger and indignation, Joe Howe swung his left hand, striking Inkpaduta across the nose! The pox-scarred Indian lost his grip on Joe's hand and pulled back, clutching his face.

Having more life than the Indians realized, Joe turned and ran back in the direction of his cabin. The knife wound in his back was severe, blood pumped out of the gaping wound with each beat of his already failing heart. His stumbling gait had only taken him a few yards when Gunn caught up with him and knocked him to the ground. Inkpaduta, blood streaming from his nose, systematically broke the bones in Joe's legs and arms with his war club and scalped the man, leaving him still alive in the snow, where he would slowly die.

Following Howe's tracks, the war party came to his cabin site. Wasting little time, Roaring Cloud, followed by Fire Cloud, Rattling and Young Inkpaduta, barged through the cabin's door, sending the inhabitants screaming in terror! There were no grown males here. Joe's wife was just climbing out of her bed. Rattling grabbed a flat iron from beside the fireplace and struck Mrs. Howe on top of the head with it. The blow caused her eyes to bulge out and fill with blood. The woman crawled under her bed and died.

In quick order, the men knifed or clubbed the rest of the family: a teenage son, two young girls and four younger children. They left the bodies where they fell and after searching the cabin and taking all of the foodstuffs, they joined Inkpaduta, who had finally stanched the flow of blood from his nose, and the band moved north up the lakeside to the final cabin of settlers. Fanning out, they surrounded the clearing.

After watching the cabin from hiding for about an hour, Inkpaduta was sure that there were only two men inside. Alvin Noble and Enoch Ryan were both Joe Howe's sons-in-law. Ryan and his wife lived in Joe Howe's cabin, but he had come to help Alvin while Joseph Thatcher was gone to Shippley. He and Alvin had cut down several trees and dragged them up to the clearing with a team of oxen. The trees pulled easier in the snow than they would in the spring mud. It was hoped that before spring arrived, they could have enough trees felled and pulled in to put up the walls of a second cabin. The two men were just sitting down to breakfast when they heard a call from outside.

Inkpaduta and his men left the scalps and plunder in the woods. They approached the cabin as starving beggars wanting food. He called to the house again and was not surprised to have the door open in answer to his call.

"Come on in," Lydia Noble shouted, beckoning to them. "We ain't got much, but we will share it with you."

The Indians pushed into the dark building and stood for a moment, letting their eyes adjust to the dimly lighted interior. Lydia Noble and her friend, Elizabeth Thatcher were busy cooking oatmeal and getting additional bowls for their guests. Alvin and Enoch sat at the table, not even bothering to look at the Indians. Inkpaduta and Roaring Cloud sat down on the chairs at both ends of the table.

Elizabeth Thatcher could hear her seven months old son fussing in his bed. She knew that it was time to feed him, for her breasts were swollen and hard. She could feel the pressure, and the sound of her child's hungry voice triggered the mothering instinct. Her breasts began to drip, causing wet spots on the front of her shirt. She was hesitant to feed the child with so many strangers present, but knew that she couldn't wait any longer. She decided to take the child to the back of the cabin in the corner and feed him while the Indians were preoccupied with their own eating. Maybe they wouldn't notice what she was doing.

She bent to pick up the child from his cradle and was startled when two gunshots rang out, the blasts echoing from the walls of the cabin. Screaming with fright, she turned to see Alvin Noble and Enoch Ryan slumped forward on the table. Rattling and Fire Cloud had placed the muzzles of their rifles at the base of each man's head and squeezed the triggers simultaneously. Pieces of bone and gray matter were scattered over the tabletop and cabin wall.

Screaming with wild excitement, Young Inkpaduta grabbed the Noble infant from where the child stood at the edge of his crib. Clutching her baby to her breasts, Elizabeth tried to run for the cabin door, but was cut off from escape by Roaring Cloud. She ran around the room still carrying her child and fought him off, each time he cornered her, kicking and biting with the ferocity only a mother can muster to protect her child.

A small hope filled her when she saw that the rest of the Indian men watching, laughed when she eluded him and shouted encouragement to her each time she stopped to fight him. But she was no match for his strength and Roaring Cloud soon grew tired of being teased by his compatriots. With a powerful blow, he knocked Elizabeth to the floor and grabbed her squalling baby from her arms. The blow dazed her, and Elizabeth was spared the sight of seeing her child's head battered against one of the trees the men had dragged into the clearing.

At the sound of the gunshots, One Leg grabbed Lydia Noble and pushed her outside, where she was forced to watch the murder of both her own and her friend's babies. She was in shock and stood barely able to comprehend what was happening. The cold air brought her senses awake as she felt her clothing being torn from her body. His Mysterious Father knocked her to the ground and Big Face, who had dropped his pants, fell between her legs and raped her first. She struggled, fighting and screaming, until there was no strength left in her. His Great Gun, One Leg and Rain Cloud each took a turn, ravishing her in the snow. Over the men's grunting and wheezing with their efforts, she could hear Elizabeth Thatcher screaming inside the cabin and knew that her friend was enduring the same indignities.

When all of the men were finished with the two young white women, Inkpaduta ordered their hands tied and Elizabeth and Lydia were dragged, naked through the snow and cold, down the same path that had brought this terror upon them. When they passed Joe Howe's body, it was so mutilated that at first Lydia didn't recognize it as her own father.

When they arrived at the Indian encampment in the Mattock Clearing, the two women were thrown into a tipi, where they found young Abbie Gardner. The three young women hugged each other and cried, but they were allowed little time to comfort one another. Hates Her Father Woman and Afraid of Her Husband Woman entered, throwing rough leather dresses, similar to the one Abbie was wearing, on the floor. Shouting, and using hand gestures, Hates Her Father Woman instructed them to don the dresses and to braid their hair in the same fashion that Abbie's was braided. After the two women were dressed, Trader's Slave Woman entered he tipi and sat a small bowl of scorched meat by the door. Too sick to eat, the women let it sit and wept throughout the rest of the day.

Again that night, all three were used by each of the men. They tried to resist, but soon found it was useless to fight. All fighting gained them was a good hard beating!

# Chapter 35
*Discovery*

The night was cold and windy, and Morris Markham was chilled to the bone. He had been traveling since early that morning and was looking forward to getting out of the weather. The nearly full moon darted in and out behind the clouds. The bright orb made travel easy when the night sky was clear, but it was almost impossible to make time when the clouds appeared. Morris was a woodsman. He made his living by hunting game and trapping fur-bearing animals. As civilization advanced into the wilderness, he found it harder each year to bag game and trap furs.

With this problem in mind, he had jumped at the chance to accompany his friends, Alvin Noble and Joe Thatcher, when they told him of their plan to follow their father-in-law, Joe Howe, to move west into the game rich area around the lakes in the wild lands of northwest Iowa.

Arriving in the lakes area and staking out their claims late in the summer had left only enough time to build two cabins, one for Joe Howe and his large family, and one for Alvin and Joe Thatcher to share for the first winter. Morris built and lived in a lean-to attached to Alvin and Joe's cabin. His hunting skills kept their cabin in meat through the fall and winter months.

Because of his travels and friendly disposition, Morris had become known to all of the settlers in the area. They were a fairly close-knit group of people, depending upon one another and always ready to help out if someone needed it. Harvey Luce had stopped by the Noble and Thatcher cabin three days before to tell Markham that he had seen oxen tracks heading south along a stream that fed into the Des Moines River east of the Lakes area. Alvin Noble's team of oxen had wandered off during an early snowstorm, and Morris thought it was possible that the tracks Harvey saw could have been made by Alvin's oxen.

His friends had already lost one ox from having its nostrils freeze shut, so Morris set out that very day, hoping to catch the animals before they wandered too far down the river or got caught in a blizzard and suffocated. But his search was futile. He had picked up the tracks one day's travel to the east and followed them all the way to the Lizard River and then followed them down the small stream until he lost all sign of them in a sudden snow fall. He had sat out the storm in a hollow tree and spent the rest of the next day searching downriver, trying to find fresh tracks, but the animals had disappeared.

He spent that night huddled near a big fire, waking every few minutes to throw more wood on. He rose with the sun and after circling the area one more time, upon finding no fresh tracks; he gave up and cut a beeline for the lakes.

Estimating the time from the position of the moon, Markham guessed it to be nearly eleven o'clock. He knew the Gardners would all be asleep, so he did not expect there to be a light when he saw the dark form of their cabin through the trees ahead of him. He was sure they would put him up for the rest of the night, and he was anxious to get in out of the cold. The moon passed under the clouds again as Morris entered the Gardner clearing. He tripped over something that felt like a small log and could sense, rather than see other forms littering the cabin's clearing. This was odd, he thought, because the Gardners were notoriously neat and never left clutter around their place.

"Halloooo the house!" he called, waiting a moment to give the cabin's occupants time to roll from their beds and answer his call. When he received no answer, he walked closer and called again, "Halloooo the house! Is anybody awake in thar?"

When there was no answering call, he moved closer until he sensed that something was wrong. He stopped and stared at the rectangle of darkness in the middle of the cabin's wall. The dark square shouldn't have been there. It was where the cabin's door should be and if the door were closed, he knew that the pattern of the cabin's wall wouldn't be broken. The door was open and that didn't make sense to Morris. He edged closer to the building until he stood just outside of the open door. He brought his gun up and was ready when he stepped over the threshold.

It was dark inside as the windowless cabin walls blocked even the filtered light of the cloud-shrouded moon. He moved carefully though the room until he felt his foot bump into something on the floor.

Bending, he felt with his free hand and found a cold stiffened body. Standing quickly, Morris backed to the door. He was sure there

334

was no use in searching the cabin further. If anyone were alive inside, they would have closed the door to keep the cold out. When he turned from the cabin door, the clouds moved, and the moon lit the scene in the clearing. He found Mary Gardner and Mary Luce and the two little boys scattered over the clearing. The log he had tripped over when coming into the clearing was the small body of baby Amanda Luce.

Shock set in and Morris's mind went blank. He began trotting down the path leading to the Mattock place with no conscious thought.

The horror of the clearing behind him, the hair on the back of his neck feel like it was standing on end. He quickened his pace until he was running. When clouds passed under the moon again, the wooded landscape was thrown back to total darkness, and he lost the trail. His feet tangled in bramble bushes and he stumbled, falling hard onto the snow covered ground. Jumping to his feet, he ran blindly on until he ran into a tree, bumping his head, and he collapsed. Sitting in the snow, he held his aching head. Warm tears squeezed from his eyes and rolled down his cheeks, freezing in his short beard.

As he sat, the shock began to wear off, and he started thinking more clearly. He knew that he needed to warn the other settlers, and he couldn't do that if he knocked himself out by running into trees. Shaking his head, he rose and walked on more carefully. When he neared the Mattock clearing, a sudden eruption of barking dogs brought him to an abrupt standstill. He could see silhouettes of the dogs against the glowing orange light of campfires.

When the moonlight broke through the clouds once again, he could see that they were wild, wolf-like creatures, standing on the edge of the Mattock clearing, sniffing the air. They stopped barking. Vicious snarls and low malicious growls emanated from deep in their chests, as they walked stiff legged with the hair on their backs standing on end. Morris realized that the wind was at his back and that the dogs could smell him, but could not see him. He backed slowly away and stood behind a large tree. The tree blocked his scent and soon the animals quieted. Some went back to chewing on the dark forms sprawled in the clearing.

Carefully peeking around the tree, Morris could make now out the shadows of the tipis. Realizing that he had almost walked right into the middle of the Indian camp, his knees went weak. He could see the still smoldering timbers of the Mattock's cabin, and his stomach churned as he recognized that the dogs were chewing on the bodies of the former occupants of the cabin.

Backing slowly away, until he could no longer see the clearing, he hurried through the timber as fast as the moon's meager light would allow. Breaking through the gooseberry brambles near the lakeshore, he ran up the lake, sliding his feet across the slippery ice. Traveling on the frozen lake was far quicker. He didn't need moonlight to see his way and the windswept lake was practically devoid of snow, making it unnecessary to trudge through deep drifts, and he was able to run.

He was sure he could make it to Joe Howe's cabin. Once there, he could rest while Joe went to warn the Nobles and Thatchers and bring them back to Joe's cabin where they could fort up. His fast, unfettered pace took a toll on Morris as he sucked great draughts of cold air while he ran.

By the time he came to the spot opposite the Howe cabin, his lungs were burning. He stopped and rested for a moment, hoping that his voice would be loud enough for them to hear.

Trudging up the snowy bank, he pushed ahead until he saw the cabin. Intending to hail the house from the edge of the clearing, he found that his voice wasn't strong enough. He went to the door and began pounding on it. When there was no answer, dread flowed through his body. He tried the latch and pushed the door open. The silent darkness within was ominous.

"Joe. Joe Howe," he croaked in a hoarse whisper.

But there was no answer. He felt his way into the room until he found a body, dressed in a woman's dress, lying on the floor near the table. With a cry of anguish, he bolted out the cabin door and even though the cold air hurt his lungs, he ran up the path toward the Noble and Thatcher cabin, his home.

Markham's cry hadn't fallen on totally deaf ears. The sound roused something in young Jacob Howe, who was lying under the bed with his dead mother. Joe's teenage son crawled slowly from beneath the bed. He couldn't see, because he couldn't open his eyes. He didn't know why. His eyelids were just too heavy to lift. Jacob could not remember anything that had happened. He was confused as to why it was so cold in the cabin and knew only that his head hurt fiercely.

Feeling with his hands, he found the door and crawled out into the cold snow. About half way across the clearing, he came to a big stump. His hands were cold from being in the snow. His head ached, and he was extremely tired. He pulled himself up and sat on the stump. Folding his hands under his armpits, he wondered again why he couldn't open his eyes. Maybe, when the sun came up, it wouldn't be so dark. He would wait and see.

Morris Markham was cold and all alone as he sat staring into the light of a small fire. He was hidden in a deep gully created by a wash that fed into the lake from the high ground on the east side. The Nobles and Thatchers had been hit too. He chanced lighting a candle in their cabin and found Alvin Noble and Enoch Ryan slumped over the table, their breakfasts untouched. He didn't look for the women. His mind had absorbed all of the horror it could stand for one day.

Totally exhausted from his long day of traveling, but afraid to stay in the cabin, he hid in the deep gully and built a small fire, needing to warm up and rest. But sleep wouldn't come. His mind wandered to the Marbles, who lived up on the big lake, and he decided that they too were already dead. He could not face the thought of finding another cabin full of dead bodies. Lying closer to the fire's warmth, he still couldn't sleep. The thought that he was the only survivor of the lakes settlement haunted him. Everyone else was either dead or scattered in the winter wilderness where they would die if help didn't come soon.

With these thoughts, he planned his next day. At first light, he would head north staying on the east side of the lakes until he came to Springfield across the border in Minnesota. There he could raise the alarm and find help to come back and rescue anyone who may have survived.

*　*　*

At first light, Inkpaduta ordered the camp to be packed up. The tipis were struck and the three new slaves were loaded with heavy packs and forced to carry them on the march to the Howe cabin. They set up camp again in the Howe clearing. Inkpaduta decided that they would camp here for one more day and thoroughly search through the cabins to find everything they could use: food, weapons, jewelry and clothing, it was all packed in bundles that could be carried. The three white slaves were shown how to fold and tie the bundles into manageable sizes. While doing this, Lydia Noble noticed her brother, Jacob Howe, sitting on the tree stump near the edge of the clearing. She was surprised that the Indians hadn't seen him and ran quickly to him.

"Run, Jacob. Run!" she hissed in a shouted whisper. When she neared him, she pulled up short. A choked cry caught in her throat at the sight of him. The boy had been clubbed and was thought to be dead the day before. His Great Gun had even scalped him. The scalping loosened the skin of his forehead and it slid forward, making it impossible for the boy to open his eyes. Jacob was dazed from his injuries and nearly frozen from his long night in the open. He was only semi-conscious, but did recognize his sister's voice.

"Liddy? Is that you?" he whimpered turning his blood stained head toward her. "I'm so cold." The muscles in his face strained as he tried to open his eyes to see her. He began shivering and tears streamed from beneath the folds of skin covering his eyes. Lydia realized the futility of his situation and she tried to stifle the sobs welling in her chest.

"Maybe—maybe they will leave ya be Jakie! Maybe they've had enough killin' and they'll leave ya alone," she whispered, her voice shaking with emotion. Looking around, she saw that some of the Indian women had noticed that she left her place, and she knew she would pay for it. "When them Injuns is done in the cabin, you crawl over there and git in outa the cold. Do ya hear me Jakie?" She could hear Afraid of Her Husband Woman shouting at her and reached out to grasp her brother's ice-cold arm. "Jakie?" She shook him gently. "Jakie, climb into Mama's bed and cover up an' maybe you'll be all right. Do ya hear me Jakie?" she finished, sobbing the words.

Afraid of Her Husband Woman came up behind Lydia before she could say more and grabbed her by the hair. Jerking violently, she pulled Lydia off her feet. She landed on her back in the snow, and the Indian woman began striking her with a stick of firewood. Lydia jumped to her feet and ran back to the camp, where Elizabeth Thatcher wrapped her arms around her and cried with her trying to hide Lydia's eyes from what was about to happen next.

After chasing Lydia back to the tipis, Afraid of Her Husband Woman walked swiftly back to the young boy sitting on the stump. Raising the stick of firewood that she had beaten his sister with, she struck Jacob Howe on the side of the head. He keeled over, listing slowly at first, like an ax cut tree, then toppled quickly, landing in a heap beside the stump. Afraid of Her Husband Women began piling brush on Jacob's quivering body. Soon several other women and some of the children were helping her until a large pile covered him.

Lydia turned away from Elizabeth and saw Afraid of Her Husband using a cooking pot to scoop up hot coals from the fire pit. She screamed when she realized that the woman was carrying the coals to the brush pile covering her brother. Crying uncontrollably, she tried to pull away from Elizabeth to go to her brother. Abbie Gardner wrapped her arms around Lydia to help Elizabeth hold her, knowing that if Lydia tried to interfere with their grisly work, they would kill her too. Afraid of Her Husband fanned the coals to flames and stood back to watch the fire build. Soon, as the three white women watched in horror, the fire consumed the brush and Jacob's body began to char.

"He was dead already, dear Liddy," Elizabeth Thatcher said, hugging her friend tightly, holding her from fainting to the ground. "He didn't feel the heat."

"He didn't cry out or move a bit when the fire hit him," young Abbie Gardner added, trying to be reassuring. "It's a sure sign he didn't feel nuthin'."

After the fire burned away, all of the women and children went back to packing the pillaged goods. The three white girls were forced to help. Lydia cried throughout the long morning. When the job was finished, they went back into their tipi and sat, hugging one another for support for the rest of the day.

When night came, they were pulled from the tipi and given boiled meat and some unleavened bread, made by mixing flour with water until a thick paste formed. The paste was spread on hot rocks by the fire's side where it cooked into a crispy mass. The result was scraped as crumbs off the rock and served in handfuls. After they were done eating, they were taken to separate tipis, all three being shared by the bachelors and any of the other men who wanted them. It would be many days before the three white captives would be allowed the simple pleasure of being together again.

In the morning, they packed up the camp and made the short trip to the Noble and Thatcher cabin where they set up camp again. Inkpaduta was in no hurry. As far as he knew, they had killed every white person living here by the lakes, except for the three young women they had taken captive. Chances that anyone would be traveling during the cold season were slim, and he felt sure that they were safe from being found out any time soon. He wanted to make sure they found everything of value that these white settlers may have hidden. He decided that they would spend the day searching through this last cabin.

Elizabeth Thatcher and Lydia Noble spent the day within sight of their dead babies' bodies. Both women tried to go to them, but were driven back by a group of women with switches, led by the old crone Hates Her Father Woman and the ever-present Afraid of her Husband Woman. Finally, Roaring Cloud picked up the two small corpses and threw them out of sight behind the cabin. It was a long miserable day and night for the captives.

They moved the next day, traveling north along the east side of *Okobooshi* until they reached a narrows where they crossed the lake on the ice. Traveling was slow, as there was still deep snow to plow through as they headed northwest. That night they camped on the south end of *mini wakan*. In the morning, they moved along the west shore of the lake until they saw smoke curling in the clear blue sky above some trees not far from the lake's western shore. Inkpaduta was surprised to see yet another white man's cabin. A sudden fear coursed through his mind. How many more white men were in the area? He had felt safe thinking they had killed them all. But now they had found another cabin. Were there cabins on the other side of this lake too?

They were about one hundred yards from the cabin when he called a halt. He ordered the women to keep the captives out of sight while he and half of the men advanced toward the cabin. Upon entering the small clearing he shouted a greeting and heard an answer from inside. The door opened and a white man carrying a rifle walked out.

"Food?" Inkpaduta asked smiling. "Jib food?"

The white man went back into the cabin and came out with three loaves of bread. The Indians were disappointed to see that he still carried his rifle. Tearing off a piece of bread, the man handed the rest to Inkpaduta, who also tore off some bread and handed the loaves to be passed among the rest of his men. They all ate in silence until the bread was gone. Inkpaduta pointed to the rifle the white man still held in the crook of his arm.

"Good gun," he stated in a complimentary tone.

The white man smiled and shook his head in agreement.

"Shoot good?" Inkpaduta asked.

"Yah, it shoots good," the white man answered.

Inkpaduta turned to Gunn and pointing to an oak tree growing near the lake shore and handed him a square of legging leather. Gunn ran to the tree and hung it from a low hanging branch. Charley took aim at the target and missed it cleanly. Fire Cloud fired and missed too. Young Inkpaduta and Gunn tried. All missed.

Laughing at their apparent ineptitude, Inkpaduta gestured to the white man to take a turn. William Marble looked at their smiling, friendly faces and thought how much like children they were. He stood and took careful aim and fired. The leather target leaped when the fifty caliber round ball struck it, and flipped loose from the branch and fell to the ground. A roar of approval from the assembly of Indians met his ears as they cheered his good marksmanship. Smiling to himself, he walked to the tree and picked up the target. He hung it from the branch again.

Turning, he saw all of the Indians were aiming their guns at him. A startled fear raced through him as he realized that because he had neglected to reload his gun he was defenseless. But his fear subsided and was replaced with relief when he saw the smiles and heard the laughter coming from the group of Indians. It was just a joke. He

340

began to laugh with them, and the more he thought of it, the funnier the joke became and he continued laughing as he walked back toward them.

But suddenly he noticed that he was the only one laughing and that the Indians were still aiming their guns at him. He stopped, and looked squarely into the pox scarred Indian's eyes, and William Marble finally understood.

"Run Margaret Ann!" he shouted just before eight lead balls struck him in the chest, knocking him flat on his back.

Margaret Ann Marble heard her husband's shout and looked out after the sound of the cacophony of gunfire to see her husband's body sprawled in the snow. She didn't hesitate and ran out the door racing for the lake, but Rattling chased after her catching her before she had made it to the end of the clearing. Big Face and One Leg quickly tied her hands and pulled her back to where the women stood waiting.

Leaving Roaring Cloud in charge of half of the men, with instructions to search through the cabin and take everything they could carry, Inkpaduta and the rest of the men returned to the women, and he led them away from this last scene of carnage. The magnitude of their sudden killing spree was beginning to worry Inkpaduta. There were many more white men living in this area than he had thought. He wanted to put some distance between this last crime scene and where they would camp. He pushed the people hard all day and that night, as he sat near a warm fire ten miles to the northeast, he examined the situation.

They had killed eleven white men, five white women and sixteen children. They also had four captive white women. He knew that the white government would want revenge, and he was sure that there would be soldiers from the forts in Minnesota put on their trail. He pondered the problem, sitting at the fire for most of the night. His cunning mind came up with a plan to help cover his trail and cause some confusion as to who had committed the killings at the lakes. In the morning, they would cross into Minnesota and visit some *Santee* villages near the white settlement of Springfield.

# Chapter 36
## *Springfield*

$\mathbf{A}$ starving and nearly frozen Morris Markham was near death when he stumbled, mumbling incoherently up to the cabin of a Springfield settler named Thomas. The Thomases quickly took him into their cabin, wrapped him in blankets and provided hot coffee and a warm porridge breakfast. It was the first food he had eaten since the morning of the day he had discovered the massacre. His feet were frostbitten, and his glassy eyes indicated a fever. Periodic shivers shook his body as he sat by the warm fireplace and tried to relay his warning to the kindly people who had taken him in. His voice was husky, almost too scratchy for them to understand. He slowly recounted what he had found at the cabins near the lakes some thirty miles south and west of Springfield three days before.

While the exhausted Markham slept, Thomas carried his warning to the other residents of Springfield.

By nightfall, twenty-one people were forted up in the Thomas cabin. The Woods brothers, George and William, and a hog farmer named Stewart and his family were the only residents of the young southwest Minnesota community to ignore the warning. They questioned Markham's story. George and William Woods were doing a thriving business through their general store, selling foodstuffs and a multitude of supplies to the local Indian population who paid with annuity money. Stewart also had a good business relationship with the Indians, trading hogs for fox skins and coon hides.

The Woods brothers and Stewart attributed Markham's wild story to the fact that he had been lost in the snowy countryside and had gone mad. But the people in the Thomas cabin had only to look into Morris's grief stricken eyes to see the truth of his words. The next morning, two men volunteered to make the long trek to Fort Ripley, far to the north, to ask the army to help protect them.

\* \* \*

The trip to Springfield took a little longer than Inkpaduta thought it would. The huge amount of supplies they had taken from the cabins slowed them down. The captive women were loaded with large packs to carry, but they were unused to such hard work and had to be constantly prodded to keep up and waited for when they couldn't. As they traveled deeper in the land of the *Mdewakanton* and *Wahpekute*, they came across many small bands of people. Each time they did, Inkpaduta ordered a feast and he and his men showed off the riches they had stolen from the whites. They recounted their acts of bravery, and Inkpaduta encouraged them to kill all of the whites and take their land back.

When the band reached Heron Lake, fifteen miles from Springfield, he called a halt and the women set up camp. A day later, Sleepy Eye and Black Buffalo and the people from their villages came to visit. Rumors of the killings at the Iowa lakes had reached their ears two days before. Supposedly, the rumor was started by a white man who had seen the dead people at *Minnetanka* and *Okobooshi*. Black Buffalo had even asked the white trader William Woods, about it. But Woods had scoffed at the rumor and said that it was the story of a wild man, made crazy by the snow. It was now evident to both he and Sleepy Eye, that the rumor was true.

The visit by the two *Santee* leaders and a large number of their people gave Inkpaduta the opportunity he was hoping for. He told Roaring Cloud to shoot the lone ox they had driven with them from William Marble's cabin. The women were set to butchering the meat and as the sun sank in the afternoon sky, a great feast was held. Everyone in Inkpaduta's band dressed in the bright clothing they had stolen from the cabins.

The men sang and danced and showed off the scalps, jewelry, guns, axes, knives and silver money they had taken from the whites. The four captive women were scrubbed clean in the frigid waters of Heron Lake and brought naked to the campfire area where they were forced to parade around in the light of the fire. Their light skin and Abbie's golden hair, rinsed of the charcoal grit and soot, shone brightly. Each of the women was hauled off, by groups of young men, who took turns using them in the bachelors' tipi.

The fires burned late into the night as the men of Inkpaduta's band continued to dance and sing, acting out the story of their conquest against the white intruders to their land. Soon, feeling the excitement as the drums beat a measured cadence that grew louder and faster as the dancers picked up their pace, the young men of Sleepy Eye's band joined in the celebration. Black Buffalo's young men were not to be left out, and the circle around the fire pit was soon trampled smooth by the dancers' feet.

Inkpaduta took part in the celebration. Standing with Margaret Ann Marble's favorite red dress folded over his arm, he told how he had outsmarted the white men and killed them. As he spoke, he felt that the fame and glory he had experienced when his father was still alive was once more his. Now, as then, his warriors were feared by their enemies. He turned slowly around the circle of young men massed around the fire pit. Their excited faces turned toward him, their eyes following his steps around the pit, drinking in each statement he made.

The women threw more wood on the fire and the flames grew high, but Inkpaduta was not blinded by bright light of the fire in the dark night. He knew of the fires that grew in young men's hearts at the thought of going to war. He also knew that the whites would be angry about the killings at the lakes. It would be called a massacre, and there would be a loud outcry for retribution.

During the night's long celebration his cunning mind formed a plan that, if carried out correctly, would place the blame for the massacre on Sleepy Eye and Black Buffalo. But it all depended upon his being able to convince the two leaders to continue the war he had started. As he walked around the circle of young men, shaking a scalp pole with four fresh scalps that danced with each thrust of the shaft, he began speaking directly to the young men.

"Warriors–*Santee* Warriors! It is time to take up your war clubs and prove that you are truly *Dakotah*! It is time to count coup and take scalps. It is time to take back what is ours. It is time to tell the White Man that we don't need his annuity money or his bright colored cloth clothing," he cried, throwing the red dress in the fire, which brought everyone to complete silence. He pointed toward the bachelors' tipi. "It is time to kill the white man and fuck his women as my warriors did at *Minnetanka* and *Okobooshi*!"

A shout of agreement rose from the crowd, and many of the young men who hadn't visited the white captives yet eyed the tipi hungrily. But before they could move from where they sat, he continued, "Those are our women." He pulled a blue shirt from beneath his buckskin shirt. "These are our clothes." He held a handful of dangling necklaces and jewelry above his head and his other hand holding silver coins high for all to see. "These are ours now. Our clothes, our jewelry, our money and our women!" He stopped and stared intently at Sleepy Eye and Black Buffalo before continuing, "You can get your own." And he pointed in the direction of Springfield.

Just before sunrise in the morning, Inkpaduta, Sleepy Eye and Black Buffalo held a council of war. It was decided that Inkpaduta and his men would accompany Black Buffalo's forces to the Woods' brother's store and to Stewart's hog farm. Sleepy Eye would lead his men to the rest of the outlying cabins. Inkpaduta could feel the excitement coursing through his veins as he and Black Buffalo walked into the clearing in front of the Woods Brothers' store. The rest of the men circled the building, cutting off any escape for the white men inside.

"Woods, come out," Black Buffalo called, breaking the quiet of the morning. He too, was excited, and his forehead had beads of perspiration on it even though the early morning air was still cool. His voice cracked with excitement, as he called again, "Woods, your friend Black Buffalo calls you."

William Woods stepped out of the cabin store onto the porch. He had heard Black Buffalo's first call, but had taken time to pull his boots on.

He noticed a stranger with a horribly pox scarred face standing beside Black Buffalo. William thought that maybe the stranger was an agency Indian who hadn't spent all of his annuity money yet. He was certainly welcome to finish spending it in his store. He stepped down the steps to the ground and walked forward, smiling, extending his hand in friendship. His hand was left hanging as neither Black Buffalo nor the new Indian raised a hand to grasp it.

Confused, he looked the two men in the face and saw no friendliness in their eyes. The rumor about the massacre at the Iowa lakes entered his mind, and fear caused the hair on the back of his neck to stand on end. He turned and walked stiffly toward the cabin door.

Standing off to the side, Roaring Cloud raised his rifle and shot William Woods through the legs. Woods fell to the ground with a startled shout on his lips. From inside the cabin-store, his brother George looked out and saw him writhing on the ground. The truth about the rumor was suddenly apparent to George, too. Believing that his brother was dead, his only thought was to try to make it to the Thomas cabin, a quarter of a mile in the distance.

George ran out the back door, heading for the trees along the creek bed. Before he had run half the way to the cover that the trees would have afforded, he was cut down by a rifle shot through the stomach.

All of the young men ran forward wanting to count coup by touching the severely wounded white man. Their excitement boiled over and soon they were pushing and shoving, arguing about who had the right to scalp the still living man, the man who had shot him, or the man who had touched first coup. Inkpaduta settled the argument by picking up some brush and threw it on the hapless William Woods.

"Burn them!" he ordered.

Excited by the thought of watching the white men burn, the warriors quickly gathered brush and branches of trees cut to make the clearing and began piling it on William. One Leg entered the cabin and returned with a scoop of hot coals from the store's stove. William screamed in terror and began trying to crawl out from under the brush piled on top of him as One Leg bent to start it on fire. Both legs were broken by the round ball that had passed through them, and he could not crawl. There was nothing in the spring-muddied ground for him to grip, so he could not even pull himself with his arms.

The flames flickered quickly through the small twigs first, tickling his feet. He struggled, pulling his useless legs away from the flames with his hands, but the fire was growing too fast. The brush was from plum trees chopped from a thicket on the edge of the clearing. Long thorns and sharp prickly branches grabbed at his clothing and scratched his skin as he struggled to escape the growing heat.

A wild howl burst from his lips in a wavering keen of pain and terror as the flames licked his legs. The fire grew in strength and crackled through the freeze-dried branches, snapping and roaring as it engulfed the pile. William's cotton and wool clothing ignited, sending a new strength to his wounded limbs. He tried to rear up, throwing the burning brush from him. But he was already a human torch, and he fell back screaming as the young men threw more brush on him.

The gut-shot George Woods was silent as the Indians piled brush on him. He had heard his brother's screams, but his own private agony held him in a tight grip of immense pain and suffering. He curled up in a ball and moaned loudly when the flames burned through the brush pile and reached him. He barely moved after his clothing started burning. Perhaps the bullet wound had put him out of his misery before the true heat of the fire could add to it.

The brothers' remains lay perfectly still by the time the fires had burned all of the brush that was on top of them. Their clothing was burnt away, and their hair was singed, with only small tufts of fragile strings left. Splits in their blackened, heat-swollen skin seeped dark red blood. Their fingers, toes and genitals were shriveled to small lumps of charred ash.

Inkpaduta ordered his sons to quickly search through the cabin-store to make sure no one was hiding there. Rain Cloud and Fire Cloud found no one and exited the building having taken a quick inventory of items that they would return for that afternoon. Inkpaduta ordered half of the men to go join Sleepy Eye. Black Buffalo then led the smaller contingent off to the distant home of hog farmer Stewart.

Stewart too, was a trusting man who held a good relationship with the Indians of the area. He had sold many hogs to Black Buffalo's people in the past and had no reason not to answer his call now. The pox-marked stranger with Black Buffalo held a small leather pouch that brought real silver to Stewart's mind.

The Woods boys didn't get it all, he thought as he walked past Inkpaduta, heading for the hog shed. It was his last thought as Inkpaduta raised his rifle and shot hog farmer Stewart in the back. The force of the blast slammed his body face down on the ground, where he lay, not moving. The ball had severed his spine, killing him instantly. Stewart's wife, carrying a small child, ran screaming from the cabin and bent to help her fallen husband.

Black Buffalo looked to Inkpaduta for a reassuring nod before he raised his stone tipped war club and smashed the woman on the back of her head. Her body cartwheeled to the ground flinging the small child through the air. The baby hit the ground screaming. Rattling silenced the child by smashing its head with his gun butt. Roaring Cloud, leading three of Black Buffalo's men, entered the cabin and caught up two small children. Carrying them outside, they dashed their lives away on the corner of the building.

A third child, an older boy, escaped by disappearing into the thicket on the backside of the clearing.

After scalping the Stewarts, the war party returned past the Woods Brothers' store to join Sleepy Eye at the Thomas cabin. They found that the rest of the white population of Springfield had forted up in the Thomas cabin.

Unlike the Woods brothers, these people were not trusting and had not been fooled into leaving the safety of the cabin. Charley and Gunn accompanied Sleepy Eye that morning and had approached the cabin dressed in white man clothing hailing the people inside in English. The inhabitants, thinking that they might be soldiers from Fort Ripley, poured out of the cabin cheering, but stopped when they saw the half-breed brothers and grew cautious. An excited young man from Sleepy Eye's band grew impatient and fired at the whites from too great of a distance for accuracy. Several other men then fired also, but they succeeded only in wounding one small child before the white people had all slipped back into the cabin.

Sleepy Eye's force tried to breech the cabin walls, but each time was pushed back by gunfire from the men inside. Each assault during the afternoon also failed.

By nightfall, most of the young men had grown bored with the siege and when full darkness came, they all returned to Inkpaduta's village to dance and sing songs of bravery. Black Buffalo's men bragged of the day's killings. Sleepy Eye's men could only wait for the next day. They planned to flush the white people from the cabin by starting it on fire, and then they would get their chance at glory.

But in the morning, they found that sometime during the night the remaining residents of Springfield had slipped out of the cabin and escaped toward Fort Ripley across the dark prairie.

Inkpaduta was furious to find that the whites were gone. His women had looted the Woods Brothers' store, replenishing the band's food and powder and shot supplies. They had begun striking their camp as soon as the men left to attack the Thomas cabin again, and they were ready to travel. His plan was to stay with Black Buffalo and Sleepy Eye only until their warriors were fully involved with the attack. Then, Inkpaduta's orders for his men were to pull back and move quietly off to the west. His hope was that Black Buffalo and Sleepy Eye and their bands would catch the brunt of the white army soldiers' anger upon finding the settlement of Springfield under attack or wiped out.

With the escape of the Springfield residents, there would be no prolonged battle to catch the attention of the soldiers. He knew they had to hurry away from the scene and hope that the murder of the Woods brothers and Stewart would distract the soldiers from their trail.

Leading twelve horses heavily laden with dry goods—flour, powder and lead, clothing, bed quilts and bolts of bright colored cloth—the outcast *Wahpekute* band headed west. All of the women also carried heavy packs. The four young captive women were loaded down heavier than before and had a hard time keeping up. Inkpaduta assigned One Leg to keep watch on them and whip them when they fell behind. It would be a full day of traveling, as he wanted to put as much distance between Springfield and his band as possible.

They didn't stop until after the sun was down, camping without fires and sleeping on the ground covered by buffalo robes and blankets.

In the morning, Young Inkpaduta returned from watching their back trail with the news that a troop of soldiers on mules was following them. Inkpaduta knew that they would not be able to out run the well-mounted soldiers. He decided to make a stand. The women hurriedly packed up the camp, and they moved a short distance away to a stand of trees. Instructing them to keep going, he set his men in a skirmish line on the inside edge of the trees. Fire Cloud and Rain Cloud pushed the four captive women to their knees and tied them hand and foot.

"If the soldiers attack," Inkpaduta said, "kill the slaves."

Watching from the trees, the Indians saw the soldiers arrive at their campsite. The white leader called a halt, and all of the soldiers dismounted and unsaddled their mules. They had been on a forced march through the night, a feat made possible by the sure-footed mules, and both the animals and men were tired. The white leader circled the camp several times. There was no fire, so he couldn't judge by the coals how long it had been since the Indians had left the camp. He had only horse droppings to look at and wasn't a good judge of them.

Finally, he shrugged his shoulders and ordered the troop to saddle their mules. When they mounted up, they rode back in the direction from which they had come, giving up the chase.

After the white soldiers were gone from sight, Inkpaduta and his men gathered up the captives and followed after their women. He wanted no fight with anyone who could fight back. The band traveled steadily for two more days, sleeping in cold camps and eating only jerky, extending the distance between them and the United States Army. When all fear of pursuit passed, they traveled at a more leisure pace, meandering aimlessly through the western Minnesota wilderness.

It was soon apparent that one of the white women had taken ill during the three weeks of captivity. Elizabeth Thatcher developed a fever and experienced constant, body shaking chills. The warming spring weather did little to alleviate her miseries. Instead, the dampness and rain worsened her condition. Each day she was forced to work hard as was a woman's duty and a slave's only means of survival. When the band was on the move, she carried a heavy pack. When they were camped, she searched for firewood, scraped hides or stripped meat for drying. There was not time to recuperate.

As the *Moon of the Red Grass Appearing* passed into the *Moon When the Ponies Shed*, her condition worsened. Her left breast grew to twice its normal size, became fevered and finally gathered and burst, a black, bloody pus draining from the hole on its underneath side. A day later, her left arm swelled and turned black from blood veins breaking. Between the two ailments, Elizabeth suffered the most excruciating pain. Only the hope of one day returning to her husband kept the nineteen-year-old woman going. Each day, she shouldered her pack and doggedly followed along. But as her ailments progressed, she began falling farther and farther behind. Abbie, Lydia and Margaret tried to help her along, but their actions slowed the band down. Inkpaduta named her Sick One.

Inkpaduta decided to head west and try to find some buffalo before the cows dropped their calves. If they could find the herds and wait for the cows to have their calves, the hunt would be more successful. Young calves were like sick women, they slowed you down. When the band came to the river that the whites were already calling the Big Sioux, they started crossing the wide stream on a natural bridge made of uprooted trees that had been deposited at a narrows by the spring flood. Half of the people had crossed when Inkpaduta held up the rest, waiting for the four slaves to catch up. Sick One was falling behind again, and the other three had dropped back to help her along. The wait angered him, and his anger helped him make a decision.

"Take care of Sick One," he directed Young Inkpaduta.

The young man approached the women and took the pack from Elizabeth's shoulders. Taking her by the good arm, he gently led her to the log bridge and started across, showing her where to step on the tricky footing of the wet logs. Abbie, Lydia and Margaret were surprised. This was the first act of kindness from their captors that any of them had experienced.

Their surprise didn't last long. When Young Inkpaduta and Elizabeth Thatcher reached the middle of the river, he took both of her hands in his and threw her off the bridge into the cold, swift running water. The water, still cold from the spring thaws, revived her fever-racked body and with superhuman strength, she swam to the bank.

Before she could crawl out, One Leg shoved her back into the freezing water. Elizabeth swam to shore again, finding a tree root to hold on to. Afraid of Her Husband Woman quickly ran to the bank and beat Sick One's hands with a stout stick until the woman let go of the tree root and fell back into the river. She let the current carry her body down stream. Many of the women and young boys chased after her, throwing sticks and rocks at her. Whooping and hollering, they enjoyed this new game. The current carried her to another logjam bridge that was not far down river. When she bumped into it, she instinctively tried to crawl out of the water onto one of the logs. She had almost made it when Rattling, tiring of the game, shot her through the body, and the hapless woman fell back into the dark water. Her body rolled under the logs and she failed to surface again.

Hates Her Father Woman and Beaded Hair Woman divided Sick One's loaded pack between the other three slaves, and they were ordered to cross the bridge their friend had been pushed off of.

## Chapter 37
### *Some Retribution*

**A**s they traveled further into the lands of their western cousins in the Dakota Territory, the *Wahpekute* became less cautious. When they met parties of *Hunkpapa, Minneconjou,* and *Ogalala*, Inkpaduta and his men bragged of their attack on the whites at the Iowa lakes. They dressed in the bright clothing, showed off the silver jewelry, and paraded their three captive women to prove that their story was true.

After traveling to the west for three weeks, the band camped on the shores of Skunk Lake. Inkpaduta's fame spread quickly through the western tribes, and he became well known at the Skunk Lake camp.

Because he had stopped trying to hide his trail, it was easy for two *Sissiton* men from the Yellow Medicine Agency to find him. The two men boldly entered his camp early one morning and announced that they were looking for the Great Inkpaduta. They had traveled many miles from the Minnesota country, trying to catch up with his band. The white men in Minnesota wanted the yellow-haired slave-girl back. The whites had given the two men many valuable items to buy her from Inkpaduta with. What they didn't tell Inkpaduta was that the Government was threatening to stop making annuity payments until Abbie Gardner was returned.

Inkpaduta frowned. He hadn't decided what to do with the girl yet. At first, he wanted to keep Yellow Hair Woman for himself. Not only was she very pretty, she was young and strong and a good worker. His old wife, Hates Her Father Woman, didn't seem to mind when he used the young girl in his bed at night. He thought also about his youngest son, Young Inkpaduta needing a wife. Of the three slave women, she seemed to fit in better than the other two. Quiet Voiced Woman got along all right and did what she was told to do with out having to be beaten. But she stayed by herself and didn't join in. She ate only enough food to keep alive and was slowly wasting away. He thought she would probably die when wintertime came. Angry Face

Woman was just the opposite; she was loud and demanding and had to be beaten often to get her to do her duties. She was a fighter, and his sons enjoyed forcing her to have sex with them, because unlike the Yellow Hair Woman and Quiet Voiced Woman, she didn't just lie back and let them do what they wanted to do. She fought them each time, giving blow for blow. But she always submitted after the fight, coupling with a fierce excitement that left both participants, though sometimes battered and bloodied, exhausted and completely satisfied.

With these thoughts in his mind, Inkpaduta refused to sell Abbie Gardner to the *Sissitons*. Instead he offered them Quiet Voiced Woman. The agency Indians decided that it was better to bring back one woman, even if she were the wrong woman, rather than return empty handed. They accepted Inkpaduta's offer and turned over the guns, powder, cloth, flour, knives and furs the Agent had given them to trade for Abbie Gardner.

The next morning, the two agency Indians and Margaret Ann Marble rode off to the east. Inkpaduta was proud of the price he had been paid for a slave who probably wouldn't have lasted long anyway.

His good feeling didn't last long, though. When Roaring Cloud and Fire Cloud heard of the sale, they were angry that they hadn't been consulted before the sale was made. They were also angry when he told them of his plan to give Yellow Hair Woman to Young Inkpaduta for a wife. The twin brothers could not control their jealousy.

It was the start of four weeks of fighting and bickering among the family. Not a day went by without one or the other of his sons threatening to leave the band but never actually doing it. When Afraid of her Husband heard that Roaring Cloud wanted Yellow Hair Woman, life became a living hell for the young white girl. As much as each of the other women of the band wanted the young girl for a slave to help with their work, they were also all envious of her beauty and the fascination caused by her blond hair. They began working her harder and harder and beating her more and more often.

Inkpaduta's frustration grew as he realized that he could not give Yellow Hair Woman to his youngest son for a wife or keep her for himself without causing his other sons to be jealous. The women in the band were beginning to act jealous of the attention their men were giving to both of the white slave women. By the end of the *Moon of Making Fat*, Inkpaduta was tired of the problems being caused by having the slave women.

While hunting buffalo with a band of *Yanktons*, Inkpaduta decided to get rid of his problem. A one-legged *Yanktoni* man named

End of the Snake had good use for the slave women. He walked with a crutch when he was on the ground, but he practically lived on his horse. He hunted small game, shooting rabbits, prairie hens and skunks with his bow and arrows from horseback to keep his family fed, and he needed the slave women to retrieve his game. When he offered to buy them from Inkpaduta, Inkpaduta sold both women to him, much to his sons' disapproval.

The *Wahpekute* traveled with End of the Snake's *Yankton* band for several days, hoping to find a buffalo herd. Both bands were small, and the more hunters there were if they found a herd, the bigger the kill would be.

Only a few days after Abbie and Lydia Noble moved into End of the Snake's tipi, Roaring Cloud came and ordered Angry Face Woman to come back to his tipi. He pushed the one-legged owner of the women aside, stating that he wanted a woman and Afraid of Her Husband Woman was in the sick lodge, having her monthly sickness. He needed a slave woman to prepare his food and scrape his skins and warm his bed until his wife returned. He had used Yellow Hair Woman the night before, while End of the Snake and Angry Face Woman were hunting. When Fire Cloud found out, he complained to their father. Inkpaduta scolded Roaring Cloud, reminding him that the slaves belonged to End of the Snake.

But the scolding only made Roaring Cloud more determined to have his way. He decided that since he had not been consulted in the sale of any of the women and did not approve of the sale, he would use them both whenever he wanted to.

"Angry Face Woman, come out now!" He demanded from outside the door of End of the Snake's tipi. Lydia Noble refused to answer his call, drawing back into End of The Snake's tipi at the sound of Roaring Cloud's voice.

"You better go Lydia," Abbie Gardner advised after Roaring Cloud's third shouted summons. "He sounds mad. Just go and do as he tells ya. It ain't so bad if ya don't fight with 'em."

"I'll not go," the little woman said defiantly. "He is awful! He beats me if I fight him and he beats me if I just let him have his way. It's almost like he wants me ta fight. This Injun we got now might make us work, but at least when he takes ya ta bed, if ya do what he wants, he don't beat on ya. I'm stayin' with this Injun. Don't want nothin' more ta do with that mean bastard out there."

These defiant words had just left Lydia's mouth when Roaring Cloud burst into the tipi. His eyes were blazing with fury. He screamed at Lydia, spittle flying from his angry mouth. She dodged around the interior of the tipi, trying to escape out the door. He caught her by the hair and dragged her out. Livid with rage at her resistance, he scooped up a sturdy stick from a pile of firewood and began beating Lydia with it. The blows to her body cracked her ribs, and she fell to the ground and passed out. Roaring Cloud sat moodily watching the unconscious woman, waiting for her to wake up. When she did he began beating her again until she was a mass of broken bones and bleeding flesh.

End of the Snake quietly crawled into the tipi, counting the woman as a loss. He sat inside the door with his bow and arrow ready to protect his investment of the yellow haired slave.

No one else in camp paid any attention to Roaring Cloud or the woman as he beat her. They were too frightened by his uncontrollable anger to get involved. But later in the morning, after Roaring Cloud left, Lydia's loud moans irritated Fire Cloud. He loaded his rifle and shot her low in the side. The force of the blast rolled her body over and a startled grunt escaped her dying lips. Fire Cloud reloaded, and he and Young Inkpaduta both shot her again. When it was clear she was dead, they returned to their own camp without looking back.

That afternoon, Inkpaduta paid End of the Snake back what he had been given for Angry Face Woman. This satisfied the one-legged Indian's anger at having lost one of his slaves. The next morning they moved on, leaving her body where it lay. The tension between the two camps over the killing of the slave woman disappeared with the sighting of a small herd of buffalo. It was a successful hunt and a time of celebration ensued. They hunted in the area of the James River for several days, coming across a large *Yankton* village on its banks. These people had never seen a white person before and were all fascinated by End of the Snake's white slave girl. They were eager to touch her light skin and yellow hair, but were much kinder than the people of Inkpaduta's village had been. While camped with the *Yanktons*, Brave Bull heard rumors of a large *Hunkpapa* village to the north and headed off to find his family.

Only two days later the arrival of three *Santee*, from the Yellow Medicine Agency caused a lot of excitement in the village. The men were *Sissitons* and held little regard for Inkpaduta and his people. Their names were Man Who Shoots Metal as He Walks, Beautiful Voice, and Iron Hawk. Iron Hawk was the spokesman, and he told End of the Snake that they had been trailing them ever since the two men had returned to the Agency with the white woman they had purchased from Inkpaduta.

"The White Father at the Agency is angry about the killings and the kidnappings committed by Inkpaduta and his people," Iron Hawk stated bluntly. "But he has a kind heart and will forgive the killings if the captives are returned. He has asked us to find the white women and has given us many goods to trade for them."

End of the Snake had also grown tired of the problems having a white slave woman caused. Everyone wanted to see her and touch her hair. Most of the men wanted to bed her, but Inkpaduta's sons were still very jealous of anyone else touching the girl, and he had found himself breaking up fights and scuffles on a regular basis. This one small slave wasn't worth the trouble she had been. He agreed to sell Yellow Hair Woman for two horses, twelve blankets, two kegs of powder, twenty pounds of tobacco, thirty-two yards of blue cloth, thirty-seven yards of calico, ribbons and a basket of beads, mirrors and other trinkets.

There was a dog feast that night, and the next morning, the three *Sissitons*, accompanied by two of End of The Snake's sons, took Abbie Gardner across the James River in a bull boat, which was the first leg of her journey back to the white world.

With Yellow Hair Woman gone, the problem of finding a wife for Young Inkpaduta once again became a focus for his father. Young Inkpaduta wanted a wife, but did not want one of the wild *Yankton* girls that were available. He decided that an agency girl would be much better. An agency girl would have beads and baubles for beauty and the knowledge of how to use white man luxuries. An agency girl would be more like Yellow Hair Woman.

When Inkpaduta heard his youngest son's desire to find an agency girl for a wife, he agreed that the thinking was probably sound. But he was cautious because of the words spoken by Iron Hawk. His plan to spread the blame for the attack on the whites at the Iowa Lakes to Black Buffalo and Sleepy Eye's bands had failed, and he was hesitant to take the band back to Minnesota. Instead, he sent Roaring Cloud and Rattling with Young Inkpaduta to search the agency for a suitable wife and bring her back to their camp on the James River.

After living for almost five *Moons* with the wild *Yanktons,* Inkpaduta realized just how much he missed some of the luxuries brought by the whites, luxuries the *Yanktons* had not yet experienced. Tobacco for his pipe was of major importance. The mellow blue smoke that smelled sweet and tasted mild just couldn't be replaced with the mixture of wild clover and dried buffalo or horse dung that the *Yanktons* smoked. And his cloth clothing was beginning to wear thin. White man clothing, while being bright and pretty and soft and comfortable, didn't hold up very well and had to be replaced often.

Flour was a white man foodstuff that he had become almost addicted to. The unleavened bread that Yellow Hair Woman had taught them to bake in a covered pot over the fireplace rocks had been a welcome addition to the wild meat diet he was used to. Also the band had used up most of their powder and shot, and it would be much easier to replace if they could live in the land of the *Santee* again. He told Roaring Cloud and Rattling to quietly visit with the *Santee* living on the Agency lands to see if it would be safe for him to bring his band back to Minnesota. If possible, he was ready to go home.

*   *   *

John Other Day was a "cut-hair." Cut Hair was the name given him and a few others like him by agency Indians who were unsatisfied with agency life. Those who called him a "cut hair" were men who took the easy living the whites gave them on the agency and then complained about their lot in life rather than doing anything to improve it.

John Other Day had learned the ways of the white man's God and became a Christian. He had taken a white woman for a wife. They were married in the agency church. He cut his hair and dressed in cloth clothing. He, his wife, and their children lived in a white frame house on a farm just outside the agency lands. He had learned English and seldom spoke his own language. He was learning to read and write with his children. He had already learned to plow and plant and harvest. John Other Day took to farming as well as most of his race took to hunting and fishing for a living. He made a good living. God had been good to John Other Day. He was blessed with a good wife, wonderful children and some of the best farmland in the state of Minnesota.

For all of this, John Other Day was grateful. He had grown up in a life that had left him hungry or frightened, each time the sun set. Either hunting was poor or some enemy was threatening, sometimes both.

But since the white people had come and taught him the true way to everlasting life in the house of the one true Lord, his life had changed. Now his house was warm, his enemies were few and his larder was full. John Other Day was a good man and felt he owed a great debt to his beloved wife's race. It was this debt that was on his mind when he rode to Fort Ridgely to report that he had seen part of the renegade, Inkpaduta's band, camped on the Yellow Medicine River not far from the Agency.

*   *   *

Roaring Cloud, Rattling and Young Inkpaduta sat contentedly around the fire, watching the sparks rise into the night sky. They were in the village of a distant cousin, Man Who Hates Fish. The camp sat one hundred yards from the river, high enough to be safe from floods and close enough to be a good source of water for the village.

Man Who Hates Fish lived with the *Wahpetons*. He had four wives, who did all of his heavy work, and he had fathered seventeen children, split evenly among his wives. The children's ages ranged from two years to twelve. Sometimes it was even hard for the mothers to remember whose child was whose. It really didn't matter because Man Who Hates Fish kept three tipis and the children slept each night wherever they felt the most welcome.

Also in the camp were the families of his wives' mothers and fathers, sisters and their husbands and their offspring. Thus, the village was alive with the constant chatter and motion only young children can provide. It was a thriving camp, but not large and important enough for the whites to keep watch on. It was just the type of village that Inkpaduta had instructed his sons to find.

Each day, the three men moved away from Man Who Hates Fish's village and visited camps up and down river. They listened to the gossip and started idle conversation with the inhabitants, hoping to find out information about how the people in the area felt about the attacks on the white people that spring. They were not surprised to hear that Black Buffalo and Sleepy Eye had ducked the blame for the attack at Springfield by steering it all at Inkpaduta's band. It was apparent that it would still not be safe for their father to bring his people back to Minnesota.

They returned to Man Who Hates Fish's camp each night to discuss what they had heard. On this night, Roaring Cloud and Rattling were paying Man Who Hates Fish for the use of his two youngest wives. Young Inkpaduta had purchased a bride from down on the Redwood River at a *Mdewakanton* town. His bride's father had too many children to feed and was glad to take payment for the hand of his oldest daughter even though he knew his son-in-law would not be joining his family in the traditional manner. As the three men sat smoking their pipes, they made plans to return to the west the next day.

The wind was calm, and it was hot. The women rolled up the bottom of the tipi to let the evening breeze pass under its walls. All of the children had been herded into the tipis with Man Who Hates Fish and his other two wives, leaving one tipi for the three outcasts and their women. Even now, Young Inkpaduta could hear the women giggling in the tipi as they teased his young bride. Rattling and Roaring Cloud joked with Young Inkpaduta, comparing their fat, experienced women to the shy young girl he had married. Roaring

Cloud offered to "break her in" for him and Rattling grinned as he offered to make sure the girl was satisfied if Young Inkpaduta needed any help.

Young Inkpaduta was as proud as any young man with a new wife, and he traded insult for insult with his older brother and brother-in-law until the moon was high in the sky. When the last of the tobacco went out in their pipes, the three men stood and entered the tipi, each going to his own bed and the pleasures he would find there.

It was nearing midnight when John Other Day met the white soldiers on a high hill half way between the Redwood Agency and the Yellow Medicine Agency. There were two detachments, one of cavalry, led by Major Flandrau and another of infantry, led by Captain Murry. John described the location of the renegade's camp and the layout of the land surrounding the village.

Major Flandrau decided that the cavalry would surround the village on the north side, and Murry and his Infantry would take up positions to cut off escape on the river side. Because of the large number of innocents in the camp, Flandrau gave orders to the men to make sure of their targets before firing. But he also cautioned them not to take any chances, for some of the men in the camp were known murderers and had to be captured or killed.

"Watch for anyone running out of the camp, they will be the ones we're after," was his last advice to the soldiers.

After the plans were made and the orders given, John Other Day led the way across the dark prairie.

After about only an hour, they approached Man Who Hates Fish's village. The soldiers moved into position as quickly and quietly as they could, but something woke Roaring Cloud. Maybe it was the squeaking of the leather saddles or jiggling of the bridles on the cavalry mules. Or perhaps it was a canteen thumping against an infantryman's hip or a whispered curse of a man who twisted his ankle. He had been a fugitive from one enemy or another for most of his life and was not a stranger to danger coming in the night. He listened for only a moment before waking Rattling and Young Inkpaduta. Soon all three could hear the movement in the darkness. Quickly, Roaring Cloud formed a plan of escape.

"Rattling and Young Inkpaduta," he whispered, "When the clouds cover the moon again, make a break up river." He took Young Inkpaduta's young wife by the arm and said, "I'll take the girl and run for the river. When we get there, we'll follow the bank down river. After you lose the soldiers, circle around and meet us on the far side."

"But what of these other women?" Rattling asked fondly, patting Man Who Hates Fish's youngest wife on her round rump.

"They can lay low here in the tipi," Roaring Cloud answered, adding, "It is not them they want."

"But why can't I take my wife to the river and you decoy the white soldiers?" Young Inkpaduta asked.

"Don't argue little brother!" Roaring Cloud hissed. "I will be better able to protect her," he added, indicating the short double-barreled shotgun he had acquired at the Noble and Thatcher cabin during the attack at *Okobooshi*. "I will take good care of her!"

Suddenly, the clouds blocked the moon and the time for discussion was over. Rattling and Young Inkpaduta jumped up and ran out of the tipi. Roaring Cloud and the *Mdewakanton* girl followed them out the door, but turned and ran toward the river. Just as suddenly as the clouds had moved to block the moon, they thinned and the village was again bathed in the light of an almost full moon.

Rattling and Young Inkpaduta had only reached the edge of the camp, and with an instinctive reaction to the sudden lightening of the sky, the two men dove into a tipi, snuggling in with the occupants, who had also been awakened by the approaching soldiers. Fearfully, they crouched, holding their silence.

The moonlight caught Roaring Cloud and the girl in the open on the grassy slope leading to the river, and they had no recourse but to keep running. The girl, realizing the danger of being near Roaring Cloud, lagged back, trying to break free from his grip on her wrist. She fell and he dragged her after him, grunting with effort and straining to keep his speed. He cursed to himself about having to pull the woman along with him.

"Halt. Stay where you are!" came a command in English from somewhere in the dark shadows along the riverbank ahead of him.

Roaring Cloud stopped and released his hold on the girl. She sank to the ground whimpering fearfully. He stood watching the darkness in front of him, wishing now that he had let Young Inkpaduta come this way with the girl. He wondered why there had been no gunfire coming from the direction that Rattling and his brother had run. Anger suddenly clouded his reason, and he raised his shotgun and fired blindly in the direction of the river. An answering volley of fourteen rifles splattered the earth around him. Two slugs took his legs out from under him, and he fell to the ground with a loud grunt.

Ignoring Young Inkpaduta's wife's screaming, he reloaded quickly. The girl had been hit in the arm and was terrified, but there was little he could do to help her now. Sensing movement to his right, he sat up and swiveling his torso, fired both barrels of his shotgun.

Again there was an immediate answering volley of rifle fire. This time, the soldiers had pinpointed his muzzle flash, and Roaring Cloud was struck several times in the body. The force of the bullets striking him knocked him back. He rolled to his stomach and tried to crawl, but because of his wounded legs, he couldn't move far. There was no place to hide anyway. With the last of his strength, he loaded the shotgun again and waited, trying to hear any movement in the darkness that might give him a target. But the screams of the wounded girl on the ground behind him made it impossible for him to hear anything else.

"Shut up, woman!" he shouted.

"Drop yer gun an' give it up, Redskin," came an order from someone who had approached from behind him.

Roaring Cloud stretched his neck in the direction the voice had come from and thought that he could see movement. Without hesitating, he raised his shotgun and fired it for the last time. The answering fire from the infantrymen, who had moved in closer and could now see his dark form on the ground against the sea of grass, riddled his body from head to toe.

Everyone in the village was awake. The women and children were crying and screaming with fear, and the men stood in groups, looking down on the scene near the river. Flandrau's cavalry rode through the village, ignoring the people standing around the tipis to join Murry by the body of Roaring Cloud. Rattling and Young Inkpaduta took this opportunity to slip out of the village and disappeared into the vast darkness of the plains to the west. They traveled back to the village on the James River to find Inkpaduta and give him the news that he would not be welcome in Minnesota and that his son, Roaring Cloud, was dead.

# Chapter 38
## *Warnings*

*My Hunter has left – I cry*
*He shall not return –I cry*
*His bones are scattered – I cry*
*I won't see him in the next life –I die!*

*I don't need his children –I cry*
*I don't need his weapons – I cry*
*I don't need his clothing –I cry*
*I don't need his shelter – I die!*
*I Die! I Die! I Die! I Die!*

**O**ver and over, Afraid of Her Husband Woman sang her mourning chant. Her voice wavered high and piercing and then low, choking with emotion. Sobbing, her cheeks streamed with tears. Her husband Roaring Cloud was dead, and her tearful lament summoned everyone in the village. The people gathered close to listen. Dragging her crying children by their hands, she delivered them to Fire Cloud. He was their uncle. Now, custom said he was their father. She gave Roaring Cloud's weapons to Rain Cloud and gave his clothing to Inkpaduta.

Methodically, as she sang, she handed out all of her possessions to friends and relatives in the crowd of people surrounding her. Piece by piece, she gave away everything except for the clothes on her back. When her tipi was empty, she pushed Young Inkpaduta over to it and shoved him inside. It was his now. She had no use for it. She planned to die.

The recipients of her gifts walked slowly away, and she began her grieving in earnest. Jerking and pulling at her hair, great clumps came away in handfuls, leaving large raw wounds on her head. She slashed her legs and arms with a hide scraper, making them bleed. Staring off in the distance, her eyes were glassy and shone with the light of the insane. With a final act of total grief, she hacked and sawed at the fingers of her left hand until she completely severed her little finger and watched it fall to the ground. Screaming in incoherent agony, she fell to the ground, her body shaking and quivering with uncontrollable convulsions.

Finally, the convulsions stopped, and she lay very still. Blood streamed from her numerous wounds and many thought she was dead. But suddenly, her voice returned to the grief chant for her lost husband:

*My Hunter is dead! – Ah-eee!*
*I am alone. – Ah-eee Alone!*
*My children are not mine! – Ah-eee!*
*My tipi is not mine. – Aheee!*

*I have no hunter! – Aheee!*
*I have no children! – Aheee!*
*I have no shelter! – Aheee!*
*I have no food! – Aheee!*
*I Die! I Die! I Die! I Die!*

Stumbling to her feet, the grief stricken woman staggered from the camp, leaving a trail of blood on the sun-dried grass. Even after the sunset and night came, her keening could be heard coming from out of the darkness.

Many of the people thought they would never see Afraid of Her Husband Woman again, but even in her deep grief, the resiliency of her strong body and innate will to live kept her alive. As the days passed into weeks, she became known as Lost Woman. She wandered the edges of the camp for days. She slept in the open without even the benefit of a blanket for shelter. Her only food was what scraps she could wrestle away from the camp dogs. She could exist this way during the warm weather but when the cold times came, she would surely die unless someone took her into their tipi and made her a part of their family.

Two weeks after Young Inkpaduta and Rattling arrived with the news of Roaring Cloud's death, Inkpaduta ordered the camp to pack. He decided that they would move back to Minnesota despite the danger. His anger over the murdering of his son would not quiet and let him sleep at night. He would try to find out who had betrayed Roaring Cloud.

The next morning found them traveling east. The rolling prairie shimmered with the sun's light glistening on the waving grass, rustling in the endless breeze of the open, treeless plain. Ever wary,

Inkpaduta watched his back trail and soon discovered that they were being followed. On the fourth day out, Lost One was still following them, and Inkpaduta knew that someone in the camp had to be giving her food. He called a halt and began asking questions. It was time for someone to take the woman in, especially if they were feeding her. He was surprised when his own wife, Hates Her Father Woman came forward, admitting that it was she who had been feeding Lost One.

"Inkpaduta," she cried, prostrating herself on the ground before him. "I am an old woman. My work is too much for me to do alone. Living with the wild Yanktons has proven it to me. There is no wood for fires, so I must find dried buffalo dung to burn. I must carry water long distances and scrape hides, make clothing, dry meat, put up your tipi, take down your tipi, load the travois and cook your meals." She was crying. "While we had the white slaves, life was easier, but now I am too old to do all of this work alone!"

"Lost One is still young and healthy," the old crone whispered, crawling on her knees to him. There was a cunning light in her eyes as she pulled him down where he could hear her whispered words. "She is experienced in giving a man pleasure. You wouldn't have to teach her your needs. Your own son bragged many times about how willing his wife was to soften his stone."

Inkpaduta stood, and his eyes traveled around the ring of faces surrounding them. Lost One would be a great help to Hates Her Father Woman, and her body under the robes would make the cold nights much warmer for himself. He found it hard to argue with such logic. He announced that they would wait for the woman to catch up. He would take her into his lodge, and she would become his second wife. Her name was to become Follows the Camp Woman.

A week later, they crossed the river into Minnesota on the same log bridge where they had killed Sick One. After crossing, they set up camp, and Inkpaduta sent out scouts. Though still several days from the Agency, he was cautious and wanted no surprises. His caution was justified early the next morning. Big Face raced into the camp with a warning that a large group of mounted men were approaching from the south. Quickly, the women hurried back across the log bridge and hid in the underbrush on the far side of the river. The men spread out and took cover behind rocks and trees along the riverbank. They aimed their rifles at the clearing where Inkpaduta sat alone by a fire, smoking his pipe.

One hundred mounted *Santee* soon rode into sight. Inkpaduta was surprised to see such a mixed force of warriors of the Eastern Fires of the *Dakotah* Nation riding together. His eyes moved over the crowd of riders, and he recognized the dress of three of the four tribes. A glimmer of hope passed through his mind, thinking that maybe the *Santee* were finally banding together to fight against the whites and drive them from their land. He would gladly join them. There were People of the Mystic Lake, (*Mdewakanton*) led by Little Crow, People of the Leaves (*Wahpeton*) led by Hole in His Nose, and People of the Swamps (*Sissiton*) led by a young man named Wakeaska, but Inkpaduta saw no members of his own tribe, the People Who Shoot Among the Leaves (*Wahpekute*), and he realized that it was not white men these warriors were looking for.

The mounted warriors pulled to a halt a short distance from his campfire site and began milling about. He could see that they were all looking at him and could hear their voices raise and lower as they argued about what they wanted to do. Finally, Little Crow and Wakeaska left the throng of riders and strode on foot slowly over to where Inkpaduta sat. Little Crow's eyes scanned the area, looking for Inkpaduta's warriors, knowing that he was not really alone. Inkpaduta could see caution in Little Crow's eyes. Wakeaska's eyes showed only anger.

"Welcome!" Inkpaduta called. "Sit. Smoke." He offered up his pipe.

The two men sat opposite Inkpaduta and took turns sucking on the long stemmed ceremonial pipe he handed them. Inkpaduta chuckled silently as each man winced when the sharpness of the *Yanktoni* tobacco bit his tongue. When each man had finished blowing the sickly green smoke and handed the pipe back to Inkpaduta, he started the council by asking a question.

"Why does a man of the Mystic Lake People ride at the front of the People of the Leaves and the People of the Swamps?"

"The sun rose high this day and warmed us all with its strength," Little Crow answered, ignoring Inkpaduta's question. He had been elected speaker for the agency *Santee,* and he knew that all of his skills of persuasion would be needed on this day. He could feel the guns of Inkpaduta's warriors boring into his back. He smiled and continued, "How have the passing of these many *moons* treated Inkpaduta's people? Are the *Yanktons* still living the good life?"

"The *Yanktons* are living the same life as always, without the curse of your white friends telling them where they can live and where they can't live," Inkpaduta stated simply. He watched the two men before him and saw only surprise at the harshness of his words in Little Crow's face, but saw a flash of anger in the eyes of Wakeaska.

"The soldiers are angry about the killings at *Okobooshi!*" Wakeaska shouted rudely, ignoring the look of warning that Little Crow gave him. He was a Sissiton leader and had enjoyed a happy life on the agency lands. "The agent has taken our annuity payments away and says he will not pay them again until we bring you or your scalp back."

"Inkpaduta, my friend," Little Crow interrupted, sensing the tension growing. "On the night that your son was killed by the white soldiers, they also took the young woman who was with him prisoner. They say they will not release her until you return to face up to the crimes you committed at the blue water lake." He stopped to clear his throat and started to continue, but was interrupted by Wakeaska.

"*Wahpekute,* you have caused trouble in our homeland. You killed the whites at the southern lakes. You took their women. The Whites want your scalp for this. They are punishing the rest of us for your crimes! For this you will pay."

When the *Sissiton* leader jumped to his feet and stood glaring down at Inkpaduta, Little Crow tensed, expecting the sound of a gunshot that would drop Wakeaska. Inkpaduta's angry eyes shot up at Wakeaska, but his mouth spoke to Little Crow.

"Leader of the People of the Mystic Lake, tell this low swamp dog to leave my council fire. He is young and foolish, so I will let him live out of respect for you. But if he doesn't leave now, my dogs will bark, and he will die!"

Little Crow jumped to his feet and took Wakeaska by the shoulder, leading him a short distance away. Angrily, he berated the *Sissiton* leader for his hot temper and warned him of Inkpaduta's men, hidden in the trees–his dogs who could bark death from the ends of their gun barrels. Then with a short push, he sent the angry young man back to the rest of the warriors and returned to sit with Inkpaduta again.

"They are angry. The white agent has shut off the annuity payments. It was the return of your sons that triggered this." Nervously, Little Crow cleared his throat again and continued, "They have the girl as a prisoner and have said that they will not release her or pay out any annuity money until we hunt you down and bring you in. I agreed to lead a party to look for you but I never thought that we would actually find you! I thought you were in the land of the *Yanktoni,* and we could tell them that it was only your one son who had been foolish enough to return to Minnesota. The only reason I agreed to lead this hunt was to appease the agent."

"I do not want to fight a war with my brothers, the *Wahpekute.* As you probably noticed, none of your tribe joined in this hunt," Little Crow stated, relaxing a little. "I have a plan. I have some old scalps and three women who were captured years ago from the *Winnebago.* We will give them to the agent and will tell him that we couldn't catch you, but these scalps and women were part of your people. In this way, we will collect our reward and get our annuity money," Little Crow finished, laughing at his plan to fool the agent.

Inkpaduta didn't join in the laughter. He stared into the fire, showing little indication that he had heard a word Little Crow had spoken. He raised his eyes to look in the direction of Little Crow's warriors, many of whom had dismounted and were talking to the angry Wakeaska.

"How many of them rode with the soldiers who killed my son?" He brought his eyes back to look directly into Little Crow's eyes and continued, saying, "I came to find any who helped the whites and kill them."

Little Crow recognized the hatred in Inkpaduta's voice, and he knew that there would be nothing but trouble if this man were to return to the agency lands. He felt a certain desperation growing.

"Stay in the west, Inkpaduta," he begged. "Do not come back to the land of lakes and rivers. Their anger will pass when the annuity payments continue."

"Annuities for your people mean little to me when my belly is empty!" Inkpaduta answered with an angry chuckle. "I have never been given my share of the annuities, and you expect me to care if you don't get yours?" He leaned back and tapped his pipe on the heel of his moccasined foot, brushing the black soot away with his hand.

"These precious annuities will one day get you into trouble, Little Crow," Inkpaduta warned. "One day soon, your young men will get tired of living as dogs of the white agent, and they will kill him. Who will pay your annuities when that happens? Then you will see that I am right. The white men should be driven out! There will be war! I only hope it won't be too late."

Little Crow groaned. There were people living at the agency now who agreed with Inkpaduta. But Little Crow had visited the Great White Father's home in the east. He had seen the power of the white army and knew that the whites were too strong to fight a war against. He also knew it would be fruitless to argue that with Inkpaduta now. Wanting to end this council, but also wanting to make sure that Inkpaduta caused him no more trouble, he stood brushing the dead grass from his leggings and offered his hand to Inkpaduta.

"For the good of all of the people," he said when their eyes met, "yours and mine, stay in the west Inkpaduta. Stay with the *Yanktons*. There are too many at the agency that feel as Wakeaska feels. There are too many who would have your scalp. It will not be safe for you there. And if they kill you, your people will avenge you. How about it old friend? If there is war, I would just as soon it be against the whites, not against each other." Without giving Inkpaduta a chance to answer, Little Crow turned and walked away. At his word, his warriors mounted, and they rode south.

Little Crow's warning to stay away from the agency lands filled Inkpaduta with stark indignation. *Minne sota*, his beloved land of lakes and rivers, was the home of his ancestors. It was a place where the *Wahpekute* had gone to seek shelter during the cold *moons* for generations, and the desire to live in that land was deeply ingrained in his soul.

It angered him to remember how eager the men of the Eastern Fires had been to follow him in killing the whites at Springfield earlier that year. Now, neither Sleepy Eye nor Black Buffalo would accept any of the blame. It angered him more to realize that he had actually brought more guilt upon himself by leading the attacks at Springfield. By leaving the area, he had led the pursuit away from the local *Santee* and put all of the blame upon his people. It was with great reluctance that he ordered his women to break camp and led them back to the west to find Long Arm's *Yanktons*. They would honor Little Crow's request for now. He would send scouts back to the agency each summer to see if the *Santee* were still happy living as the white agent's dogs. When they tired of licking the white man's boots and finally became warriors again, he would return.

# Chapter 39
## *Uprising! (1862)*

Following the council with Little Crow on the banks of the Big Sioux River, Inkpaduta led his people back to the James River to live with the *Yanktons*. Each summer after the year of Roaring Cloud's death, Inkpaduta sent a pair of scouts back to the agency to test the mood of the agency Indians. Charly and Gunn were sent the first summer.

They returned to report that the annuity payments had been reinstated after Little Crow turned over the Winnebago women and bragged to the Agent about chasing Inkpaduta's outlaw band back to the west.

Rain Cloud and One Leg went the next year and reported that the *Santee* were content and not interested in having Inkpaduta's band return. Fire Cloud and Big Face reported the same after their visit on the third summer. Charly and Gunn went again in the fourth summer. When they came back, they brought news that the whites were fighting each other in a great war. The battles were far to the south, but the war was drawing soldiers from the Minnesota forts, leaving fewer soldiers to watch over the reservations.

Rattling and Young Inkpaduta made the trip east in the summer of the fifth year arriving at Man Who Hates Fish's village early in the *Moon When The Cherries Turn Black*. When they rode into the village, they were surprised to find it nearly empty. A young woman sitting alone by the fire quickly told them that Man Who Hates Fish expected trouble and had moved his wives and children to another village farther from the traders' cabins.

She said the trouble began the year before when the annuity payments were late in arriving. The agent couldn't pay them their annuities, but convinced the traders to allow the *Santee* people to run a line of credit so they could buy their food supplies. When the government money shipment did arrive, it was less than it was supposed to be, and the annuity payments were only half of what they should have been. Unfortunately, most of the people had used credit with the Traders for the full amount of what the annuity payments were supposed to be and could not pay off their debts.

With hunting growing poorer and poorer each passing year, the *Santee* had become dependent on the trade goods they purchased with their annuity money. The annuity payments were late again this year, but since most of the debts had been left unpaid, the Traders cut off all credit. The people were hungry, and the children cried themselves to sleep each night.

Little Crow tried to talk the new man in charge of the agency, Agent Galbraith, into ordering the traders to extend credit again. Galbraith was new to the job and unsure how to handle the situation. He called a council inviting the *Santee* leaders and the white traders. When everyone had gathered at the Redwood Agency, he asked the traders to consider extending more credit to the Indians.

A man named Andrew Myrick stood to speak for the rest of the Traders. Myrick was a bad-tempered little man. He had trouble collecting the *Santee* debts the year before and cared little for the reasons why they had not been able to pay.

"Honorable men pay their debts," Myrick stated flatly. "These Indians did not do that. We gave them credit, but they did not pay it back. They are not honorable, trustworthy men."

"The annuity payments were short last year because of the cost of the war," Galbraith stated. "And the money shipment is late again this year for the same reason. The Government will make it right with you. You know that," he added.

"Do I?" Myrick questioned, looking around at the rest of the traders. "The war is not going all that well, Galbraith. You know that as well as any of us! What if the North loses? Who is going to pay these debts if that happens?" he sneered.

"But if you won't extend them credit, how do I feed these people?" Galbraith asked in frustration, adding, "They are hungry."

"If they are hungry," Myrick brashly cried before the assembly of white traders and *Santee* leaders, "let them eat grass. Or, if they are real hungry," he continued with an angry grin, "let them eat their own shit, for they'll get no credit from me!" and he turned and stalked off.

The *Santee* leaders left the meeting screaming with anger and frustration and returned to their villages to report the disappointing outcome to their people.

Rattling and Young Inkpaduta moved to the village of a *Mdewakanton* man called Red Middle Voice. They shared a tipi with Rattling's cousin. Remembering the many enemies they had living at the agencies, they tried to keep a low profile, but were instantly recognized by Young Inkpaduta's wife who had been wounded when

Roaring Cloud was killed. She was disappointed that he didn't return for her, but since had married another man.

She ran off to spread the word that the men who had killed the whites at *Okobooshi* had returned. The two men began hurriedly packing their belongings, expecting trouble. But before they could flee, they found themselves surrounded by a throng of young warriors, all wanting them to relate the story of how they attacked the whites and killed them. That night, they told and retold the story of their attack on each of the Iowa cabins and at Springfield in southern Minnesota five years before, to a growing group of young warriors, who were tired of living under White Man rule.

Two nights later, four young *Wahpeton* men who had taken *Mdewakanton* wives and were living in Red Middle Voice's village with their wives' parents, thundered into the village on horses they had stolen from a white farm, just outside of the agency lands. The horses were lathered, and the young men, Brown Wing, Breaking Up, Killing Ghost, and Runs Against Something When Crawling, were excited and frightened. They told Red Middle Voice that on their way back to the village from another unsuccessful hunt, they came across a chicken nesting along the road.

"Brown Wing warned me not to steal the chicken's eggs because the chicken belonged to a white man," Killing Ghost related. "I told him that he was a coward if he did not want to steal the eggs. I told him he was a woman and afraid of the white man."

"To prove he was not afraid of the white man," Runs Against Something When Crawling continued the story. "Brown Wing led us to the white man's cabin. We talked the white men there into a target shooting match and when their guns were empty, Brown Wing shot one man. Then, Breaking Up and I shot two more white men. Killing Ghost shot a woman and Brown Wing went into the cabin and shot a younger woman, but we did not kill her baby."

"We were excited. We tricked them like Young Inkpaduta said they killed the whites at *Okobooshi*," Brown Wing said, "but now we are frightened. We don't know what to do."

Red Middle Voice rushed them out of his village, taking them to the village of a man named Shakopee. Shakopee had been present at the council when Trader Myrick made his statement about feeding the hungry children grass, and his young men were eager for a fight with the whites. The two leaders decided that a council of war should be called immediately. They sent runners to the villages of Mankato, Wabasha, Traveling Hail and Big Eagle to summon them to Little Crow's village.

Rattling and Young Inkpaduta could hardly believe what was happening and knew that their father would be pleased. He had predicted a war with the whites for many years. They traveled through the dark night to Little Crow's village and attended the war council. Little Crow was reluctant to make war on the whites. He related to the assembled warriors about how powerful the white man army was.

The other leaders all reminded him that the white army was fighting a big war against another white army and was much weaker than they had ever been. If ever they were going to drive the whites out of Minnesota, now was the time! Realizing that he was losing the argument, Little Crow finally agreed to lead the *Santee* into battle against the whites.

Soon after sunup the next morning, three hundred *Mdewakantons* and *Wahpekutes* arrived at the Redwood Agency. It was a small settlement of trader's stores, Agent Galbraith's quarters and government barns. Screaming a war cry, Little Crow raised his war lance and threw it at the door of Andrew Myrick's cabin. Gunfire began, and the traders and government employees began to die. The first to fall died behind their counters or in the stables, performing their daily chores with no knowledge of the coming tragedy.

The sound of gunfire was deafening. Andrew Myrick's helper was one of the first to die behind the trader's counter. Myrick was quick to dash out the back door and ran north for the river. He had run only a few yards when Rattling shot him through the legs. The wounded trader climbed to his feet and tried to hobble on but was knocked down by a charging Young Inkpaduta. Before he could get to his feet again, three men from Little Crow's village jumped on him and held him down. Another man raced up and shoved handfuls of grass and horse dung into his mouth. He gagged, choking on the dried offal and stared in wide-eyed terror as Rattling shoved his rifle into Myrick's stomach and pulled the trigger. Trader Myrick, gut shot and choking on a mouthful of grass and horse dung, died slowly.

Approximately twelve white men were killed at the onset of the attack. After the initial onslaught, the hungry *Santee* began plundering the stores and warehouses. This preoccupation with the foodstuffs and other goods allowed many other whites to escape across the Minnesota River to the north and travel the eighteen miles of prairie to Fort Ridgely. After looting the buildings at the Redwood Agency, the warriors spread across the frontier, raiding isolated farmsteads and killing every white person they met.

When the day ended, there was a wild celebration by the young warriors. Rattling and Young Inkpaduta took part in the dancing and singing of war songs, but were called aside to meet with Little Crow. He wanted them to travel back to Inkpaduta and inform him of the war right away.

Little Crow planned to attack Fort Ridgely early the next morning. With a victory over the white soldiers at Ridgely, he thought it would be easier to recruit more warriors from some of the *Santee* bands that were showing reluctance to join them. He thought that capturing a fort might even help get their ancient enemies, the Chippewa, to rise up against the whites in the northern parts of the state. After Fort Ridgely, they would attack Fort Ripley. He also planned to send a force to the Dakota Territory to attack Fort Abercrombie on the Red River. He told Young Inkpaduta and Rattling that he wanted Inkpaduta to meet up with that force and lead the attack.

If the *Santee* could get some quick victories over the white military and at least get them to abandon the forts in Minnesota, he planned to sue for peace before the white army could shift their soldiers from the war against their white brothers to the south. He would offer the White Father his forts back for more annuity payments and fairer treatment from the traders who the government licensed to trade with the *Santee*. With this message, Young Inkpaduta and Rattling left immediately to find Inkpaduta and give him the good news.

*       *       *

They rode into Long Arm's *Yankton* village several days later on worn ponies. They were tired and hungry, but word of their arrival spread quickly and soon everyone in the village had gathered to listen as the two young men delivered Little Crow's message to Inkpaduta. He was overjoyed that his prediction of a war with the whites had finally come true! He called a council and invited the young men of Long Arm's village to join him when he went to meet with Little Crow's force of *Santee* to attack Fort Abercrombie.

A great roar of approval met this suggestion, and the next morning they rode into the rising sun. It was a large force, well mounted, but poorly armed. They carried but a few firearms. Most had only bows and arrows, and some relied only on their war clubs and knives. But most were young men who knew no fear and worried little about their poor armaments.

Two days later, they came upon the first sign of white existence. They topped a rise and saw a small cabin nestled by a stream at the bottom of the hill. They rushed down upon the cabin, screaming wild cries of battle, but were disappointed to find it was abandoned. News of the war to the east had arrived ahead of them, and each cabin they came to that day was empty. They ransacked and burned these lonely buildings each time they found one. They pushed on, and fifteen miles south of Fort Abercrombie, they arrived at the small community of Breckenridge.

Approaching the town from the west, they could see that it had been evacuated. There were no signs of life. The buildings were dark, and some had the doors boarded up. At least the abandoned town held more promise of plunder than the lonely cabins and barns of the countryside.

Plundering was new to Long Arm's young men, who had never even seen many white people. They ran through each building, taking everything from bright colored clothing to preserved foodstuffs. They had never seen such finery, and after finding a supply of whiskey in one of the buildings, went wildly out of control. Several young men raced to the largest building in town. It was a two-story hotel, and they were sure it held riches beyond anything they had ever seen before. When they burst through the door, screaming with excitement, a shotgun blast greeted them! The double loaded charge caught Long Arm's nephew, Leaps On His Horse, full in the chest, knocking him back out of the building, where he landed in a crumpled heap on the steps.

At the sound of the gunshot, the rest of the fighting force rushed to the hotel and upon entering, found Leaps On His Horse's friends surrounding three white men and a woman with a baby. The man with the double-barreled shotgun had not reloaded. He held the gun by the barrel, ready to use it as a club. It appeared that it was the only weapon they had as the other two men stood behind him, their fists up, ready to defend the woman and child. The young *Yanktons* stood at bay, not knowing what to do.

When Inkpaduta arrived, he laughed with contempt and shot the man with the shotgun. Fire Cloud and Rain Cloud each shot one of the other men and all three men dropped, dead or dying in an instant.

The woman jumped to her feet, screaming in terror and clutched the baby so tightly it began to cry. Young Inkpaduta swung his war club, striking the woman behind the ear and snatched the child from her stunned arms as she staggered backwards, trying not to fall. Laughing, he threw the child across the room, where it bounced on the floor and began crying louder.

Fire Cloud picked the infant up by the heels and smashed its head against the stone fireplace. Young Inkpaduta tore the injured woman's clothes off and knocked her to the floor and raped her. She struggled weakly as each of the young warriors took turns with her. She died long before her ordeal was finished.

376

The war party spent the night in the empty buildings of Breckenridge. In the morning, scouts reported a large force of Indians approaching from the south. Inkpaduta led his men out to greet them. It was the war party of *Santee* sent by Little Crow to attack Fort Abercrombie. A Sissiton named Sweet Corn led them.

The fort sat on the west bank of the Red River in the northern Dakota Territory. It was a fort in name only. There was no stockade to protect the enlisted men's barracks, officers' quarters, a commissary, guardhouse, Sutler's Store and stables. The buildings were scattered across a small knoll just above the flood plain. Without advanced warning, Fort Abercrombie would have been highly indefensible against a force of several hundred armed warriors. But the news of the "Sioux Uprising" had preceded the attackers by several days in the form of an influx of refugees.

The commander ordered his few troops to build a barricade between the main buildings using overturned wagons, furniture, barrels and building material. The stables, housing not only the army's horses, but also all the livestock, including cattle, chickens and hogs, brought by the civilian population, were outside of the barricade, as was the fort's only source for drinking water, the river.

On a cool morning in the *Moon When the Calves Grow Hair,* Inkpaduta led his men silently, crawling toward the stables. They had watched the fort for two days and noticed the activity around the stables, which indicated that there were horses, cattle, chickens and hogs in the stables.

Inkpaduta planned to take the livestock from the stables and use it to feed his men while they fought, and their families for many *moons* after the battle was over. He expected it to be an easy raid. They would quickly run into the stables, release the animals there and drive them out, before the white defenders knew they were even there.

As they crawled quickly through the tall grass, a sharp-eyed sentry spotted one of the *Yankton* warriors, who carelessly stood up to look ahead at the stables. The sentry fired his rifle in warning. The bullet passed close over some of the young men's heads, and the sound of its whining snap frightened them. Five jumped up and ran away. Afraid that the panic would spread, Inkpaduta charged toward the stables shouting encouragement, and most of his force followed him.

The sentry was calling for help and after reloading, took cover behind a rain barrel. The sentry from the other end of the stables was also calling for help, and soon soldiers and armed civilians, who had been sleeping with their loaded rifles, poured from behind the barricade to join the two sentries in the stables. Inkpaduta's men managed to open one pen and drive five cattle out of the stable before gunfire from the reinforcements forced them to take cover. They returned the gunfire while trying to move deeper into the building, hoping to release more animals. But through the noise of the frightened bellering of the cattle and neighing of horses, Inkpaduta could hear evidence of even more fighters from the fort as the soldiers from inside the barricade shouted questions. He was hoping that Sweet Corn would lead a charge on the fort to take some of the attention away from the stables. But no attack came, and as the morning wore on, and the sun rose higher, its rays grew warmer. The air inside the stable was stifling from the heat. Soon the overpowering smell of heated manure made it hard for the Indians in the building to breathe.

When it became evident that there was no imminent danger of an attack on the fort, a patrol of several more soldiers left the barricade and concentrated their gunfire on the Indians occupying the stables. The odds in the battle were sharply against him, and Inkpaduta knew it. He had no choice but to pull his men out and retreat.

It was a bitter defeat for Inkpaduta. Two of his men had been killed and another one wounded. The warriors left the stables dragging the dead men and carrying the wounded man. They had gained only a few head of cattle and one pair of workhorses. Inkpaduta was not anxious to fight a fortified enemy again.

Two days later, Sweet Corn and a *Yankton* leader named Crane Legs convinced him that an attack from all sides at once with their entire force might be successful. Once again, Inkpaduta led his force on the stables. Sweet Corn led his men from the north and Crane Legs' force attacked from out of the west trying to gain entrance to the Sutler's Store.

The attack started going wrong, even before their plans could be put into motion. The soldiers brought into use a weapon that not even Inkpaduta had seen used before. As Sweet Corn massed his men on the flat plain to the north of the fort, well-directed cannon fire landed amongst the mounted men. The cannon balls exploded on impact, sending hot chucks of lead into the Indians. Searing fragments slammed into men and horses alike, maiming and killing with each blast. In a matter of only moments, Sweet Corn's entire force was in complete disarray; dead, wounded, or running away! The attack from the north never materialized because Crane Legs' men saw the destruction of Sweet Corn's force and dropped their plans to attack altogether.

Not knowing what the loud blasts from the cannon shots were, nor the effects they were having on the other attacking forces, Inkpaduta started leading his men against the stables once again. This time there was an even larger force of soldiers and civilians in the stables, and they defended it so well that Inkpaduta stopped his men before they even reached the buildings. Dodging from one bit of cover to another, he led his men back out of rifle range and went to look for Sweet Corn.

More than twenty men had been killed, and several more were wounded. It was not known if any of the enemy had been killed, or wounded. Inkpaduta refused any further attacks. He would be content to lay siege to the fort.

Day after day, they sniped at the occupants of the fort from long range and kept the whites from sending messengers for help. They harassed the water detail sent to the river for water, but could not stop them from filling their water barrels, because each time they tried to attack, the fort's cannons began raining shot at them.

Two white men were killed when a detachment guarding a messenger was ambushed as they tried to leave the fort. The two men fell from their horses and were captured, but the rest of the detail made it through and rode off to the east. In their anger and frustration, Inkpaduta's men shot the prisoners full of arrows and chopped them to pieces. As the siege wore on, many of the young men grew bored and went home.

Inkpaduta's force grew smaller and smaller with each passing day. A *Sissiton* messenger arrived looking for Sweet Corn with the news that Little Crow had failed to take Fort Ridgely, and that the attack on Fort Ripley never had came about because too many *Santee* refused to take part. The war in the east had gone badly, and Little Crow and many of his men had scattered or were in hiding.

That same afternoon, a force of four hundred and fifty soldiers and civilians arrived in relief of Fort Abercrombie, and Inkpaduta sadly recognized defeat. As Sweet Corn and the *Santee* rode back to the east to see what they could salvage at the reservations, Inkpaduta led his force of *Wahpekutes* and *Yanktons* back to the west, knowing he would never go home again.

# Chapter 40
## The Prairie War

*"These miserable wretches, who among all devils in human shape, are among the most cruel and ferocious . . . I will sweep them with the besom of death!"* – Brigadier General Henry H. Sibley to Minnesota Governor Alexander Ramsey

*"It is my purpose to utterly exterminate the Sioux if I have the power to do so . . . They are to be treated as maniacs or wild beasts."* – Major General John Pope, Commander of the Military, Department of the Northwest

On December 26, 1862, thirty-eight *Santee* leaders were simultaneously "hanged by the neck until dead" in Mankato, Minnesota. Hundreds more were imprisoned. Many of the prisoners became sick and died while waiting to hear their fate. Hundreds more escaped to the west or were torn from their ancient homes and herded unwillingly to the western territories, banished from the State of Minnesota forever. Still, nearly five hundred settlers and soldiers were killed in the Sioux War, and public outcry by the white residents of Minnesota demanded more action against the *Santee* people.

Feeling this pressure from the white populace, Major General John Pope struck orders from his office in St. Paul for a final expedition against the *Santee* that would punish those who had escaped and would rid Minnesota of its Indian problem, once and for all.

Pope's orders included a two-pronged movement. One force of two thousand men, led by the experienced Civil War officer, Brigadier General Alfred Sully, marched out of Sioux City, Iowa, marching up the Missouri River. Another force of three thousand men, led by the recently promoted hero of the Sioux Uprising, Brigadier General Henry H. Sibley, departed from Fort Ridgely, marching west across the plains. The two forces were ordered to move slowly toward one another, pushing the Indians between them. The plan was to harass the fugitives' campsites and disrupt their hunting, thereby forcing them together, while at the same time isolating them into one group that could be found and contended with. Sully and Sibley were to rendezvous on the Missouri River. Their orders after joining forces were to capture or destroy the entire *Santee* fighting force . . . a job both officers were eager to do.

*     *     *

It was a hot night. The tipi walls were rolled up. Inkpaduta rolled away from Follows the Camp Woman's naked body to look out over the shadowed plains. Needing to urinate, he stood and looked down at his son's widow. She murmured softly and rolled into a tight ball as a slight breeze swept through under the tipi walls, cooling her sweating skin and raising goose flesh across her hips.

Grinning, he threw a robe over Follows the Camp Woman. She was a good worker and helped Hates Her Father Woman with all of her chores. She was especially good at performing her wifely duties in bed, something Hates Her Father Woman wasn't interested in any more. He was proud that a man of his age could keep a woman so young as his son's widow sexually satisfied. She seemed genuinely grateful that he had taken her into his lodge and used her as a wife.

He left the tipi and walked to the small stream they were camped by. Standing on a high bank, he relieved himself into the slow moving water. As the pressure left his body, he sighed a contented sigh and contemplated his situation in relationship to what had happened over the past year. He was strong and healthy, and his position among his people had improved since the *Santee* war against the whites in Minnesota. He was no longer considered an outlaw among his own people. No longer were the people who followed him known as outcasts. He was one of the few *Santee* leaders left. Most had been imprisoned or hanged, and the few leaders yet alive were scattered far and wide.

There were hundreds of refugees who left the Minnesota country to find safety from the white man's retribution with the wild tribes in the west. Almost every day, for several weeks after the failed uprising, more people came wandering across the plains, looking for a leader to join up with. They reminded him of the people who came to follow his father back in the days when Wamdisapa chose to fight against the Sauk and Fox and Winnebago people, rather than sign treaties for peace among the tribes that the white men wanted him to sign. He felt a grim satisfaction, thinking that those people who had shunned his father were either dead or incarcerated now. He also felt secret satisfaction in knowing that the *Santee* leaders who had looked down on him and his people for so many years, were fugitives from the whites, much in the same way he had been after the killing of the whites at *Okobooshi*. He remembered the council with Little Crow and Wakeaska shortly after the death of Roaring Cloud. Anger still grew within his breast at the memory of Wakeaska's insolence and bad manners at that council. Many times since that day, he had wished that he had killed the man then and there. But it looked like the white men had taken care of that for him. According to some of the *Santee* refugees, there had been no sign or news of Wakeaska or Little Crow since the end of the war. They were probably dead.

It was a bad war for the *Santee*. Those not killed or put in the white man prisons were herded up and placed on reservations in the Dakota Territory and treated as prisoners of war. Life on the reservations was not good during the winter of 1862. Many people slipped away early in the spring looking for the one *Santee* leader who had not been caught or humbled by the white man, Inkpaduta! His village of *Santee* and *Yankton* people tripled in size during the early *moons* of the year following the war.

They spent the early part of the next summer between the James and Missouri Rivers, chasing small herds of buffalo. It was going to take a lot of dried meat to last this great village through the coming winter. His hunters had to keep on the move, and the women had to lug the meat great distances to keep the meat drying racks full and set up in the sun for a long enough time to dry. Everything was going well until in the middle of the *Moon of Making Fat,* some of his hunters returned and reported seeing a long column of soldiers marching slowly in a direction that would bring them close to the village. Inkpaduta, Sits In the Sun and Long Arms rode out to observe the soldiers.

The three leaders crawled to the top of a low rise and watched the white men. Two officers on horseback rode in front of two single-file columns of slowly marching men. Following behind were several wagons pulled by teams of mules. The entire procession stretched for over a mile. The three *Dakotah* leaders watched the advancing soldier columns for two days before deciding that the whites truly were following a track that in a matter of time would lead them to their present village site.

They decided it was time to move. The village was struck, and the *Dakotah* traveled south and east away from the Missouri River. Inkpaduta and the other leaders decided that they would try to avoid confrontation by keeping ahead of the soldiers, hoping that the whites would get tired, give up, and go home. But with the women and children in tow, they couldn't move fast, and the soldiers clung stubbornly to their trail.

Hunting became hard, and many times a promising chase had to be abandoned because the herds moved toward the white soldier column. Many times the village had to be picked up and moved before the meat was sufficiently dry. Rotting meat would taint their winter food supply.

Soon, everyone was tired from the constant running, and fear began to set in. Fear was stronger in the newly arrived *Santee* than it was in Inkpaduta's people or in the *Yanktons* for they had not yet seen the full wrath of the white man. But fear was contagious and began growing in all of the people. Even Inkpaduta felt a slight twinge of fright when a second column of white soldiers was spotted. After keeping ahead of the soldiers coming from the south for a full *moon*, they were being hemmed in by another column of soldiers coming from the east, cutting off an escape to the north.

Inkpaduta called a council, and the leaders finally decided that they should approach the soldiers to find out why they were following them. Near the end of the *Moon of Red Cherries* at a place called Big Mound, Inkpaduta led a contingent of warriors on horseback to meet with the white leaders. It was his intention to tell the whites to go home and leave them alone or they would fight.

But the chance to talk never came. An excited young man from Sits In the Sun's people pulled up his rifle and fired into the group of white men who were riding out to parley with them. Without hesitation, the white soldiers attacked with an infantry charge that fanned out, gaining the high ground of the land. Though they were outnumbered nearly three to one, the *Dakotah* warriors fought hard, slowing the soldiers' attack and allowing their women and children to flee to the west. In the late afternoon, the warriors gave up the fight and followed after their women.

Three days later at Dead Buffalo Lake, Sibley's column of soldiers caught them again, and a similar battle ensued. Again the *Dakotah* men fought a holding battle, allowing their families to flee before escaping themselves. Two days later, at Stony Lake, the soldiers hit them again. Inkpaduta's people lost most of their possessions, while escaping to the west once again. This time they crossed the Missouri River, and Sibley ordered his men to stop pursuing them at the river.

The soldiers returned to their base camp at Big Mound. Sibley had chased the hostiles to the west of the Missouri and felt that in the three battles, he had defeated them soundly enough to permanently damage their conditions for survival in the coming winter. His men were worn and tired and bloodied from the fighting. The next day, pushing his disappointment at not meeting up with General Sully aside, Sibley ordered his men to begin marching back to Minnesota.

When he was sure the soldiers were gone, Inkpaduta brought his people back across the Missouri to the village site at Stony Lake. They were disappointed to find that the soldiers had gathered and burned the possessions they had left there and knew that they would have to replenish their supply of dried buffalo before winter came. Inkpaduta led them back to the east to the hunting grounds between the Missouri and James Rivers again. It would be hard to replace what had been lost during the three battles with the white army. Over one hundred warriors had been killed or wounded, which would leave fewer hunters.

On this warm summer night, he sat on the edge of the stream looking at the moon's light reflecting off the white stone ledges of the hill rising high above the camp. After they crossed back to the east side of the river, his scouts immediately reported that the slow moving column of white soldiers that they had first seen was still marching up the Missouri River. Because of their slow pace and the fact that their course hadn't varied from the river, Inkpaduta was sure that these white soldiers would continue to follow the river on some business having nothing to do the *Dakotah* people.

Circling far to the north, he had led the people in a fast race back to their hunting grounds. In the morning, they would begin hunting in earnest. He stood and looked up the hill. The ledges of Whitestone Hill glistened in the moonlight. Tomorrow would be a good day. His people had survived once again, and he had decided that from now on, he would avoid the whites entirely.

He walked back to his tipi and crawled into his bed. As he snuggled up to his dead son's wife, he vowed that he would look for no trouble and would try to live in peace, leaving the whites alone and them leaving him alone. He had a new young wife to keep him warm at night and wanted to enjoy her attentions without having to worry about what the next day would bring. Suddenly, he felt safe, warm and content.

\* \* \*

The men of Brigadier General Alfred Sully's column were tired. They had been marching up the Missouri River all summer. They had left Sioux City in July and did not have to carry packs, because their supplies rode in the steamboats and their food supplies and sleeping blankets had only to be ferried to shore each evening. But by the time they reached Fort Pierre in the Dakota Territory, low water levels in the big river made steamboat travel slow and the boats couldn't keep up with the marching men.

They waited at Fort Pierre until the steamboats arrived. During the wait, Sully fussed and fumed at the delay. If he was going to meet Sibley up river, he had a schedule to keep. There were supplies on board the boats that Sibley's men would need for their return trip across the prairie, so every effort had been made to get the boats up river. But it was finally apparent that it would not be possible for the boats to continue further, and Sully made a command decision. Two thousand men were outfitted with packs and issued supplies to last them thirty days.

On the morning of August 21, Sully's command marched away from the Fort carrying fully loaded packs and leaving the boats tied to the moorings. The rest of the trip up the river would be an exhausting nightmare of one forced march after another for the men.

One week later, they reached the rendezvous point, only to find that Sibley had already been there and left. Sully cursed the slow steamboats and the decision he had made to wait for them. His scouts reported seeing signs where a large Indian village had crossed the river only a day or two earlier. Hoping to salvage something of his expedition, Sully ordered another forced march, following the trail left by the Indians.

For three days, they rose before the sun and marched until well after it set. Sully ordered cold camps with no fires and the men ate only dried jerky and hardtack washed down with a few sips of tepid water from their canteens. The soldiers were tired and angry. They were angry with Sully for marching them so hard, but they were angrier still at the Indians for causing the trouble that made it necessary that they march themselves to exhaustion on these dry, inhospitable plains. The column was made up of mostly Iowa and Nebraska volunteers. Some had already seen action in the Civil War. Others who had avoided the draft felt more inclined to volunteer to fight Indians close to home, rather than travel far to the south and fight men of their own race and creed.

Some of the men had seen action in the Sioux Uprising the summer before, a conflict already being called the Dakota War of 1862. Other members of the troop were men who had been with the relief force that had gone to the Spirit Lake region to bury the victims of the massacre that took place there in 1857. Memories of the dead and the mutilated bodies and small children and babies with smashed heads were still as fresh in their minds as if the slaughter had happened only yesterday. The anger that they had felt then, resurfaced and grew into extreme hatred as the fatigue caused by the forced marches of this campaign began setting in.

On the third day of their march from the river, Sully called a halt with orders for another cold camp. A ripple of excitement ran its course through the troop, as word that a large Indian encampment was only a few miles ahead. This night, they would not only camp without fires to heat their coffee, they would also not set up their tents. It was to be a quiet camp with no singing or loud talk. Their only comfort would be to roll in their woolen, army issued blankets. They would sleep in ranks, with loaded rifles at their sides. Knowing that they had finally caught up with their quarry put them on edge, and despite their exhaustion, most of the men found only fleeting sleep. With the coming of dawn, they expected to finish what they had started out to do.

*       *       *

The morning dawned clear and warm. Flicker birds called their wild cries from the top of a tall cottonwood tree growing beside the shallow spring seeping from the foot of the white stone hill. It was the only tree for miles and its great size attested to its great age. For those who survived the day, the cottonwood would bear witness to an event that would last long in the memories of the men, women and children camped beneath it.

Inkpaduta, Sits In The Sun, and Long Arms decided to remain camped by the white stone hill. There was considerable buffalo sign in the area and with the fresh spring water available, this site would make a good base camp.

They sat back, smoking their pipes and watching as the village came to life. The morning passed slowly as the children began running and shouting and the women began stretching and scraping all of the flesh, fat and membrane from the hides of the buffalo taken in their last successful hunt. When the hides were clean, the women would rub salt and brains into them, and let them dry in the sun. The next day they would soak the hides in salt water and twist and pound them until they were dry and keep repeating the process until the thick hides were soft and pliable. It was peaceful and quiet in the village, and the men were content to sit and think about which direction to go looking for buffalo the next day.

About mid-day, a sudden cry came from some of the boys watching the horse herds. *Wasichu* soldiers were marching toward them from the south rise! By the time Inkpaduta and Sits In The Sun could gather their weapons, the white soldiers had formed a skirmish line on the rise just above the camp. Quickly, Inkpaduta, Fire Cloud and Rattling, along with Sits In The Sun and some of his most trusted men walked slowly toward the soldiers.

"Be brave." Inkpaduta told the men as they slowly walked up the hill. "I will tell these men to leave us alone." Inkpaduta said. "Do not draw your weapons. It will frighten the *wasichu*." He glanced over his shoulder and saw that Follows The Camp Woman was directing the women to begin striking their tipis.

Long Arms was a *Yankton* and felt that he should stay out of the negotiations. The war with the whites had been a *Santee* idea, and he would leave it up to the *Santee* to work out their problems. He stood with the rest of his people at the north end of the camp, watching Inkpaduta approach the soldiers. Inkpaduta moved ahead of Sits In The Sun. He knew more about the ways of the white soldiers, and since he could speak some white man talk, he would do the talking for the *Santee*. He stepped up to the soldier he thought was in charge. To show friendship and that he was not frightened, he stuck out his hand in the manner of white men.

The young white soldier met him by taking his hand in a firm grasp, and the two stood looking into one another's eyes.

*This is a man I can talk to,* Inkpaduta thought to himself. But the thought had barely crossed his mind when muffled rifle shots drew his attention to the east end of the village. Puffs of smoke from gunshots wafted above the tipis. The screams of terrified women and children, intermingled with more gunfire, reached the ears of the men standing on the rise.

Inkpaduta jerked his hand and turned to see the young officer still holding it tightly. He could see the surprise in the young man's face and upon trying to pull free again, felt his hand released. Without further hesitation, he turned away and raced down the hill following Sits In the Sun, and the rest of the men who had taken off running as soon as the gunshots reached their ears.

"Hold your fire!" he heard the officer shout as he ran down the hill. Even so, Inkpaduta expected to be fired upon by the soldiers but gained the tipis in the village without hearing any shots from behind them. The village was in chaos! Women and children were running wildly away from a charging line of uniformed soldiers. Sully's men were out of control. Weeks of building hatred along with the sounds of gunfire and smell of fear had whipped them into a frenzy. They raced head-long into the Indian town firing indiscriminately at every Indian they saw, paying no attention to gender or age.

Follows the Camp Woman was shot through the head in the first volley of rifle fire. Worn Moccasin Woman was wounded through the side and fell to the ground, not able to run away. Three Nebraska volunteers grabbed the prostrate woman, dragged her into one of the tipis and took turns raping her.

When they were finished, they clubbed her with their rifle butts. A man from Fort Dodge deftly sliced off one of Follows the Camp Woman's breasts. He would scrape it, tan it and make a tobacco pouch out of his "souvenir." Hates Her Father Woman was quickly chased down and shot in the back at the edge of the camp. Sick From Her Babies, Beaded Hair Woman and Cuts Her Hair Woman were captured and herded with their children to the center of the village, where they were shoved roughly to the ground. Almost one hundred other women and children were captured and put in the charge of one of the officers with orders to protect them.

Inkpaduta and Sits In The Sun's warriors tried to mount a resistance, but found themselves overwhelmed by the crush of retreating women and children before a large force of blue clad soldiers. They fired their rifles, but many had no powder or lead to reload with. Big Face and His Great Gun were wounded, one in the arm, and the other through the side.

An officer wielding a saber killed Rain Cloud as he tried to reload his rifle. The *Santee* men fought hand-to-hand, but were soon over run! Their only recourse was to flee!

The *Santee* who were not killed or captured fled away from the village and spread out on the plains. Sully's soldiers chased them for several more days with more being captured or killed. Most of the *Santee* women and children were either dead, wounded or taken prisoner. Sully ordered the tipis, food, clothing, and weapons burned. Winter would soon be upon those who had escaped. Without shelter, warm clothing, and food, they would not survive.

Finally, Brigadier General Alfred Sully claimed victory and ordered his soldiers to march to the south, herding their captives with them. He would return triumphantly proclaiming that the Sioux would no longer be a problem to the people of Minnesota. Over three hundred *Santee* had been killed and two hundred more were taken prisoner. Only nineteen of his soldiers were killed. Thirty-four more were wounded. What he did not mention was that not even half of the dead Indians were men of fighting age. The battle of Whitestone Hill was the first case of total warfare used against the plains Indians. It was a strategy that would be used in future years and in the end, be recognized as the means with which to bring the mighty *Dakotah* nation to its very knees.

Three months later as the winter winds began to blow, the last of the *Santee* surrendered. With their heads hung low in defeat, starving and in need of medical assistance, they moved onto the Dakota

Territory reservations. There, they were reunited with their loved ones who had been captured at Whitestone Hill. Upon finding most of his family dead or missing, Inkpaduta surrendered also and accepted his position as the last of the *Santee* chiefs.

## Chapter 41
### Hang Around The Forts

At the reservation, the agent gave them small bundles of clothing and canvas tents for shelter. Rattling found Beaded Hair Woman. Their small daughter hadn't survived the march to the reservation. His Great Gun had died from his wounds three days after the battle. His wife, Corn Stalk Woman, was marched away with the captives. Both of their children were killed during the battle. Fire Cloud had managed to save his daughter and both of Roaring Cloud's sons, but barely kept them alive during the arduous weeks of traveling across the prairie until they reached the reservation.

During the following months on the reservation, he took Corn Stalk Woman for his wife. Young Inkpaduta had refused to follow his father to the reservation. Instead, he set out to find Long Arms and his *Yanktons,* as he had taken one of Long Arms' many daughters for his wife.

The reservation was a bleak place, open and windswept. There was no game to hunt, but it didn't matter, for they had no weapons. Rain Cloud's widow, Trader's Slave Woman and her young son shared the small gray army tent that was provided for them, with Inkpaduta. But he slept alone and shivered through the long cold nights of winter with only a thin trade blanket to cover him.

Each day Trader's Slave Woman waited in a long line with the rest of the refugees to collect rations for herself, her son and her father-in-law. She cooked the food and served it to him. She mended his worn clothing and filled his pipe. She did his work, as was her duty, for he was a man and a leader of the people, but she refused to lay with him at night, not even for warmth. She shared a blanket with her son on the far side of the tent. She would use her body to keep her son warm, not to pleasure her old father-in-law.

It was a long, cold winter. The food and garments provided to the *Santee* by the soldiers were adequate for existence but not comfort. Colds, influenza and pneumonia ran a course through the reservation, and many young children and old people died. Inkpaduta remembered the bad winter in his youth when they had starved and froze on the lakeshore in Minnesota. It gave him hope because there had been no one to give them food then. Yet, they had survived. But he could see a change in the people. The whites had changed them. Suddenly, they had lost the ability to survive without help from these enemies.

Though there were not many of his original followers left, there were many who listened to his words. He was the oldest of the *Santee* leaders left. The pox marks on his face, scars from numerous wounds and his dried, wrinkled skin were all quiet testimony to his years of experience and wisdom acquired. Each day, the men gathered around a large fire set before Inkpaduta's tent. They smoked their pipes and complained about this new life in the shadow of a White Man fort. They were unhappy with these thin, cloth tents. They didn't really like the clothing they were given to wear. Even though it was soft and comfortable against their skin, it didn't cut the wind like the skin of a bear or buffalo. The food was not good either. There was usually lots of flour, but there was little meat except for some rancid, barreled salt pork and an occasional beef cow the agent released to them from a quickly dwindling herd.

The days were long with nothing to do, and the cold nights were even longer. As the grip of a cold winter passed into spring, their dissatisfaction grew even stronger. Before they had been forced onto this reservation, when they were free, they spent spring days preparing for hunting buffalo or preparing to fight their enemies.

But it was soon apparent that these age-old rituals were not necessary, nor were they allowed on the reservation. The Agent had made it very clear. They would not have to hunt because the Great Father in Washington would provide them with food. And they would not have to go to war any longer because the Great Father in Washington would protect them from their enemies. This last statement made Inkpaduta laugh with bitterness in his heart.

"If the Great White Father in Washington is promising to protect us from our enemies, where was he when Sully and his men were killing our women and children?" he asked the assembly of men smoking around his fire on the morning after they had killed and butchered a single cow the soldiers had driven from the pen at the fort to the reservation. "If the Great White Father is going to supply us with food, where is the meat?" He looked over both shoulders, then stood and turned in a full circle. "I see no meat. It is gone. One stringy cow and a few bags of mealy flour every ten days to feed three hundred people is not what I call 'providing us with food.'" He sat back down and stated, "I am hungry now, but it will be many more days before there is more meat." He folded his arms across his chest.

Many men nodded their heads in agreement.

"What can we do, old Father?" One of the younger men asked. Inkpaduta raised his eyes to the young man's face and he smiled.

"Ten days from now," he said in a quiet voice, "when they drive that sorry excuse for a beef cow out here and give one of you a gun to shoot it with, there will be more meat to go around because I will not be here to take my share."

It was a simple statement, but its meaning rang like the clear tone of the church tower bell in the fort. Their leader, Inkpaduta, could no longer stand the restrictions of reservation life. He would be leaving. Those who would follow him started hoarding their meager food supplies and waited.

Nine days later, Inkpaduta and over two hundred followers jumped the confines of the reservation. They left in the dark of night, taking their tents, blankets and every available horse. The next morning when the soldiers drove the cow from the pen at the fort to the reservation, there were only very old men and women and a few young mothers with small children left. Without the usual ceremony of lending one of the Indian men a rifle to kill the cow with, one of the soldiers drew his sidearm, placed the barrel behind the cow's ear and shot it. He remounted his horse, and the soldiers hurriedly rode back to the fort to report the missing Indians.

*       *       *

Inkpaduta led his followers west into the wild lands. They searched for Long Arms and his *Yanktons* through the spring and found them before the end of *The Moon When the Ponies Shed*. It was a joyous reunion when Young Inkpaduta rode out to greet his father. The previous summer's warfare against the *Santee* had awakened the Western Council Fires to the menace of the whiteman. There were many *Dakotah* on the move. A gathering of *Hunkpapa, Sans Arcs, Minneconjous, Yanktons* and free *Santee* held a council and decided to defend their territory by blocking the upper Missouri River and closing the northern immigrant trail from the wagon trains of white settlers.

Contrary to Brigadier General Sully's claim, the battle at Whitestone Hill wasn't the end of the white army's problems with the *Dakotah* people; it was only the beginning of a war on the prairie. When the *Santee* jumped from the reservation and joined with other hostiles in causing problems for white immigrants to the west, General Sully was sent to lead another expedition onto the plains.

393

Again, his was a two-pronged exercise, but the timing was better, and his two armies met as planned and built Fort Rice on the Missouri River. After Fort Rice was complete, Sully led his main force up the Cannonball River Valley in pursuit of the tribes. The *Dakotah* fled ahead of his vastly superior force, trying to hide their trail. But Sully tracked them doggedly, and near the end of *The Moon of the Red Cherries*, he caught them near Killdeer Mountain.

Once again, the Indians were outnumbered and completely out gunned. Their only weapons were bows and arrows and a few shotguns with limited ammunition. Sully's men had some of the newest weapons designed to help end the Civil War. His intent was to utilize the weapons to finish the war on the prairie. But this time, the *Dakotah* led Sully's army away from their women and fought him from hidden wooded ravines refusing to be caught on the open prairie.

Sully's command lost only five men killed and ten wounded. The *Dakotah* had thirty-one men killed and wounded and again lost some of their tipis, pemmican, and buffalo robes. But their defeat was not total, and as Sully pulled his command back, the remaining warriors followed, sniping and harassing the blue clad army all the way across the badlands until it arrived at Fort Union on the Yellowstone River. The *Dakotah* left Fort Union and disappeared into the vastness of the territory before reinforcements from Fort Rice could arrive. Inkpaduta's followers joined with these wild cousins and strengthened their resolve to resist the advancing white men.

When the War Between the States came to an end, there was a sudden vast emigration of mustered out soldiers and displaced southerners to the gold fields of California and the farming valleys in Oregon. The immigrants' paths led directly across *Dakotah* lands, and violent confrontations between them and the Indians became commonplace.

A cry for protection by the travelers was heard in Washington, and in 1866 troops were sent to build a line of forts along the most heavily traveled trails. Cavalry units were stationed in the forts. The forts were in direct violation of treaties the United States Government had signed with the *Dakotah* Nation. The tribal leaders demanded that the treaties be honored and that the soldiers stationed in the forts be withdrawn. When the *Dakotah* demands were ignored, immediate warfare broke out.

Spotted Tail's *Brules* fought the whites and lost, but Red Cloud's *Ogalalas*, led by the brilliant young war chief named Crazy Horse, annihilated Captain W. J. Fetterman and a force of eighty men near Fort Phil Kearney. The Whites were not yet ready to pay such a big price in blood for the land, and they sued for peace, promising to keep the immigrants from trespassing on *Dakotah* lands.

In 1868, Red Cloud traveled to Washington D.C. to sign the peace treaties. While there, he learned the true strength of the white invaders and, like Little Crow before him, realized the futility of fighting them. The treaties set up a large reservation covering the western half of the present state of South Dakota. Five separate agencies were assigned to see to the needs of the peaceful Indians living on the reservations.

Red Cloud, awed by the power and never-ending numbers of white men, moved onto the reservation and advised his followers to do the same. Crazy Horse and those who chose to follow him moved west, leaving the reservation lands to join with the *Hunkpapa*, Sitting Bull and many other tribes not yet ready to bow down to the white master.

As winter was coming, Inkpaduta opted to follow Red Cloud back on to the reservation and live off of the White Man for the cold season. Provisions proved to be much better on this reservation than the one set up for the *Santee* people five years before. But even so, when summer came again, Inkpaduta led his followers off the reservation and joined up with the wild tribes again.

There were Northern *Cheyenne, Arapaho, Blackfoot Dakotah, Hunkpapa* and *Ogalala* roaming the region stretching from the Black Hills in the east to the Big Horn Mountains in the west. They hunted the diminishing herds of buffalo and attacked wagon trains of white settlers that slipped past the Army posts charged with keeping white trespassers from entering *Dakotah* lands. When gold was discovered in the Black Hills, the task of keeping gold seekers out was too much for the army, and a sudden onslaught of white men seeking gold poured into the hills. The *Dakotah* were quick to react, and the hills ran red with blood. Desperate for a peaceful solution to stop the warfare, the Great White Father decided to buy the Black Hills from the *Dakotah* people, and the order to negotiate the purchase of the Black Hills was passed down to the reservation agents with little consideration as to how tough of a job it may be.

The area called the Black Hills by the white government was considered to be *Pa Sapa* (Sacred Ground) by the *Dakotah* people. The agents knew they had their job cut out for them. During the few years the Indians had lived at the agencies, the agents developed a policy of giving men who carried great influence with the people favors.

Men like Spotted Tail and Red Cloud were honored by each having their home reservation named after them. Other leaders were given extra food or warmer clothing. This policy of favoring the leaders turned once great warriors and fighting men into jealous children, who strove to please the agents instead of looking out for the good of their own people. Spotted Tail and Red Cloud were both issued clapboard houses on their respective agency in place of the canvas tents the rest of the people were provided with.

There was never a shortage of food for the chiefs, and soon the agents began rewarding first one, then the other for small favors in controlling the people. Animosity between the two men grew and in time, they began trying to out-do one another in pleasing the agents. Red Cloud and Spotted Tail and their followers became known as "Hang Around The Forts" by the *Dakotah* who had refused to move onto the reservation lands. The free *Dakotah* were staunchly against selling their sacred ground to the whites. The emissaries sent by the two reservation leaders, asking them to attend a council to discuss it, were sent back alone.

Therefore, only reservation Indians attended the council held at night a short distance from the fort on Spotted Tail's Agency, and even among them, there was a great division of opinion on the proposed land sale. For some it would be no great loss, for they didn't need the hills to hunt in any more. But for others, *Pa Sapa* was still the home of their ancestors and should be kept sacred. The agents begged the Indian leaders to convince their people that selling would be a wise thing. It was a warm night, and there was almost no wind. The council fire was lit and each man lit his own pipe with a brand taken from it. They sat in silence until each man had smoked his pipe empty and knocked the ash from it by gently tapping it on the sole of their moccasin. When each man was finished, Spotted Tail rose.

"Welcome to Spotted Tail's Agency. It is a warm night, and many have traveled a long distance to attend this council." He spoke softly, drawing everyone's attention. "We have an important decision to make, and we must make it even for our bothers who chose not to attend this council. The *Wasichu* want to buy *Pa Sapa*. Their young men have found the yellow stone that they prize, and even the power of the Great White Father can not stop these young men from going into *Pa Sapa* to hunt for it. This is causing much fighting between our people and the young *Wasichu*. The time for fighting is past!" he stated boldly as he glared at the faces of the assembled people.

The men were circled close, all sitting cross-legged, some still holding their empty pipes, others with their arms folded across their chests. Behind the seated men stood the women, quiet and solemn, listening to every word he spoke. Spotted Tail walked around the circle of people. His eyes searched their faces, seeming to dare anyone to disagree.

"The *Wasichu* came to this country many seasons ago. At first, they just traveled through, hurting no one. They were friendly. They gave us presents. Then more and more *Wasichu* came. They built roads and forts and brought the iron horse. The buffalo have been shot or scattered widely over the plains and are hard to find. When we grew hungry and tired, most of our people decided to live here around the forts, where the *Wasichu* provide us with food and protection."

He stopped speaking again for a moment and stared out into the growing darkness, his eyes reaching beyond the ring of light from the fire. The growls and snarls of fighting dogs down by the tipis came to his ears and seemed very loud in the calm quiet night.

"There were times when we were treated badly by the *Wasichu*." He nodded his head up and down as if agreeing with someone's statement. "And . . . we fought them," he continued, sad eyes turning back to the people, head nodding up and down again. "We fought them . . . and lost." He hung his head as if totally defeated by the thought. A low murmur rose from the assembled men, but went silent when Spotted Tail continued, "Yes, we, the mighty *Ogalala, Minneconjou, Hunkpapa, Brule, Yankton* and *Santee* fought them . . . and we all lost!"

He glanced around the circle of light, his eyes searching again for anyone disagreeing with him and then continued, "But even after fighting them and killing their young men, we are invited to live here at their forts. They give us food and blankets in the winter, when we are hungry and cold. We no longer need to chase the buffalo. We are given cattle, tobacco and clothing!"

Hitching up the cloth trousers he wore in place of the traditional leather leggings, he walked full circuit around the fire once more. He stared out into the darkness, as if looking for someone to come from there with all of the answers to the questions in his soul. Nervously, he cleared his throat, hawked up phlegm and spit into the fire.

"The *Wasichu* want to buy *Pa Sapa*. I say we should sell it to them for a very high price. If we are going to live on agency land, we don't need *Pa Sapa*. The *Wasichu* give us what we need. If we sell *Pa Sapa*, we can continue to live here on the Agency forever and have everything we want. The *Wasichu* will keep our bellies full, our lodges warm and our enemies away." Once again, he glared at the assembly of men. "*Pa Sapa* is nothing to us anymore. Our future is here. Our future will be better if we make the *Wasichu* happy."

Spotted Tail walked to where he had left his pipe at the edge of the fire-lit circle and sat down. As he settled into place, a murmur arose once again from the assembled people. It was like a slow wind, quiet and low at first but gaining strength with duration. The minutes passed, and the voices grew in number and volume until nearly everyone was talking at once, arguing, some for, and some against. Even the women were taking part in the discussion, each trying to determine which side of the issue her man was on. Everyone had an opinion and the right to express it.

When it seemed that the noise would continue to grow until loud enough to be heard by the soldiers at the fort two miles distant, Red Cloud stood and raised his hands. In a short time all of the men and most of the women became silent in respect for his age and his station in life, for he was known as the man who had fought the whites and won! Red Cloud bent, reaching for some sticks and threw them on the fire, causing it to flare high and give off more light.

Finally, all of the women quieted, and only the growls, snarls and yips from the fighting dogs could be heard. A small frown creased his face, and he waited, hoping the dogs would stop fighting. It would be a good sign.

Suddenly, there was a loud yelp, and the dogfight abruptly stopped. Red Cloud waited for a few moments to see if it would start up again. But the silence held, and he brought his hand up to his mouth and coughed to hide a small, satisfied smile.

"My people," he called, his voice loud and strong. "Do not quarrel among yourselves. Let us be united in this important decision. I know that *Pa Sapa* is sacred. It hurts to lose it." He stopped, and his eyes swept the circle of people, "But lose it we will. I have seen the power of the *Wasichu* army. I have defeated that army with the help of many of you and with the help of those who chose to stay away tonight." He paced the circle as had Spotted Tail, searching for the right words, words which would bring the majority of the people over to his way of thinking, thus increasing his popularity with the people and at the same time, raising himself in the favor of the white agents.

"We defeated the *Wasichu* in a time past, but we will defeat them no more. I have seen their army's true strength. Their warriors are as many as there are leaves on the trees. And like the leaves, when one season's crop dies, in time, another crop grows back. They have cannons and guns, and if they lose them or have them stolen, they know how to make more. We do not!" he stated flatly. He stopped and listened as an owl began to hoot in the distance. He waited until it stopped, and the night quiet was again complete. Even the wild creatures listened when the great Red Cloud spoke. It was another good sign.

"We have fought wars with the *Wasichu* and won. But even when we win, their ability to replace their lost warriors turns our victory into defeat. We must not fight them again!" he shouted. "We must not fight them again, or we as a people may lose everything!" He gritted his teeth and again followed the path around the fire, stopping to look at the people on each side of the circle before continuing. "They have come here now to make us sell the *Pa Sapa*. We can refuse and kill all of the *Wasichu* in that fort!" he stated, pointing through the darkness toward the fort. "But it would only bring more *Wasichu* to take their place. More and more!" he shouted again before continuing quietly, "Then it would be us who would be killed. Then they would have *Pa Sapa* for free." He sighed heavily and continued.

"We should sell *Pa Sapa* to the *Wasichu* for the most we can get. We should bury the hatchet and live in peace with them. Let them feed us and clothe us and protect us." His eyes blinked, and his voice was barely above a whisper when he finished, "I have said this . . . and I will say no more." He sat back down and waited.

No one had expected the old fighting leader to side with Spotted Tail, for it was well known that the two men seldom agreed on anything. There was a shocked silence for a time. Both of the principal leaders had spoken in favor of selling the sacred ground to the whites. The people sat quietly searching their souls for an answer. Their hearts screamed to keep the land, but the wisdom of their leaders' statements confused them. Was selling their only option?

There was a surprised rattling of voices when the old *Santee* leader, Inkpaduta, climbed to his feet and walked to the center of the circle, stopping to sprinkle tobacco on the fire and watch as the thin wisps of smoke rose into the darkness.

Few people had been aware that Inkpaduta was present. He and the *Santee* appeared on agency lands one day, only to disappear the next. No one, least of all the white agents, could keep track of him. He was an enigma, living on agency lands around the forts, accepting food and blankets from the whites during the wintertime, and then leaving with the coming of spring to roam the vast prairie and make war on any whites he happened to come across.

When the cold time came, he was quick to return to the reservation and blend in with the "Hang Around The Forts." Inkpaduta had emerged from a man once considered an outcast who was looked down upon, to become the main leader of the ancient Eastern Fires (the *Santee*) of the *Dakotah* Nation.

The silence continued, and the light from the fire reflected a red tint in the old warrior's hair as he began to speak.

"I have fought the white man longer than any man here. I am old, and it has been my way to war against the enemies of my people." Inkpaduta didn't pace back and forth, or circle the fire as had Spotted Tail and Red Cloud. He felt no nervousness. His eyes didn't search the crowd, for his sight was failing, and he could see little in the darkness anyway. He stood in one place and looked straight ahead. He knew there was no good answer to the problems facing his people, but the leadership of Red Cloud and Spotted Tail sickened him.

"I have killed the *Wasichu*. I have killed their men with arrows and bullets. I have killed their women with my knife and my war club. And I have killed their children by smashing their heads against tree trunks. And they have killed my people in the same ways." He stopped and glanced balefully in the direction of Red Cloud and then turned to face Spotted Tail. "But there are some here tonight who tell you of the strength of the white army. They say we have fought and lost. This is true. They say we can never win. This also may be true."

There was a low rumble of voices and the bobbing of heads in agreement, especially by those who sat near Red Cloud and Spotted Tail.

"Do as your two wise leaders advise . . . sell *Pa Sapa* to the white skins! Take all you can get for it! Sell *Pa Sapa!*" he shouted with a cry in his voice. "Sell it for all you can get, and enjoy whatever it is you get, for it will be the last thing you will get from the whites!" Anger shone in his watery, ancient eyes. His voice was shrill but steady. "But I wonder what they will want to buy next? The *Santee* sold their land to the whites long ago. We took their food and clothing and . . . protection. Ha ha ha," he laughed in a quiet voice; all of the anger was gone. "We collected a good price, but I wonder what kind of price you can charge for your own self respect? Look at the *Santee* now." He raised his arms in the general direction of where his people sat on the outer edge of the circle. "Where are the great benefits we got for selling our souls to the *Wasichu*?"

"Sell *Pa Sapa,* and our gods have no home." His voice dripped with scorn and his half blind eyes burned into the darkness touching all who sat there. "Sell *Pa Sapa,* and our home has no gods."

The crowd sat in silence as the old leader turned and left the council fire. His teenage grandson led him through the darkness. When he reached his tipi, he instructed Trader's Slave Woman to be ready to leave in the morning. She dipped her head in respect and began packing. She had stayed with the man these thirteen years since the death of her husband and had grown to respect him as a father. She married a man called Walking Horse, thereby bringing a hunter into the lodge as a good daughter would, gaining Inkpaduta's respect and gratitude. She felt no need to ask where they were going, for she knew. They would travel west to find the old medicine man, Sitting Bull, and the young war leader, Crazy Horse. They were men who didn't sit around asking for the answer to the question as to whether they should sell their souls to appease the white skins or fight for their honor.

Horse Woman's Child didn't need an answer, for to him there was no question!

## Chapter 42
### *The Last Battle (1876)*

The setting sun glared in Inkpaduta's squinting eyes as he rode directly into its glowing red light. It was a hot afternoon. Sweat ran from his body, trickling down over his hips to soak into the blanket-saddle covering the back of the horse he rode. The many days of hard riding since leaving Spotted Tail's Agency had caused the skin on his inner thighs to chafe from the motion of the animal. His back ached, and he had to grit his teeth at the pain that burned his knees when he kicked the horse with his heels to hurry the animal along.

He and his people had traveled far and were now nearing the end of their journey. He was anxious to reach the great camp at the river just ahead because the aches of his body reminded him of his age. The long trip in the hot weather was making him feel very old.

It was a huge camp, stretching for two and one-half miles along the winding banks of a small river the *Dakotah* called the Greasy Grass. It flowed out of the north end of the Big Horn Mountains. The white men had named it the Little Bighorn River, after the mountains. When Inkpaduta led his people into the south end of the camp, they were greeted by an old acquaintance. Sun At Night's grandson, Brave Bull, walked forward extending his hand in welcome. The young warrior had grown to full manhood. His name had been changed to Gall, and he proudly told his old protector that he had taken his place among the *Hunkpapas* as a war chief. Gall showed the *Santee* and *Yanktons,* who had followed Inkpaduta away from Spotted Tail's Agency, where to set up their tipis.

While the tired people made camp, he led Inkpaduta across the huge village to join a council being held in the lodge of the medicine man, Sitting Bull. As he entered the dimly lit interior, Inkpaduta could not see the faces of the many men assembled there and asked Gall who everyone was.

"Crazy Horse and Big Road of the *Ogalala,* Sitting Bull, myself, Black Moon and Crow King are here representing the *Hunkpapa,*" the young man said quietly with pride in his voice. "Spotted Eagle of the *Sans Arc*, Younger Hump and Fast Bull of the *Minneconjou*, are here and our friends, Dull Knife and Ice Bear of the *Shyela* (Cheyenne). There are some *Blue Clouds* (Arapaho) traveling with the *Shyela*, but their leader was killed. Now, Inkpaduta, you have arrived with the *Santee* and *Yanktons* you lead."

Inkpaduta grunted his thanks and accepted a seat of honor beside Sitting Bull. A pipe was passed, and each man offered its smoke to the four directions and to their Father in the sky and their Mother in the earth. After the pipe, Sitting Bull once again related the details of the vision he had experienced at the Sun Dance ceremony that spring.

"I danced the Sun Dance as a young man," the old medicine man began, proudly pointing to the two deep scars just above the nipples on his breasts. "When I danced again as an old man, I cut fifty pieces of skin from each of my arms." He pointed at the numerous white scarrings running up and down his arms. "I danced for two days without stopping to eat or drink or sleep. I danced until my Medicine Helper took me to his world where I could see into the future." Sitting Bull glanced around at the faces circling his tipi walls. In his hunger and exhaustion-induced stupor, a vision had come to him. "When I returned to this world, I remembered what I had seen while in my Medicine Helper's world. Hundreds of blue coat soldiers were falling, head over heels into this camp on the Greasy Grass River. It was a sign of a great battle to come." The old Medicine man smiled a thin smile before continuing.

"I believe this dream," Sitting Bull stated firmly. "But know this, we will need strong medicine to win the coming battle against the *Wasichu* army. Crazy Horse says his scouts have reported columns of soldiers on the move to the north, east and south of this camp. Even the great number of warriors we have here will be out-numbered if the white armies all converge on us at the same time."

"Eight days ago," the wrinkled old Medicine man continued, "*Hunkpapas* and *Ogalala* attacked a column led by Three Stars (General Crook) on Rosebud Creek. It was a hard fought battle that lasted all day, and both sides left the field with no clear winner. Only a few of our men were wounded." The old man glanced around the crowded tipi until his eyes came to rest on a young war leader, and he smiled. "But Crazy Horse and his men captured a wagon full of many boxes of bullets and new rifles that will shoot many times. This is a good sign!"

"It is rumored that the soldier column to the north is led by *Pahuska* (Longhair Custer). Is this true?" Dull Knife, the *Shyela* leader asked. Longhair Custer had led an attack on a Cheyenne village on *Washita* creek eight years before, and the 7th Cavalry killed Chief Black Kettle and many women and children in that attack. The few survivors had been herded together and held at gunpoint. In an attempt to further incapacitate the Cheyenne people's ability to retaliate or to even survive, Custer ordered his soldiers to shoot all of the Indians' hunting ponies. "If this is true, we must leave enough warriors in the village to protect the women and children," Dull Knife stated solemnly.

"The white soldiers killed many *Santee* women and children at Whitestone Hill also," Inkpaduta stated, adding, "I believe these white men have decided to kill off all of our children and young women, so that in time, they can end our existence without ever having to fight our men. It is time to stop these white men." Sitting Bull and several other men voiced their agreement.

"We must act quickly to keep the three white armies from coming together," Crazy Horse stated. "Go back to your camps, and ready your men for war. Tomorrow, we will make our plans to take these white armies one at a time before they come together. Dance tonight! Tomorrow will be a good day to die!"

Fires were built high, and the young women turned out to dance around the flames. Many excited young warriors joined the dance, singing war chants of bravery and brandishing their war clubs. Most of these young men had never been tested in battle, but they belittled their enemies while dancing around the fire and built up their own courage at the same time. The dancing went deep into the night with many young men falling out near dawn, exhausted.

Early in the morning, Sitting Bull ordered his wives to take down his tipi and move it to the far north end of the encampment. As medicine man, he would not join in the battle, but stay in his lodge praying for guidance. Even though it was midmorning, many people were just rising from their beds because the celebration of the coming battle had gone on so late into the night.

Crazy Horse asked Gall to find Inkpaduta and bring him to the war council. He was curious to know if the people at Red Cloud's Agency and Spotted Tail's Agency would support them in a war against the whites? Inkpaduta and Gall were walking across the village looking for Crazy Horse when they heard screams coming from the south end of the camp and changed their course to find out what was happening. Women who had been digging for roots by the small stream south of the camp were running into the village screaming!

"*Wasichu! Wasichu!* They come!" the running women were shouting and pointing back in the direction they had come from.

A column of blue-coated soldiers could be seen slowly advancing toward the encampment. Smoke puffed from the ends of their rifle barrels and soft, popping sounds could be heard as the soldiers fired into the camp. One of the running women was struck between the shoulder blades, and the force of the bullet slammed her forward onto her face. She landed at Inkpaduta's feet and lay groaning in agony.

Panic erupted in the village. Screaming women ran back and forth dragging their crying children with them as they tried to seek shelter from the danger! Warriors, shouting in anger, armed themselves and tried to push through the growing throng of panic-stricken women and children milling about in the open areas between the tipis. Adding to the confusion were those who heard the shouting and came running to find out what was going on. Inkpaduta felt a hand on his shoulder and turned to see Gall.

"Defend this end of the village, Old Man," the *Hunkpapa* war chief said, grinning with excitement. "I'm going to get my war-pony and find Crazy Horse. We will take the fight to them. You just stop them from coming any closer!" Gall then ran into the village, weaving a path between the crying groups of frightened women and children, calling for the men to follow him.

Inkpaduta's failing eyesight kept him from seeing the approaching white soldiers. He knew the general direction they were coming from and strode bravely toward them, gripping only his war club. Many other older warriors and young men not yet tried in war followed him and soon passed him, shouting their war cries and firing their single-shot rifles and arrows wildly in the direction of the soldiers.

The small force of soldiers split into four groups of five and dismounted. One man in each group held the reins of the horses while the other four men knelt in the grass to shoot at the rapidly approaching Indians.

For a short time, this tactic seemed to work as the attacking *Dakotah* had to drop down into the grass where they couldn't be seen by the soldiers and advanced more slowly. More warriors arrived. Many were mounted, and they rushed their horses, en-masse, at the kneeling soldiers. The *Dakotah* gunfire hit three of the soldiers' horses, and the men holding their reins lost them. The wildly plunging animals, squealing in pain and fear, broke loose and ran back in the direction they had come from, leaving their soldiers afoot. The soldiers began retreating, some trying to drag their wounded compatriots with them. Others dropped everything, even their rifles, and ran.

The men with Inkpaduta rose up from the grass and chased after the fleeing soldiers. Inkpaduta could feel the old excitement pumping through his veins as he tried to run along to keep pace with the younger warriors, but he soon fell behind. A sudden concentration of gunfire erupted from the east side of the village, where the easy ford across the river lay nearest the camp. Inkpaduta stopped, watching and waiting, until finally a young boy came running from the village carrying a small ax.

"What is going on back in the village?" he asked the boy, "and what are you doing with that ax?"

"Some soldiers were caught trying to cross the river into the village." The boy stopped and stared up into the old man's face. "Black Moon and Crow King and their warriors saw them coming and ambushed them. Crazy Horse and Gall have led the rest of the men out to meet the *wasichu* soldiers that have been spotted circling over there," he said, pointing to a low hill running to the east of the camp. "I am going to kill the blue-coats with this ax!" He pulled free of Inkpaduta's grasp and ran after the warriors who were chasing the retreating soldiers.

Without their horses, many of the fleeing soldiers were caught. They were shot and clubbed. They were scalped, and their bodies were mutilated. Inkpaduta found the boy with the ax hacking at a large, red-haired soldier who had been wounded through the left leg.

The man had thought to play dead but saw that even dead men were not safe, and he was trying to hide in the tall grass. The boy found him and was trying to chop him with the ax. The man, who had dropped his rifle in his panic to get away, was dodging and kicking at the boy with his good leg, as he tried to crawl away dragging his broken leg.

Inkpaduta could see that the boy was getting tired from swinging the ax and was afraid that the man might take it away from him. He walked up close on the opposite side of the man from where the boy stood. Both the soldier and the boy were panting from near exhaustion. The wounded soldier was not aware that Inkpaduta was approaching and didn't see the old Indian swing his war club in a mighty arc that smashed into the side of his head, just below his temple. The soldier slammed to the earth on his back and quivered like a dying rabbit. The boy raised the ax and drove its head through the man's neck, severing his head and systematically began dismembering the man by chopping his feet and hands off.

Inkpaduta walked on, finding more and more scenes of death and mutilation each time his men caught up with one of the soldiers. He crossed the creek and came upon a group of young men who were discussing what they should do next at the base of a high bluff that led up out of the valley. On the flat plain at the top of the bluff, the soldiers had formed in a large circle. They had shot their horses and were using the animals' bodies as breastworks to lie behind for protection from the *Dakotah* gunfire. The young men turned to Inkpaduta for advice, but before he could answer their questions, a thunderous eruption of gunfire began over the rise on the east side of the river.

It was clear that the white soldiers' leaders had planned for these decoys to attack the village from the south and hold the warriors' attention until another, larger force could circle to the east, staying on the low ground between the rolling hills and then sweep into the village in a surprise attack.

Upon discovering the direction the true attack was coming from, Gall led a large contingent of warriors to attack them from the south, driving between them and the ford near the village. His force of warriors, superior in number, quickly pushed the whites toward the top of the rise. Crazy Horse led the rest of the warriors up the back side of the rise and caught the whites from behind and above. The crescendo of gun blasts grew in a continuous rumbling of a thousand rifles being fired over and over. Wounded horses screamed in pain and fear, and men shouted curses and prayers. There were cries of fright and cries of exultation adding to the clamor that lasted for only a few minutes before a sudden, perverse and total silence prevailed over the prairie.

The quiet was so complete that Inkpaduta could hear the murmuring voices of the white soldiers forted up behind their dead horses at the top of the bluff. A pall of dust torn loose from the earth by the churning hooves of the Indian ponies, rose slowly into the quiet sky over the battlefield and drifted gently to the south before falling back to the earth.

The warriors, riding their tired ponies, returned to the village and reported that all of the large force of white soldiers who had tried to attack the village by circling in from the east, were dead.

The women broke the quiet as they left the safety of the village ululating in celebration of the great victory. They searched the prairie, falling upon the bodies of the dead soldiers, the enemies of their people who had come to kill their husbands, brothers and children, with a vengeance. Stripping the clothes from the corpses, they completed the mutilation of the bodies, hacking with their hatchets and slicing with their knives. They continued the age-old practice of mutilating dead enemies to ensure that they would not enter the next life whole, until every white soldier, except for a small group that had fallen halfway up the rise, felt their wrath.

Most of the men who came to view this group of white men thought that their leader was indeed, *Pahuska*. His hair was not as long as they thought it would be, but he was dressed in buckskins instead of a bluecoat uniform. When Dull Knife arrived to view the bullet-riddled body, he confirmed it was the dreaded village attacker. While a great feeling of exultation spread throughout the warriors, it was agreed that no one would scalp *Pahuska*. The women were ordered to leave his body without mutilating it. His medicine was known to be powerful and though they hated this man, they also feared him, even in death.

Inkpaduta told the young men to leave the soldiers forted up behind their dead horses. At a council of leaders, it was decided that it would not be worth chancing even one man's life to kill them. It would be better to leave them alive, so that they could return to the Great White Father and tell him about this defeat of his famous war leader. They would tell him that the *Dakotah, Shyela,* and *Arapaho* were still powerful people who would fight, if he didn't leave them alone!

The entire village celebrated the great victory! Large fires were built, and the young warriors danced and sang and told the stories of their bravery over and over. Several, including Young Inkpaduta, claimed to have been the one who killed *Pahuska!* The women were proud, and the children felt safe and happy. All seemed good to the people, but Sitting Bull was worried. In his dream, the soldiers had fallen into the camp dead, but none had appeared to have been mutilated.

"It bothers me that in my dream these dead men were whole," he stated, looking around the circle of leaders. "I am afraid that it could mean more soldiers will come. We won a great victory today. But most of the bullets for the rifles that shoot many times are gone. Can we beat the soldiers led by Three Stars or Bear Coat without bullets for these rifles?" he asked. "There is not enough grass to feed the horses for this large of an encampment for very long," he stated when no one answered his question. "I will be leading my people away from this place tomorrow. It is a good place, but I feel we must leave."

Inkpaduta, feeling ties with the *Hunkpapas* because of his relationship with Gall, decided to follow Sitting Bull. The contingent of *Santee* and *Yanktons,* who had followed him off the reservation, split up, each man choosing another leader to follow. Fire Cloud and Young Inkpaduta chose to follow Crazy Horse and the *Ogalala*. They were accompanying the *Shyela,* heading to the south where they hoped to find buffalo.

With the largest contingent of followers, Sitting Bull headed west intending to circle back to the south through the Bighorn Mountains. But after only a few days, his scouts discovered that a large troop of white soldiers was following them.

The soldiers were not hampered by the necessity of carrying all of their worldly goods with them. They had no old people or women and children to slow them down and quickly closed the distance. They were led by General Crook, a man the *Dakotah* called Three Stars, a man known to be particularly anxious to carry out his orders to eliminate the Sioux problem.

Sitting Bull changed direction and turned into the mountains, hoping to lose the soldiers in rough terrain. The tactic slowed Crook, but the white leader continued to dog at their heels, closing in one day, only to lose the Indians' trail the next, then finding it again the day after. This cat and mouse game of hide and seek continued for almost a year.

The *Hunkpapa* leader could see that the hardships the pace required to avoid the white army following them was taking a toll on the old people and children. Many of his exhausted followers simply dropped out or fell back and died. He knew that without their families, his warriors could easily outdistance and lose the army following them. He also knew that with their families it was impossible to hide their trail and that they could not keep ahead of the soldiers forever. When it became apparent that Crook would not give up and leave them alone, in desperation, Sitting Bull led his people across the border into the land of the Great Mother, Queen Victoria. In Canada, they would be safe from the white soldiers of the United States.

## Chapter 43
### *The Final Journey*

Inkpaduta sat in his tipi staring through the smoke hole at the wan sunlight of yet another foggy morning. He wondered if the sun ever shone brightly in this land called Canada? The People were camped along the edge of a shallow, swamp-like lake that stretched for miles in the lowlands below the foothills of the mountains. This was a less than desirable village site, but it was where the Old Mother's officials told them they would be welcome to stay.

It had been a long, bitterly cold winter, and Inkpaduta was contemplating the situation he found himself in. The hard traveling to escape from Three Star's army had taken its toll. The long days of traveling with little or no food for those many months had caused him to lose his healthy weight. He was thin and bony and had no body fat to help keep himself warm. The nights were cold, and the wind in this northland was even more biting than the wind on the open prairie of his traditional homeland. He dozed.

Inkpaduta woke shivering uncontrollably. He pulled the thin trade blanket up to his chin and tried to warm himself. He moved slowly, feeling pain in each of his joints. He coughed hard, spitting up bloody mucus and could hear a rattle in his chest. With each breath he took, he felt a burning sensation as the air tried to fill his ailing lungs. He felt hot and cold at the same time. His legs and arms ached, and he could feel numbness in his feet. His already failing eyesight had grown even dimmer, and many of his teeth were broken or had fallen out while chewing the tough smoke-dried meat that had become their main staple during the long months of exile in Canada. A sense of unease overcame him as he thought about this change in his health.

He now wished that he had chosen to follow his sons and their families who had followed Crazy Horse to the south after the Great Battle. None of his family lived in Sitting Bull's village, and in his heart he knew he would never see them again. His daughter, Beaded

Hair Woman and her husband, Rattling, had gone their own way, turning to the east after Sitting Bull led them into Canada. Rattling wanted to try his hand at trapping and was heading for Chippewa country by Lake of the Woods. Thinking of his sons and daughter left him feeling lonely and depressed. It seemed that the fire warming his heart had cooled with these dark thoughts, and by the time the town crier passed, calling out the news of the day, he had made a decision.

"Gall and Sitting Bull," the crier shouted, "have decided not to spend another winter in the Great Mother's land. They are returning to the buffalo prairie in the land of the Great White Father. They are leaving tomorrow."

The man shouted this news over and over as he walked through the entire village to make sure everyone heard it. What he left unsaid was that anyone who wished to follow the two leaders should begin packing their belongings and be ready to go the next morning. After the crier passed out of hearing, Trader's Slave Woman rose from her bed and began packing their things. She and her husband Walking Horse, were unhappy living here in the Old Mother's Land too. Inkpaduta cleared his throat and called to her to stop packing.

"Are we not going to go back home with Gall and Sitting Bull?" the woman asked.

"You must go with Gall and Sitting Bull back to our homeland," Inkpaduta answered. "But I will not be leaving the land of the Great Mother. Gather your possessions and leave this tipi," he added sternly.

Nodding his head in understanding, Walking Horse picked up his weapons and medicine bag and stalked out. Trader's Slave Woman spent the rest of the day packing their gear and dragging it from the tipi. They would move into her son's tipi and help support his wife's family until they obtained enough hides for their own lodge.

The next morning Inkpaduta rose early, and after going outside to relieve his bladder with a disappointingly weak stream, he sat down near the door of his tipi. His aching shoulders slumped under the tattered blue and white trade blanket that hung down, loosely covering his crossed legs. His milky eyes looked up, following the memory of slowly rising smoke wafting from the fire pit, up the conical ceiling to where it swirled out of the smoke hole at the peak. How many years he had lived, he didn't really know. It mattered little to him. His had been a long, hard life, and he was tired of the struggle. In his memory, it seemed that he had spent his entire life fighting. He had fought the Sauk, the Pawnee, the Omaha, the White Men, and even his own brothers, the *Santee*. Many times he had risked death, but always before he had cheated the coyotes and crows. Thinking of it failed to lift his spirits. He just felt very tired.

"It is a good morning, old Father." The lilting voice of Trader's Slave Woman turned his head in surprise when she entered the tipi. "The sun shines brightly. The wind blows warm from the south."

She removed the blanket from his bony shoulders and gently helped him stand and walk to his bed of buffalo robes, where she helped him lie down. Rolling the blanket, she placed it under his neck, propping his head up.

This done, she went to the cook fire and dipped a tin cup of thin broth from one of the two pots sitting on its coals. Slowly, she spooned a nearly clear liquid into his mouth. He swallowed, smacking his lips occasionally and running his tongue around their perimeter to gather in every drop of the warm juice. When the cup was empty, the woman filled it again. This time, she fished pieces of meat from the soup and taking them into her own mouth, chewed them into small, mushy bits before spooning them into his mouth. Failing to line up two teeth to chew the meat with, Inkpaduta laboriously gummed the already masticated chunks of meat a few times before swallowing them.

"This meat is the flesh of Feeds Her Pups In The Morning," the woman stated proudly. Inkpaduta knew what a sacrifice it had been for her to butcher her favorite camp dog to feed him this meal. Dogs were important to normal village life, and the People only ate them in times of extreme hardship or for special occasions. Recognizing the significance of this meal, he felt honored and ate until his stomach was bloated before turning his head to the side, refusing the offered spoon.

Trader's Slave Woman pulled back her long, graying hair and tied it in a horse's tail behind her head. She had lived many years with this man she had once hated. He was a harsh man with cruel tendencies in his younger years. But he had mellowed some in his old age and had provided her with a home to raise her son in. She owed him for that and would perform this one, final duty to show her respect.

She removed the rolled blanket from under his head and laid him flat on his back again. Lifting the second pot from the coals, she bumped it against one of the rocks that circled the fire pit. A metallic tone rang with a wavering quiver that roiled the water in the pot until she set it down by his side. Etched into the side of the fire-blackened pot were the words, *U.S. Army,* plunder taken from the wagon of the soldiers who had died from smallpox many years before.

She dipped a square of blue cloth, cut from a soldier uniform, into the warm water and wrung it out, letting the water squeeze back into

413

the pot. Lifting his head, she wiped his face and neck clean and methodically proceeded down his chest and upper torso, alternately dipping the cloth and wringing it out before the rag could cool. She removed his clout and washed his privates, hiding her surprise at the red-brown color of the small patch of pubic hair, before moving down his legs, paying particular care to his feet, washing each toe separately.

By the time she was finished, goose flesh covered his arms and legs and he shivered. She covered him with the trade blanket and placed a heavy buffalo robe over it to warm him. His half-blind eyes stared up at the smoke hole again, and he silently wished he could see the blue sky through it.

The woman moved the pot of dog soup from the fire and placed some small sticks on the coals. She fanned the white embers with the dried wing of a prairie hen. Soon, the twigs burst into flame. She laid larger sticks of wood on the fire, and the light from the rising flames flickered on the tipi walls.

Trader's Slave Woman bustled about, picking through articles of his clothing. Those made of white man's cloth, she fed to the fire and others of leather tanned from deer, buffalo or white man's cows, she hung on pegs driven into the lodge poles. When finally she was finished, she pulled the buffalo robe and blanket from Inkpaduta's shrunken form. With great ceremony, she dressed him, pulling beaded leather leggings over his feet and tying them above his knees. She placed moccasins, intricately decorated with dyed porcupine quills on his feet and retied his clout around his skinny waist. Last, she sat him up and pulled his painted war shirt over his head and arms. He sat for a moment while she pulled the shirt down past his hips, and then lay back on his bed again.

The woman placed his war club near his right hand, his bow and arrows near his left and leaned the ancient flintlock rifle that had been his father's against the lodge pole nearest the door. Its cherry-wood stock was cracked, and its barrel was rusty, but it still held a place of honor in his heart. She propped his long-stemmed pipe, carved from sacred red stone mined in the *minne sota* country, across his chest and placed a twist of tobacco in his hand. The fire burned down, and she set the pot of dog soup back on the heating rocks at its edge. At last, the young woman with the graying hair turned to look down at the old man's wasted form. Tears slipped from her eyes, and there was a catch in her throat when she spoke, gesturing toward the fire.

"There is firewood to keep you warm, and soup, rich with the flesh of a faithful helper, to stop your hunger." Then spreading her arms, she said in a choked whisper, "You are dressed for your final battle. Your best and most trusted weapons are here to help you. Now it is time for us to leave, old Father." With one last, lingering look, she stooped through the tipi door and tied it shut from the outside.

Inkpaduta lay there for a few minutes, wishing that he had spoken to the young woman with the gray hair. She had never let him lie in her bed with her, but she had cared for him over these last many years, even though, he knew, she had never really liked him much. Now, she had prepared him for his final journey, and he would have liked to have thanked her. He thought of rising and going after her to tell her, but an overwhelming weakness overcame him, as he listened to the muted sounds of departure coming from outside the tipi. Whickering horses, yipping dogs and solemn voices of the people talking in subdued tones as many filed slowly past his tipi. They were leaving him to find his own way to the next life.

When all sounds of the village departing were silent, Inkpaduta began to softly chant his medicine song. It was a song he had prepared many years before, and the disjointed words of bravery and victory over his enemies brought him a peaceful feeling. When his song was done, he listened for more sounds of the people leaving, but only silence reached his ears. In the silence, his mind wandered back, taking him to times in the past. He remembered people and places and legends that had brought him to this wizened old age . . . he slept.

*    *    *

His dream from years gone by returned. *A large fire grew out of the darkness. A circle of relatives stood around it: His father Wamdisapa, his brother Sidominadota, women he had used for wives; Runs Like The Wind Woman, Hates Her Father Woman, and Afraid Of Her Husband Woman, and his sons Roaring Cloud and Rain Cloud stood shoulder to shoulder and all were crying. The circle grew with the faces of Sun At Night, Big Face, Little Crow and many other men he had called friends before their deaths. Even men he had called enemies and men he had killed himself; Tasagi, Buffalo Calf Man and New Grass Woman took their place in the circle. Even the Sauk who had cut off Sidominadota's fingers in that first battle so many years ago was there!*

*The circle was full around the fire, leaving only one space blank. Just outside of the circle stood his birth mother, tall on her horse legs. Her long dark hair framed her beautiful face and hung loosely about her shoulders, covering her small breasts. She was crying. Tears of fire dripped down her face and fell as sparks, landing by her hooves. A pile of black ash grew from them and took the shape of a human that walked to fill the last space in the circle. Rain Dance Woman suddenly appeared beside his mother, a bright light shining behind her. She reached for him, drawing him toward her full bosom where he had felt safe and warm so many times as a small child and the fear he had felt growing in his soul began to melt away.*

*Suddenly a loud laughter drowned out all other sounds. He could see Rain Dance Woman's lips moving, but could not hear the words she spoke. Irritated, he turned to look at the source of the laughter coming from the center of the circle. Growing from the flames was his red-haired, white-skinned father, who had haunted his dreams with loud laughter for years. Just as suddenly as it started, the laughter stopped and complete silence followed. His mind cleared, and he could see that the last figure, who had grown from the ashes of his mother's tears and taken the last place in the circle, was himself. Darkness prevailed.*

Horse Woman's Child was dead.

THE END

## ABOUT THE AUTHOR

Roger Stoner's love of history was deeply ingrained after a grade school field trip to the Gardner Cabin on the south shore of West Lake Okoboji in northwest Iowa. The frightening tale of violent murder commonly known as *"The Spirit Lake Massacre"* affected him deeply. His desire to know the whole story resurfaced years later and he began researching the life of *Inkpaduta*, the man named as responsible for the outrage. *Horse Woman's Child* is the culmination of over twenty-five years of research.

His first book, *Life With My Wife: The Memoir of an Imperfect Man*, is a compilation of 50 out of more than 800 humorous observations about day to day frivolities between a man and his mate that were published during his fifteen and one-half years as a columnist.

His short stories have been published in anthologies about growing up in small towns in the Midwest, *Knee High by the Fourth of July*, *Amber Waves of Grain*, and *True Cow Tales*, and he has had magazine articles published in *Fishing & Hunting Iowa* and *Successful Farming*.

He has worked as a farm hand, carpet cleaner, a grain elevator employee, a factory machinist, a columnist and a newspaper publisher. Roger and his wife, Jane live in Peterson, Iowa, where they live a simple life, enjoying their six grandchildren and . . . keeping each other on their toes.